USA Today and *New York Times* bestselling author Catherine Cowles has had her nose in a book since the time she could read and finally decided to write down some of her own stories. When she's not writing she can be found exploring her home state of Oregon, listening to true crime podcasts, or searching for her next book boyfriend.

Praise for Catherine Cowles:

'Heartfelt, hopeful and emotionally gripping'
Lauren Asher

'I'm ready to enter my Catherine Cowles era!'
Elsie Silver

'No one writes twisty smalltown romance like Catherine Cowles' Elle Kennedy

'The queen of steamy smalltown suspense'
Helena Hunting

Also by Catherine Cowles

Sparrow Falls

Fragile Sanctuary
Delicate Escape
Broken Harbor
Beautiful Exile
Chasing Shelter
Secret Haven

Across the Vanishing Sky

CATHERINE COWLES

PENGUIN BOOKS

PENGUIN BOOKS

UK | USA | Canada | Ireland | Australia
India | New Zealand | South Africa

Penguin Books is part of the Penguin Random House group of companies
whose addresses can be found at global.penguinrandomhouse.com

Penguin Random House UK,
One Embassy Gardens, 8 Viaduct Gardens, London SW11 7BW

penguin.co.uk

First published 2026
001

Copyright © Catherine Cowles, 2026

The moral right of the author has been asserted

Penguin Random House values and supports copyright.
Copyright fuels creativity, encourages diverse voices, promotes freedom
of expression and supports a vibrant culture. Thank you for purchasing
an authorised edition of this book and for respecting intellectual property
laws by not reproducing, scanning or distributing any part of it by any
means without permission. You are supporting authors and enabling
Penguin Random House to continue to publish books for everyone.
No part of this book may be used or reproduced in any manner for the
purpose of training artificial intelligence technologies or systems. In accordance
with Article 4(3) of the DSM Directive 2019/790, Penguin Random House
expressly reserves this work from the text and data mining exception.

Printed and bound in Great Britain by Clays Ltd, Elcograf S.p.A.

The authorised representative in the EEA is Penguin Random House Ireland,
Morrison Chambers, 32 Nassau Street, Dublin D02 YH68

A CIP catalogue record for this book is available from the British Library

ISBN: 978-1-911-74630-0

Penguin Random House is committed to a sustainable future
for our business, our readers and our planet. This book is made from
Forest Stewardship Council® certified paper.

For all those looking for belonging, for a true home. Never give up hope. You might just find it in the unlikeliest of places.

PROLOGUE
Braedyn

ONE YEAR EARLIER

"IF I GET POISON IVY ON MY HOO-HA, MY REVENGE WILL BE VAST, Braedyn Winslow," Nova threatened as we rounded a curve in the trail with an especially thick patch of underbrush. "I'm talking putting your hand in warm water while you're sleeping, Sharpie-ing something distinctly inappropriate on your face, and possibly dyeing your hair purple. Peeing in the woods is not for me."

I couldn't help the soft laugh that escaped as I turned around to take stock of my best friend, who'd just returned to the trail from a mid-trek bathroom break. She'd committed to the hiking bit, seeking out secondhand finds at Goodwill that made her look like she conquered dozens of miles in the backcountry every weekend. Her dark hair was pulled into an artful knot atop her head, and her gray eyes had that tinge of silver that only came when her emotions were heightened.

Right now, I couldn't decide if Nova was more annoyed or amused. It only made my smile widen.

Nova stopped mid-trail and pointed her colorful water bottle at me—the one she'd decorated with stickers that would've painted a picture of who she was to a stranger: A girl with her hands in a meditative prayer position in front of her chest with the words *Namaste in bed* scrawled below. A little chicken nugget with sunglasses that said *Nugs not drugs*. A pink cooler that read *Don't hate me because I'm a little bit cooler*.

There were also more typical ones: one for both the yoga studio and coffeehouse she worked at in Oakland, a shooting star, a holographic butterfly... Each thing was a little piece of Nova's sparkly personality, as was the gold, heart-shaped locket dangling from her neck.

"I don't appreciate that smile," she bit out.

It only made the curve of my lips grow. "Don't worry, princess. I'm looking out for your delicate sensibilities."

Nova scowled in my direction. "We live in a city. We grew up in a beach suburb. How did you get to be so at one with the woods?"

She was right. Oakland was about as far from Starlight Grove as you could get. Not in distance—that was only about four hours—but everything else about them was night and day. Our home, about thirty minutes outside of San Francisco—at least when it wasn't rush hour—had a population of about half a million people. Starlight Grove, about an hour south of the Oregon border, had about one thousand.

It was one of the reasons I'd picked this spot for our girls' weekend—the weekend that was supposed to be a thank-you for everything Nova had done for me these past seven years. But on second thought, the hike up Three Creeks Canyon might not have been the best gratitude gift.

Just the thought of *seven years* had me wanting to pull my phone from my shorts pocket to see if I had an update from the Cub Scout leader in charge of the camping trip not more than an hour from here. I'd gotten one this morning before we left for our hike, letting me know everything was great. Owen had slept well and was super excited for their fishing expedition that day.

But worry still niggled. This was his first time away from me for more than one night. What if he got sick or scared or—?

"Don't tell me you conned me into this so-called adventure because of your Bigfoot obsession," Nova grumbled and dropped her gaze to my shirt.

I knew exactly what she was looking at: the image of Bigfoot with a sunset sky behind him and the words *Believe in yourself, even when no one else does.*

I shook off my worries for Owen, picturing his blond hair in a shade so similar to my own. The slope of his nose with the smallest upturn was all me, too. Really the only thing that was his father were his eyes—green irises that felt like they could see right through you. But those eyes were the only thing Vincent had given our son.

"Earth to Braedyn," Nova singsonged.

"Sorry, I swore I heard a Bigfoot call," I teased.

Nova whirled around. "It's probably a goddamned bear. And if I get eaten—"

"You'll shave off my eyebrows and tattoo your vengeance across my forehead," I finished for her.

She turned back, hands on her hips. "I will haunt your ass."

I burst out laughing and pulled her into a hug. "I'm so glad because I'd be lost without you."

I held on a little longer than necessary, and my action had Nova hugging me tighter. More like a sister than a best friend, she always knew when I needed a little extra something. Knowing each other practically since birth had given us that—the kind of bond that didn't even need words.

Still, she gave me them. "What's going on?"

I gave her one last squeeze before releasing her. "I don't know. Owen's first big overnight trip...it has me remembering everything you've done along the way. You're the best friend a girl could ask for. That *anyone* could ask for."

Nova's face went soft as she squeezed my hand. "I didn't do that much."

I made a face. "Supernova," I began, using the nickname my son had given her, "when my world exploded, you were the one who picked up the pieces. You moved across the country with me. You were my birth coach—"

"Because Vincent the douche is the prick of the century."

She wasn't wrong there. Vincent had been what I thought was forever. Six years older, wealthy, charismatic—he'd used all three things to charm his way into my pants. But when I ended up pregnant at nineteen because he refused to wear a condom, he'd wanted nothing to do with our baby. Told me, *"Get rid of it or I'll get rid of you. I'm not marrying you just because you're trying to trap me."*

And I'd seen for the first time who he really was. I'd ended things then and there. Vincent had given me an NDA and an offer of half a million dollars to never reveal the father of my baby. I'd told him to go fuck himself as I ripped up the NDA and then kneed him in the balls as an extra parting gift. But I could never quite bring myself to hate him. Not when he'd given me the best gift I'd ever received.

Owen.

"You're a way better parent than he could ever be," I swore. Because Nova was. She was his auntie but more like a second mom than anything else.

"My Bubs is the dopest kid around, and I'm honored to be his cool aunt."

"The coolest."

I pulled out my phone, all this talk of Owen breaking the last of my reserve to keep from checking. Zero bars. *Damn.*

"Brae-Brae..." Nova said in a warning tone. "He's fine."

"I know, I just..."

"You just worry anyway because you're the best mom in the universe."

"I highly doubt that," I mumbled. At least one day a week, I felt like a complete failure. More than once, I'd cursed myself for not taking that half-a-million-dollar payout. But it had felt too much like someone stripping my voice from me. And if there was one thing to know about me, it was that I'd never be silenced.

"Facts," Nova argued. "Never seen anyone work harder to give their kid everything."

But Nova did, too. She'd given up the life of a young twenty-something to help me raise my little miracle. And I never would've been able to do it without her.

"You make that possible," I whispered.

"Stop trying to make me feel my feelings," Nova muttered.

Her remark had a laugh breaking free of my throat. Nova might've been a yoga devotee, but she was out the second someone tried to make it about feelings. Maybe it was how she'd grown up. Neither of us had come from money, but as strict as my parents had been, they always made sure I had the things I needed. Nova had pretty much raised herself, and I knew there were things she didn't share about her childhood.

"I love you," I said with a grin.

Nova sent a mock-glare my way. "Yeah, yeah. You know I have those affectionate feelings toward you and the Bubs, even if I will never say the L-word."

"Loooooooooove you to the moon and back, sister."

Nova flipped me off but then lifted her pinky to me. I hooked mine around hers, and then each of us kissed our closed fists, the friendship bracelets she'd made us touching. It was the oath we'd created in the third grade at the top of the jungle gym as we vowed to give Johnny Cooperson his comeuppance.

We'd succeeded. I'd distracted him while Nova poured salt in his water bottle. He hadn't picked on either of us again.

And our oath remained eighteen years later. We'd always have each other's backs.

We released our grip, and Nova swatted my ass. "Hurry up, lazy-bones. That massage you booked us later today is calling my name."

"Making note: Hikes, no. Massages, yes," I said, laughter in my voice.

"And wine. Wine is a *big* yes."

"Good thing I booked us a winery tour tomorrow," I called as I hurried down the path. We were only about twenty minutes from the trailhead now, if my guesstimate was correct.

"Thank the Bigfoot gods."

I chuckled as I caught sight of the breathtaking river below through the trees. The May sun sparkled on water that looked too clear to be real. Nothing like the water in the bay where we lived. And then I saw them—the stunning, little, peachy-pink wildflowers peeking out through the trees, leading down the steep bank to the river.

"Look." I grabbed Nova's arm without taking my eyes away. "Wildflowers."

"They're super pretty. Just like the twenty-five others we've seen along the way," Nova grumbled.

"I want to get a picture," I said, already slipping off the trail and into the underbrush.

Nova groaned. "You've taken at least two hundred already."

"Last ones. Promise," I called as I navigated around bushes and through trees, lifting my voice above the roar of the water.

"I'm in danger of getting hangry," Nova yelled, but I could barely make out her words over the thundering river.

I laughed as I pulled out my phone. No one wanted Nova hangry. It was not a pretty sight.

The roar of the water intensified as I moved farther down the embankment. The sound was deafening but in a beautiful way. It was one of the things I loved most about nature—the power of losing yourself in the sights and sounds, forgetting everything that weighed so heavily on you.

As I moved farther and farther away from the path, I saw an even more elaborate display of flowers closer to the riverbank. I stepped over fallen logs and around scrub brush, and then I was surrounded by blooms.

Crouching down low, I took shots of the little peach buds my city-girl self had no idea the name for. Then I took a more artistic shot where the river was in focus and the blooms were blurry in the foreground. That would be a framer for sure. Maybe I could get it printed on canvas and hang it in my bedroom—the bedroom that barely had space for my twin bed, a dresser, and a nightstand.

I straightened, but as I did, my foot hit a root. I stumbled back a step, then two, my arms windmilling. I barely managed to heave myself forward so I wouldn't fall straight into the river.

My heart hammered against my rib cage as my hands and knees hit the ground. Blood roared in my ears louder than the rushing of the river, and I pressed a palm to my chest. "Note to self: don't go down to the riverbank."

I swallowed, my hand shaking as I pulled it away from my chest. Far too close a call. I picked up my phone from where it had fallen. It was covered in dirt, but the screen was still intact. Relief swept through me as I started to make the climb back up to the path. I'd gone farther than I realized and winced, knowing Nova would be annoyed.

"You'll be glad to know that's my last picture for real," I yelled up toward the path.

There was no answer.

Ruh-roh. That meant the hangry had taken hold. When Nova was truly annoyed, she went silent, those gray eyes sparking silver. She told me that my amber ones flashed gold in a similar fashion. Silver and gold, a bonded pair, just like we were meant to be.

I scrambled up the side of the embankment. "I'm sorry. I'm hurrying. I nearly lost my life in the pursuit of wildflowers. I wonder if Bigfoot would've saved me. Right out of one of your monster romance novels—"

My words cut off as I reached the trail and found it empty. "Nova?" The only things that answered me were the wind swaying the branches and the river roaring behind me. I moved a few steps one way, peeking around a bend, and then went in the opposite direction. Nothing.

A scowl pulled at my mouth as realization dawned. "This isn't funny."

Still nothing.

I turned in a circle, looking for any sign of my friend. I was sure she was behind some tree or boulder, planning some elaborate scare as revenge for me keeping her from the snacks we had in the car.

Starting down the path, I took a handful of steps and braced for Nova to leap from either side of the path. One time, she and Owen had scared me so badly by jumping out in monster masks at Halloween, I'd peed my pants. She was vicious.

"If you don't come out, I'm going to eat the Wild Berry Skittles I brought just for you." That should've done it. If Nova had a weakness, it was those damn Skittles.

When I hit step thirty, unease slid through me. "Nova," I yelled louder.

The only response was the water and the soft call of some bird.

My stomach twisted. Would she have gone back to the car because she was annoyed? I had the keys, so it wasn't like she could get in.

I turned around one more time, but there was no sign of her. Not the khaki shorts with their elaborate stitching, the purple tank with the flowers dotting the hem, not the matching purple bandana she'd tied in her hair as a headband. No gleam of the gold heart locket she always wore around her neck, the one I'd scrimped and saved to give her.

A tingle lit in my limbs, the kind that told me I wasn't breathing. I sucked in air, trying not to inhale or exhale too quickly. And then I picked up to a jog. My backpack bounced against my tailbone and shoulder blades as I ran along the trail. Not full-out. I could still scan the trees on both sides and the packed earth below my feet.

But there was nothing.

The twenty minutes I'd estimated it would take us to make it back to the trailhead only took me twelve. The six-or-so-vehicle parking area was empty except for the tiny sedan Nova and I shared. But I didn't see her anywhere.

Real panic set in. Like when Owen ran from me in the Super Target back in the Bay Area, thinking we were playing the best game known to man. I'd lost half my life in the handful of moments he was out of my sight.

When I found him, I'd burst into tears as I held him to me. A nice older lady had come over, rubbing my back, her dark skin crinkling as she gave me a kind smile. *"They'll give you five hundred heart attacks before they graduate, but you got this, Mama."*

There was no kind lady here now. And there was no sign of my missing friend.

"Nova!" I yelled it as loud as I could this time, spinning in a circle and praying she would miraculously pop out from somewhere. "You're scaring me!"

And Nova wouldn't do that. Not for real. Not for more than a brief *boo!* or a jokey jump scare. Because she cared about me too much.

My circles slowed as hot tears pricked the corners of my eyes. I didn't know what to do. Go back and look on the trail? Stay here?

I pulled out my phone, wiping dirt from the screen. The second I took in the upper right corner, I cursed. Still no bars.

I bit my lip so hard I tasted blood.

Swallowing, I ordered myself to think, to make a plan. I'd take one more trip out on the trail. If I didn't see her, I'd drive back into town. I knew we weren't on federal land, so I guessed there wouldn't be a ranger station, but maybe there was something similar.

I was starting back toward the trail when a flicker of color caught my eye—the pink and teal hues of a familiar water bottle. It was speckled with dirt, as if it had rolled or been thrown. A glimmer of the holographic butterfly sticker shone through the dirt, sparkling in the sun.

Nova's water bottle.

A lump caught in my throat, making it hard to breathe. I still managed to scream. I screamed Nova's name until I was hoarse, but she never answered.

CHAPTER ONE
Braedyn

ONE YEAR LATER

MY HEART GAVE A STUTTER STEP, THE KIND THAT MADE ME wonder if I'd developed a heart condition in the three hundred and seventy-two days Nova had been missing. Not one sign or sighting beyond things that were wishful thinking. So maybe it was a heart condition.

A *broken* heart.

My fingers tightened around the steering wheel as I fought against worst-case scenarios and nightmares that took root in my mind. I would not let the what-ifs win.

The used SUV I'd emptied my savings for had seen better days, but it hugged the road like a dream as the worn sign came into view: *Welcome to Starlight Grove.* The wood was weathered, but you could still make out the stars carved into its grain at the top and the ornate trees along either side.

It was rustic and charming, like the town itself. But all I could feel were nerves. My stomach gave a jolting rumble as my gaze flicked to my wrist and the pink-purple-and-teal friendship bracelet Nova had made me during one of her crafty phases. I hadn't taken it off in the three hundred and seventy-two days she'd been missing, and it was starting to fray in places.

There were times when the bracelet felt like one of those hourglasses filled with sand—a marker of what was left. And time was running out. Those final grains swirling around and around, threatening to tell me I was out of options. And Nova was out of time.

"I'm not an idiot, right?" I whispered to no one. Not to Owen, who had his headphones on, glued to a show on his tablet. Not to my sweet, mischievous dog, Yeti, whose nose was pressed to the glass, dying to smell all the new scents.

Nova had always been the recipient of all my questions and doubts. The one I talked through every problem with. But now...I didn't have a single soul. Not really.

As the road curved again, I sucked in breath but for a whole new reason. Mount Lupine sprang up over the fields and forests like a beacon guiding us home—to our new home, anyway.

Starlight Grove might hold shadows, but it also gleamed with unending beauty. Every corner you turned, there was something new to discover. Sagebrush and tall grass-filled meadows. Ponderosa pine- and spruce-packed forests. Countless bending rivers and streams. And that mountain as a backdrop to it all.

Yeti shoved her head between the front seats and licked my cheek at the sound of my intake of air. I couldn't help the soft laugh that bubbled out of me. "You ready, girl?"

She barked as if to say, *You've had my furry butt locked in this car for four hours. What do you think?*

Owen brushed his headphones off, and I heard the faint sounds of that robot show he loved emanating from them. He shoved his glasses-clad face through the opening between the seats, too.

A more full-bodied laugh left me at the sight of the two of them in my rearview mirror. Owen and Yeti had become besties since I brought her home from the shelter a little over a year ago. A mix of Labrador, Saint Bernard, coonhound, and pit bull, she carried traits of all four. But most importantly, she had the nose of the first three, making her an excellent search dog and a pretty dang good guard dog to boot.

"Are we here?" Owen asked, bouncing in his seat as much as his seat belt would allow.

"Just about. What do you think?"

My eight-year-old cocked his head to the side, examining the landscape in front of him. "It's big."

My mouth curved, and I held on to the way it felt. The lingering tendrils of warmth from the laugh he and Yeti had created. After Nova went missing, I'd had to fake every laugh and smile for months. For Owen. So he wouldn't know the truth of what had happened. So he'd believe the story that Nova had been forced to return home to help her family. That she'd try to come back.

But one day, Owen had been painting on his activity table and accidentally exploded the blue paint all over his face. His glasses had blocked the worst of it from getting into his eyes, but he'd looked like a blue burglar.

I'd laughed for real for the first time and knew then that you could find humor amid pain, and joy amid agony. And I'd vowed to hold on to every sprinkle I could get.

"Mountains tend to be big, kiddo."

"I *knoooooow*, bruh," Owen said in that voice that was eight going on eighteen. The *bruh* thing was new. I hadn't been *Mommy* in years, but I'd hoped to hold on to *Mom* for a little longer. Now, I was *bro* or *bruh* more often than not.

"All right, *bruh*." I reached back and tickled his neck, making him squeal in a tone that was still 100 percent little boy. And I clung to that, too.

Yeti let out another bark and licked Owen, sensing some sort of game being played.

"Gross, Yeti! You're a slobberfest."

I chuckled as I made the turn into downtown Starlight Grove. I braced, waiting for the memories to hit—the handful I had of Nova and me here. The Grove Griddle, the diner where we'd had some incredible French toast. Barrel & Branch, the wine bar where we'd sampled local creations. The adorable little B&B where we'd stayed.

But because I'd braced, the memories didn't hit as hard. They liked to surprise—a sucker punch of grief when you least expected it.

"It looks like one of those old movies you love," Owen remarked, taking in the downtown.

It did look like a set from an old Western, with not a single stoplight in sight, so opposite from our life in Oakland. But I guessed you didn't need lights when you went from a population of almost half a million to just over a thousand.

The downtown area's aesthetic was rustic with endless character—the kind of thing stores in urban areas paid a whole lot of money to look like. Sort of shabby chic. Some stuck with the Old West vibe, others had brick facades and antique glass windows. Still more had an old-farmhouse feel.

Planters adorned just about every storefront, erupting with color. The bakery had a sign that read: *Order your Fourth of July pies!* in artsy script. An aged wood building, so dark it was almost black, read *The Boot* and looked like an honest-to-goodness saloon. I spotted the bookstore, craft shop, and plenty of little tourist shops before my GPS told me we'd arrived.

I snagged an empty parking spot and marveled at the fact that there were no meters to pay. At least I'd be saving money there—*and* on the rental I was about to pick up the keys for. But I was also jobless.

My gig as an office manager at a tiny accounting firm had been about as exciting as watching paint dry, but at least the paycheck had been steady and they'd allowed me to work only the hours Owen was in school. I wasn't sure I'd be as lucky here.

But the Starlight Grove school system had an excellent rating, despite the town's small size. The articles I'd read praised it for being highly supported by the community, with a low student-to-teacher ratio. It also had what looked like an amazing after-school program if I needed it.

We'd make it work. I gripped the wheel a little harder as if to cement that promise to myself.

Turning off the engine, I twisted around in my seat. "How about you pack up your backpack with your tablet, headphones, and water bottle? I'm not sure how long the paperwork will take."

Owen groaned. "More sitting."

He had a point. "Looks like there's a park down the block. Why don't we walk Yeti first and get out the wiggles. Then, after we get the keys, burgers and milkshakes?"

I didn't tell him we'd also have to get groceries. That could wait until my boy had been fed. Just like Nova, you didn't want to mess with him when he was hangry.

"Chocolate milkshakes?" Owen asked, hedging.

I gave him a comically exasperated expression. "Do I look like an idiot? Of course, chocolate."

Owen started doing a shimmy shake in his seat, singing some made-up song resembling the cha-cha tune. "Cho-co-late shake, yeah! Cho-co-late shake, yeah!"

Much to my amusement, Yeti started copying Owen's shaking movements. A laugh forced its way out of me, and I held on to the warm vibrations. "All right, dance king. Pack up your bag so it's ready."

As he started what I knew would be at least a ten-minute process, I reached for my phone. There were no text messages. No missed calls.

I swallowed the lump in my throat. Nova and I never went anywhere without checking in with each other half a dozen times. But I didn't have that anymore.

Shoving all those feelings down, I toggled over to my photo-sharing app and waited for the interface to load. The moment it did, I tapped my profile.

SearchingForSunrise.

The account was dedicated to Yeti and me and followed our journey since I'd brought her home from the shelter. I'd had guidance from an amazing woman up in Cedar Ridge, Washington, who was involved in training dogs for search-and-rescue operations. When I told her why I wanted to train a search dog, Maddie had helped me for free. That was just the kind of generous soul she was.

It hadn't been easy, but the training had given me a place to focus all my angry, sad, hopeless energy. And so had getting plugged into the missing-persons community.

Until a loved one went missing, you had no idea just how many people *disappeared* every single year. Over six hundred thousand in the United States alone. And so often, people weren't searched for.

I knew damn well I was the only one looking for Nova.

The sheriff's department headquartered in Starlight Grove had put in a mixed effort. There were officers I could tell truly *cared*, and others who were phoning it in at best. The sheriff himself wasn't exactly my favorite person.

It had taken begging and pleading for them to involve Juniper County Search and Rescue two days after Nova's disappearance, but with a rainstorm that week, they hadn't found a thing. Neither had the state police when they joined the investigation. And Sheriff Miller certainly hadn't been thrilled with how often I called to check on the case. But the nail in the coffin had been his call to me a few weeks ago.

"Nova's case is cold, and I'm reassigning the officers on it. You have to stop grasping at straws and wasting taxpayer dollars when they could be spent on cases where they might actually do some good. There's nothing left to find. It's time for you to move on."

Sheriff Miller thought Nova had slipped and fallen into the river or been attacked by a wild animal, possibly one of the cougars who roamed the woods. But I *knew* in my bones that wasn't true. Just like I knew Nova was out there somewhere, waiting for me to find her.

A couple of the officers had gone above and beyond, two of them continuing to keep the case on their desks, but there wasn't much they could do when the sheriff wanted them focused on cases with real leads.

I fought the scowl that wanted to rise, inhaling deeply. If you hadn't gone through losing someone this way, you'd never understand the brutal blow that was *"There's nothing left to find."* And I refused to believe it.

I clicked on the image I'd uploaded before we left that morning: a shot of Yeti in the redwoods after a search exercise. I never posted places I'd been until after I left, and I never showed my face on the feed—safety precautions I'd learned from getting involved in the missing-persons community.

The caption of the image read: *Yeti loves new adventures.*

There were about ninety-eight comments. A few familiar names of people I knew from the missing world.

> **TheGamerGirl13:** *Yeti is the goodest girl! All the bones for you!*
>
> **PDustan88:** *What did you have her searching for this time? I tried the sock exercise yesterday and it took Bingo three tries but he got it and his peanut butter reward.*
>
> **DogLuverX8:** *What kind of pupper? I'm in love with that face.*

That drooly face, I thought to myself. As I caught the next comment, my blood chilled.

> **V.Fabes911:** *New adventures, huh? I wonder where…*

It wasn't threatening. Not exactly. But I still clicked the profile. Private. No profile photo. Just like always. Every time, it was a different incarnation of Vincent Faber's name. It was like he got some sick pleasure out of my knowing that, even though he hadn't wanted us, he was still keeping tabs.

I hit *block* and locked my phone. He didn't get to steal this from me like he'd stolen so many other things. I wouldn't make my profile private to keep him out because he didn't get to keep me from the community I'd built. He didn't get to win.

Vincent had been letting me know he'd been *watching* since the moment I left. Anonymous emails. Even texts until I changed my number. And now, this.

It wasn't exactly a shock. He'd always had a petulant side, the kind of personality that meant he just had to have the last word. When we started dating, I'd found it amusing, even adorable. But that was before I saw the other side of it.

I shoved all my anger and hurt down into the same cavern I kept my Nova emotions in. Locked away where they couldn't take over. Where they wouldn't affect me or Owen or the new life we were building. Because we were going to build something beautiful.

And I would find Nova. So she could share in the beauty with us.

CHAPTER TWO

Dex

My SUV made the final turn into Starlight Grove as if on autopilot. Or maybe it was me who was. My hands moved with the kind of knowledge that came from years upon years of making the same turns, even after almost a decade away.

It wasn't that I never came back. I did. Made the visit at least three times a year. Sometimes more. Christmas. Anytime Great-Uncle Waylon had a follow-up scan after kicking cancer's ass. My niece Skylar's birthday as often as possible. And always Mom's birthday... or what would've been.

But there was always a cost. Coming back here, to a place where people knew exactly what my brothers and I had come from. Exactly *why* our great-uncle had taken us in.

The reactions varied: pity, disgust, fear. But there was *always* a reaction. I hadn't had to deal with it in DC—not in a city where I was practically invisible, just one of the many filing through the streets and metro stations. That anonymity had become a comforting blanket, and I'd just ripped it clean off by deciding to move back here.

I eased my car to a stop as a woman I recognized stepped into the crosswalk. People never worried about cars coming to a stop for them in Starlight Grove. There was blind trust around here, a belief that people would do the right thing.

Maisy Carmichael, one of the ladies who worked at the Yarn Barn, the local quilt and craft shop, slowed a fraction as her gaze met mine through my windshield. Her pale-green eyes widened, making the endless wrinkles on her face deepen.

Fear.

That was what those eyes held. It was as if she thought I'd gun the engine and run her down right then and there. Part of me didn't blame her. She knew whose blood ran through my veins. But another part of me *did* blame her—her and every other person who looked at my brothers and me with wary eyes.

Instead, I forced a smile I'd donned more times than I could count. The kind that said *I'm nothing like the monster who makes up half my DNA.* And then I waved. A little finger wave that was beyond ridiculous but made to tell her I was no one to fear.

Maisy sent me a tight smile and a nod, then scrambled the rest of the way across the street. I didn't think I'd seen the woman—who had to be deep into her eighties now—move that fast in years.

Guilt swamped me. I was an asshole. And that assholishness had been made worse by the fact that I'd just spent the past four days driving cross-country, sleeping in crappy motels, and drinking awful coffee, and I was pretty sure I'd pulled something in my back.

I wasn't sure how you could pull something in your back by doing nothing but sitting for forty-two-plus hours, but I'd managed it. Was this what it was like to get old? If it was, it sucked. And the fact that I was feeling the effects at thirty-one was concerning.

I waited until Maisy was deep onto the sidewalk before easing off the brake, but I couldn't stop my gaze from flicking over to her. A scowl twisted my lips when I saw a cell phone pressed to her ear, no doubt telling her sewing circle that all five Archer boys were back in Starlight Grove now.

As I forced my focus back onto the road, I had to slam on my brakes as a maroon SUV backed into the street, not a care in the world. I resisted the urge to lay on my horn. But the last thing I needed was

Maisy telling the world I had a rage problem on top of all the rumors she was helping along.

I didn't—at least not that I ever let anyone see—because I did everything to combat it. I meditated. Had a gratitude practice. Did things to counterbalance all the evil my father had bled into the world.

The SUV kept right on backing up, and I realized it wasn't a fuck-you move; the woman likely couldn't see over the piles of suitcases and boxes in the back. I could only tell it was a woman by the flash of long, blond hair I saw as her head turned. Oblivious to me, she started down Mountain View Way on her way out of town, a dog shoving his or her massive head out the window.

"Tourists," I muttered. Always completely unaware of their surroundings unless stopping to take a selfie and bringing more crap with them than they'd ever need for a two-week vacation.

I cracked my neck and eased off the brake yet again. If I could make it to the ranch without getting into a wreck or biting someone's head off, it'd be a miracle. I needed a meal that didn't come from a vending machine or a fast-food drive-through, a cold beer, and a scalding-hot shower to scrub off the road. Not necessarily in that order.

But I still didn't let myself drive even three miles over the speed limit. Couldn't risk it. Not with my history. Not with my family's reputation.

Instead, I tried to take stock of all that had changed in downtown Starlight Grove since my last visit. My brother Wylder's bar, the Boot, looked damn good. He'd added some color in the form of flowers in water troughs out front, and they worked against the dark, almost-black stain of the wood building. Countless people were crowded into picnic tables around the diner, opting for the Grove Griddle's walk-up window in the deep May warmth. And the bookstore looked like it had gotten a facelift, too.

My brain stayed occupied until I reached the edge of town and could breathe a little more deeply. Luckily, my hands stayed on autopilot, taking me on the fifteen-minute drive out of town to the place that was more home than anything else I'd ever had. The estate I'd grown up on in Greenwich, Connecticut, sure as hell hadn't been home. I'd thought it was, but it had been a house of horrors. My apartment in DC had barely seen my face other than for me to grab fitful patches of sleep. And the only thing my college dorm room had been was the backdrop for my arrest by the FBI.

But Twisted Oak Ranch. That was home. The perfect fit for the misfit Archer brothers. And it all centered around the ramshackle house my great-uncle had built with his friends and added onto year after year. The house he'd been determined to build with a massive, living oak tree at the center of it.

The tree house. That was what my brothers and I called it. There was even a swing off one of the branches in the living room.

But it was more than the house itself. It was the land and all the things on it. Over a thousand acres with everything but what most people raised around here: cattle. Not Uncle Waylon. The only cows he had were those of the mini-Highland cow variety. He had alpacas, an extra shaggy breed of sheep, goats, and a small herd of yaks.

Even the land itself seemed to fit us. Rustic and wild, a little ragged around the edges. Fields and meadows punctuated by brambles and sagebrush, framed by endless forests with that staggering mountaintop in the distance.

Beauty and home.

My SUV slowed as I reached the gate, the rusted metal complete with Uncle Waylon's true love in the middle…a clock. And not just any clock. A Bigfoot clock.

A soft chuckle left my lips as I rolled down my window and punched in the gate code—the same one we'd had since we'd come here to live. It sure as hell wasn't secure to not change it in two decades, but every time I brought that up to Waylon, he said he'd never be able to remember a new one.

The gate swung open with a creak, and I eased my SUV over the familiar bumps of a cattle guard. Each vibration sent a spasm of pain through my back. *Damn.* I needed a soak in the hot springs on the property.

I guided my vehicle around the bends in the bumpy-as-hell dirt road, cursing every divot and ridge. But finally, the tree house came into view. Its sage-green siding almost matched the oak tree leaves that sprang out of the roof. How Waylon had managed to make that work without a leak of some sort was beyond me.

But then again, he had all sorts of mechanical tricks up his sleeve. And like a magician, he always refused to share his secrets.

Slowing to a stop, I cut the engine and climbed out of the SUV. I stretched and cracked my back, groaning with the movement.

"Uncle Dex!"

The two words had me searching out the source. Skylar ran at me full-out. Her blond hair flew behind her in a tangle of waves, the crown atop it sliding to one side. She wore a pink princess dress paired with cowboy boots covered in pink flowers and mud, and wielded a play sword.

I couldn't help the chuckle that left my lips as she launched herself into the air. I caught her with an *oomph* as pain flared in my back and my glasses nearly flew from my face. "Did you grow on me, Little Princess?"

"Duuuuuuh, I'm seven now," she shot back.

"Driving yet?"

Skylar sent me a sly smile. "Sometimes, on the tractor."

Oh Jesus. I bet Kol didn't have a clue about that one. My brother put the *over* in overprotective, especially when it came to his little girl.

"Damn it, she's fast," Maverick called on a wheeze as he ran around the side of the house.

I choked on a laugh as I took in the youngest of our bunch, adjusting my glasses. He wore a cowboy hat, a hot-pink feather boa, and held a shield and sword. Behind him charged a mini-Highland cow decked out in fairy wings.

"I thought hotshots were in better shape," I yelled back.

Mav flipped me off. "Smoke jumper now, you asshat."

"Swear jar!" Skylar chastised.

Mav scowled. "You're always getting me in trouble."

I arched a brow as I deposited Skylar back on her mud-caked boots. "Pretty sure you don't need my help in that department."

Maverick did everything he could to live up to his name: reckless to the bone and always searching for his next dose of adrenaline. Uncle Waylon blamed Maverick for his white hair.

Mav rolled his eyes. "The FBI really did make you boring as shit."

"Swear jar," Skylar singsonged again.

Without warning, I dove for my brother, trying to get him into a headlock and attempting a noogie at the same time.

Maverick instantly retaliated by thwacking me with his plastic sword as Skylar giggled.

"Shots fired on an unarmed man!" I accused.

An ear-splitting whistle pierced the air, which had Maverick and me releasing each other.

"Do I need to turn the hose on you two?"

I grimaced as I took in Uncle Waylon, clad in his favorite Carhartt overalls complete with a Bigfoot patch on the bib, work boots, and his worn ball cap that read *The truth is out there*.

Lucy, the sweetest Irish wolfhound known to man, ambled down the porch steps after him, making her way toward me.

"He started it," Mav complained.

I crouched low to give my old girl scratches. "There she is," I cooed.

"Mav," Waylon began, "you start shit nine times out of ten."

Skylar giggled. "Swear jar, Grampa Way Way."

She'd called him that from the moment she learned to talk. Because he was a grandfather to her in all the ways that mattered and the only grandparent she'd ever have.

A door slammed. "I ask you two to keep an eye on my daughter for two hours," Kol grumbled as he ambled away from his Forest Service truck.

Maverick clamped his hands over Skylar's ears. "Newsflash, buzzkill, she already knows more than a couple of four-letter words."

This was *not* the thing to say to Kol. You did not expose his daughter to anything that might harm her in any way, even if that was just a curse word.

"Boy," Uncle Waylon warned in Mav's direction. "You wake up on the stupid side of the bed this morning?"

I pushed to my feet, dropping my hands from Lucy's scruff. "Pretty sure that's every morning."

Mav released Skylar to take a swipe at me that I dodged with a laugh, and I turned to Kol, pulling him into a back-slapping hug. "How the hell are you?"

"Language," Kol warned.

"Is *hell* really a bad word?" I asked.

"It's on the no-no list," Skylar helpfully informed me.

"Whoops," I muttered as I released Kol.

He clapped me on the shoulder. "It's good to have you back."

I took a second to really take Kol in. His dark scruff was thicker, edging on beard territory, and he was just as broad and tall as he'd always been, but it looked like he'd put on more muscle. With his job as an investigator for the Forest Service, he could resemble a lumberjack. But those hazel eyes, which leaned toward the dark side, were the same ones we all had—the ones we all hated. Because of what they reminded us of.

I shoved that thought down. "It's good to be back. Wylder and Orion around?"

"Wylder's at the bar like always," Maverick offered about our eldest brother.

"Orion?" I asked.

Mav and Kol shared a look, and my gut sank like a boulder in a lake. Orion hadn't been what I'd call *good* since the day our whole world imploded. But Orion's world had fractured more than the rest of ours because of the higher price he'd paid for our survival.

"He's been sticking to his place more than usual," Kol hedged.

All my brothers lived on ranch property except for me, while I'd been working for the FBI in their tech wing, what I lovingly referred to as *Hackers Anonymous*, and Wylder, who lived above his bar. But Orion's house, which he built with Waylon's help and moved into the second he turned eighteen, was as far from the rest of the residences as he could get.

My jaw worked back and forth as worry set in. I'd be paying him a visit before long. And his cantankerous ass *would* be talking to me, in whatever way Orion was willing to talk these days.

I cracked my neck. "I need to get over to the guest cabin, unload my stuff, and take the longest shower known to man."

Maverick eyed my back seat. "You mean unload your two duffel bags?"

"Hey," I shot back. "I also have three boxes."

"Let me guess," Mav continued. "Computer crap?"

I narrowed my eyes on my brother. "Do not demean Betty Lou."

"Who's Betty Lou?" Skylar piped up. "Did you get a kitty?"

Maverick snorted. "It's his nerdtastic computer."

"I'd watch your tone about Betty Lou, or I'll make sure you can't access a single bank account, social media profile, or email."

"Dexter," Uncle Waylon warned. "We have a deal."

"No hacking on your property," I grumbled.

"Speaking of this property," Kol interjected, "what guest cabin do you think you're staying in?"

I blinked back at my brother a few times. "The one and only guest cabin on the ranch."

Mav and Kol shared another look.

"What now?" I groaned.

CHAPTER THREE
Dex

I STOOD IN THE OPEN DOOR OF THE GUEST CABIN. THAT WAS AS far as I could make it when every single inch of the small cabin was piled high with crap. Uncle Waylon wouldn't see the items as such, but I sure as hell did. Especially when it was between me and the shower I desperately needed.

Waylon scratched his thick beard. "I thought I cleaned this place out."

I pinched the bridge of my nose. "You thought?"

"Well, I had it on a to-do list somewhere. I didn't see it, so I assumed I already did it."

"Pepper probably ate it," Maverick said, laughter in his voice.

I turned and scowled at him. "*You* probably fed it to that damn goat."

Mav held up both hands. "Whoa, grumpy much?"

"There are five hundred million clocks and clock parts between me and a hot shower, so yes, yes I am," I groused.

"There's a buncha trail cams and Bigfoot calls in there, too," Waylon amended.

Of course there were. Clocks and Bigfoot, the true loves of Waylon's life.

Kol's lips twitched. "Take a drive by Blaze's. He might have a rental you can use."

"In the height of tourist season?" I challenged.

Kol just shrugged.

"You can stay in the main house with me," Waylon offered. "There's plenty of room."

There were also four dozen cuckoo clocks that went off every hour on the hour, all day and all night. I tried to fight the grimace rising to my mouth. "Thanks, Uncle Waylon, but I'll try Blaze first. It would be nice to have my own space while my place is getting built."

Waylon let out a huff. "Still don't know why you hired that fancy builder. Me, Blaze, and Zeke could've built it for you."

I was sure they could've—complete with eighty-seven clocks, thirteen secret passageways, twenty-two trapdoors, and a layout that made no sense to anyone but them. "You've got enough on your plate," I hedged.

Mav started laughing, and I sent a hard elbow back into his gut, which changed the laugh to a cough.

"All right. Well, I'm here if you need me," Waylon muttered.

I crossed to my great-uncle and pulled him into a hard hug. "You always are."

And it was true. When everything fell apart, not a single relative wanted to touch the Archer brothers with a ten-foot pole. No one but my dad's uncle, who might not have been a man of many words but was a man of swift action. He'd made us all rooms and set us up with school, sports if we wanted, and a local therapist. He'd given us a home.

Waylon thumped me on the back. "Love you."

"Love you, too," I said as I released him. "I'll be back after I see Blaze."

"Good luck," Kol said, lifting Skylar onto his hip.

"Bye, Uncle Dex," she said, waving. "When you come back, we can play dress-up war games."

I let out a soft chuckle. Being raised by six men since her mom had dropped her on Kol's doorstep as a baby, without him being aware of her existence, meant Skylar was the perfect blend of princess and commando.

"Can't wait, Little Princess," I called as I got into my SUV.

I made the drive back into town much faster than when I'd left it, almost breaking my three-miles-an-hour-over-the-speed-limit rule. But I was desperate. Downtown was more crowded now, and I eased off the brake and put on my blinker when I saw a station wagon with bikes on the back pull out.

But before I could snag the parking spot, a maroon SUV turned in from the opposite lane.

Seriously?

My back molars clamped down as I realized it was the same damn one as earlier. Half a dozen silent expletives left my lips as the dog shoved its head out the window, tongue lolling as if sticking it out at me.

Movement a block down caught my attention, and I bolted for the new space opening up. I slid in right on the heels of the sedan, not leaving anything to chance, and made my way to the brick building that housed Blaze's rental company.

I took the wooden stairs two at a time, praying that by some miracle, he'd have an opening. I'd take a cabin with an outhouse as long as I could set up my Wi-Fi.

The door was one of those wood-and-glass deals where the glass was rippled, so you couldn't see through. The lettering read *Amazin' Blazin' Rentals*. One corner of my mouth kicked up as I knocked.

There was a long pause and then an almost musical, "Come in."

I opened the door and stepped into the sun-filled office. The rays caught on suncatchers, crystals, and an endless array of house plants, including some with distinctly shaped leaves.

Blaze stared straight ahead, his head tilting to one side and then the other as he examined a pink crystal.

"Blaze?" I asked cautiously.

His head slowly turned toward me, his long, gray hair tied back in a braid by a rainbow bandana. "Dex. Heeeeey, Little Dude. Good to see you."

Blaze had gotten his nickname for his affinity for the recreational pursuit. But he looked a little more out of it than usual.

"You okay?" I asked.

"Totally." He grinned. "That friend of yours, Lolli, asked me to sample her new blend of the good stuff, but her homemade grows might be a little stronger than mine because I don't think you have pink hair in real life."

I tried not to laugh. Connecting him with one of my best friend's soon-to-be grandmothers might have been a mistake, given her penchant for brownies with a little something extra. "I do not have pink hair, but I am hoping you can perform a miracle."

"Talk to me, Little Dude."

Blaze had called my brothers and me *Little Dude* since we came to live with my great-uncle and continued to despite the fact that I was now six feet four and over two hundred pounds.

"Do you, by any chance in tourist hell, have a cabin I could rent? Even just for the summer?" I asked.

Blaze blinked a few times, moving slowly and then suddenly speeding up, jumping out of his chair and heading to a board of keys. "Miracles abound, Little Dude. Just gotta open your eyes to truly see them."

My lips twitched. "And to see the pink hair?"

Blaze grinned. "Pink's your color. A couple just canceled on one of the Creekside Cabins. They were gonna be here all summer."

Relief washed through me fast and fierce. I loved my family. Wanted to spend plenty of time with them. But I also needed my space—all of us Archer brothers did in our own ways.

I clapped Blaze on the shoulder. "You are my hero."

He sent me one of those lopsided grins. "I'm just happy as hell you're home. Waylon missed you."

Guilt pricked at me. Ever since I'd gotten arrested at twenty-one and was given an ultimatum by the FBI—come work for them or do the time for hacking into one of their servers—I hadn't been home much. My three-times-a-year trips had been shorter, and my stays distracted because my head was usually stuck in a case.

One for the FBI or one of the *others*—the ones my brothers and I worked in the quiet, anonymously trying to help where we could. I didn't need to be a profiler to understand why. We were doing penance for crimes that weren't ours.

"Little Dude?" Blaze pressed.

I blinked a few times, clearing away the ghosts—no, the demons. "I'm happy to be back, too."

"Good." Blaze's voice went a little dreamy again.

I shook my head and accepted the key. "How much do I owe you for first and last?"

He just waved me off. "I'll invoice you."

My brow about hit my hairline. "You using a computer now?"

"I got me one of those tablets. Granddaughter taught me."

Laughing, I shoved the key with the cabin number on the chain into my pocket. "Small miracles."

"They are *everywhere*, Little Dude."

I gave Blaze a wave as I headed out, moving down the stairs and into the sunshine. I started down the block toward my SUV, which was in a parking place much farther away, thanks to the spot-stealer.

Just as I hit the curb to step down, something hit me. Right on top of my head with a force that spoke of heat-seeking missiles or air-dropped bombs. It was a bomb, all right. As I felt the top of my head, my face screwed up in a scowl.

Bird poop.

More than half a dozen curses left my lips. But as a familiar face spotted me from down the block, a man who always looked at me and my brothers with wariness in his eyes, I shoved those curses down. Swallowed them like I did all the things I wanted to give voice to but didn't.

Instead, I climbed behind the wheel of my SUV, wiping away the worst of the bird crap with some fast-food napkins and water from the bottle in the cupholder. I ground my back molars the entire ten-minute drive to the cabins along Clover Creek. It wasn't until I saw that not another person was in sight near the three cabins along the winding water that I truly breathed.

But I still couldn't take in the beauty around me. All I could think about was a shower and some painkillers for the headache I was now rocking. I hauled the one duffel I'd need out of the back seat and started for the cabin's front door. They weren't fancy, but I knew Blaze had a crew that made sure they were clean. And he could handle any repairs.

Cabin Two was bigger than expected. Three bedrooms. Two baths. A living room and kitchen that flowed together. And a yard with an epic view of the creek, the fields, and the forest beyond.

But I only cared about the shower.

I went straight for the bathroom, dumping my bag; shucking my shoes, glasses, and clothes; and climbing into the spray. There were a couple mini-bottles of shampoo, and I washed my damn hair twice, rolling my neck under the stream and hoping it would unlock some of the knots.

Finally, the water started to turn lukewarm, and I forced myself to climb out of the antique-looking shower/tub combo. It sure as hell wasn't made for a man my size, but I made do.

A noise caught my attention as I rubbed the towel over my hair. Scraping. *Someone trying to pick a lock?*

Everything in me went on alert. I grabbed my glasses, shoving the frames onto my face as I glanced down at my open duffel and cursed. I wasn't usually this careless. I was always prepared because I knew better than anyone what could hide…in the day or dark, behind a warm smile or a sinister scowl.

It didn't matter that I hated guns—weapons of any kind, really. I'd become a master with all of them. But the small and varied arsenal I maintained was in a travel gun locker in the back of my goddamned SUV.

Hinges squeaked—the front door opening. There was no time to wait.

I wrapped the towel around my hips and stalked out of the bathroom and down the hall, only to come face-to-face with a woman whose golden-amber eyes had gone wide with shock.

The expression appeared genuine, but I knew people could be good actors. The best.

Those wide doe eyes matched lips forming a perfect O of surprise. Her hair was pulled back into a high ponytail, and the long, wavy blond strands hung around her like some sort of teasing curtain. She wore cutoffs—the denim kind with threads that dangled and danced across tanned, toned thighs—and a tank top in a dusky pink that only heightened the sun-kissed quality of her skin.

And the shoes. They looked like they'd once been white high-top Chucks, but they'd been colored all over. And not by someone with a deft hand. I could just make out what appeared to be a cookie, a heart, and something that looked like a bear.

I took in every tempting, alluring inch of the woman—took in those facts and filed them away in less than ten seconds, knowing every single one of them could be a lie.

I let the scowl rise to my lips. "What the hell are you doing in my house?"

CHAPTER FOUR
Braedyn

I HADN'T BEEN STUNNED SILENT MANY TIMES IN MY LIFE. WHEN I accidentally broke a neighbor's window at age nine. When Vincent told me he didn't want anything to do with me or my child. When I finally held Owen in my arms. The first time I saw the Pacific Ocean.

And now.

This moment. As a man who looked like some cross between a professor and a biker with mountain-man height and shoulders prowled toward me.

I should've been scared. I told my brain as much. Said to reach for the pepper spray in my pocket. To call Yeti.

But I didn't. I was too busy ogling him.

It wasn't just his rugged beauty—though he had that in spades. It was something else. An energy that clung to him. The same kind infused into his skin by way of his tattoos. It wasn't as if he was covered from head to toe, but he had a healthy dose of ink.

Art that ghosted over his forearms and hands led to bare biceps and then gave way to a piece on his chest that stole my breath. I couldn't help but study the image that pulled taut over toned muscle.

A phoenix.

My mouth went dry as the design on my own rib cage seemed to heat. The man's phoenix was surrounded by wisps of smoke and ash, and I swore the creature's eyes glowed as they burned into me.

"What the hell are you doing in my house?"

The barked words had me pulling back to the here and now, regaining some sense of sanity as I heard my little boy's laugh outside as he played with Yeti. Just because this man had a tattoo similar to mine didn't make him a friend.

But I wasn't the only one who heard the words spoken with an edge of anger. Yeti did, too. And she didn't appreciate them directed at her human.

As I pulled out the pepper spray, Yeti tore up the steps of the cabin and charged in front of me, letting loose a ferocious growl. She didn't attack the man, just stayed between him and me, but the surprise of it was enough to have him stumbling back a step—stumbling back and losing his towel.

The shock of the sequence of events was enough to have my jaw dropping right along with the terry cloth. And I suddenly didn't know where to look. I didn't want to take my eyes off him in case he made a move, but I couldn't look anywhere on his very toned body without flushing to the shade of a tomato.

The man swiped up the towel and covered himself as Yeti bared her teeth. He cursed, backing up another step as a new voice joined the chaos.

"Mom?" Owen asked.

Normally, I'd revel in the fact that my son had called me *Mom* instead of *bro* or *bruh*, but all I could think about was that this situation had just gotten so much worse.

"Why is there a shirtless dude in our new house?" he continued, completely unshaken.

I let out a strangled sound, clamped a hand over my son's eyes, and backed out of the doorway. "I'm not sure why there's a shirtless dude in our house." But it was better than the naked one from thirty seconds ago.

The man let out a strangled sound as my dog growled low in her throat. "It's *my* house. Blaze rented it to me fifteen minutes ago."

Crap on a cracker.

When I picked up the keys, the landlord had seemed a little out of it. I really hoped he wasn't some scam artist. "He rented it to me two months ago, and I have a year's signed lease."

The man muttered another curse. "Can I move to get dressed and get my phone, or is your dog going to rip off an appendage I'm fond of?"

Owen giggled at that. "Yeti won't bite you. She's supes friendly."

"I wouldn't be so sure about that," I hedged. "Better move quick or she could get hungry."

The man made a choking sound.

"*Viens ici*," I commanded Yeti. She slowly moved back to me.

The man tilted his head to the side. "French?"

I shrugged, not wanting to share my answers with him. "You'll want to get dressed."

I turned then, trusting Yeti to watch my back as I got Owen down the front steps and back toward the SUV. I nibbled on my lower lip, wondering if I should call the sheriff's department. I quickly dismissed that thought. The authorities in Starlight Grove already thought of me as a nuisance.

But I'd be a thorn in every single side if it meant they'd help me find Nova.

Owen tipped his head back. "That guy has glasses like me."

I brushed some blond strands away from his face as I tightened my grip on my pepper spray with my other hand. "He does."

Owen hated his glasses. Had hated them since some kids in his class were cruel about them. But he also always noticed when someone else wore them.

The screen door slammed against the frame, and I instantly braced. I whispered another command to Yeti, telling her to be on guard. She wouldn't make a move unless I asked, but she would also not let the man get anywhere near Owen and me. It was one of the things we'd worked on, along with the search-and-rescue training. And right now, I was damn glad I had.

I lifted my gaze as I released my hold on Owen and shifted so I was another layer of protection. Even with as much as I'd been through, raising Owen as a single mom, I hadn't truly been suspicious of the world around me until Nova disappeared.

Everything changed in that single second. Afterward, I couldn't help but see everyone with an air of suspicion until they proved themselves trustworthy.

Now that the man was dressed, I could take in some other things about him. Sandy-brown hair that was drying with a wave to it. Dark-hazel eyes that held an edge to them, like a forest just before a storm. He was clad in jeans, a worn tee that read *The Boot*, and work boots. But it was the tortoiseshell glasses that had me curious. Everything about the man said he refused to be just one thing.

He was also clearly astute because he didn't miss how our little group aligned itself. The dog, then me, then my son. Something passed over those stormy eyes. *Pain?*

He stopped a good ten feet away, making sure we had plenty of space, and scrubbed a hand over his face. "Sorry about earlier. I just drove cross-country, found out I didn't have a place to stay, got shat on by a bird, and thought someone was breaking into my house."

A little tension bled out of me, and I eased my grip on the pepper spray. "Sounds like a no-good, very-bad day."

One corner of the man's mouth kicked up. "The absolute worst." Suddenly, his eyes narrowed on something behind me. "*You're* the worst. You're the one who stole my parking spot. You're the reason the damn bird pooped on me."

Owen giggled. "Harsh, Mom."

I glanced down at my son as he moved closer, before scowling at the man. "Excuse me, but I hardly think I control the sphincter muscles of our avian friends."

"Should've recognized the dog right off. He stuck his tongue out at me after you swiped the spot. Then I had no choice but to take the bird-poop spot."

"You're not even making any sense. And *her* name is Yeti. And she *is* capable of appendage ripping like you were afraid of, so I'd watch your tone."

The man moved as if to cover himself, wincing. "Adding insult to injury."

"You're the one who said I was the worst," I shot back.

"A bird *shat* on my head."

"Buck up, Buttercup. And if I'm the worst, you're the worstest."

His eyes narrowed on me at the word *buttercup*, clearly affronted.

"Sussy," Owen chimed in. "You both are."

"Sussy?" the man asked, brows pulling together.

I sighed. "Language of the youth."

"Prolly comes from suspect or suspicious. You can also say sus," Owen explained helpfully.

The man's mouth twitched in a movement so quick I wondered if I'd imagined it. "Understood. Well, I'm gonna call Blaze because he is the one who's actually sus."

I watched as he tapped something on the phone screen.

"Yeah. You rent the same cabin twice today, Blaze?"

I could hear muffled grumbling on the other end of the line.

The man pinched the bridge of his nose, shoving his glasses askew. "Yeah, it's a damn *oops*. I just scared the hell out of some woman and her kid. I was fu—" He eyed Owen. "I was freaking naked, Blaze."

Loud laughter boomed from the other side of the line.

He pulled the phone away from his ear and glared at it. "Not funny. I'm gonna report your stash of Lolli's brownies to the cops, then we'll see how much you're laughing." A pause. "Yeah, yeah, I know it's legal. I'm coming for the right key. Don't go anywhere."

He hung up without saying goodbye to the landlord.

I almost felt bad for Blaze if he had to come face-to-face with this cantankerous ass. He might be hot, but he was *grumpy* and slightly unhinged.

"Figure it out?" I asked hopefully.

The man shoved his phone into his pocket. "Gave me the wrong key. Looks like we're neighbors."

Oh shit.

CHAPTER FIVE
Dex

MY BOOTS THUMPED AGAINST THE SIDEWALK AS I WALKED away from Blaze's office, giving away my annoyed mood even as I tried to keep a pleasant expression on my face. When you carried the kind of history I did—my father, my arrest—you didn't have room for bad moods or scowls. So it was surprising that the woman whose name I hadn't gotten had pulled so many out of me.

I couldn't help trying to put the pieces together when it came to her. The way she shielded her son. The fact that she had a damn guard dog. None of it spoke of good things.

Guilt ate at me. And I'd been an asshole. I needed to apologize, make things right.

What was the right apology for accidentally flashing someone when you thought you were at risk of your dick being bitten off by a ferocious dog? Flowers? Wine? A candle?

God, I sucked at this sort of thing.

"He doesn't call. He doesn't write. He doesn't even tell you he's moving back to town."

I looked up at the sound of a familiar voice. Roger Oakley wore the same sheriff's department uniform he'd donned since graduating from the academy straight out of high school. And judging by the fact that his patch now read *sergeant*, he was moving up the ranks.

I wasn't surprised. Roger had always been one of the golden gods of Starlight Grove. Quarterback for the only football team in a decade to make it to state. Head of the student council. But hanging around with profilers so much at the FBI helped me pinpoint that he had something to prove. Maybe it was because his dad was a drunk and his mom had taken off when he was in middle school. He needed to prove he was worthy.

"Hey, man. Good to see you."

"Wylder said you were coming back. Didn't know it would be this soon."

"Small towns," I muttered.

Roger chuckled. "You had to miss it a little."

Had I? I wasn't sure. Losing the veil of anonymity I'd had in DC made me feel like I was standing naked right on Mountain View Way. Or maybe it was my earlier encounter with the mystery woman. Hard to say.

"It's nice to see some familiar faces," I half lied.

"You want to get a drink at the Boot later? Trav will be happy as hell you're back. He might even be able to get the ball and chain to let him off the hook for the evening."

"Travis and Cora got married?" I asked, not shocked that the high school sweethearts had tied the knot but that I hadn't gotten an invitation. Then again, it wasn't like I'd kept in touch with my friends here.

Roger shook his head. "Just engaged. But who needs that tight a leash?"

I let out a quiet chuckle. "I guess your lack-of-commitment ways haven't changed."

He held up both hands in mock innocence. "I just know who I am and who I'm not."

"Fair enough." It wasn't as if I had *future husband* tattooed on my forehead. Too much damage and mistrust had been laid in my formative years for that. I had the occasional partner, but even my female companions had grown farther and farther apart.

I was in that weird place where I couldn't handle something truly serious—the kind of relationship where someone saw all your secrets and scars—but something casual felt unfulfilling at best and cheap at worst.

"So, beers tonight?" Roger asked, rubbing his hands together.

"Sorry, man. I gotta unpack and desperately need a good night's sleep."

"Debbie Downer," Roger complained. "I'll hit up Mav and see if he's game."

"Unless he's on duty, you know he will be."

Mav was always up for a good time in all forms. BASE jumping. Mountain biking. A death match round of shots—or hot sauce. But then again, all the Archer brothers had an affinity for the spicy stuff.

"Next time," Roger called as he headed back toward the station.

"You got it."

I moved toward my SUV, the correct cabin keys now in my possession, and allowed myself to enjoy the journey a bit more this time. The wide-open landscapes reminded me of what I had, in fact, missed.

The wild edge to those expanses made me feel a little less alone, as if some part of me recognized myself in them. A tumbleweed rolled across the road ahead as the wind picked up, reminding me of the weird games of soccer my brothers and I had played with them after coming to live with Waylon.

As I made the turn onto Briarwood Lane, I took in the raw beauty of it. It was so different from the landscapes in and around DC. There was nothing manicured or refined, no white picket fences or perfect yards, just raw, authentic, powerful beauty.

I'd missed that: the land, my brothers, Waylon, Skylar. It was all I needed.

As I climbed out of my SUV, I heard a shout and braced to run when a peal of laughter came after it. The panic in me eased. Not the screams of a terrified little brother but the shrieks of a happy little boy.

A blur of movement caught my attention as I walked toward my cabin. I could just see a snatch of the yard behind Cabin Two. The little boy raced around, a water gun in his arms, the dog happily chasing after him.

Then there was a flash of blond strands. "Prepare for defeat, dark lord."

The boy let out a maniacal cackle. "Nevaaaaaaah!"

I stood there for a moment, watching them chase each other, occasionally hitting the other or the dog with a stream of water. Everything about them reminded me of simple joy. Innocence. Something I hadn't had in so damned long.

So I stayed, longer than I should've, soaking up that happy. And then I forced myself to unlock the door to Cabin Three and step inside. This one was smaller, with no bells and whistles, but it would be just fine. There was a bedroom, a kitchen, and a living area that I'd make my office. It faced Clover Creek and the meadows and forest beyond. It might not have a mountain view, but that meant cheaper rent. Given that I didn't have an actual job at the moment and would be seriously cutting into my savings to build my house, that was a good thing.

I made quick work of unloading my SUV but didn't bother unpacking my two duffels full of personal items. Instead, I went straight for the tech gear.

Surveying my furniture options, I headed for the smallish dining table and shoved it against one of the back windows. I'd need to order a gaming chair, or my back would seriously hate me. I started to unpack one of my monitors but paused as the woman caught her son, rolling with him to the ground as the dog barked and leapt over them in glee.

A ball of emotion lodged in my throat as I set the monitor down. My back molars answered that flare of emotion by gnashing together in frustration. Maybe they were too damn good to be true. Maybe it was all a show.

I hauled my laptop out of my messenger bag and settled on the couch that was more than a little lumpy. *Thanks for that, Blaze.* Flipping it open, I glanced at the laminated paper on the coffee table. It had a Wi-Fi network and password that was to be shared by all three cabins.

I shivered at the thought of shared Wi-Fi, but it would help me find a little of what I needed. As I logged into my VPN, I made plans for setting up my own satellite Wi-Fi. Within seconds, I could see every single device connected to the shared network.

"Bingo," I muttered, seeing an iPhone I knew wasn't mine.

Another handful of seconds later, I was into her device. The lack of text messages raised my hackles, and I instantly moved to her social media apps. Some people thought they had anonymity there. They were wrong.

With half a dozen keystrokes, I was into one of the photo-sharing apps people loved—people who weren't aware of all the ways it let others into their lives.

I wasn't sure what I expected of her profile, but it certainly wasn't an artsy array of photos and the handle *SearchingForSunrise*.

I frowned as I clicked on a picture, reading its caption.

Yeti loved the bone-fragment exercise. She's getting better and better at searching for older remains.

"What the fuck?" I whispered at my screen as I quickly went from one image to the next, a clearer picture emerging.

Yeti was a search dog, trained in both trailing searches for live human beings and human remains detection—HRD. And you didn't just decide to train a dog for that sort of thing randomly. You did it for a reason. That had my head lifting, my gaze searching for the woman with the blond hair and secrets in her golden eyes.

"What the hell is your story?"

CHAPTER SIX
Braedyn

SO THE HOT, SLIGHTLY UNHINGED MAN WAS MY NEIGHBOR. Definitely neighbor status given that he was currently shirtless, sitting on the side of the next-door cabin's roof and attaching some sort of gadget to it. I'd seen him coming back from a run this morning. Shirtless again, revealing far too many glistening muscles in the sunlight and that captivating tattoo. But missing his glasses.

I found I missed the tortoiseshell spectacles, which was absolutely bonkers since I didn't even know the man's name and he seemed about as fond of me as a rabid raccoon. But I guessed being neighbors was better than accidental roomies.

"Mooooooom," Owen called from down the hall.

I jerked away from the window as if someone had just caught me shoplifting. *Note to self: Don't ogle the hot, unhinged, grumpy neighbor.*

Grabbing my iced coffee, I headed in search of my son. I halted in his doorway, leaning against one side of the frame. "You bellowed?"

Owen rolled his eyes as Yeti lifted her head from her spot on Owen's bed. "What do I need to bring to camp again?" he asked.

I'd enrolled him in a summer-long local day camp, hoping it would give him some new friends for the start of school in the fall. It would also provide me with childcare for the job I was manifesting.

I did a quick sweep of the room and tried not to mentally calculate the time it would take me to get it organized. I'd managed to get Owen's bed and some of his clothes settled last night, but he'd opted for throwing items all over the room instead of putting them away.

"Well...I can tell you that you aren't going to need every item of clothing that has ever touched your body."

Owen sighed and dropped a thick coat he *definitely* didn't need. "Bruh."

"Bro," I shot back.

A soft giggle left his lips. It was the kind that made my chest ache because it reminded me just how young he still was—a little boy but getting older. Another pang hit as I thought about everything Nova was missing. Owen would be barely recognizable to her now.

Suddenly, he looked a little unsure. "I don't know what the other kids wear around here. I don't wanna take the wrong thing."

This time, my heart cracked. God, being a new kid sucked. I waded through the piles of clothes and toys to my boy and wrapped an arm around him. "Worst case, best case."

Owen let out a long breath. "Worst case, they think I'm a huge dork and no one wants to be friends with me. Best case, they think I've got sty because I'm from Oakland and everyone wants to chill with me."

I had to translate that sty meant style. It was a miracle I didn't need a dictionary at this point. At least Owen was giving my brain a workout.

Brushing the hair back from his face, I gazed down into his green eyes. "Worst-case plan?"

I'd learned over time that it didn't help to tell him that the worst case would likely never happen. It belittled his feelings and sent him the message not to trust himself and his emotions. Instead, we made plans—plans that would help him deal with any of his fears.

Owen tugged his lip between his teeth. "Move back to Oakland?"

"Never back down, what?" I challenged.

"Never give up," Owen grumbled. He snatched up a bathing suit. "If they hate me at first, I'll win them over with my gaming skills and Bigfoot knowledge."

A laugh bubbled out of me as I pulled him into a hug. "Dang straight. Best-case plan?"

"Best-case plan, I'm king of the school until I graduate and get to go learn coding."

I grinned. "*And?*"

"And I remember how it feels to be on the outside and make sure to include other kids," he mumbled.

I wiped invisible tears under my eyes. "They grow up so fast."

Owen tickled my side. I squealed but quickly sobered and cupped his cheeks. "Proud to be your mom."

"Proud to be your kid," he echoed.

I left a smacking kiss on his forehead before heading for the door.

"Sick!" Owen called after me. "And not in a good way."

"You've got fifteen minutes before we need to leave for camp, rizz king!" I called back.

"You're not using it right," Owen yelled back.

I shrugged. *Rizz* was supposed to loosely mean charisma. I thought I was close enough.

Heading down the hall, I slipped into the third bedroom. Just like in our house in Oakland, I'd always keep the door closed but would also never tell Owen he couldn't come in. If I did that, he'd instantly become interested—too interested. For now, he thought what dotted the walls were exercises for Yeti.

They weren't.

The room itself was the largest in the cabin. Not huge but with enough wall and storage space to create a headquarters. In Oakland, I'd slowly turned Nova's room into that headquarters. Now, I had a space that would turn into her room once I found her.

And I *would* find her.

I'd been told time and time again that what I found might not mean happily ever after and a sweet reunion. And I knew there was a chance I might not find Nova alive. But I couldn't help clinging to hope and the knowledge that I would *feel* if Nova had been wiped from this earth.

Either way, I would bring her home. I would bring her peace.

I crossed to the massive map of Starlight Grove and the surrounding areas. There were already a couple of pins in the map and a dish with more on the nightstand I'd placed below it. There were half a dozen colors with different meanings.

Yellow for the places Nova and I had visited on our trip before she disappeared. Green for the stops we'd made along our hike. Red for the last place I'd seen her and where I found her water bottle. Purple for reports of women who matched her description. Orange for where women with similar victim profiles had vanished.

There weren't many oranges. But there were a few. And I hoped like hell some of their loved ones would be at the support group meeting this weekend. Because maybe there was a common thread here that law enforcement had missed.

But that didn't matter because I was about to be a serious pain in their asses if they wanted to cold case Nova.

"Never back down, never give up," I whispered to the wall.

And I would never give up on Nova.

CHAPTER SEVEN
Braedyn

ROLLING MY SHOULDERS BACK, I IMAGINED SLIDING INVISIBLE armor into place. I'd need every piece of chain mail for the battle about to ensue.

Taking in the double glass doors and the sign above that read *Juniper County Sheriff's Department*, I sucked in a deep breath and reached for the handle. The moment the door opened, I heard the din of conversation and work. It wasn't the sort of noise that came from emergencies but from everyday business.

As I stepped inside, a woman in her mid-thirties looked up from behind the counter. "Afternoon, can I help you?"

"Hi. I wondered if Sheriff Miller was in?" I kept my voice steady and my expression neutral.

"Can I get your name to let him know who's here?"

I tried not to tense at the question. Of course, she'd ask. The problem was, my name would give Sheriff Miller warning. But I didn't have any other option. "Braedyn Winslow."

There was no recognition on the woman's face; she simply lifted the phone on her desk and hit a couple of buttons. "Sheriff, there's a Braedyn Winslow here to see you."

I watched as the woman's demeanor changed. The easy welcome slid away millimeter by millimeter, replaced by a hardness that had lines settling around her mouth and eyes. Not a glare exactly, but not nearly as friendly.

Still, I didn't let my expression change. Professional. Neutral. And unmovable. I'd sit in this reception area all day if I had to. I'd done it before on one of the occasions I'd managed a trip up here for the day while Owen was with a friend's family.

"Understood, sir," the woman said, lowering the phone to the receiver. She looked up with brown eyes gone guarded, making her skin seem paler than it had been just moments ago. "You'll have to wait."

"No problem," I said easily, moving toward the hard plastic reception chairs. What was it with law enforcement offices and hospitals? Always the worst chairs when you needed a moment of kindness.

I eased into the uncomfortable plastic shell and set my tote bag on the chair beside me. It was the one Nova had made me, complete with an embroidered Bigfoot in the top corner and the word *believe* next to it. I pulled out my book on scent training.

I wanted to start training Yeti on air tracking. It would allow her to move more quickly, and now that her recall was nearly perfect, I trusted her enough to release her without a lead. I'd just need to make sure she had her bear bell and a GPS collar.

"You know, I'm hurt," a familiar voice said. "You ask to talk to the big guy and don't even bother to stop and say hello."

"She emailed me and told me she was coming in," another voice said, a teasing edge to it.

I shut my book and looked up, a smile tipping my lips. The Juniper County sheriff might've been on my shit list lately, but that didn't mean his officers were.

My gaze settled on the owner of the first voice. "I might not have requested your assistance, but that doesn't mean I came without gifts." I pulled out a cellophane bag I'd tied with ribbon and handed it to Roger.

The tall man with sandy-blond hair took it easily, studying the contents. "Donuts, coffee, and speeding ticket cookies?"

The second man barked out a laugh, his green eyes twinkling. "I'll be damned."

I fished in my tote and retrieved a second bag. "One for you, too, Travis."

He grinned at me, patting his flat stomach as his gaze flicked to Roger. "Don't tell Cora she gave me these. I don't want to share."

"You never want to share," Roger mumbled as he untied his bag.

Travis quickly broke off a piece of cookie. "Sharing is for non-food-related items only."

"Not even with *Cora*? That's not very nice," I teased.

Roger popped a piece of cookie into his mouth. "Especially since they just got engaged."

My eyes went wide. "Seriously?"

A little pink hit Travis's cheeks, making his auburn hair look a little redder. "About a month ago."

I pushed up and out of the chair, giving the man a hug. "So happy for you."

And I was. Roger and Travis had both been on the original callout for Nova. And when Sheriff Miller started going longer and longer between updates, they'd kept me in the loop. But I knew I had to get Miller on my side if I wanted real law enforcement effort on Nova's case. I had to find something that would make him believe Nova was still out there, that there was hope.

"Looks to me like my boys got too much time on their hands," a loud voice boomed.

Both Roger and Travis tensed. Miller's tone was teasing, but I got the sense the words carried the jerk of a choke collar. The sheriff's hair had gone snow white with age, and while the bushy mustache should've been grandfatherly, his tone made it come across more sinister than anything.

A muscle flickered along Travis's jaw. "Just saying hello."

Roger was better at playing the game. He shot the sheriff a grin and held out his bag. "Cookie?"

Miller eyed the contents, and I could see he wanted one, but he shook his head. "No."

I bent, fishing out my third and final bag. "I brought one for you, too, sir. Home baked."

"You poison 'em?" Travis muttered under his breath.

Roger choked on a half laugh, half cough.

Miller just scowled but swiped the bag from me. "What do you want, Braedyn? There are no updates. I told you I'd call if there were."

"I know. But I wanted to let you know that I moved to Starlight Grove."

All three men went silent and stock-still.

"What in tarnation were you thinking?" Miller bellowed. "You think you can move to town and start riding my ass every week? I will bar you from this building. We got real cases to tackle. Your friend's gone. Tourists fall prey to all kinds of fatal accidents in these woods and mountains. I'm sorry for your loss, but you gotta let her go."

I bit the inside of my cheek so hard I tasted blood. "She's not gone. I found her water bottle in the parking lot. Someone took her."

"She probably dropped it on your way out on the hike—"

"She didn't. I saw her drink from it," I shot back.

Miller shook his head. "You *think* you did. Mind plays tricks. Guilt plays tricks."

His last statement was the truest thing I'd ever heard him say.

"I'm not wrong. And even if I don't have your help, that doesn't mean I'm going to stop. Ever."

Snatching my bag off the chair, I stalked out of the building and onto the sunbaked sidewalk. My breaths came in ragged pants until I got my temper under control.

"Brae."

I stiffened at the sound of Roger's voice but forced myself to turn around. The pity I saw written across his face was a sucker punch to the gut. "You think she's gone, too."

His blue eyes shifted to the side. "What I think doesn't matter."

"It does to me," I said quietly.

Roger studied me for a long moment. "I think she likely fell into the river and it took her under. I don't want to think she was kidnapped. Because if she was, she's gone, and it's not a pleasant way to go."

My stomach twisted at the thought. Delving into the world of missing persons after Nova disappeared, I'd heard all the horror stories. Human trafficking. Serial killers. Rapists. I didn't want any of that for my friend and sister.

"But," Roger went on, "sometimes, we have to look for *us*. We need to go down every possible road so we can let go. So tell me, what do you need?"

He might not believe, but he'd still help. I'd take that. "I need resources. I have maps of movements and possible sightings. I have similar cases of missing persons. But I need…I need access to camera feeds from that time period and the reports of possible sightings."

Roger winced and scrubbed a hand over his face.

"Miller won't let you," I surmised.

Roger shook his head. "Said he'll can my ass if I use company time or resources." He let out a long breath, glancing over his shoulder as if checking to make sure we had a modicum of privacy. "I'm not sure why Miller's taking such a hard line on this but he's heaping more work on anyone's plate who says they have time to look into Nova's case."

Anger stirred, a hot flush rising to my cheeks. I understood that they were a small department with limited to resources, but this was flat out cruel. "Then how am I supposed to get my hands on that footage?"

Roger studied me for a long moment. "It could've been erased by now. But…"

"But what?" I pressed, hope flaring.

"I've got a friend. He's damn good with computers. Might be able to find some workarounds. Let me see."

I stretched up, laying a smacking kiss on Roger's bristled cheek. "Thank you."

"Careful," Roger warned. "You keep kissin' me like that, I'm gonna keep askin' you to dinner."

"Sorry, pal. That particular shop is closed." And it would stay that way. Sometimes, trust had been broken in too many ways to let yourself go down that road. It wouldn't be fair to you or whoever you attempted it with.

Roger let his gaze sweep over me for a moment. "Damn shame."

I laughed, starting down the sidewalk. "I'm taking that as a compliment."

"It is one," he called back.

I gave him a wave and turned to head down the block. I took my time, looking in windows to see if there were any *Help Wanted* signs. The one in the window of Barrel & Branch was a bust. They were looking for someone who could work nights. I dropped off a résumé at the bookstore and an art gallery before pausing in front of the dark wood facade of the Boot.

A bar almost certainly was looking for someone who could work nights, but when I peeked in through the open saloon doors, I saw that it was half-full at three in the afternoon. That had to mean something.

Brushing my hair back, I took stock of myself in the reflection of the front windows: blond hair pulled back into a high ponytail with a few wisps framing my face, the light makeup I'd taken time to apply this morning—something I rarely did in the summer months when Owen and I were outside more. I'd picked dark-wash jeans and a white boho blouse that read casual but professional and paired them with sandals.

I needed to get cowboy boots if I wanted to fit in with the locals. I hadn't missed how about 75 percent of them wore the footwear or work boots, even though the temps had raised into the seventies.

Straightening my bag on my shoulder, I gave Nova's friendship bracelet a tap for luck and headed inside. I quickly scanned the patrons and marked a variety of folks—a table of guys who were likely locals, given they looked as if they'd recently kicked off from a construction site. I took stock of a couple poring over a hiking guidebook and had to stop myself from a warning lecture. A family piled into a booth, along with a few other groups. Two guys and a woman sat at the bar.

The space itself had real character. Two walls were adorned with local signage, while a third had nothing but license plates. The fourth was dedicated to the spectacular bar. The woodwork looked hand-carved and expertly done. And the bottles lining the shelves were various shapes, sizes, and values.

A dark-haired man standing behind the bar looked up from his phone as if he had radar for people approaching his domain. He quickly swept me from head to toe, not in a lascivious way but in an assessing one.

That sort of thing didn't bother me. I did the same, looking for any red flags or other alerts. So I gave him an easy smile. Not overly forced but warm. "Hi."

"Afternoon. Looking for a table?" he asked, those dark eyes never leaving my face. He was tall, leanly muscled, and had a hint of scruff. When he moved, I saw that his dark eyes had a golden-green cast.

"Actually, I was hoping I could talk to someone about a job opening."

Brown brows lifted in surprise. "Summer gig?"

I guessed that some tourists who stayed through the summer liked to find part-time work. It made sense, something to line your pockets while you were away.

"I'd take it for as long as you'd offer it."

The assessing stare was back. He double-checked my features as if he might've misplaced them somehow. "New in town?"

I nodded. "Just moved here from Oakland. I have restaurant experience, though it's been a minute. I worked in a bar and grill for about five years back in Rhode Island. In Oakland, I worked as an office manager at an accounting firm."

"Far from home," the man assessed. "Little bit of a different vibe up here."

It wasn't a question, but I understood what he was asking. He wanted to know if this was a fluke and if I would bail on him the second I realized we were in a small-as-hell town without the comforts of city life.

"Different is just what I'm looking for," I told him. And it wasn't a lie. The past year had fundamentally changed me in ways that made me crave quiet, peace, and the knowledge of who your neighbors were.

"Well," the man said, leaning against the back bar, "what are you looking for in a job?"

This was my chance. "Anything I can do from nine to four. I'll clean, serve, sous chef, wash dishes, mix drinks, clear tables. I've got some bookkeeping experience, so I could help in that area if you're looking for it."

He was quiet for a moment, then shoved off the bar and reached out a hand. "Wylder Archer. This is my bar, and it just so happens that I think bookkeeping is the seventh circle of hell."

A laugh bubbled out of me as I took his offered hand. "Braedyn Winslow, but my friends call me Brae."

"Well, Brae, there a reason you can't work past four?"

I swallowed. This could be the breaking point. "I have a son. He'll be in camp Monday through Friday, eight thirty to four thirty. I need to be with him the rest of the time. Once school starts, the hours will be similar."

"That's as good a reason as any." He glanced to his left, his gaze settling on a woman who looked to be in her early thirties with tanned skin and a sleek fall of light-brown hair. "Cora," he called.

She looked up as she set the final plate down on the table. The ease of the motion said she'd done it thousands of times before. "You called, boss man?" she said as she tucked her tray under her arm and crossed to us.

"Cora, this is Brae. She's new in town. How do you feel about training her for day shift?"

Cora's green eyes lit like a kid's at Christmas. "Hot damn. Best news of my day. Welcome to Starlight Grove, Brae."

"Thank you. And nice to meet you," I greeted. And then the light dawned. "Are you the Cora engaged to Travis by any chance?"

Her whole face lit up then. "I am. Do you know Trav?"

"A little." I struggled to explain just how I knew her fiancé without trauma-dumping on all of them. "He, uh, helped me out with an incident last year when I was visiting."

Cora simply nodded. "He's a good one."

But Wylder had that assessing look again. He didn't give voice to his curiosities. Instead, he pointed to a pass-through window where I could just make out a woman with salt-and-pepper hair and kind eyes. "That's Fiona in the kitchen. She's a sometimes cook and sometimes waitress."

"And all around keeping your asses in line," she called back. "Hi, honey. You can call me Fiona or Fee, I answer to both."

"Nice to meet you," I returned.

"Did I hear fresh meat?" a male voice called as it got closer.

I turned to see a man who looked to be in his mid-thirties but had the boyish expression of someone much younger. He was definitely handsome, with dark hair and blue-green eyes, but he wore it in a way that said he knew it and used it to his advantage.

"Aidan," Wylder warned.

"What?" he asked, affronted. "What did I do?"

"It was what you were *about* to do, which was hit on my new waitress and bookkeeper."

"Stop using your psychic abilities on me," Aidan muttered. He held out a hand. "Don't listen to the lies these two tell you. I'm misunderstood, that's all."

I took the hand, laughing as Aidan executed some sort of bow where he touched my knuckles to his forehead. I glanced at Wylder. "Psychic, huh?"

Wylder rolled his eyes in a movement that mirrored one of Owen's. "Hardly. Worked in bars since the second I turned eighteen. I know people."

That made a little more sense. And that sort of experience gave you a kind of wisdom that was hard to come by.

"He uses his gifts for evil," Aidan grumbled.

Wylder stiffened at that, and Cora sent Aidan a death glare.

He winced. "You know what I mean. He always knows when I'm lying about calling in sick."

The tension in Wylder's shoulders eased a bit but not all the way. "You're just too easy to read. You call in sick anytime you're here with friends the night before or the fish are biting."

"Yeah, yeah, keep your psychic powers away from me," Aidan

said with a laugh. "Even if you do look all hot as hell when you're mind-melding people."

There was something here—something in the interplay that had just occurred, the reaction to the word *evil*. But I wasn't sure what it was.

"So," Wylder said, bringing my focus back to him. "Can you start tomorrow?"

A grin split my face. "Seriously?"

"One-week trial. You do good, you become a permanent hire. You in?"

"I am so in," I agreed quickly.

Cora patted my shoulder. "Welcome aboard." She glanced down at my feet. "I recommend sneakers tomorrow."

"Noted." The fact that I could wear my lucky Converse that Owen had decorated for me was a definite bonus. I glanced at Wylder. "Is there a dress code?"

"Dress code for what?" a deep voice asked—a *familiar* deep voice. Something about the tenor. It had a frequency all its own that made my skin pebble in anticipation.

I turned, taking in my hot, unhinged neighbor. He'd obviously showered and wore jeans that hugged thick thighs—likely a by-product of those morning runs—and a worn T-shirt with writing so faded I couldn't make it out. And the glasses were back. Damn, those glasses.

But beneath them, I took in the dark-hazel eyes full of suspicion. The emotion was only amplified by the lines of tension bracketing his mouth. Apparently, my neighbor was just as unhappy to see me here as he was at the cabin he'd thought was his. The only problem was, I was here first.

"Are you following me?" I accused, a hint of humor lacing my words. I couldn't help poking the grumpy bear.

The man glowered in my direction. "It's my brother's bar. What's your excuse?"

Oh, hell.

That meant my hot, grumpy-as-hell neighbor would be in here.

Possibly a lot. But I didn't let that make me falter. I jutted out my chin. "I work here."

"You hired her?" the man demanded, clearly disbelieving.

"Jesus, Dex, what's your deal?" Wylder asked.

Dex. It fit him somehow. Short, to the point, and a little harsh but still sexy as hell.

"Newsflash, neighbor, just because *you* think I'm the worst doesn't mean everyone does," I informed him.

Cora let out a strangled laugh. "What'd you do, Dex?"

"*I* didn't do anything," Dex began.

"He broke into my house and flashed me," I said, completely nonchalant, knowing it would just piss Dex off.

He gaped at me. "That...that isn't even remotely true."

"Dude, you can get arrested for that shit," Aidan muttered.

I arched a brow at Dex. "Isn't it true?"

He glared at me. "You are the worst."

I grinned. "I'm afraid that's you, Bird Poop Boy." I shot Cora and Wylder a wave. "See you tomorrow."

And with that, I left Dex to explain. It served him right, the grumpy pants.

CHAPTER EIGHT
Dex

MY ELDEST BROTHER STARED AT ME FOR A LONG BEAT AND then burst out laughing. "Bird Poop Boy?"

I scowled at him. "It's a long story."

Aidan slapped me on the shoulder. "It always is, man. Looks like that one's keeping you on your toes."

I didn't miss the unspoken question beneath his words—one that had my skin suddenly feeling too tight for my body. But Wylder saved me from having to say anything.

"Aidan…if you cost me another waiter or waitress because you broke their heart, I will put you on bathrooms for the rest of the year."

It was Wylder's dumb luck that his biggest flirt of a staff member had interest in both men and women. It doubled the potential issues if the relationship didn't work out.

Aidan's jaw went slack. "The rest of the year? Cruel and unusual punishment, boss man."

Cora rolled her eyes. "More like you're on your ninth life."

One corner of Aidan's mouth kicked up. "Just call me cat boy."

"Both of you, get back to work before I decide the stockroom needs a full reorg," Wylder shot back at the two of them.

Aidan saluted and took off for one side of the restaurant, while Cora just shook her head and moved toward the other.

Wylder's focus zeroed in on me, his dark-hazel gaze so similar to mine—and someone else's. A person we wanted no ties to. But there was a different quality to Wylder's. Something sharper than the rest of ours. He put together pieces others missed and could give my profiler friends in the Behavioral Analysis Unit a run for their money.

"Beer?" he finally asked.

Of course he didn't go in with whatever question he actually wanted to ask. I gave him the play. Sliding onto a stool, I rested my arms on the bar. "Pass on the beer but wouldn't mind a Coke."

Wylder's hands moved without him looking. He could've poured half the drinks in this bar with a blindfold. But that's what happened when you worked in the same place for a couple years shy of two decades.

He slid the soda over the worn but gleaming wood. "You turning into me?"

It was a fair question. Given the end of my tenure with the FBI and the couple of cases I'd helped my ex-profiler friend, Anson, with in Sparrow Falls, the demons had been rustled up, to say the least. "You know booze isn't my answer."

Wylder's mouth twisted in a lopsided grin. "Nope, you prefer vengeance via keystrokes."

I chuckled and took a sip of the crisp Coke. "I'll never know why you kept the place."

Wylder leaned against the back of the bar, running a towel between his fingers. "Sometimes, you have to face it. Just to prove you can. That it didn't get the best of you."

He'd done that and more. Gotten sober. Worked a program. Even mentored others going through the program now.

I met my brother's gaze, not looking away. "Proud of you."

He didn't hold my focus for long, always uncomfortable with any sort of praise. "So," Wylder began, finally settling into what he wanted to know. "What is it about Miss Braedyn Winslow that has your knickers in a twist?"

Braedyn.

I could've looked up her name. The moment I got into her phone, I could've looked up every damn thing about her. But I'd stopped myself.

The one profile I'd found was already too tempting. I'd lain awake for hours last night, scrolling photo after photo, memorizing every detail. And I couldn't deny that her putting me in my place was starting to feel like a game I didn't want to stop playing. Only, that was the last thing I needed.

"She doesn't." The two words came out gruffer than my normal voice.

Wylder simply arched a brow. "You aren't typically a grumpy bastard who scowls at everything that moves. Brae just bring it out of you or something?"

I scrubbed a hand over my face. *Shit.* My inner asshole kept rearing its ugly head. "Rough day when I met her. Blaze messed up the rental keys. I ended up in her cabin. I thought she was breaking in—"

"And you were naked?" Wylder asked, amusement in his words.

I glared at my brother. "I had on a towel. I was getting out of the shower. Then her dog lunged at me and—"

"You gave her one hell of a show?"

"It wasn't my finest hour."

"Dex, I hate to break it to you, but you're not exactly doing a great job of remedying that."

Everything he said was so very Wylder. He was the peacekeeper, the one always trying to soothe others' hurts and wounds.

"Got a few submissions for us to look through," I said, taking a sharp right into new territory.

Wylder's eyes narrowed on me. "I know what you're doing."

I shrugged. "Let me do it anyway."

"For now," Wylder grumbled, always wanting to excise the wound.

I pulled my phone out of my pocket and navigated to the app I'd created to hold all the website submissions for missing persons cases. Three had come in over the last week alone, and given that people only found us through word of mouth, that meant something.

"Missing woman outside Coeur d'Alene. Disappeared while hiking. Teen boy in Dayton, Ohio. Parents think he might have run away, but they're not sure."

A muscle along Wylder's jaw twitched. "I hate the kid ones."

I didn't have to agree audibly for Wylder to know I felt the same way. "Father of two went out for drinks one night and never came home. That one's in Houston."

"Last two you might be able to give some insight on the tech side alone," Wylder said.

He wasn't wrong. With a handful of careful hacks, I could tell whether that father of two was truly gone or if he'd just decided to bail on his family. The teen might be harder, depending on whether he had a debit or credit card or a phone he was still using.

It was just a hell of a lot riskier now. My old boss had warned me that I would no longer have their protections if I chose to leave the FBI. She wasn't an idiot. She knew what I did on the side, what had become a compulsion—not just for me but also for my brothers.

"I'll do some preliminaries before I present." That was how it always went. I ran initial searches and verified data, then brought it to my brothers, and we decided as a group. If one person had concerns, we didn't take the case. We all had a role to play, and if someone was uncertain, we couldn't work as a unit.

Wylder rubbed at a mark he spotted on the bar. "Not like you don't have time on your hands. When are you going to get a job?"

I flipped him off. "I've got time. Savings." I'd worked more than a few side gigs while putting in my decade at the FBI. It had given me a decent-sized nest egg. And I could pick up more consults anytime I wanted to.

Some might suggest I dip into the wealth our father had left behind from his import/export business, but none of us had touched it for any reason but to fund our work. It had become our unspoken vow.

The work was how we dealt with everything. How we came to terms with all the horrors our father inflicted, things so dark and twisted it seemed impossible that we'd missed the signs. But we had. Until it was too late.

Now, we tried to right the wrongs in small ways. To find those who had gone missing. For families that didn't have answers. Just like the torment our father had inflicted on so many. But when you were a serial killer, you didn't care about the hurt you caused. Worse, you liked it.

And our father? He loved that kind of pain.

And *that* was the DNA running through my veins. The genetic makeup that always left me wondering if I would become like him one day.

CHAPTER NINE
Braedyn

PULLING INTO THE HALF-FULL PARKING LOT, I TOOK IN THE recreation area. Yeti let out a happy bark as she did the same.

"Playground. Sweet," Owen muttered.

We were on day eight in Starlight Grove and slowly adjusting to our new home, even if I'd had to find a noise app that played city sounds to fall asleep. Work had been surprisingly…fun. Aidan was a hoot, Cora was someone I could see myself becoming real friends with, Wylder was a kind boss, and Fiona kept us all in line. I hadn't seen much of my hot, unhinged neighbor and didn't want to look too closely at my disappointment at that fact.

Owen's camp experience had been positive overall. Even with a couple of kids who sounded like bullies, he was making friends. Yeti was *thrilled* with her new surroundings and primed for adventure.

And me? I was…hopeful.

For the first time in a while, I was excited for what might happen now that I had access to the area where Nova had disappeared. And today was a big part of that.

Compass was a national organization that formed local support groups for people with missing loved ones. It was a way to access resources but also emotional support. And Juniper County had its own chapter.

I rubbed my palms over my jeans, trying to clear away the dampness. I'd been super involved with the Bay Area chapter of Compass, but new people meant opening myself up all over again and sharing some of the most painful moments of my life with strangers.

But they wouldn't stay strangers. With time and vulnerability, they'd become community. At least, I hoped.

I took a moment to stare down at the pink, purple, and teal threads woven into the friendship bracelet Nova had lived up to every day I'd known her. Now, I had to do the same.

Rolling my shoulders back, I turned off the engine and slid out of my SUV. I opened the back door and gave Yeti a soft command to stay at my side. She did but quivered as Owen bounded out after her.

"I wanna swing and then do the monkey bars," Owen said, practically bouncing.

My mouth curved, loving every moment he still felt like my little boy instead of an almost preteen. "What are the rules?"

"Bruh, I know the rules."

"Then it'll be easy for you to tell me, *bruh*."

Owen smiled, even if slightly grudgingly. "Stay in sight of you at all times. If I want to go anywhere but the playground, I have to ask. Don't talk to adults I don't know unless you're there." His lips twitched. "And I bet you don't even want me to take candy from strangers."

I drilled a finger into his side. "Could be losing candy privileges altogether with that smarty-pants response."

He laughed, trying to dodge my tickles. "Fine, fine! I'll play by all the rules. Can I go?"

"Fly free, my son."

With a roll of his eyes, Owen took off for the swings. Yeti pranced next to me as if asking *Can I go? Please?*

I dropped a hand to give her floofy head a scratch. "Sorry, girl, you gotta stay with me." I clipped on her leash, which she stared at indignantly. "Sorry about that, too, but rules are rules," I said, pointing to a park sign.

Sliding my Bigfoot tote bag over my shoulder, I took in the group assembling in the pavilion between the playground and what looked like a soccer field. Someone had hung a sign with COMPASS in big, printed letters. Why did this feel like the first day of school?

I took a deep breath and started toward the pavilion. There were about ten or so people in a wide range of ages and appearances. Even a few kids ran around. At least Owen wouldn't be alone in coming along. I just had to be careful with what he overheard.

As I approached, a woman who looked to be in her mid-thirties with blond hair caught sight of me. A warm smile tipped her lips as she crossed in my direction. "Are you here for the Compass meeting?"

I swallowed, my tongue suddenly feeling heavy in my mouth. "Yes. I'm Brae."

"Oh, Brae! I'm Holly." The woman was already moving in for a hug. "It's so nice to finally meet you. And this must be Yeti. I've heard a lot about you."

"Clive?" I asked with a relieved laugh. The head of the Bay Area chapter of Compass had said he was going to reach out to the woman who headed up this chapter. Apparently, he'd given her a complete rundown.

Holly beamed. "He's your biggest fan. Where's your son? You're always welcome to bring him, too."

I inclined my head toward the playground. "He's here and ready for play duty."

Holly nodded knowingly. "Always good to have an activity."

"Always," I agreed.

"Come on." She waved me toward the pavilion. "I'll introduce you and Yeti around."

The picnic tables had an array of sandwiches, cookies, and drinks, along with other snacks. Some people had brought camp chairs to set up, while others opted for the picnic benches. Curious gazes lifted to me as we approached.

"Everyone, this is Brae. She moved here from the Bay Area, where she was involved in Compass. And this is her dog, Yeti, who also happens to be trained in search and rescue," Holly said, that same bright smile on her face.

A series of greetings reached me, and a few people pushed to their feet, crossing in my direction. A man in his mid-forties with a hint of gray at his temples extended a hand. "Welcome. I'm Jack."

"Nice to meet you, Jack."

"Search dog, huh?"

I nodded. "Trained in trailing searches and HRD."

His brows lifted. "HRD?"

I glanced around in deference to any little ears, but the couple of kids I'd seen had run off toward the playground. "Human remains detection."

"Whoa," Jack muttered, assessing Yeti with new eyes.

"Hi, Brae. I'm Alma," a woman in her sixties greeted, lines deepening in her tanned skin as she smiled. "And those three little ragamuffins are my grandchildren."

"That little troublemaker is my son," I said, pointing out Owen on the swings. "Lovely to meet you."

As people got settled, a new face appeared. She looked about my age, with the palest blue eyes I'd ever seen. Her light-blond hair was pulled into a loose braid that hung down her back, and the requisite cowboy boots peeked out from beneath her jeans.

She extended a hand to shake. "Hi. I'm Aster."

"Nice to meet you. Brae."

She had the kind of smile that instantly put you at ease. "I'm the resident therapist. I help provide additional support if needed."

Suddenly, more pieces clicked into place. The waiting until I'd gotten my bearings for an introduction. The welcoming smile.

It wasn't out of the norm for a therapist to help out at the Compass meetings. When a loved one vanished, plenty of trauma came on its heels, and big feelings could come up as you processed.

"Nice to meet you."

"You, too. If you need anything at all, just let me know. Even if it's only a recommendation for where to find the best cup of coffee."

"*That* I will take you up on," I said with a quick grin.

Aster laughed. "Oh, I've got you covered. For simple, I actually love the diner. If you're feeling like a latte or a blended drink, the Cozy Cup next to the bookstore is perfect."

"I'm taking mental notes."

"All right, everyone," Holly began, clapping her hands together. "Let's find our seats so we can get started."

I glanced around at the group, trying to settle on the best spot. A familiar face with light-brown hair and green eyes looked up, surprise lighting her expression. "Brae." Cora greeted me. "There's an open spot here."

"Thanks," I said, taking the camp chair next to her. I waited for her to press, ask questions. But she didn't. And the fact that Cora was here should've told me she wouldn't because she'd lost someone, too.

"Hello, gorgeous," she greeted my dog. "This must be the infamous Yeti. Can I pet her?"

"You'll be her favorite person forever."

Cora instantly sank her hands into Yeti's fur, giving her all the scratches. "What an angel. Goodest girl in the world, aren't you?"

I laughed. "Only sometimes."

"All right, settle in, everyone," Holly commanded.

Every Compass chapter leader had a slightly different style, but I could already tell that Holly liked being at the center of things. That wasn't necessarily bad. Most groups needed a leader. And it was clear Holly wore that badge with pride.

As she went through the opening business, I felt eyes on me. My gaze lifted to find a man in his early seventies studying me. Not in an inappropriate way, more of a curious one. The moment our eyes met, he gave me a quick grin. I understood the curiosity about what someone's story might be, but I hated it just the same.

As the opening business concluded, Holly took a seat next to Aster. "Does anyone have a case update for us?"

Compass meetings usually happened once a month. Occasionally, there was a call for volunteers to help if a member needed boots on the ground for something. To search an area. To hand out fliers. But mostly, it was monthly meetings, which meant there were usually a fair number of updates.

The man in his seventies who'd been studying me earlier cleared his throat.

Holly's gaze snapped to him. "Go ahead, Bruce."

His throat worked as he leaned forward with his elbows on his knees. "We, uh, my daughter and her husband, they found my grandson."

The circle reacted in various ways. Next to me, Cora inhaled sharply. A few folks made audible sounds of concern or hope.

Bruce clasped his hands together tightly, knuckles bleaching white. "He's living on the streets down in San Francisco." His voice hitched. "My daughter and her husband went down there when the private investigator called. And Shawn...he didn't want to be found."

A few more sounds of heartbreak filtered through the air.

Tears swam in the older man's eyes. "He'd rather sleep on the cold cement with nothing but a tarp to keep him dry. He'd rather that existence than a warm bed and hot meals, just so he can have his drugs."

Cracks erupted in my chest as my gaze sought out Owen on instinct. He was racing up the jungle gym with a little girl. I couldn't imagine what I would do if faced with the same fate.

Jack clapped Bruce on the shoulder, holding his grip but not saying anything.

Bruce hiccupped. "He doesn't give a damn that he turned our lives upside down for the past nine months. That we've spent endless time, resources, worry."

"Selfish," Holly bit out. Not directed at Bruce but at the person hurting her friend.

The vehemence in Holly's single word caught me off guard. It was so at odds with her warmth from when I first met her. But we all had our triggers. Maybe this was one of hers.

Aster reached out with a light hand, resting it gently on Holly's arm for a moment before turning to Bruce. "Hurts like hell when someone chooses that."

The way she said the words spoke of experience, which had me curious.

"Like a damn brand," Bruce rasped.

"And all we can do is remind ourselves that it has nothing to do with us. Addiction is a disease—one with no easy cure. And the only one out there requires *choice* from the afflicted," Aster went on.

Alma made a clucking sound with her tongue, nodding in agreement. "My Maya. She was in that life, making choices that put her at risk. And now, I constantly have to battle being terrified for her out there and furious she left her children behind without a second thought."

Bruce scrubbed a hand over his face as he turned toward the woman. "I don't want to hate my grandson, but that anger…it's so fierce."

"It'll always be there," Alma told him. "Flashes of it so potent they steal your breath. But they come further and further apart. Time."

"How can we help?" Aster inquired. "What do you need?"

"I don't fuckin' know," Bruce muttered. "Now that I know he's alive and wasn't taken by some monster, that he's not dead, I just… feel lost. Like I don't belong here. Don't belong anywhere."

Holly leaned forward, dipping her head to meet Bruce's gaze. "You'll *always* belong here."

I found myself softening toward Holly's earlier harshness. There was more than a good heart underneath it all. And when you lost someone, you sometimes needed to channel it into purpose.

Bruce sucked in a stuttered breath. "He's not missing anymore."

Holly's eyes misted. "Neither is my boy. But I'm still here."

Hell. With as young as Holly was, she had to have lost her son at far too young an age. Suddenly, I wanted nothing more than to pull her into my arms and hold on tight. Which was the ultimate lesson, wasn't it?

Someone might not be your kind of people, there might be something about them that annoyed you or that you disliked, but they were a *human being*. Someone with losses and triumphs, traumas and loves. And, most of all, they deserved support when they needed it.

"We all have a place here," Cora said softly next to me.

Aster nodded. "That's right. We all belong because of shared experiences and the commitment we've made to support one another however we can. You think you can still do that?"

Bruce lifted his head and met Aster's pale-blue gaze. "I can do that."

Her mouth curved into a soft smile that told him he was seen. "Good."

Holly leaned back in her seat, wiping her hands on her dark jeans. "Anyone else?"

I felt Cora shift next to me. Her gaze dropped to her lap, where she plucked at a loose thread on her jeans. "Tomorrow's the anniversary. Eleven years since my mom disappeared."

This was different. It was the kind of share that didn't come with news or developments. The kind that was only put out there because it needed someone to bear witness. Over a decade without someone you loved…

A different sort of ache took up residence in my chest—the kind borne of fear. The kind that asked if I'd still be here ten years from now, saying the same sorts of things. The kind that wondered if I, too, would never find answers.

"Sometimes," Cora began, clearing her throat, "sometimes I wonder if she just decided to leave, peaced out on me and my dad and started over somewhere without the complications of family. I don't know which would be worse: her choosing to leave or her being stolen from us."

Bruce made a sound of agreement in the back of his throat.

Cora's head lifted, her eyes finding his. "Either way, it's pain. Part of you is frozen—the you that you were when they went away—and part of you is this whole different person."

An invisible match lit the ache in my chest then. As if soaked in kerosene, it flamed to life. "Like they wouldn't even recognize you if you passed them on the street," I whispered.

Cora turned to me, her expression pained but somehow relieved at the same time. Because I'd seen her, because I knew her pain. And that was the magic of Compass.

"Exactly," she agreed.

I felt another gaze on me and looked up to find Aster's understanding eyes studying me. She sent me a gentle smile. "Do you want to share what brings you to Compass, Brae? There's no pressure—"

I shook my head as if shaking off that suggested pressure. The longer I waited, the harder it would be to open that wound. My fingers dug into my jeans-clad knees. "My best friend—more like my sister. The person who helped me raise my son."

My gaze flicked to Owen, and I watched for a moment as he raced around the playground, glasses bouncing up and down on his nose. I swallowed hard. "We were here, in Starlight Grove, on a girls' weekend a year ago. She disappeared on a hike."

There were a few sounds of pain or intakes of breath around me, but I didn't search them out. It would be harder if I did. Instead, I let my vision go blurry as I watched my son have the time of his life.

"I stepped off the trail to take a stupid picture. Wildflowers. I tripped and almost went straight into the river. It took me a few minutes to right myself and get up the embankment—no more than five. And she was gone."

My fingertips began to tingle, and I ordered myself to breathe. "There was no sign of her or her pack. We were less than a mile from the trailhead, so I ran back there. Nothing. Not until I found her water bottle on the ground."

"I remember reading about that in the paper. They said law enforcement suspected accidental death, but you think she was taken?" the man named Jack asked, his eyes going hard.

My throat worked as I tried to dislodge the emotion making itself at home there. "I do. The sheriff thinks she somehow fell into the river from fifty feet away or got mauled by a cougar but managed to leave no blood behind."

Jack's dark eyes flashed. "Practically that whole department's a fucking joke."

"Jack," Aster warned.

"Yeah, yeah. Helpful, not harmful." His gaze flicked to Cora. "Not Travis. He's actually marginally useful."

Cora's lips twitched. "I'm gonna take that as the ultimate compliment it is."

Jack barked out a laugh. "True enough."

Alma looked at me. "So you're just visiting, then? Trying to help?"

"No, I, um, moved here."

Bruce let out a low whistle that I was sure spoke for the surprise of the whole group.

"She's my family." My voice hitched on the last word. "She was there for me when no one else was. I'm never going to give up on her."

Cora reached over tentatively and squeezed my hand. "She's lucky to have you."

The meeting continued with more shares and talk. Holly asked if anyone needed volunteers for search projects of any kind. I'd be taking the group up on that offer at some point—once I had a better idea of where to focus the volunteer hours.

As Holly closed the meeting, Yeti looked up at me balefully as if to say, *Can I play now?*

Aster grinned as she walked up. "Your girl has all the personality."

I chuckled. "She's very annoyed that we came to a park for something other than playtime."

Aster crouched and got on my dog's level. She sifted Yeti's fur with her hands, finding the spots that sent her into a state of pure ecstasy. "You get a gold star for behavior, Miss Yeti." Aster's pale-blue gaze flicked to me. "Think you could train my dog? He's great with cattle but has a mind of his own the rest of the time."

"Trust me, Yeti can be the most stubborn dog on the planet when she has a mind to."

Aster moved to scratch behind Yeti's ears. "You? Never."

The way she handled Yeti, looked for all the tiny responses, told me she had plenty of experience with animals. But the mention of cattle meant she likely lived on a ranch—a life full of animals.

Maybe I'd find that for myself one day. A tiny patch of land with an array of dogs and other animals. Maybe a goat. I felt like a goat would be fun.

"So," Holly began as she walked up, "what did you think?"

I scanned the group, which was now snacking and chatting, the mood lighter. "Everyone seems pretty amazing."

I swore Holly's chest puffed up with pride. "They really are. We're lucky."

Aster pushed to her feet. "Let me give you my number. We can all meet up for dinner or a drink one evening."

My gaze moved to Owen yet again.

"Or lunch or coffee," Aster quickly amended.

I shot her a grin. "That whole childcare thing."

She smiled back. "I get it. I have a nephew who spends his summers with me."

Pulling out my phone, I opened the contacts app and handed it to her. "That'll keep you on your toes."

"Eli?" Cora asked with an amused grin.

"The one and only," Aster said as she punched in her contact information. "You know he's probably only a year or two older than your son. We should get them together."

"I'd love that."

Aster handed me back my phone. "We'll set it up."

"Is there anything else you need?" Holly asked. "Anything with your friend's case?"

It was incredibly kind of her to offer, and I could tell this group did more than just listen to each other. They lent a hand whenever it was needed.

"I'm still figuring that out," I told her honestly. "I think the next thing is getting some tech help. I was hoping the sheriff might be looking into some camera feeds, but that's not going to happen. Roger at the sheriff's department said he has a friend who might help."

"Not..." Holly began but trailed off, sending my spidey-senses tingling.

"He's back," Cora said quietly. "Maverick told Trav he's back for good."

Aster stiffened.

"What's with the tension?" I asked, cutting through the veiled words and hushed tones.

Aster rolled her shoulders back. "Sorry. Roger's friend, he's a hacker. Or *was* one. Got arrested in college and then got scooped up to work for the FBI. But he's a good guy."

Holly made a sound in the back of her throat that said otherwise.

"He was a black-hat hacker wrapped up in the dark web, and we *know* what goes on there."

Aster's eyes narrowed on Holly. "He was there trying to help people. People like us."

"That's what *he* says. And given who his father is…" Holly argued.

A muscle fluttered in Aster's cheek. "Don't," she clipped. "Don't be like the rest of the narrow-minded assholes in this town."

There was a story here—one that ran deep. But the anger that flashed in Aster's eyes told me it was a tender one, and now wasn't the time.

Holly's jaw tightened, molars grinding together. "You're right. I shouldn't." She turned to me. "But you should still be cautious. I don't want you getting wrapped up in something illegal."

Nerves flitted through my belly. But what other choice did I have? The legal avenues of investigation weren't exactly on my side. "I'd still like his help."

Holly's lips flattened into a hard line.

"You look like you sucked on a lemon, Holls," Cora chided.

The expression only deepened.

Cora laughed. "Come on. Dex is a good guy. And you know it."

It was my turn to stiffen. "Did you say Dex? Glasses? The guy whose hotness is only matched by his grumpiness?"

Aster looked confused. "He does wear glasses, and he's definitely hot. But the only asshole in that family is Maverick." Her mouth tightened on the name, and I realized her earlier tension wasn't at the mention of Dex but Maverick, who had to be his brother.

But I was still stuck on one thing. The black-hat hacker whose help I desperately needed? He was my hot, unhinged neighbor who hated me.

Great. Just great.

CHAPTER TEN
Dex

THE SOUND OF TIRES ON GRAVEL HAD ME LOOKING UP FROM MY desk. I couldn't help the pull of my attention, the need to get a look and find out just a little more about my neighbor. I didn't want to even think about how much time I'd spent scrolling her photos.

Or the number of times I'd replayed our encounter at the Boot. God, she was pure fire. A hellion, honestly. The truth was, I was worried she'd become an addiction. But I hadn't given in to the urge to dig deeper. I hadn't run a background check or looked into her financials or personal communications. It would've been so easy. But wrong. And risky.

Still, I let myself take the look I wanted now. Turning around, I watched out the cabin's front windows as she let the beast dog and her son out of the SUV. The little boy practically leapt from the vehicle, making the dog bark and the woman laugh.

Brae.

Making Brae laugh. I had her first name. And her last. I could plug them into a simple search engine and—nope. No. No. No.

Brae's head lifted as though she sensed someone watching her. Long, blond hair caught on the breeze as she glanced around, her focus landing on my cabin. There was no way she could see me, given how we were both angled, but I swore she looked right at me.

She tugged a plump, berry-pink lip between her teeth and took a step toward my cabin before stopping. She shook her head, talking to herself as she did, then turned around and headed toward her own cabin.

Disappointment flared. And why the hell was that? I didn't need to get mixed up with a neighbor, in any way, shape, or form. They were too close. Had the potential to see too much. And I had more important things to focus on.

But I couldn't help but wonder why she'd been tempted to walk my way. Another verbal sparring session? Did she need something? It wasn't like people borrowed a cup of sugar these days. Maybe she needed someone to let her wild beast out while she was at work.

My phone dinged, making me realize I'd been staring at the place where Brae had been, even though she was gone.

"Get a grip," I muttered as I swiped up my phone and saw a group chat name flash.

Maverick has changed the name of the group to 50 Shades of Slay.

I scowled at the screen. This was Mav's way, making light of anything serious, taking trauma and laughing in its face. But not everyone in our brotherhood felt the same.

> **Kol:** *What the hell is wrong with you?*
>
> **Maverick:** *Where do you want to start? So damn good-looking I can't get through the day without a woman hitting on me?*
>
> **Me:** *Head so big it makes it hard to fit through doors?*
>
> **Maverick:** *I mean, my dick is so big it can make it hard to walk.*
>
> **Wylder:** *Dude. TMI.*
>
> **Kol:** *Someone change the name back.*

It was a toss-up who would hate Mav's group name more, Kol or Orion. But Orion had been mostly silent in our brother chat lately. And I worried about what that meant.

> **Wylder:** *I dunno. It's kind of funny.*
>
> **Me:** *Your lack of tech know-how is truly terrifying to me. Where did I go wrong?*
>
> **Kol:** *Fuck off, computer nerd.*

I laughed but took pity on him and changed the group name back to what it had been before: *Hot Sauce & Hot Goss.*

> **Maverick:** *Second-best group name, but I'll take it. This text is to tell Orion that his brother has returned from his sentence with the FBI and that his presence is required at family dinner tonight.*

No texts came in for a moment, and that earlier worry intensified. Orion had ended up the most changed after that night nineteen years ago. He'd paid the highest price. And it had been to save the rest of us.

> **Orion:** *Working.*

Orion had a gift when it came to mapmaking. His creations were infinitely unique, no one exactly like the other, and their uniqueness was only matched by their intricacy. So, it was no wonder people paid high into the six figures for each one.

> **Maverick:** *You're always working, asshole. But you also have to eat. So stop whatever project you're on for an hour and come see your family. If you don't, I'll let Dex hack all your devices and turn every alert to the Hannah Montana theme song.*
>
> **Me:** *I'm not your weapon, Mav.*
>
> **Wylder:** *And don't diss "The Best of Both Worlds." It's a bop.*
>
> **Kol:** *You've been watching reruns with Skylar again, haven't you?*
>
> **Wylder:** *Miley Cyrus should've gotten an Oscar for that performance.*

I barked out a laugh.

Me: *You should start a letter-writing campaign.*

Wylder: *Maybe I will.*

Orion: *If you shut up, I'll come for an hour.*

Maverick: *VICTORY IS MINE.*

Me: *I think it's actually Miley's.*

Maverick: *I can share the crown with her.*

Orion: *Turning off my phone.*

And he would. Silence was Orion's preferred state of being. No music. No talking. And certainly not the sound of his own voice.

Working alongside the Behavioral Analysis Unit on case after case, I'd gotten to know shrinks who had unique insights into the human mind. Some of them were snobby, thinking us techies were beneath them. But others were good people. And my friend, Anson, had been the best.

He'd given me more than my fair share of psychological education. And as I put the pieces together, I realized that all of my brothers and I had a version of PTSD. But Orion's was the most severe. Now, any stimuli could end up being too much for him.

A shout—sharp and fast—caught my attention. I instinctively looked out the window, expecting to see Brae and her son. The shout had sounded like the little boy—Owen. I'd heard Brae call him in for dinner. But I didn't see him anywhere now. Brae either.

And it was quiet. *Too* quiet.

I didn't wait. I grabbed the Taser I'd stashed behind my computer and strode out the back door.

Unease slid through me as I crossed the open space between the two cabins. Everything was still. Not even a breeze rustled the tall grasses at the edge of the creek.

My fingers tightened around my Taser, and for a second, I wondered if I should get my 9mm from the gun locker in my SUV. Even thinking of retrieving the weapon had nausea rolling through me. Because those weapons killed. I knew that better than most.

Taser. That was good enough. Protection without fatality.

But a million what-ifs swirled in my mind as I crept closer to cabin number two. Each possibility was worse than the one before, the price of all the dark places I'd investigated over the years. I reached the side of the cabin, pressing my back to the wall and listening.

Wind. A bird. Rustling.

I stiffened, poised for whatever might come. The sounds moved closer. I didn't wait.

I surged around the corner, only to be hit square in the chest. The impact stung and then instantly exploded, soaking the front of my shirt with...water?

My gaze dropped to my now-soaked tee and then met the jaw-dropped Brae standing in front of me. Her hand flew to her mouth, her amber eyes wide. She was soaked. Her blond hair was stuck to her face in places, mascara ran beneath her eyes, and her white T-shirt was plastered to her body, her nipples pebbled, pressing against the fabric, and—

Shit.

I jerked my focus upward just as Brae dropped her hand from her mouth.

"I'm *so* sorry. I thought you were Owen. I didn't—" She shook her head. "What are you doing here?"

The scowl came to my mouth on instinct. "I heard a scream," I gritted out.

Brae winced and gave me a little shrug as she pointed to her shirt. "It was me. Owen's got surprisingly good aim for an eight-year-old."

My gaze dropped just for a second before I forced it up again. *No wet T-shirts. No nipples. Just, no.*

"You shouldn't scream," I gritted out. "I could've called the cops."

Brae's lips twitched, the action drawing my eyes there now. The way they were almost stained red as if she'd been devouring raspberries. How they curved when she smiled, one side just a bit higher than the other. "But you didn't call the cops," she challenged.

"I could've," I clipped. "And you might've been arrested for disturbing the peace."

A laugh bubbled out of her throat, husky and just a little bit raw.

She held out her hands. "Cuff me, Officer. I dared to yell when hit by a water balloon."

All sorts of images flew through my mind at the words *cuff me*, none of which should've been there. *Fuck*.

"I could call them now. Feels like this qualifies as assault with a deadly weapon."

"A water balloon is a deadly weapon now?"

"Could be when you're wielding it." Because she was hell on wheels.

Brae really laughed then, and the sound hit me square in the chest. The vibrations it carried moved through me like a wave of waking up. She laughed like she was truly free—a laugh that reached from the tips of her toes to the top of her head, and I couldn't remember the last time I'd let myself feel something so completely.

"You're funny, Buttercup," Brae managed through her laughter.

My scowl was back. "Buttercup?"

She smiled so widely that it lit up her whole face, turning those amber eyes gold. "It fits your sunny personality."

"Fuck me," I muttered.

That only made Brae's grin bigger. "Come on, live a little. Haven't you ever wanted to have a water balloon fight to celebrate the start of summer? A little mischief might be good for you. It's a reminder that we're alive."

There was something beneath her words. A depth to them. *It's a reminder that we're alive.* It only raised more questions. Had there been a time when she thought she wouldn't be alive? Had she lost someone? One thought spiraled into another until a Tarzan-like cry split the air.

"You're going down!" Owen yelled.

A water balloon landed directly on the back of Brae's head, dousing the rest of her. She let out a comical, mock-pain yelp and then turned, stumbling toward her son. "I've been hit."

"Death blow," Owen said with a toothy grin.

Brae grabbed him in her arms, taking them both to the ground and rolling as the beast dog ran around the side of the cabin, letting out a happy bark and joining in on the fun. Owen laughed as Brae tickled his sides. "That's cheating!"

"I've gotta use all the weapons at my disposal."

Owen laughed harder until he finally escaped his mom's grasp and scrambled to his feet, staring up at me with curiosity in his green gaze. "Did you come to play, too?"

Brae grinned, leaning back on her hands in the grass, soaking wet from head to toe. "Yeah, Dex. Did you come over to play? Or are you running scared?"

Some part of me wanted to join in. To grab a water balloon and chase them both around the yard. To remember what it was like to laugh as freely as they did. But I couldn't.

"I've got a thing," I said dumbly. As if that was an explanation. But it was all I could manage. Until I saw the disappointment on Owen's face.

I leaned down, speaking in a stage whisper. "I saw her secret stash of balloons by the planter. Give her hell."

A huge smile stretched across Owen's face as he ran for the balloons.

Brae scrambled to her feet. "You're a traitor, Buttercup!"

"That's what you get for calling me Buttercup," I yelled back.

But I stayed there for a moment longer than I should've, watching the battle rage. The pure joy on both their faces. The part of me that wanted to reach for it flared again, but I knew I couldn't.

Because opening yourself up to the good meant you had to open yourself up to the bad just as much. And that wasn't something I could risk. Not with all the demons swirling in my past.

CHAPTER ELEVEN
Dex

Slamming the door to my 4Runner, I took in the tree house in the golden light just before sunset. It made the sage-green siding look even richer and the image of the house itself that much warmer.

But Twisted Oak Ranch didn't need the sun to make it warm. It had that because of the refuge it had always been. No place on this earth would ever feel safer to me.

I started for the front door, taking stock of Kol's Forest Service truck and Wylder's pickup. Of course, Mav, who'd required everyone's presence, still wasn't here. And I knew Orion wouldn't show until he was damn sure everyone else had arrived. He wasn't about to let someone come in at his back.

My boots hit the front porch steps, and I grinned at the thought that those boots would be getting their intended use now. It was a reminder that I needed to hit some trails. Maybe tomorrow morning, before the tourists packed some of my favorite spots.

Opening the screen door, I reached for the doorknob. But I knew I'd get no resistance. It didn't matter how much Kol or I tried to get Waylon to lock his damn doors—he never did.

I shook my head as I stepped inside. "The front door was open," I called.

"I meant for it to be," Waylon grumbled, his voice coming from the kitchen.

But I didn't hurry toward it. I took my time, savoring the feeling of home. Most would find it cluttered and a little odd, but I took in the walls full of clocks Waylon had created and random bits of art, and felt like I could breathe a little deeper.

The furniture in the living space was mismatched in a way that only made sense in Waylon's brain—a brightly striped chair paired with a pastel, flowered couch and a couple of antique wooden chairs. And I was pretty sure the bench on the far wall had been a church pew at one point.

I moved through the space, past the tall grandfather clock whose painted base featured a battle between gnomes and fairies. Whimsical, ornate, and so very Waylon. I moved deeper into the house and paused to place my hand on the tree at the center of it. The trunk managed to be both smooth and rough at once, but it was the ultimate reminder of home.

"Took you long enough," Waylon muttered from where he stood at the stove, stirring something in a pot.

A low moo sounded, and my gaze snapped over to the mini-Highland cow standing by the back doors—but most definitely inside—and the goat next to her.

"Seriously?" I asked Waylon.

"You want me to be safe. That's my attack cow and my goat of protection."

The two creatures ambled over to me as if responding to their duties being stated. The cow nudged my hand, and I knew exactly what she wanted. "I missed you, too, Tink. Even though you shouldn't be in the damn house."

The goat began nibbling on the edge of my shirt.

"Pepper," I warned.

She simply headbutted my side.

"Tinky!" Skylar called, running in from another room. The cow was her favorite animal on the ranch, likely because Tink let Skylar play dress-up with her.

"Why are they inside?" Kol moaned. "It's gotta be some risk for disease or contamination."

"It's definitely against the health code," Wylder muttered, an amused look on his face.

"Who knew you lot were so touchy?" Waylon said, turning away from the stove and revealing that he was wearing an apron that made him look like Bigfoot itself.

Wylder choked on a laugh while I managed to stifle mine. Kol just stared at him in horrified awe.

"I loooooove having Tinky and Pepper over for dinner," Skylar assured him. "I can make them salads, and they can eat at the table right along with us."

Kol pinched the bridge of his nose. "I draw the line at eating with livestock."

Skylar sent her dad a furious glare. "They're not livestock. They're my bestest besties."

"Dude," I said, my voice low. "Do *not* insult the Little Princess's bestest besties."

"Baaaaaad move," Wylder agreed.

Skylar crossed her arms over her tiny chest. "That's right."

Kol scowled at me and Wylder but let the expression ease as he raised both hands in defeat. "Apologies, bestest besties."

"That's better." Skylar's stance eased.

Kol lifted her into the air, ruffling her hair. "I'm still not sharing a table with them, animal whisperer."

Skylar giggled.

"What's cookin', fam bam?" Maverick called as he made his way into the kitchen.

Waylon gave one of the pots on the stove a stir. "Three-chili challenge."

My brothers and I all met each other's stares, grins starting to form. But Wylder muttered a curse. "I didn't bring Tums."

"Tums are for weaklings," Mav accused.

"Tums are for people who don't want to be shitting pure fire for the next twenty-four hours," Wylder shot back.

"Swear jar, Uncky Wy," Skylar singsonged.

"Yeah, yeah," Wylder grumbled as he pulled out his wallet and stuffed a dollar bill into the massive mason jar Mav had painted with all sorts of starred-out bad words.

I patted my stomach as I crossed over to the stove. Inhaling, I swore my nostrils even recoiled at the ferocity of the spice. "Jesus. I think I'm out of spicy shape."

Waylon looked up from his work. "Disappointed in you, boy. What've they been feeding you in DC? Rabbit food?"

"Something that's not going to corrode my insides."

Waylon guffawed. "I took it easy on this round. And you can stay with the beginner pot if you're scared."

Mav snickered. "You're so going down."

My brothers and I all had a thing for spicy food, but it had turned into a vicious competition somewhere along the way, each of us trying to one-up the others.

A clock let out a gong, signaling the top of the hour. But it wasn't alone. Within half a second, dozens of others chimed in with everything from beeps to dings, birdcalls to songs, and bells. There was even a Bigfoot call.

As it ended, I stuck a finger in my ear, trying to get the reverberations to stop. "Someone tell me how we slept through that growing up."

Mav snickered. "You always slept like the dead." He carefully left out the fact that I slept like the dead until a nightmare grabbed hold. "Remember when I drew all over your face?" he asked with a shit-stirring grin.

My eyes narrowed on him. "With freaking Sharpies? Yes. Yes, I do. I had to go to school with *foot licker* written on my forehead for a week."

Mav simply shrugged. "Shouldn't have stolen my Oreos. Payback had to be made."

Skylar stretched on her tiptoes, trying to see into the pots, revealing a T-shirt that read *Feral like my uncle*. "I think I'm ready for two chilis this time."

Wylder hoisted her into his arms so she could get a better look. "You sure about that, Little Princess?"

She nodded with confidence. "Sometimes, you gotta grab 'em by the balls."

The entire kitchen went silent and then erupted into laughter—everyone but Kol.

"Who the hell taught my daughter that one?" he demanded.

"Bad word, Daddy. And Uncle Mav said sometimes you gotta grab life by the balls. Balls isn't a bad word. We play with them all the time at school."

Kol's face got redder and redder the longer Skylar spoke. "You aren't playing with any balls."

Mav started coughing, and Wylder smacked him on the back a few times. "You really know how to influence the youth, Mav."

Mav winced as he looked at Kol. "Sorry?"

"Not yet, but you're gonna be," Kol growled.

"Now, boys," Waylon warned.

The back screen door slammed against the frame, and we all looked up. Orion filled the doorway, his gaze sweeping the space, taking in every detail as if searching for enemy combatants before finally settling on me.

I couldn't stop staring at him. He'd gotten bulkier since I saw him last. We were all pretty close in height, but Orion had gained an inch or so on everyone right around the time everything had happened, and he hadn't lost it. Only now, he carried more muscle on that six-foot-five frame.

But it was more than that. The shadows under his eyes were more pronounced, and his eyes themselves were shot through with red streaks, telling me his sleep had gotten even worse.

Fuck.

Annoyance flitted through me that none of our brothers had shared just how bad things had gotten. But I also understood why: Orion wouldn't let us help. He wasn't open to assistance in any way.

"Hey, man. It's damn good to see you."

His throat worked as he swallowed, the scruff along his jaw

shifting with the movement. For a moment, I thought he'd speak. But that was a false hope.

Instead, Orion's hands lifted, moving in the sign language he resorted to when he didn't have the option of texting or writing on a pad. *"You, too."*

We'd all slowly learned it over the years as we gave up hope of Orion using his voice. At least this way, we could meet him where he was, in the ways that worked for him.

His hazel eyes, a shade darker than the rest of ours, scanned the room again. He stopped for a moment on each face, analyzing as if he thought any one of us could turn on him the same way our father had.

"How's work?" I asked, testing the waters, hoping for a little more.

Orion's gaze narrowed on me, hands lifting one more time. *"Fine."*

"Geez," Mav muttered. "Stop monopolizing the conversation, Orion. It's a little much."

It was Mav's way of helping, getting the focus off our middle brother—the one who'd saved his life. The one who hadn't spoken since the day he killed our father.

CHAPTER TWELVE
Braedyn

"WHY DO THOSE COOKIES LOOK LIKE BOY BOOBIES?" Owen asked, coming up beside me at the kitchen counter and studying the cutouts that looked like male torsos.

My lips twitched. My boy and I had a unique relationship—likely a touch more honest than some parents would be with an eight-year-old. But we'd sort of grown up together. I'd had to learn on the job with limited people to ask for advice.

My parents had kicked me out the moment I told them I was pregnant. They didn't want a damn thing to do with a daughter who was having a baby outside of marriage. And Vincent had all but crushed my world when I told him. Nova was the only person on the planet who stuck by me.

The familiar ache took root in my chest, and I laid a hand over my ribs and the phoenix tattoo there. The one that was all about hope for me *and* her. That we would make it out of the ashes.

"Mom?" Owen pressed, his tiny brow furrowing.

"Sorry," I said, calling on the smile I needed. "I'm in an icing haze."

I set the piping bag down and bent to tickle Owen's sides. He squealed and danced away, bringing Yeti to investigate.

"You want to help?" I asked him.

"Only if I get to eat the leftover icing," Owen hedged.

My kid was smart, and he wasn't above a good haggle.

I put my hands on my hips. "One spoonful."

"Two."

I sighed. "You drive a hard bargain."

He grinned wide.

"Hands," I instructed, sending Owen to the sink to wash up.

"You never said what's up with the boobies."

I choked on a chuckle, picking up my icing bag. "I'm making apology cookies."

Owen quickly dried his hands and climbed onto the stool for a better vantage point. "Boy boobies. Birds. Balloons. A house…" A ridiculous smile spread across Owen's face. "Is that a poop emoji cookie?"

"Maybe…" This was probably teaching my kid awful things. Like potty humor. *Oh well.*

"Bro, I gotta have some poop emoji cookies for camp."

"Brooooo," I said, drilling a finger into his side. "I'll save you one, but the rest belong to someone else."

"You gotta apologize to someone's boobies?" he inquired.

A laugh bubbled out of me. "Kinda."

Owen studied the cookies, not missing a trick. "You gotta apologize to Mr. Dex's boobies?"

"I guess I do." And now, I owed the apology twice over, since I'd doused him with a water balloon.

As if Owen had summoned my hot, grumpy neighbor, headlights swept across the front of our cabin, settling in front of Cabin Three. A tumble of nerves rolled through me, snippets of today's earlier conversation at the Compass meeting echoing in my head.

For the fifty-millionth time, I thought about googling Dex, finding out what Holly had been talking about when it came to his past and father. But it seemed unfair. I wouldn't want someone glancing at single moments of my past and deciding who I was because of them.

And I wasn't sure Dex's arrest record mattered. If he'd worked for the FBI, he couldn't be *that* much of a risk. And I needed someone who could wade into the gray for me—needed someone who wasn't afraid of the shadows.

"You missed a spot," Owen informed me, breaking into my swirling thoughts.

I tapped a finger on his nose. "Thank you, my sous chef."

"I'd rather be your taste-tester."

Grabbing the white icing, I deposited some onto a spoon. "For your troubles."

"Finally."

"You helped for like two seconds," I argued.

Owen grinned. "I got high rates 'cause I'm a genius."

I chuckled and began plating the cookies on one of the older platters the cabin had been stocked with. "You are pretty dang smart."

Yeti let out a bark as I finished up.

"No frosting for you, my girl. But you can have a cookie, too." I reached for the jar on the counter. Turning to face her, I made a series of hand gestures.

She instantly sat and then balanced on her hind legs, crossing her front paws.

I made the release command and tossed her the cookie. "Such a good girl."

A few lights went on in the cabin next door, and I swallowed hard. *Now or never.*

Washing my hands, I glanced at Owen. "I'm going to run next door to give Mr. Dex the cookies. I'll lock the door after me. Don't answer for anyone but me. Yeti will stay with you."

Owen frowned. "I wanna go over to Mr. Dex's."

"Maybe next time."

He studied me for a long moment. "Adult talk?"

I wrapped an arm around my kid. "Yup. We gotta talk about the real boring stuff like taxes and turnips."

Owen's face screwed up. "Gross."

I laughed. "Just trying to save you pain and suffering, kiddo." I snatched the plate and my keys. "Be back soon. I have my phone."

Owen had one of those kids' phones that could only call out to approved numbers and 911. He'd had it since Nova disappeared. I wanted to be able to get ahold of him at any time.

"Gonna play my Switch," he grumbled, heading for the couch.

I gave Yeti another hand signal, along with a command in French, calling for a loose guard. She wouldn't attack anyone who came into the house unless provoked, but she also wouldn't let anyone get close to Owen.

"Don't set anything on fire," I called as I headed out.

"You never want me to have any fun!" Owen shouted back.

I laughed as I locked up and headed for Cabin Three. Each step wound my nerves tighter and tighter, as if they were a rope and I were being slowly strangled.

I slowed as I reached the bottom porch step and stared up at the cabin. Maybe this was dumb. Monumentally stupid. The last thing I needed was to get in trouble for some sort of illegal computer move.

But then I pictured Nova—the way she was the day she disappeared. Her cheeks flushed pink from our hike and her eyes a stormy gray. The way they lit up when she teased. So full of life. An infinite future in front of her.

She'd have done anything for me. And I'd do the same for her.

I climbed the stairs, and the door opened before I reached the top. But not before I noticed the camera tucked into the eaves of the overhang. There wasn't one of those at my house, and I couldn't help but wonder if Dex had installed it.

He leaned against the doorjamb, making his dark-gray tee pull taut against his chest. "Yes, Hellion?"

One corner of my mouth kicked up at the new nickname. "Stalking me through the windows?"

Dex's gaze flicked up to the eaves. "I have a motion detector. Lets me know when there are intruders on my property."

I let out a soft huff of breath and held up the platter. "Do intruders bring cookies?"

"Depends. Are they poisoned?"

I couldn't help the chuckle that slipped free. "Damn. I should've thought of that."

Curiosity won out because Dex leaned over the plate. Confusion quickly swept over his face. "A torso, which is kind of creepy, I might add. Birds. A house. Balloons. And smiling shits?"

I beamed up at him. "An apology for your absolutely worstest day, for rubbing it in at the Boot, and for accidentally exploding a water balloon all over you."

Dex's lips fluttered, bringing my gaze down to them. The action made me realize just how full they were. He suddenly lost the battle, and a smile overtook his stubbled face. It changed everything about the man.

It put light behind those dark-hazel eyes. It transformed his face from scary hot to devastatingly gorgeous. And something about it made me want to lean just a little closer.

"Bird shit apology cookies," Dex said, humor lacing his words.

I shrugged, struggling to reel in my reaction to the man opposite me. "Might as well make the apology personal."

He stared down at the plate for a long moment. "I owe you an apology, too. I was a grumpy bastard when we had our run-in."

"And after," I chided.

Dex chuckled softly, the sound skating over my skin and eliciting a pleasant shiver.

"And after. I'm sorry about that." He took the plate of cookies. "Thank you for these."

I nodded, twisting my fingers in front of me. Suddenly, I didn't have the first clue how to segue into what I wanted to ask. *Hey, I heard you're a supersecret computer hacker. Want to break into parts of the internet that could get you arrested?* I wasn't sure cookies bought me that much goodwill.

Dex frowned. It was the scowl I'd grown used to with him, but there was also a hint of something I swore was concern lining his face. "Did you need something else?"

I sucked in a breath. "I heard you might be good with computers and wondered if I could get your help with something."

Tension wove through Dex's muscles, erasing all the ease that had come with that beautiful smile. "Who told you that?"

I twisted my fingers tighter, all but cutting off the blood supply. "Um, Roger from the sheriff's department, kind of. And then—"

"Nosy bastard," Dex muttered.

"He was trying to help. I've figured out a lot on my own, but tech has never been my strong suit. Owen helps me nine times out of ten—"

"Owen helps?"

"He might be eight, but he's good with just about every device known to man—"

"Hellion?"

My gaze jerked up to his face. "Yes?" There was something about Dex giving me a nickname. It had an intimacy to it, even though we didn't know the first thing about each other. It set me on edge. But at the same time, I couldn't deny I loved that he'd given me a moniker with a ferocity to it—something I so desperately needed.

Dex's gaze skimmed over my face, assessing. "What do you need help with?"

I squeezed my fingers even tighter. "My best friend. She's missing."

CHAPTER THIRTEEN

Dex

THE WORDS BRAE SPOKE WERE THE LAST I'D EXPECTED. *"My best friend. She's missing."*

I'd figured some laptop emergency. Even considered that she might be hiding out from a douchebag ex. But the word *missing* had everything in me weaving so tight it was as if my muscles had turned to cement.

I knew what it was to miss someone. To have no idea if they were alive or dead. To replay every single memory of them over and over until they grew fuzzy around the edges and you wondered if you'd invented the memory.

When my mom vanished from our lives, our father had told us he'd gotten an email. He even showed it to Wylder. A letter sent the day she supposedly took off that said she was sorry but life had become too much for her. Five boys, a massive house to maintain, all the social obligations her husband's station required of her as the head of a multibillion-dollar import/export conglomerate and so-called pillar of the community. She needed a fresh start.

We'd believed him. Hook, line, and sinker. And so had everyone else in his life. They'd felt so bad for the suddenly single father, abandoned by his flighty wife.

But now, I knew just how easy it was to access someone's email. To lay a false trail. To fake everything.

When the truth about my father came to light and everything exploded, people looked at my mother's disappearance through new eyes. But it was too late. The trail was too cold. We never found out if she left or if my father stole her, too.

"Missing?" The single word I managed to give voice to had an animalistic edge. As if I'd gone feral and Brae had me cornered.

She studied my face for a moment, trying to read the tone as I struggled to hold on to my mask. Her fingers braided together as her knuckles bleached white. "A year ago, on the Three Creeks Canyon trail. We were here for a girls' weekend—the first I'd taken since Owen was born. It was supposed to be a thank-you for all she'd done to help."

Brae's words tumbled over each other as she struggled to get them out. "Nova basically raised Owen with me. When everyone else in my life bailed, she stuck around. She moved cross-country with me. Started over. Helped me with middle-of-the-night feedings, changed diapers, cooked when I could barely see straight. I don't think I would've survived without her."

Fuck.

"Family isn't always blood," I muttered. I'd learned that the hard way. Sometimes, blood was anything but family. Sometimes, blood betrayed.

Brae nodded, and I saw pain weave through those golden eyes. "She's the best person I've ever known, and I'm the only one really looking for her. Roger and Travis try to help, but Sheriff Miller thinks Nova just took a tumble down the riverbank, even though she was nowhere close. He designated it a cold case, and the state police followed his lead."

A scowl twisted my lips. Miller was the leader of the narrow-minded-asshole club in Starlight Grove. He was also lazy as hell. He enjoyed the prestige that came with being the sheriff in a small community but let others do the heavy lifting when it came to casework. Right before he took all the credit.

"I'm doing everything I can," Brae went on, releasing her hands. "As soon as I realized there was only so much law enforcement could do, I started learning. I got involved with volunteer and support groups for missing persons. I papered message boards with fliers and mailed them to local businesses. I reached out to the media and shared Nova's case, getting as much press coverage as possible, hoping that someone would realize they'd seen something that could help. I started a website where people could leave tips. I learned about geographic profiling and started mapping what I could."

I couldn't help the slight flare in my eyes at that and the curiosity that went along with it. I wondered if she could give our map king, Orion, a run for his money.

"I got involved with K-9 search and rescue. I adopted Yeti and trained her from the ground up with the help of a woman in Cedar Ridge, Washington."

My gaze flicked to Brae's cabin as if I could see the dog through the walls. Suddenly, her social media profile made a hell of a lot more sense. *SearchingForSunrise*. The exercises with her dog. Everything.

"When Miller told me he now considered Nova's case cold, I knew I had to move to Starlight Grove. I knew I needed boots on the ground so I could keep the pressure on. So I could keep the search going."

She'd turned her life on its head. For her friend.

"But I suck at tech," Brae went on. "I've tried. But I can never get past the basic stuff."

My gut twisted as I thought about her venturing into some of the darker places on the internet. With the lack of security software on her computer, she'd be asking for sick bastards to infiltrate her system. Hell, they could hack into her camera and watch her whole life. And so much worse.

"What are you trying to find?" I did my best not to let my emotions bleed into my voice. Not to give myself away. But the words came out strangled at best.

My brothers and I had three rules when it came to missing persons cases: Don't get dead. Don't let anyone know our true identities. And never take a local case.

It was too risky. The last thing we needed was the press getting wind that the sons of one of the world's most prolific serial killers had created a sort of vigilante search group. And we needed law enforcement on our asses even less. Because the lines of legality got a little blurry when you were trying to help find the people the rest of the world had forgotten about.

Little lines formed on Brae's brow as she tried to decipher my tone. "I need camera feeds."

"Law enforcement didn't check them?"

She gave a little shrug, making the wide neck of her slouchy tee slide off one smooth, tanned shoulder. "Sheriff Miller said they did, but…"

"You don't think it was thorough."

"No." Brae let out a long breath. "There is only one road in and out of that canyon. And there are at least a dozen road-condition cameras set up along it."

I set the plate of cookies on the table just inside the door, needing the freedom to move. To do what, I didn't know. Run? Pull Brae inside and make her tell me everything? Slam the door in her face?

I scrubbed a hand over my face, doing some mental math. "Even with a dozen cameras on that road, they only take snapshots. They update every thirty seconds. You could catch one vehicle but miss a dozen more. And that's *if* anyone saved the footage for this long."

Brae tugged her lip between her teeth. "But it could be something. An avenue I haven't been able to explore because I don't have the tools."

Fuck.

It would be so easy. The State of California didn't exactly have its road cameras locked down tight. I knew because I'd hacked them before. But it would break a promise to the people I *never* broke promises to.

The bond I had with my brothers wasn't just a simple blood tie. It was so much deeper than that. It had been cemented in terror and torment. In exile. In being so damn alone in the world aside from one another.

"I'm sorry," I rasped. "I can't."

The defeat in Brae's eyes was like a blade to a kidney or lung. Brutal and agonizing, even after the knife had been pulled free. "Because I'm the worst?"

I knew she was trying to make a joke, but it was so far from funny.

Fucking hell.

"You are the worst, Hellion. But that's not why. I can't risk it. The FBI gave me a strong warning when I left, and I don't exactly have room to fuck up again. Because I didn't end up working for them because I graduated from MIT." All true, just not the complete story. And leaving so much unsaid felt like a betrayal to a woman I hardly knew yet couldn't stand disappointing.

Brae's slender shoulders slumped, making her look even smaller. "I understand. I'm sorry I put you in a bad position. I don't want you to get into trouble because of me."

Her understanding was like a one-two punch to the places that had just been stabbed. "I really am sorry."

She shook her head, already backing down the steps. When the porch light caught her golden-brown eyes, I saw why. They glittered with unshed tears, and it was the last thing she wanted me to see.

"I'll see you around."

She didn't wait for my answer, all but bolting back to her cabin.

God, that killed me. Not just the tears but her fight to keep them at bay, to keep me from seeing them. She was so damn strong. But even the strongest people needed someone to lean on. And Brae had no one.

My back teeth ground together as I tugged my phone from my pocket and pulled up the *Hot Sauce and Hot Goss* chat. Not even seeing that Kol and Mav had gone to war with the name half a dozen times in the past few hours made me smile.

> **Me:** *Case to bring to the group. A personal favor.*

It only took seconds before a name popped up.

> **Wylder:** *If it's someone you need to help, you know we're there.*
>
> **Me:** *There's a complication.*
>
> **Kol:** *What kind of complication?*

Zero-risk, play-by-the-rules Kol would, of course, focus on that.

> **Me:** *It's local.*
>
> **Kol:** *We can't. You know why. It's a nonstarter.*

Maverick: *We might be able to figure out a way to keep our identities under wraps.*

Orion: *No.*

I scowled at my phone. I owed Orion everything. Down to the air still flowing in my lungs. But his finality was pissing me the hell off.

Me: *I wasn't aware this had become a dictatorship.*

Kol: *It's not, but we've always worked on a one-vote veto system. And we do that for a reason.*

I knew he was right, but I couldn't get Brae's face out of my mind. Golden eyes darkened as grief streaked across her expression.

Wylder: *Who is it?*

Of course, he'd be the one to zero in on the important question.

Me: *Brae. Her best friend went missing at Three Creeks Canyon a year ago.*

Kol: *I remember that case. I thought they closed it. I heard from my boss they thought she fell into the river. Got swept away.*

Annoyance flickered through me as my cheek fluttered.

Me: *Miller says that's what happened.*

Wylder: *That's why she moved here? To look for her friend?*

Me: *Get the sense the friend is more like a sister.*

Wylder: *Fuck.*

Maverick: *Who the hell is Brae?*

Me: *My new neighbor and Wylder's new waitress.*

Maverick: *Brae's a hot girl name. Maybe a little hippie. She hot?*

The now-familiar scowl was back on my face.

Me: *Don't be a jackass.*

Maverick: *That's a yes. I see a visit to the Boot in my future.*

I bit the inside of my cheek. It didn't matter. Mav could hit on whoever he wanted. Brae wasn't for me for a million reasons. Neighbor meant you couldn't escape them when things were done. Kid meant commitment and family, something I'd never risk after the hell I lived through. And the way everything about her had me leaning in had my red-alert signs flashing.

Wylder: *I'll pay to see this. Brae's gonna put you on your ass in two seconds flat.*

That had a different sort of alert flaring.

Me: *There a problem at the bar?*

Wylder: *Sloppy, day-drunk tourists. Never seen someone put entitled assholes in their place faster.*

My fingers tightened around my phone. I *hated* the idea of guys creeping on Brae while she worked. I knew Wylder would have her back, but that didn't change the fact that it shouldn't have happened in the first place.

Kol: *You like her.*

I stiffened.

Wylder: *She works for me. You know I don't go there.*

Kol: *Not you. Dex.*

I glared at my phone as if I could make Kol feel my annoyance.

Me: *She's a good person.*

Orion: *No.*

A wave of true anger surged.

Me: *Fine. You guys are out, but I'm in. I'll work this on my own.*

It was stupid and goddamned risky, but damn it, I was going to help.

CHAPTER FOURTEEN
Braedyn

THE DOOR CLOSED BEHIND ME WITH A SOFT *SNICK*. LOGICALLY, I knew the sound was quiet, barely audible, but it sounded like a cannon. Or a nail in a coffin full of hope.

I heard the sounds of a video game coming from the small living room to my left, Yeti's bark in response to one of Owen's cheers. But I couldn't go in there. Not yet.

Instead, I leaned against the door and slowly slid to the floor. Pulling my knees to my chest, I hugged them as tightly as I could, hoping that would keep all my grief, fear, and agony from spilling out over the worn hardwood.

I couldn't break. Because if I broke now, I wasn't sure I'd be able to pick up the pieces again.

The sound of the game cut off, and Owen's curious face popped out from around the corner. I reached for reserves that were empty, trying to bring a smile to my face, but it wobbled around the edges.

Owen frowned and crossed to me, Yeti bounding over behind him. He slid to the floor, too, looping his arm through mine. "Are you sad?"

Yeti flopped on my lap, refusing to believe that her 142-pound self wasn't a lap dog.

"Yeah, I'm sad." The one thing I'd made damn sure to do raising Owen was let him know all feelings were valid in our house. And he was safe to talk about any and all of them. I didn't want him to be raised like I was, where the only acceptable state of being was perfection, and emotions were seen as weaknesses.

Owen squeezed my arm tighter. "Did Mr. Dex not like your boobie cookies?"

One corner of my mouth kicked up. "No, I think he really liked them, actually."

Owen's head tipped back so he could study my face. "Then why are you sad?"

My throat suddenly felt painfully dry. Like I'd just taken a ten-mile trek through the Sahara without water. "I miss Nova."

I was constantly walking a perilous tightrope when it came to Nova and Owen. For those first few months, I was so sure she'd be found at any time that I hadn't wanted to lay that on my seven-year-old. And then the lie just grew. It weighed more and more the longer it went on. And now, I wasn't sure if I was protecting Owen or myself.

Hurt flickered over his expression. "Does she not like us anymore?"

The words turned agonizing pain into something unbearable. My heart fractured into the sort of pieces you could never put back together again, and if by some miracle you did, it would never look the same. It would be misshapen with ragged edges and missing parts. Barely functioning anymore.

"She loves us more than anything," I croaked and swallowed against my desert-dry throat. "Something's keeping her from talking to or seeing us. It's not her fault."

Owen's tiny brows pulled together. "Like she's grounded?"

"Kind of." I couldn't think of any better way to explain it.

A scowl with more heat than I would've thought possible erupted on Owen's face. "Whatever that thing is, it's stupid."

Normally, I didn't allow that particular s-word in my house, but I couldn't agree more in this case. "It really is."

Owen laid his head on my shoulder. "I love you, Mom."

A different sort of pain flared then. The beautiful kind. The staggering beauty of a real moment with the person you loved most in the world. "I love you, too."

And that would keep me going. Because it had to.

I stared at the coffee machine, willing it to brew faster as Owen raced through the cabin in circles, Yeti barking at his heels.

Dear God, I needed caffeine—all the caffeine the world had to offer. I laid a hand on the top of the machine. "Please, don't leave me hanging today. Give me all your beautiful life force."

Because sleep had been fitful at best. Reopening my deepest wounds twice in one day was bound to bring out the demons, but they'd come full force. Nightmares where Nova called out for me, asking why I hadn't found her, demanding to know why I'd abandoned her. I'd finally given up around four in the morning.

The sound of the doorbell rang through the cabin, sending Yeti barking and Owen changing directions. "I'll get it!" he yelled.

"Owen, not yet," I said, hurrying after him.

But it was too late. He yanked open the door, revealing six feet and four inches of towering muscle with a little more scruff than last night and dark circles under his eyes.

Owen's hands went to his hips. "Did you not like my mom's boobie cookies?"

I had the sudden urge to pull my sweatshirt up over my head and stay there.

A low chuckle slid through the air, hitting me with a wave of invisible vibrations.

"I loved the boobie cookies," Dex assured him.

Owen's eyes narrowed on the man in my doorway. "She was sad when she got back from your house."

"All right," I said, wrapping an arm around my son's shoulders. "Owen, what's the rule about opening the door to strangers?"

"It wasn't a stranger. It was Mr. Dex. He's kinda scowly, but I don't think he's a bad guy."

Truer words had never been spoken.

Dex's lips twitched. "Sorry about the scowly. But your mom's right. You shouldn't answer the door until she gives you permission." His gaze flicked up to me. "If you had a camera, you could see who was at your door before answering it."

Owen practically started dancing at my side. "Mom, we should totally get a camera. That would be bussin'. I could make it talk in a robot voice!"

"Bussin'?" Dex asked.

A soft chuckle left my lips. "Basically means it would be cool."

He shook his head. "I'm old."

"You're telling me," I mumbled.

Owen looked between the two of us. "You're both kind of old. Did you even have TV when you were growing up?"

Dex staggered back a step, clutching his chest in mock injury. "Direct hit."

The action made Owen giggle, but I couldn't help but wonder why Dex was even here.

As if sensing my question, his hazel gaze lifted from Owen to my face. "I want to help."

Owen's gaze ping-ponged between us. "Help with what?"

"One of my Yeti projects," I hurried to say, guilt swarming at all the Nova-related lies piling up.

Dex nodded slowly and dropped his hand for the dog to sniff. "Yup."

A bubble of excited hope escaped its prison. "Why don't you come in? The caffeine is in the kitchen."

Dex chuckled again, the sound reaching out like the caress of featherlight fingertips. "Give me all the caffeine."

As I moved to the fully brewed pot of coffee, Owen peppered Dex with questions. How old was he when he got glasses? Did he have any brothers or sisters? I nearly balked at the fact that he had *four* brothers. What was his job?

"Well, I guess I don't have one anymore. But I used to work for the FBI in their cyber division, helping on the computer side of things," Dex said as he settled at one of the stools in the kitchen.

"You. Worked. For. THE FREAKING FBI? Did you hack stuff for them?" Owen shrieked.

I winced as I set a mug in front of Dex. "Apologies for the lack of volume control. We're working on it."

Dex grinned. "No worries."

"Wait," Owen said, disappointment hitting him. "You don't work there anymore?"

Dex shook his head and then took a sip of coffee, ignoring the cream and sugar I'd placed on the table.

"Why would you stop doing the coolest job ever?" Owen demanded.

"Owen," I warned.

"What? I wanna know."

Dex held up a hand. "It's okay. I made them a promise. I told them I'd work for them for ten years. My ten years were up, and I was ready to do something else."

"Something not as cool as the FBI, though," Owen mumbled.

I pinched the bridge of my nose. "Owen, why don't you go get dressed?"

"Aw, man. I always miss the good stuff."

Dex leaned forward conspiratorially. "I'll catch you up on the good stuff later."

"Promise?" Owen asked excitedly.

"I promise." Dex lifted a hand, holding out his pinky finger to my son.

Owen hooked it instantly, and they shook. The image was so simple, but it knocked me sideways. Memories of my and Nova's shake flashed in my mind—a million little pinky promises.

"I'll be back," Owen yelled, running for his bedroom, Yeti fast on his heels.

The moment he was gone, a wave of nerves hit me. For countless reasons. But most of all because there was the possibility of hope. New roads to go down. New leads to follow.

Dex lifted the coffee mug to his lips and drank. His mouth tightened at the corners, lines of strain digging into his stubble.

"Not your kind of coffee?" I asked, trying to fill the now-deafening silence.

One corner of his mouth pulled up in a sheepish smile. It made him look years younger for just a second. "I don't like coffee. But I love caffeine."

A chuckle bubbled out of me. "What do you normally drink?"

"Energy drinks, mostly. Lightning Energy is my favorite."

My jaw went a little slack. "Isn't that the drink that sent a bunch of people to the hospital with heart palpitations?"

Dex took another pull on his coffee. "Amateurs."

"Maybe you should try green tea."

Dex's whole face screwed up. "I'd rather just go chew some grass outside."

My lips twitched, but the action quickly slid away. "I don't want to get you in trouble."

Dex's hazel eyes caught and held mine. "You won't."

"You sound sure." I tugged my lower lip between my teeth and worried it. The last thing I needed on my conscience was getting Dex in trouble with the FBI. He might've been a grumpy, occasionally stalkerish neighbor, but there was kindness beneath it. And his showing up here and offering to help proved it.

"I'm damn good at what I do, Hellion. I won't get caught."

He didn't look away as the words spilled into the space between us. The nickname was a tiny piece of intimacy we hadn't earned, but I still found myself wanting to hold tight to it. Because I yearned to be known in that way. The kind of way that meant someone knew you inside and out. Was aware of all your secrets and eccentricities. But I didn't have that. Not anymore.

I swallowed down the yearning. Tucked it away where I put all my other hard things. My parents' abandonment and disapproval. Vincent's rejection. Nova's disappearance. It was as if I couldn't hold on to anyone in my life. They all vanished in one way or another.

"You're sure?" My voice dipped on the words, a rasp coating them that Dex didn't miss.

His gaze tracked over my face and down to my neck as if seeking the source of tension. "I'm sure. Started getting the lay of the land last night, but it would help to know what you've found so far."

This was happening. I shoved off the counter, my fingers tingling the slightest bit, telling me to breathe. "Okay, I..."

Dex's hand loosened around his mug as if he might reach out to touch me. To comfort me? "You don't have to do it today."

"No, I want to," I said quickly. But it wasn't a want; it was a need. Not to leave Nova alone any longer. "I just...yesterday was a lot. Talking about it to you. To a support group. I'm not used to quite that much sharing."

The words tripping out of my mouth made me feel almost naked. But Dex deserved my honesty. He'd earned it with his offer of help despite all the risks it posed to him.

Dex studied my face for a long moment. "Didn't sleep well?"

I shook my head, wisps of blond hair fluttering around my face. "Nights are the hardest. So much silence. Too much room for memories."

Understanding swept over Dex's features, and beneath it...pain. For me? I wasn't sure.

"The quiet's the hardest when the memories are loud," he said softly.

He spoke as if he truly knew. As if he'd experienced the same things I had. I wanted to ask but didn't have any right to. And he was already giving me so much. Instead, I gave him what I could. "Thanks for helping me, even though I'm the worst."

One side of Dex's mouth kicked up in that lopsided grin, and something about the off-kilter smile knocked me sideways.

"You're the *worstest*. But I think I like your worst, Hellion."

A buzz lit beneath my skin at his words, a faint hum that was an early warning system. Because I didn't go there anymore. Not with anyone. If you touched a hot stove, you learned because you had the scars to prove it.

But still, I headed for my Nova room, knowing Dex would follow. Playing with fire all over again.

CHAPTER FIFTEEN
Dex

MY THUMB SWEPT ACROSS THE SCREEN OF MY PHONE, ALL THE data I'd gathered in the last twelve hours flying past. I'd built a casefile app from scratch for my brothers and me. It gave us the ability to store any information we found in a place where we could all access it.

The app was different from what law enforcement used because we had different needs. It also had a handy self-destruct button in case anyone we didn't want sniffing around got too close.

As I skimmed the words, images of Brae flashed in my mind: her blond hair woven into pigtail braids, swinging as she spoke; those warm amber eyes, flashing gold with hope or anger, deepening to nearly black with sorrow or grief.

The woman was a war. A study in opposites. She let all those emotions fly yet held so much close to the vest—layers of secrets she wasn't ready to let me or anyone else in on.

And that was fair. It wasn't as if I'd been honest with her. All I'd given her were half-truths. Something about that had guilt digging in.

I looked up, taking in the sign carved into the wood above the double doors: *Juniper County Sheriff's Department*. My back molars ground together. It was the last place I wanted to go but the first place I needed to be.

Shoving my phone into my pocket, I grabbed the stack of papers on the seat next to me. If the sheriff had moved Nova's disappearance to cold-case status, then there was no reason for them not to share their files. But it was going to piss Miller the hell off. That was just a bonus.

I climbed out of my 4Runner and headed for the station, calling on my mask that wouldn't let anyone know exactly what I was thinking or how I was feeling. It was the ultimate protection.

But it slipped into a grin the second I stepped inside and caught sight of Travis holding a box of donuts and talking to whoever was on duty at the desk.

"A cop and donuts. Isn't that a little cliché?" I asked.

Trav's head jerked up, and a huge smile split his face as he set the donuts down. "I heard the rumors, but I don't think I believed 'em until I saw your ugly mug."

I chuckled and pulled him in for a quick back slap. "You're jealous of my chiseled jawline, don't lie."

He barked out a laugh. "You caught me."

The man behind the desk eyed me with a cross between suspicion and derision. It wasn't anything new, but it still clawed at me. I tried to remember his name. Gus or Gary, something with a G. He'd been in Wylder's grade, if I remembered right.

"What are you doing here?" Travis asked, bringing my attention back to him. "Don't tell me you already have parking tickets to pay off."

My lips twitched. "That's why it's good to have friends in high places, right?"

Travis just shook his head. "If you parked in the diner's five-minute spot too long, I can't help you. You know Susie will lock that down with an iron fist."

He wasn't wrong. The owner of the diner wouldn't take any flack. And she wasn't afraid to shoot someone with a soda gun if they got out of line.

I gave an exaggerated shiver. "No way, man. She scares me."

"As she should," Trav said with a chuckle. "So what's up?"

I tapped the papers against my free hand. "Got an open records request."

His brows lifted, and I saw Gary or Gus stiffen behind the counter. Travis quickly pulled the surprise from his expression. "What's the case?"

"Nova Monroe."

A hint of wariness found Travis's face, maybe even worry as he glanced at the man behind the counter. "Rog said he was giving your name to Brae. I just didn't think there was a chance in hell you'd actually help."

Didn't that make me feel like the world's biggest asshole? But wanting the world to think I'd never get involved with this sort of thing, letting them think all the Archer brothers would do anything to avoid being on someone's radar, was by design.

And here I was, drawing a big red target around us again. Because we were all linked with the kind of brand that having a serial killer for a father gave you.

"Well, she pleaded her case," I muttered.

A hint of amusement entered Travis's expression. "Roger's asked her out no fewer than twenty-one times. Brae's shot him down for every single one. Might be fun to watch you shoot your shot."

I glowered at him. "I'm not interested in her like that."

But something stirred low in my gut at Travis's words and the idea of Brae and Roger. Something unsettling.

Travis just grinned. "Oh, of course. Too close to home."

"What the hell is that supposed to mean?" I clipped, annoyance digging in deeper.

"Come on, Dex. Your whole MO through high school was nothing within a ten-mile radius. Every homecoming date and field-party hookup was someone from another town. Every summer, you went for the tourists, never a local. Never someone close. It pissed every girl at Starlight Grove High way the hell off."

My skin felt too tight for my body, like a million eyes were on me. Because Travis was right. Never letting anyone too close was my MO. I just hadn't realized it was so damn obvious.

"I think a thing or two has changed since high school. At least, I hope to hell it has," I grumbled.

The grin on Trav's face only widened. "Unless you hit perfection the first time around."

"Oh, fuck off," I shot back. "I swore Cora would realize she could do so much better."

"Thank God she hasn't," he said with a laugh. "Come on, let's get that request filed for you. Grady can help."

Grady. Apparently, *Gus* and *Gary* were both wrong.

The man scowled as we turned to him, but Travis wasn't in any way affected. He just shook his head. "Stop looking like someone poured salt in your coffee. It's just a records request."

"You know," I said, sliding the paperwork across the counter, "my legal right."

"It your legal right to stick your nose where it don't belong?" Grady shot back.

I didn't miss that good ole Grady hadn't progressed past deputy rank while Roger and Travis, who were both younger than him, had. I didn't mention that fact. Instead, I pasted on a bland smile. "It's my legal right to be a pain in the ass, and it's one I take seriously."

"That's always been your way, hasn't it?" a new voice asked.

Sheriff Miller sauntered out of a back hallway as if some Bat-Signal had gone out announcing my presence. I took a second to study the man I hadn't seen in years. Lanky with a thick mustache—now pure white—and more lines in his face than the last time I'd seen him. But a kind of ugliness that had nothing to do with appearance shone through his eyes.

Miller had never liked my brothers and me. Hated that Uncle Waylon had taken us in and brought the media's attention. Their fascination with us had waned, only popping back up on anniversaries now and then, but Miller took it as a personal attack on *his* town.

Or maybe he just thought we were all serial killers in the making. That we would turn into our father. That we would systematically stalk women. Abduct them. Torture them. Murder them. Keep souvenirs of our kills.

Even just thinking it had my gut roiling. But the fact that Sheriff Miller suspected us gnawed at me. Because a tiny part of me wondered what darkness lay dormant beneath my skin that my father had left behind.

But I didn't let him know any of that. Instead, I just beamed at him, throwing the man off-kilter. "Sheriff Miller, it's so good to see you."

Travis snickered, trying to hide it with a cough.

Miller's scowl deepened. "What are you doing in my house?"

The fact that he called the station *his house* told me everything I needed to know about him, but I just kept my smile pasted on. "Funny. I swore this was a place of county services. I guess I could go to the state level and—"

"What do you want, Dexter?" Miller ground out.

"All reports relating to Nova Monroe."

Miller's eyes flashed, turning a golden color. But it wasn't anything like the gold in Brae's eyes. His was all anger and meanness, no life in it at all. "Why am I not surprised she got mixed up with the likes of you? I wonder if anyone's told her who you really are. What runs in your veins."

It took everything in me not to let his blows show on my face. Not to let the rage take hold. But I kept a smile fixed in place as I tapped the papers on the counter. "I trust you'll respond in a timely fashion. I'd hate to have to see if my FBI colleagues have any contacts at the California Department of Justice who might be interested in a case of negligence and corruption."

Splotches of redness erupted on Miller's neck and cheeks. "Get the hell out."

I gave him a mock salute, knowing it would only piss him off more. "I'll be seeing you, Ezra."

And with that, I stalked out into the bright May sun. I sucked in air the moment I was outside. Cleaner than DC air. A hint of pine clung to every molecule of oxygen, even downtown. I tried to focus on that, picturing it cleansing me from the inside out.

If only it could. If only it could wipe away every infected strand of DNA. If only it could cure what lay in wait.

But it couldn't. And I had to live with that.

I wasn't ready to climb back into my SUV or sit behind a computer screen. I needed to move. My fingers twitched at my sides, and I knew I needed to ask Kol about the gym a town over that he worked out at. Or hit a trail. There was nothing like climbing up the side of a mountain to burn out everything that was eating you up inside.

Instead, I found myself walking down the block until I reached the black wood siding of the Boot. I told myself I stepped inside with the goal of seeking out my brother, but I was a fucking liar.

The place only had a couple of patrons now that it was past the lunch rush and before the dinner crowd. Aidan refilled condiments at one end of the bar as Cora rolled silverware into napkins next to him. I could just make out the cook, Fiona, through the pass-through window, washing dishes. I didn't see Wylder and knew he was likely in the back, cursing over order forms or bookkeeping. But then, I saw her.

Brae's hair was out of the two braids now, but her golden strands still held the wave of their earlier arrangement. They cascaded down her back, falling around her in the kind of curtain I ached to sift through with my fingers. I wanted to tug the strands so her face tipped back and I could take that perfect damn mouth and—*fuck*.

I tried to think of anything but what Brae would taste like. Would her morning coffee still cling to her tongue? Or would she taste like pure sunshine?

Because that was what she looked like. A braid at her crown held the waves back, khaki shorts exposed tanned, muscular legs, and she had on those shoes that were an explosion of color. I couldn't help but wonder if it was Owen who had doodled all over her white high-top Converse.

As if sensing eyes on her, Brae lifted her head. She took me in for a beat of one, two, three as she paused mid-wipe at a table. And then she was striding toward me, tucking the rag into her back pocket.

She might've been tiny, but she crossed the distance in the blink of an eye. "What's wrong?"

"What makes you think something's wrong?" But my voice was too tight, my throat strangling every word.

"Oh, I don't know, Buttercup. Maybe it's the fact that you've got storms gathering in your eyes. Or that your hands are fisted so tightly, you look like you're going to break a knuckle. Or that you're making your earlier glowers and glares look like sunny smiles."

I wasn't sure how, but she somehow made me want to smile in that moment. Her no-bullshit, cut-straight-to-the-point-while-giving-me-shit way eased something inside me. The honesty of it.

"Sheriff Miller is a prick." It was the most honesty I could manage, but it was something.

A hint of surprise hit Brae's golden eyes. "Tell me something I don't know." But those eyes searched deeper, pulling together pieces I both wanted her to see and desperately wanted to hide. "Something he said got to you."

Right to the point. That was my hellion. Never pulling a damn punch.

"He goes for the jugular every time." But that wasn't exactly right. "No, he goes for the sucker punch."

"He goes for the tender spots. The injured ones," Brae said softly. Her slender throat worked as she swallowed, and I swore I could feel her warring with herself to let something go. "He almost made me quit looking once. Got me that good."

"What'd he say?" I had no damn right to ask, but the words tumbled out anyway.

Those golden eyes lifted to mine, darkening with pain and doubt. "Told me I shouldn't be taking time away from a son who needed me to chase a ghost because I felt guilty. That my kid deserved better."

A different sort of rage caught fire in my veins. Because I saw exactly the kind of mother Brae was. She was the kind who gave *everything* for her kid but still second-guessed if it was enough. Because she cared. And that bastard had twisted her up about it.

"He's a goddamned fool. But a manipulative one. And he loves to get in a kidney shot," I growled.

Brae's lips pressed together in a half smile. "Felt more like an ovary punch, but he certainly fights dirty. And he's smart enough to get in the kill shot, take a half-truth and twist it. Because I *do* feel guilty."

Those golden eyes turned glassy. "Because I wasn't there when Nova needed me."

I stared at her for a long moment and felt the sudden urge to tell her about my past. The excuse my mind made was that *someone* would. Hell, Miller had just threatened to do as much. And countless other residents in Starlight Grove could do the same. Maybe someone had already let something slip. As my gaze slid around the mostly empty bar, only a couple of lunch stragglers in a far corner left, I could still *feel* the possibility of someone telling Brae their version of my story.

But none of that was the *real* truth. I wanted to give Brae something that would show her she wasn't alone, even if I couldn't exactly give that to her. "Half-truths turned to lies," I rasped.

Brae studied me for a long moment, peeling back the layers I'd become an expert at keeping in place. "What truths does he twist for you?"

That urge to tell her intensified. I'd never wanted to tell a soul. I'd only wanted to bury it deep. But Brae's vulnerability made me want a piece of that bravery, too. And I didn't want her to be alone in her pain.

I didn't look away as I gave her ammunition I *never* gave people. Because they could use it the way Miller did. The way so many others did—by accident or on purpose. But I handed it to her anyway. "My father…was a serial killer."

CHAPTER SIXTEEN
Braedyn

A BUZZ LIT MY EARS, BUT BENEATH THE HUM AND VIBRATION, Dex's words played on a loop. *"My father...was a serial killer."* Over and over again.

To most, the words would've sounded almost flat. But I knew the tone. Knew because I'd used it many times when talking about where Owen's father was, why my parents hadn't helped when I had him, and where I'd been when Nova disappeared.

Sometimes, it felt like shame was carved into the very fabric of my being. All those secret brands—the ones I'd carry forever. The pain that never truly ended.

But I hid all of that with emotionless tones and masks of nothingness when I had to talk about them for one reason or another. Waiting for a reaction. To know if I would be greeted with pity or disgust. Occasionally, there was true understanding, and *that* was a gift. One I wanted to give Dex right now.

Because I understood the weight of what he was giving me. Just like I now understood all those short interplays I'd overheard during my time in Starlight Grove. The way Wylder reacted to being called *evil*. Holly's comment about who Dex's father was.

"That's a hell of a thing for Miller to use against you. But since he's a prick, it doesn't surprise me. Maybe he has chronic diarrhea. That would make anyone cranky."

One corner of Dex's mouth kicked up, that lopsided smile just starting to show at the edges.

"Do you think if I gave him Ex-Lax, he could recover? I bet the town would make a statue of me in thanks. Maybe I could even get a parade."

That hint of a grin grew. "Hellion."

I shrugged. "It's worth a try."

Dex studied me for a long moment as the humor faded from his expression, but a little glow of warmth remained. "You don't want to know about my father?"

I thought about how to answer that for a handful of seconds and what I *truly* wanted in that moment. "I want to know what you want to share. But I know it costs to tell those truths. And I don't want to cause you any more pain."

He was quiet; the only sounds were Cora and Aidan's soft bickering across the bar. "You really mean that, don't you?"

I scuffed my shoe against the floor. "It's not going to change what I think about you, Buttercup. You're still my hot, unhinged neighbor who has perfected a scowl and glower that could freeze water in the Sahara."

That tilted smile came back. "All I heard is that I'm hot."

I made a *pppffft* sound. "You know you're too damn good-looking. If anything's freaky about you, it's that. Maybe it's the glasses."

Dex barked out a laugh. "I'll keep that in mind."

I met that dark-hazel gaze, not looking away. "The only thing you sharing with me will change is how much I understand you. How much I respect what you've overcome."

Dex's gaze shifted to the side. The moment the connection broke, I missed it. He rocked back on his heels slightly, his eyes tracing the grain of the wood floor. "You might run away. Never want to be alone with me. Or even if you don't, some part of you might end up waiting for me to turn on you."

"Dex?"

His gaze lifted as if he didn't have control over it returning to me.

"I mean this in the nicest way possible. What the fuck?"

He jolted slightly, my response clearly unexpected. "You wouldn't be the first."

"Do you think I'm stupid?"

Dex's jaw went slack this time. "Excuse me?"

"Do you think I'm stupid? Because I'd have to be to think any of those things just because of who your father was. And that's just rude."

A hint of that familiar scowl was back, but I sensed it wasn't directed at me. "His DNA is half of mine. He raised me until I was twelve years old."

"And my parents kicked me out when I refused to hide my pregnancy and give my son up for adoption. Does that mean I'm gonna abandon my son when he does something I don't like?" I shot back.

That scowl only deepened, but again, I sensed it wasn't a glower for me. "Of course it doesn't."

"Good," I clipped. "Then you aren't stupid either. But you should apologize for thinking I was."

Dex gaped at me. "You're serious, aren't you?"

"You don't have to bake me apology cookies, but I wouldn't mind if you hacked into my cell phone plan and gave me some extra minutes or something."

Dex just stared at me.

"What? Cell plans are expensive."

That half smile was back, and I wanted to memorize every twist and curve. He shook his head. "You really are the worst, you know that, right?"

I beamed back at him. "If I'm the worst, you're the worstest."

And then Dex did something that knocked me sideways. He reached out and took my hand. The move was so quick that part of me wondered if it had even happened. It was the briefest squeeze of fingers, his large, callused ones sending a riot of sensations rocketing through me. And then they were gone.

"Always so damn unexpected, Hellion. Thank you."

I was so stunned I couldn't find words, but it didn't matter because a throat cleared. I jolted like someone in a creepy clown mask had jumped out at me in a haunted house.

"Sorry," Wylder said, his gaze flicking back and forth between his brother and me. "I thought you heard me walk up."

Heat flooded my cheeks as I realized my new boss had witnessed the moment. Not exactly something I needed.

"Guess I'm just oblivious. I, um, better get back to work. Those chairs aren't going to wipe themselves down." I booked it to the farthest possible table and didn't look back.

But I could still feel Dex's fingers curved around mine. The pressure. The heat. And I wondered when someone—other than Owen—had taken my hand last.

I couldn't remember. And that just drove the ache in my chest deeper. Because for the first time in forever, I realized I wanted that. But I also knew I'd never risk what it took to get it.

CHAPTER SEVENTEEN
Dex

WYLDER WAS THE BROTHER I *NEVER* GOT MAD AT. I could honestly count on one hand the number of times I'd lost my temper with him. The times I'd yelled or tried to deck him. And four of them were when I was under the age of ten.

But I was angry now, my temper bubbling to the surface. And it wasn't just because he'd scared Brae and had her scampering off. It was because he'd sent her away. He'd broken the first moment in forever that I'd felt seen.

By someone who hadn't lived through what I had. My brothers understood because they carried the same scars.

But for someone who hadn't lived it to understand? That was a gift. And Brae had understood without me sharing a single detail.

Wylder studied me for a long moment.

"What?" I clipped, the anger bleeding into the word.

His brows lifted. "Just wondering what that was about."

"So you had to stick your nose in?"

"When did you become such a grumpy bastard?" Wylder asked.

I sighed because he was right. I took a moment and sucked in air as if it could coat all my raw and ravaged edges. "Since I came back here and had to deal with narrow-minded assholes."

It was a half-truth at best, but Wylder still went on alert. "Who?"

The word had an edge to it that would've been surprising to anyone except our brothers. Wylder gave off an easygoing, nonthreatening vibe to the world. It was his defense mechanism. A protection. But my brothers and I knew that if something tripped his justice trigger or threatened one of us, Wylder could become a completely different person.

"Breathe, hulk man. Just Miller being his prickish self, as usual." My gaze flicked to Brae, and there wasn't a damn thing I could do to stop it.

And Wylder, being who he was, didn't miss the minuscule movement. "He being an ass to her?"

I didn't move my eyes from Brae. Couldn't. Every moment I studied her gave me another piece of the puzzle. Like now. She was stronger than you would think. She might be small, but she could flip chairs and shift tables with the ease of someone twice her size.

Good.

Something about her being strong put me at ease. The knowledge that she could protect herself. Even though I knew the truth: everyone was at risk if someone knew the angles to hit.

"Dex," Wylder growled.

My gaze finally snapped back to my brother. "Yeah, he's being an ass to her. Stonewalling, mostly."

Wylder's gaze flicked to Brae, and I saw him assess her in a new way, pain flicking through dark-hazel eyes nearly identical to mine. Wylder wasn't just the peacekeeper; he was our patron saint of lost souls. He took in anyone who needed an extra hand, and it had bitten him in the ass more than once.

But he never let it stop him. He'd offer jobs, counsel, a place to get your feet back under you. And he was a protector.

"That's the last thing she needs," he muttered.

I followed his line of sight, watching as Brae wiped down one final table and quickly moved on to refilling condiments. "No shit."

An arm slid around my shoulders and Wylder's, pulling us into a huddle. "What're we talking about? Hot town goss?" Maverick asked, humor in his tone.

"Jesus," Wylder muttered.

I shoved Mav off us. "You need a second job."

He brushed invisible dirt off his U.S. Forest Service tee with the smoke-jumper logo. "Already got two. That's enough for me."

"Two part-time jobs," I shot back. "You need at least double that to keep you out of trouble."

It was true but not exactly fair. From late spring through early fall, Mav worked with the smoke jumpers, who had a station just outside of town. The rest of the year, he had to settle for the boring old Starlight Grove Fire Department. But he made up for the lack of action by seeking out every death-defying hobby he could find, from BASE jumping to whitewater rafting to free climbing.

A part of me wondered if all those hobbies and jobs that put him in the literal line of fire were part of him coming to terms with almost losing his life all those years ago. He'd come the closest. Maybe now, he needed to prove that he was no longer afraid.

Mav's mouth twisted into a grin. "But then I couldn't come spend time with my *favorite* brothers."

"You mean mooch food off us because you just got off a shift?" Wylder asked.

Mav's grin only widened. "I can do both. Now, tell me what you two were whispering about." He scanned the bar, his gaze halting on Brae. "Wait, is that her?" He let out a low whistle. "No wonder you're breaking all the rules."

"I'm not breaking any rules," I grumbled.

Wylder's steady gaze landed on me. "No, just laws."

I tried not to shift in place, knowing Wylder would pick up on any slight movement. Because he was right. I'd broken half a dozen already. But my silence gave him the answer he needed.

Wylder let out a curse. "Seriously, Dex? This is exactly what Kol was worried about."

A muscle along my jaw started to flutter in a staccato beat. "And that's not a little hypocritical? You know I use the same tactics in cases we work."

"But they aren't local," Wylder bit out, his voice dropping low. "It won't get us on local radar."

"Me. I'm the one doing this. The rest of you bowed out. So if anyone pays a price, it'll be me." And I'd pay it. Just so I didn't have to see that gutted look on Brae's face ever again. The one that said she was totally and completely alone.

Tiny divots appeared in the hollows of Wylder's cheeks, his jaw clenching tight. "You know it doesn't work that way. Not for us. One of us gets on the radar, all of us do."

"I'm not hiding from narrow-minded assholes," I clipped.

"Boys, boys, boys," Maverick cut in. "Let's take a breath, okay?"

I didn't take my gaze off Wylder. Instead, I gave him the truth, playing a card I knew would trump everything. "You didn't hear her. How torn up she is about her friend. She's had *no one*. No one helping her raise that kid except her friend. Nova might as well have been her sister. Her *only* family. And now, she's been alone for a year, doing everything she can to find that sister. You might not want to take the risk of helping her. But I will."

A feeling of *rightness* swept through me. I'd battled with myself last night—even this morning. Guilt had mixed with my need to help. But now, I knew. This was the right thing. The good thing. More, it felt a little less like I was hiding in the shadows. Which felt damn good.

Wylder stayed quiet, his expression going blank in the way I knew meant his brain was exploring every angle. I felt Mav's gaze ping-pong between us as he waited.

Finally, Wylder scrubbed a hand through his hair. "Fuck me."

Victory and relief washed through me.

Mav grabbed both of our shoulders. "Does this mean we're in?" He sounded like a damn kid hopped up on too much sugar.

Wylder's focus didn't stray from me. "We're helping. Just try not to get us arrested. Or exposed."

I knew what that last piece meant. We didn't need the world at large to know what we were up to. "I think we can trust her."

My brothers stilled because they knew what that meant. Trust didn't come easily for any of us. But Brae had proven herself again today. The way she met me in the shadows. How she'd shown me her shame in an attempt to soothe mine.

"I hope you're right," Wylder muttered.

A faint ringing had me seeking out the sound. I looked up to see Brae behind the bar, drying glasses. She held one in her hand while she fished out her phone with the other, a smile on her face as she waved to Travis, who'd just appeared at the hostess stand.

But the moment her eyes locked on the screen, everything changed. The rosy pink on her cheeks went stark white as if all the blood had drained from her face in an instant.

Glass shattered, the sound like an explosion in the empty room. And I was already running.

CHAPTER EIGHTEEN
Braedyn

BLOOD ROARED IN MY EARS AS I STARED AT THE PHONE. A NAME flashed across the screen that I hadn't seen in over a year. Hundreds of days when I would've given anything to see *Supernova* appear. The photo of her, Owen, and me at a beach with ice cream cones, pure joy on our faces. Everything faded as I stared at the name.

Supernova Calling.

The glass I was holding slipped from my fingers, shattering on the floor as my phone fell with it—like I didn't have any control over my hands or body at all.

Fear flared and mixed with desperation as I dropped to my knees, not giving a damn about the glass biting into my legs and palms. I fumbled for the phone, snatching it up and jabbing at the screen.

It took three messy tries to hit Accept and shove it against my face. "Nova! Where are you? Are you there?"

My words tumbled and jumbled as if one tangled with the next, but there was no response. Only the sound of rushing water.

"Nova?" I croaked, my voice breaking.

I heard it then. Breath. Raspy. Ragged. The kind of heavy breathing you heard in slasher movies.

A second later, the phone was being pulled from my hand by a man with a thunderous expression. Some part of me recognized Dex as he pressed the phone to his ear. The moment he heard what I had, his expression went from thunderous to murderous.

I'd seen grumpy on Dex's face. Even pissed off. But I'd never seen cold.

A tiny piece of my brain told me I should be fearful. But I wasn't. Something about that coldness was comforting.

I watched, transfixed, as Dex pulled out his own phone, tapping on the screen and holding it up to my device. All I wanted to do was to crawl through that cell and into Nova's—to get to her.

My phone flashed and then went black. Dex cursed.

I let out a pained sound, trying to grab for the device.

Dex quickly set it on the bar out of my reach.

"No," I croaked. "It was her. I need to know where she is. I need to find her. I need—"

Pain streaked across Dex's face. "I don't think it was her."

"You don't know that!" I bit out. "Maybe she couldn't talk. What if she's hurt? What if—?"

"Hellion," Dex said softly.

Tears filled my eyes. "Where is she?"

The muscle that ran along Dex's jaw twitched wildly. "We're gonna find out. But I need to help you first. Okay?"

My brows pulled together. I didn't need help. Nova did. We had to find Nova.

As if understanding my confusion, Dex spoke again. "You cut yourself. You're bleeding."

I looked down at my hands. Cuts of varied lengths and depths crisscrossed my palms, and blood smeared my knees. But I didn't feel anything—not a damn thing but the gaping hole in my chest.

"Can I lift you out of the glass?" Dex asked, his voice so gentle it hurt.

I had the faint awareness of nodding, and Dex didn't wait; he scooped me into his strong arms as though I weighed nothing. When had someone last held me? I couldn't remember.

Through the numbness, I felt Dex's presence. The steady beat of his heart. The silent fury coursing through him that was a balm to my agony. The feeling of not being alone.

Some part of me was aware of Travis putting *his* phone to his ear and Cora and Aidan looking on worriedly. But they were all fuzzy.

Dex set me on a chair at one of the tables as Wylder moved in behind him. I knew I should be embarrassed, having this kind of meltdown after just starting a new job. But I couldn't find it in me.

That embarrassment should've flared brighter as Travis and Cora moved closer. "Called for backup," Travis said quietly.

That had a fresh scowl twisting Dex's lips, but he nodded.

A man I'd never seen before with the same eyes as Dex and Wylder moved in, setting something on the table. "Got the first-aid kit." He sent me an easy smile. "Hate meeting this way, Brae, but I'm Maverick. These two idiots' younger, hotter brother. My friends call me Mav."

My mouth tried to smile but couldn't get there. And I swore I heard a faint growling noise come from Dex.

Maverick held up both hands. "All right, all right. I get it. No flirting."

Dex's hand cupped my cheek. "Is it just your hands and knees that hurt?"

"Nothing hurts," I croaked. "I don't feel anything."

Maverick frowned as he glanced at Dex. "She's in shock." He moved to the first-aid kit, briskly pulling out supplies as Dex grabbed for some gloves and quickly donned them.

Maverick moved in closer. "Why don't you let me—?"

"I've got it," Dex clipped.

Maverick's brows lifted, but he nodded slowly. "I'll be your assistant, then. Even though I'm the one with the medic training."

"Mav," Wylder warned.

"Can we do anything?" Cora asked softly, Aidan moving in beside her in a silent offering of help.

Dex's gaze flicked up. "Help Trav corral the deputies when they get here."

I heard the sound of multiple people arriving and Wylder greeting them. There were so many voices, but I didn't have it in me to try to identify any of them. I was suddenly exhausted. So damn tired I could've slumped in the chair right then and there.

Dex sank to the floor in front of me, his eyes lifting to mine. "I'm going to treat your knees, okay?"

I gave a jerky nod of assent.

Those strong fingers moved quickly but gently, almost tenderly, as he carefully prodded my knees. A soft curse filtered out into the air between us. "Tweezers?" Dex asked, his voice tight.

Maverick handed him something.

"This might hurt a little, and I'm so damn sorry," Dex said. "But we've gotta get the glass out, okay?"

I frowned down at the man in front of me. He was so...worried. "It's all right. It doesn't hurt."

I wanted to assure him, but my words just seemed to make Dex mad. Still, he focused on the task in front of him. One gloved hand cupped the back of my calf while the other plucked tiny shards of glass from my knees.

"We need to speak with Braedyn," a gruff voice cut in—one I recognized from all the times he'd shut me down or sent me packing: Sheriff Miller.

Dex didn't move from his spot, but the look he sent the sheriff would've had me peeing my pants. Or at least rethinking my life choices. "You will talk to Brae *after* she's received medical treatment and when she's goddamned ready," he snarled.

Red spots hit Miller's cheeks. "You aren't in charge here. You're not even a first responder. You're a criminal, who—"

"Who knows a victim's rights include receiving medical treatment and not talking until she damn well wants to. Talk to Travis. He has the phone," Dex barked.

"Got it here, Sheriff," Travis called from behind the bar.

Miller looked between the phone and Dex, a battle playing out on his face as his jaw worked back and forth. Finally, he relented, stalking across the bar toward Travis and the phone.

"Looks like you got yourself a bulldog, B," Roger said with a grin, but I could see the worry in his gaze as he walked up. "You okay?"

"I'm okay." I tried to send him a wobbly smile but flinched instead as Dex pulled another shard from my knee.

Dex's gaze jerked up. "Too much?"

I shook my head. "No. I just feel it more now."

My fingers and toes tingled as sensation slowly swept through me. It was like I'd fallen asleep in an awkward position and my limbs needed to regain feeling.

"That's good," Maverick assured me.

Dex's head bent as he focused on my knees again. "I'm almost done. Two more pieces."

I tried not to wince as he retrieved the final glass shards from my flesh. But I couldn't help the grimace as he swept some hydrogen peroxide over my skin.

"I'm sorry," Dex whispered.

"You're helping."

"Hate having to hurt to help," he muttered.

I felt Roger's eyes on us, the back-and-forth energy of curiosity as Maverick handed Dex some antibiotic ointment and a bandage.

Dex stroked the back of my calf as if he needed to give a gentle, soothing touch to combat the others. "This should help ease the pain."

"It's not that bad." I'd had so much worse. When I broke my arm in the fifth grade. When I got bashed against the rocks by a vicious wave in high school. Childbirth.

Dex didn't seem convinced as he used a gloved finger to spread the ointment across my knees and then my palms. He carefully bandaged one knee and then the other, then wrapped gauze around my hands to cover the cuts there.

"You know, D-man, you could have a future as an EMT. You won't do it with nearly as much style as me, mind you, but you'd be decent," Maverick said with a shit-stirring grin.

Roger barked out a laugh. "He could always work in tech support at the senior center. Bet he could help those grannies figure out how to videocall their grandkids, no problem."

"I hate you both," Dex grumbled.

I saw what they were doing. Trying to lighten the mood, ease the swirling tension. But as I came back to myself more and more, I remembered why.

"Nova," I whispered.

The three men in front of me stilled. Roger shifted, pulling out a phone as he motioned Miller, Travis, and a female officer I didn't recognize over.

"Is it okay if I record you?" Roger asked. "That way, you won't have to go over it again and again."

"Sure." I knew I'd spoken the word, but it didn't sound like my voice.

"Walk us through what happened," Roger prodded gently.

I swallowed, feeling like some of those glass shards had somehow made it into my throat. "I was drying a few glasses left over from the lunch rush, and my phone rang. I leave it on for emergencies because of my son, but…"

"It wasn't Owen," Dex filled in.

"We need to hear from her. Not you," Miller barked.

I bit down on the inside of my cheek so I wouldn't bite the sheriff's head off. "It wasn't Owen. It was Nova's name on my screen. I…I've kept her cell phone plan paid, just in case. I thought it was a stretch, but what if the phone got turned on? What if we could find her?"

A look of sympathy passed over Travis's face. "The phone isn't on anymore. I had a tech try to trace it as soon as I realized what was going on, but nothing came up."

I fisted my hands, instantly regretting the move when a fresh wave of burning pain erupted in my palms. Dex reached down and gently unfurled one fist and then the other. "Easy, Hellion."

"Was there anyone on the other end of the line?" Miller asked, his voice tight.

"At first, I just heard water. Rushing like a river, not trickling. And then…then there was breathing. But no one spoke."

"I heard the breathing, too," Dex added. "No voice, just heavy breathing. Like whoever was on the other end was trying to freak her out."

Roger and Travis shared a look—the kind that told me none of this spelled good things. I knew that. Someone had Nova's phone. Something that had been with her when she was taken. And that person thought it would be fun to scare the hell out of me. What did that mean for Nova?

Sheriff Miller shifted, his hands resting on the front of his gun belt. "And you don't think it's interesting that the day Dexter files an open records request, you just happen to get a call?"

I frowned, not understanding the point Miller was trying to make.

His hard gaze flicked to Dex. "You bored, coming back to small-town life after a decade with the FBI? Think you'll run a prank to liven things up?"

My jaw went slack as Dex's entire form hardened to granite.

"Sheriff," Maverick began, pushing to his feet.

"I'm not talking to you," Miller clipped. "I know there's all sorts of tech bullshit you can use to copy a phone number."

"Spoofing a number," the female officer suggested.

Travis's eyes narrowed on the woman. "He was standing right here when the call came in. I saw him."

"Probably could pay someone to make the call," she shot back.

"You both better watch yourselves," Wylder's voice cut in, cold as ice as his gaze cut to the female officer and Miller.

But me? I felt nothing but heat.

A burning rage ignited by ignorance and cruelty. "Are you serious right now?" I growled.

"Hellion," Dex said softly.

"No," I clipped. "Not for a damn second." I shoved out of my chair, still feeling a little shaky. "You do a half-assed job when Nova goes missing. You won't help me follow up on leads. You tell me her case is cold. And now you're trying to drag down a good man who offered to help me when your selfish, lazy ass couldn't be bothered?

Don't you dare try to pull him down in the mud just because that's where you live."

Those red spots crept up Miller's neck and onto his face. "I followed procedure. I got countless open cases in my county. I can't waste time chasing a ghost. Because Nova Monroe is a ghost. She fell into the river or got taken out by large game. And you're so hellbent on saying it was something else. Even if it was…she's gone. I'm not wasting my officers' time or my county's resources because you can't accept reality."

A ringing lit in my ears. "I would know." My voice trembled with each word. "I would know if she was gone. I would feel it."

Miller made a *pssh* noise. "Feel it. Woo-woo, Bay Area bullshit. I'm not wasting thousands of taxpayer dollars 'cause you got a *feeling*."

"Maybe you should do that because she got a call from a phone *you* think belongs to a dead woman," Dex ground out.

Each back and forth was like a stinging slap that startled all the air from my lungs. But *dead woman* was a knockout punch. *Dead*.

My fingers twisted in the strands of my friendship bracelet as I tried to feel Nova. *I'd know*. I told myself that over and over. I'd know if she no longer walked this earth. I'd feel it.

Miller's eyes narrowed on Dex. "Oh, you bet your ass I'll be lookin' into it. And when I find out you're involved, I'll make sure we throw the goddamned book at you. Get you in a cell where your father should've been all his fuckin' life."

"Get. Out." Fury burned through each word as they shot out like bullets, landing square in Miller's chest.

Anger burned through his brown eyes, shooting right back at me. "You don't got the right to say that, little lady."

"She may not, but I do," Wylder said, his voice deadly calm. "This is my establishment. No laws have been broken here—"

"That we know of," the woman next to Miller muttered.

"I'm asking you to leave," Wylder pressed. "Or I can file a complaint with the county. The state. Police harassment. Might make for a nice news story."

Something told me that was a lie, that he wouldn't want it in the news. The Archer brothers clearly kept the tie to their father as quiet as possible. But Miller still folded.

His glare swept across the lot of us. "You'll be hearing from me."

"That'd be a first," I muttered.

Travis met my gaze, a million apologies in his. "Here's your phone back. We don't need it since we already have the caller's number." He handed the device to me as if it were a piece of delicate china. *"I'm sorry."* He mouthed the words, but I just shook my head. None of this was his fault.

Roger squeezed my shoulder and made a motion that told me he'd call me later. There was nothing he or Travis could do. Their hands were tied by a douchebag dictator.

Quiet reigned when the last officer walked out the door. Nothing but the sound of my breathing remained. Until Dex's voice broke the silence.

"No one's ever stood up for me like that."

My neck twisted, head tipping back to take him in. There was a different sort of fire in those dark-hazel eyes now. Some emotion I didn't quite have a name for.

Dex's throat worked as he swallowed. "No one but my brothers."

The pain of that slid through me like another wave of glass shards. "Not going to let someone lie about you right to my face." One corner of my mouth kicked up in the barest of smiles. "Even if you are the worst, Buttercup."

CHAPTER NINETEEN
Dex

BRAE WAS TRYING TO MAKE LIGHT OF THE SITUATION NOW—all she'd given me in that mere handful of seconds, everything she'd offered with her fire and fury.

"You're trying to drag down a good man who offered to help me when your selfish, lazy ass couldn't be bothered?"

Her words echoed in my head. No, they *branded* themselves there.

"Don't you dare try to pull him down in the mud just because that's where you live."

And Miller did live there. In the mud—in worse than that. But Brae wouldn't let him get that mud on me. More than that, she fought for me. Stood up for me when only my brothers and Waylon, in his own way, had ever done that before.

"Hellion," I rasped.

Brae flicked her wavy, blond hair over one shoulder, but I didn't miss the slight tremble in her hand. It belied what still lived underneath: the trauma she'd just lived through. But you'd never know it by her voice. "He needed to be put in his place."

I opened my mouth to thank her, to say something—anything—that would show her just how much what she'd done meant to me, but an alarm cut through the air.

Brae fumbled with the cell phone in her hand. "I'm gonna be late getting Owen. I'm never late. I need to find my bag and my—"

I moved in, resting my hands on her shoulders. "Breathe, Hellion. I'll get you to pickup. Just breathe."

It was the least I could do. And the last thing I'd be able to do right now was leave her. The tremble I felt beneath my hands only solidified that fact. Everything stirring deep should've had me running for the hills, but it didn't. And that was the most dangerous thing of all.

"You've got this," I said, my voice dipping low. "One thing at a time. Where's Owen?"

"Camp," Brae rasped.

"The adventure camp run through the county?" Maverick asked.

She nodded, pink hitting her cheeks, clearly embarrassed at having all of us witnessing her meltdown. But Maverick—in true Mav form—appeared unaffected by it all. And I could've hugged him for that. He simply pulled out his phone and pressed it to his ear. "Kol."

A pause, and then Maverick's face screwed up.

"No, I didn't get another flat tire four-wheeling."

Another silence.

"Will you shut up for two seconds? Dex's friend, Brae, has a kid in the same camp as Skylar. Name's Owen. Will you guys chill with him until she gets there? She's running a few minutes late."

Quiet again, this time for longer, but I could hear the buzz of a stream of words on the other line.

Finally, Maverick cut him off. "I'll explain later. Thanks, man." And then he hung up without a goodbye, his gaze finding Brae. "Our brother has a little girl in the camp. They'll hang with your dude until you get there."

"Thank you," she whispered, her gaze dipping. I hated losing that golden amber, even for a second.

Wylder shifted. "I know you have the weekend off, but if you need more time, just let me know. We can cover you."

Brae struggled to swallow as she forced herself to look up at Wylder. "I already cost you hours of business."

One corner of Wylder's mouth kicked up. "We'll open back up in a few, and we'll be flooded because people will want to know why the cops were here. We'll make double what we normally do."

A pit settled in my stomach at the thought of Brae being at the center of the town gossip. God, I knew what that was like, and it was the last thing I wanted for her.

Aidan shot Brae a grin as he strode up. "I'm gonna tell them the FBI called in a tip that we had a sleeper spy in our midst, and I bravely took him down in a citizen's arrest." He glanced at me. "You can back me on that, right? Tell me the FBI lingo."

My lips twitched, grateful for the humor I could always count on him to bring. "I got you."

Cora moved in, rolling her eyes at Aidan and then sending Brae a conspiratorial smile. "I'm going to tell everyone Aidan accidentally slept with a mobster's wife, and they took out a hit on him. More believable."

"I'm going pure aliens," Maverick said, his eyes finding mine. "The truth is out there."

The tiniest laugh bubbled out of Brae. It wasn't a sound I expected to hear given the circumstances, but my hellion was full of surprises. "Thank you. All of you."

Fiona handed Brae a tote bag with a tiny Bigfoot stitched in the corner. "Go get your boy and text me if you need anything, honey."

Aidan's blue-green eyes twinkled. "I'd be happy to stay over tonight if you want some company and—"

Wylder slapped him upside the head. "Get back to work."

I glared at the too-flirty-for-his-own-good waiter. If anyone was staying over, it would be me.

Fucking hell. That was the last thing I needed to be considering. The last thing I normally *would* be considering.

Aidan rubbed the back of his head. "You know, if I get brain damage because of your constant abuse, I'm suing."

"Don't be an idiot, and we won't have a problem," Wylder shot back.

"Keys," I demanded, my voice gruffer than I meant for it to be.

Brae's head tipped back as if in search of the voice. Her golden eyes held questions I didn't have answers for.

I extended a hand, palm up. "Keys."

Because while I may not have answers, I could take her to pick up her kid. Make sure they got home safely.

"Why?" she asked.

"Because you're not driving."

Her jaw went a little slack. "Excuse me?"

"Hellion," I said, my voice dropping low. "You're shaky. I don't want you behind the wheel. Don't want you driving Owen home. You'll be distracted. He'll be talking your ear off about boobie cookies and—"

"Boobie cookies?" Maverick cut in. "How do I get some of those?"

I shot him a look that promised vast retribution if he didn't shut the hell up. "You don't get them. They're mine."

Mav held up both hands. "Touchy, touchy about the boobie cookies. Noted."

My scowl only deepened.

Brae just shook her head as she slid a hand into her bag and pulled out her keys, dropping them into my palm. "You can drive."

A small thrill of victory slid through me. "Thank you."

I didn't wait for her to change her mind. I ushered Brae out the back amid a chorus of goodbyes and into the small parking lot behind the Boot. As she pointed us toward her small maroon SUV, my scowl reemerged.

Really taking in the vehicle—if you could call it that—for the first time, it looked like it was held together by duct tape and a prayer. Okay, maybe it wasn't that bad. But it was clearly aged in spots, and the tires were pathetic.

"Are you still traumatized from the bird-poop incident?" Brae asked.

My head jerked up. "What?"

"Still traumatized that I stole your parking spot and you got pooped on?"

I shook my head. "It was seriously scarring. Living next to you should mean I get hazard pay. But no."

Brae's mouth curved like she found my annoyance adorable. "Then why are you scowling at my car? Got an issue with the color maroon now?"

"I'm scowling at your goddamned tires. They're practically bald. You need to get new ones before winter."

She frowned, studying the SUV. "I just got this. Used, but all the checks came through."

"You ask when they last replaced the tires?" I pressed.

She tugged her lip between her teeth, pressing down. Like I'd just dropped the final straw that would break her.

Shit.

My hand found the small of Brae's back on instinct, like that would somehow make it all okay. "We'll deal with it. Just get in."

We'll.

I didn't think I'd ever used the word *we* with a woman. Yet it had slipped right out with Brae.

It seemed to take her by surprise just as much as it did me. She rolled her shoulders back as if heading into battle. "I'll get new ones before the winter. These are good for now."

I eyed her as I opened the passenger door and ushered her in, but I didn't say a word. Because I got it. She'd ask for all the help in the world when it came to Nova but never for herself.

As we made our way to the parks-and-rec area where the camp was being held, I could feel and see Brae's nerves: the drumming of her fingers against her thigh, the way her gaze jumped from place to place, never landing on any one thing for more than a second or two.

I couldn't stop myself from touching her, trying to ground her. My palm curved around her forearm—nothing forceful, just gentle reassurance. "It's okay to let someone help you every once in a while."

Brae's golden eyes cut to me, going glassy in the afternoon sunlight. "Everyone I've ever leaned on has vanished."

My hand on her forearm tightened for the briefest moment. My emotions, the ones I normally kept so carefully under wraps, broke through. "Hate that for you."

She blinked away some tears as she watched her son climbing on the jungle gym outside the rec center. "Me, too."

I would've done anything to change that for her. To tell her parents they were narrow-minded assholes with a side of idiot. Tell her ex that he'd ruined his damn life by missing out on the magic that was Brae and Owen. Go on that cursed hike so her best friend never would've vanished into thin air.

But I couldn't do any of that. I *could* try to be her friend.

Friend.

What a joke. Friendship didn't exactly seem like an accurate term for Brae. I'd try to live out that lie anyway.

Brae shoved out of the SUV, forcing a smile as I hurried to follow. Owen's laugh pierced the air as Skylar chased him around the castle-like play equipment.

Kol stood watching them like a sentry as a few other parents, kids, and camp staff milled about. They were all in small groups, laughing and chatting. But not my brother. He stood with his arms crossed, a hard look on his face.

"Kol," I called out.

He turned, but nothing changed on his expression: hard, wary, and maybe a little bit worried.

Brae forced her smile wider, but it trembled at the edges. "Thank you for hanging with Owen."

Kol's gaze dipped to her hands and then her knees. "What happened?"

I gave him a small shake of my head. "I'll explain later."

The tension in Kol's face intensified.

"Mom!" Owen shouted, racing toward Brae. "Did you know Mr. Kol has the coolest job ever?"

Her smile became a little more genuine. "Cooler than a coder?" she asked as Owen came to a screeching halt in front of her.

"What about the FBI?" I cut in, a little offended that I'd already been dethroned.

Indecision warred on Owen's face. "Okay, they're all tied. But he looks for poachers and people doing bad stuff in the forest. He gets to go hiking, like all the time. And knows how to find people *anywhere*. Sky told me."

My niece popped up then, and Brae's smile widened. I couldn't help but grin. Sky was freaking adorable in a fluffy, pink skirt paired with combat boots. She had a T-shirt with a picture of a raccoon that read *Cute but feral* and rainbow necklaces I knew she'd made herself.

She grinned up at Brae, revealing a missing tooth. "Never play hide-and-seek with my dad. He wins *every* time."

Brae laughed. "I'll keep that in mind. I'm Brae, by the way. Thanks for hanging out with Owen."

Sky just beamed. "I'm Skylar. And that's my dad."

Kol simply grunted.

I rolled my eyes. Always big on polite chitchat, my brother.

"Skylar, I absolutely love your outfit. You have fabulous style," Brae told her.

She twirled to show it off properly. "Thank you. I love your shoes."

Brae's focus dipped to her high-tops. "Thanks. Owen decorated them for me. He makes me a pair every year."

"That's *so* cool. Daddy, we should do that. I can draw hearts and Nerf guns all over them for you. And use my glitter markers."

Kol gave his daughter a pained smile. "Nothing I love more than glitter hearts."

"Samesies," Sky agreed earnestly as Brae fought a laugh.

"Mom, what happened to your hands?" Owen asked, frowning at her.

I didn't miss Brae's wince, but she covered it quickly. "You remember when I tripped over Yeti and gave myself a black eye?"

Owen giggled. "But you told everyone you got into a fight with a ninja and kicked their butt."

She grinned at her son. "It was a much better story."

"Only when you showed off your moves while telling it," Owen added.

"True," she agreed. "Well, I dropped a glass at work, and I got all cut. But I think we need a better story. Maybe I dove through a window to escape a pack of wild wildebeests."

It was Skylar's turn to giggle. "Or to hide from invading aliens."

I ruffled Sky's hair. "You sound like Mav."

"Uncle Mav has the *best* stories," she pointed out.

"Just as long as you remember that none of them are true," Kol muttered. His gaze flicked to Brae, landing on her hands again. "Are you okay? You get those looked at?"

Annoyance and pissed off were basically Kol's love languages, so I knew he was softening toward Brae, even if she didn't know it.

"Dex treated them with Maverick's help. I'm all good," she assured him.

Kol's mouth thinned, but he gave her a quick nod.

That was the most we could hope to get from my surly older brother, so I turned to Owen. "Ready to hit the road?"

Owen grinned so wide I thought it would split his face in two. "You're driving us?"

"I am. And I say we need milkshakes along the way. What do you think?"

"Yeeeeeeessssss!" Owen cheered, doing a little dance.

Skylar's pigtails whipped around. "Can we get some, Daddy? Pleeeeeease?"

Kol glowered at me. "If she won't go to sleep tonight because she's all hopped up on sugar, I'm calling you to babysit."

CHAPTER TWENTY
Braedyn

"So," Dex prodded, a hint of mischief in those dark-hazel eyes.

I took a sip of the milkshake, letting the flavors play over my tongue as Owen raced ahead of us toward my SUV. "It's like blackberries and raspberries combined in some sort of delicious goodness."

Dex chuckled, the sound skating over my skin in a different sort of deliciousness. "I'm taking that as a good thing," he pressed.

"Definitely."

I studied him as we walked, milkshakes in hand, and was struck by something. Dex cared. Despite his gruff, sometimes-cantankerous exterior, he cared. And he didn't show it with flowery words and false promises. He did it with his actions. Somehow, that was more powerful.

Apparently, the gruff caring act was an Archer brothers' trait. Because despite Kol's wariness of me and the whole situation, he'd wanted to make sure I was okay, too. The only thing I couldn't figure out was what about me set Kol on edge.

"They put like a bazillion Oreos in this milkshake," Owen cheered. "It's the *best*!"

I groaned. "Can't wait for bedtime tonight."

One corner of Dex's mouth kicked up. "Sorry about that."

"You're not sorry at all," I grumbled.

Owen chattered away, asking Dex five million questions as we made the drive home from the diner. What started with the FBI inquiries turned to computers, and I couldn't understand half of what Owen was asking.

"You know," Dex said, pulling onto Briarwood Lane, "you have way more computer knowledge than I did at your age."

Owen bounced up and down in the back seat. "Really? Do you think you could teach me stuff? I really want to learn how to brute force attack."

Dex let out a laugh. "I think your mom might not love me teaching you that. But I can teach you how to build firewalls."

My gaze slid to the man next to me, studying the way his forearms flexed as he turned the wheel. The easy smile he had for my son. How effortless it was for him to step in and be just what we needed today. "If you teach my kid to hack into the Pentagon, I will steal all your gadgets, dump them in the creek, and dye all your clothes bubblegum pink."

"Bro," Owen said, clearly annoyed I wouldn't let him do something that could get him imprisoned for all of eternity.

"I'm such a buzzkill, I know. Worst mom ever," I commiserated.

Dex barked out a laugh as he pulled up to the cabins. "See, even your kid thinks you're the worst."

I stuck my tongue out at him in response.

"Who's that?" Owen asked, leaning forward.

My heart skipped a beat as I turned to the front windshield. Through it, I caught sight of two figures sitting on our front steps. I wasn't sure what I expected to find. Another bomb dropped on my life? The cruel mystery person taunting me through Nova's phone? The monster who'd stolen her from me? But the moment their faces came into focus, I let out a breath.

"That's Holly and Cora," I explained. "They're friends from when I took you to the park. And Cora works with me."

Owen's mouth thinned. "They're okay, I guess. Not as fun as Nova, I bet."

Pain slid through me as I reached back and squeezed Owen's knee. "They're all amazing in their own way, but no one will ever replace our Supernova."

"No one's as awesome as Supernova," Owen muttered.

"No," I whispered. "No, they aren't."

I felt Dex's eyes on me but couldn't look at him. It would be too much. And if I broke now, it would all fall apart. Instead, I climbed out of the car. "Hey, guys."

Holly and Cora were already on their way to me. Holly pulled me into a hug. "Are you okay? Have they traced the call? What are—?"

"I'm fine," I said quickly, then tipped my head to where Owen was climbing out of the back, widening my eyes meaningfully.

Cora moved in then, squeezing my arm. "I thought you might need dinner. How do you feel about lasagna, salad, and garlic bread?" She gestured to some takeout bags on the front stoop.

The burn behind my eyes was back for a whole new reason. It wasn't just Dex who cared. I was finding a whole community in Starlight Grove. I swallowed against the ball of emotion gathering in my throat. "Thank you."

Holly rubbed a hand up and down my back. "It's what friends do."

"Mom, can I let Yeti out?" Owen called.

"Sure, have Dex help you. He has the keys."

Dex arched a brow at me. "Your dog gonna go for the family jewels again?"

My lips twitched. "Only if you shake them in her face."

Cora choked on a laugh. "I feel like this might have something to do with your first run-in."

"Ask her about the boobie cookies," Dex said as he started up the walk, Owen running ahead of him.

Holly's mouth pursed as she watched them go. "You two seem to have gotten…close. I thought you didn't know him."

I tried not to bristle, but the weight of the day made it hard. "Dex lives in the cabin next door. He also had my back today and is going to help me with Nova's case."

"In other words," Cora began, "don't be a dick, Holls."

Holly's jaw went slack. "I-I wasn't... I—"

I placed a hand on her shoulder. "There was a little judginess in there."

Her lips pressed together. "I just don't want you mixed up in anything that could get you in trouble," she said softly.

A little of my annoyance eased. "I think I'm already in trouble. And if it means finding Nova, I'll gladly go to jail or the fiery pits of hell."

A wave of grief passed over Holly's face, and her gaze shifted to Owen. She watched as he laughed and chased Yeti around the front yard. "I would've done anything for my boy."

Cora squeezed Holly's hand in a silent show of support. "We do everything we can for those we love."

Holly sighed and straightened her shoulders. "We do."

"Come on," Cora said. "Let's go inside, and I'll warm up dinner. You can tell us what you need."

For her, it was as simple as that. Whatever I needed, she'd try to give.

As they headed in, Dex met me on the walkway. His gaze skimmed over my face as if checking for injury. His fingers twitched at his sides, making me wonder if he wanted to reach out and touch me but was stopping himself.

"Will you be okay with them for a little while?" he asked. "I need to check on a few things."

"I've been on my own for a long time, Dex. I'll be fine." I said the words for myself as much as him. I needed to remember just how strong I was. That I could stand on my own two feet.

Shadows swirled through his dark-hazel irises. "Just because you've been on your own before doesn't mean you have to be now. I'll be back, Hellion."

Each word felt like a carefully placed blow—the gentlest yet most brutal cut. But his vow to be back was the hardest to take. Because sometimes, people didn't return, and you were left to live with the ghosts of their promises.

CHAPTER TWENTY-ONE
Dex

IT KILLED ME TO WALK AWAY FROM HER. MAYBE BECAUSE everything in me screamed she was in trouble. Maybe because it was clear she was too damn used to people bailing on her—whether by choice or not.

Each step I took toward my cabin hurt, like muscle ripping away from bone with each stride. But I forced myself to do it anyway. Just like I forced myself not to look back. Because if I did, I'd go to her. Nothing could stop me.

Unlocking my front door, I stepped inside and pulled out my phone. Half a dozen text threads flashed on the screen, and I had to take a second and breathe. Closing my eyes, I went through a list of priorities in my mind.

Running the recording through sound-recognition software. Getting Nova's phone number plugged into my backdoor triangulation software no phone company wanted me to have. Cameras and an alarm system for Brae—something I was sure she'd fight me on. Talking to my brothers.

Sometimes, my brain felt like a computer overloaded with too many files, and I had to do a hard reboot, choosing only the most important things to focus on. With one last deep breath, I opened my eyes and instantly went for my texts as I strode into my makeshift office. I opened a new message to Blaze and started typing.

> **Me:** *How do you feel about a free alarm installation at Creekside Cabins, including cameras?*

Three dots appeared and then disappeared, then appeared again.

> **Blaze:** *Little Dude, working for The Man has really changed you.*

> **Me:** *It's a safety precaution. I'm not trying to spy on whatever crystal light show you put on here when the cabins aren't in use.*

> **Blaze:** *Maybe I'm entertaining female company. Someone would pay big money to put that on the interstellar highway.*

My whole face screwed up.

> **Me:** *There's a kink for everyone, but I'm not putting cameras INSIDE the cabins, just outside.*

> **Blaze:** *Oh. Why didn't you say so? Run with it, Little Dude. Then maybe I'll catch those jerks who like to have keggers back there but don't invite me.*

I just shook my head and eased into the desk chair.

> **Me:** *I'll get you justice.*

Blaze just sent a *power to the people* raised-fist emoji in response that definitely was not intended for righteous indignation about being left out of a party.

Pulling up the recording I'd taken of the call, I air-dropped the video to my desktop and uploaded it to the sound-identification software. It might not give me more than my ear had, but it was worth a shot.

One thing was clear: Someone was messing with Brae. In a way that meant they got joy out of causing pain. And I knew just what sort of dark roads that could lead you down.

As the software got to work, my phone let out another ding.

My brothers' chat flashed on the screen, and I realized I'd missed more than a few texts from them.

> **Wylder:** *Let us know how Brae's doing once you get her home.*
>
> **Maverick:** *Brae's a badass, and I have no doubt she's totally fine. A hot badass. D, want to take my place on the ranch? I'll move into your cabin. I can play bodyguard.*

I scowled at the screen.

> **Kol:** *Someone tell me what the hell is going on.*
>
> **Maverick:** *You meet the little badass yet? You'll like her. She cut Miller down in three blows, then kicked him to the curb. Thing of beauty.*
>
> **Kol:** *Why the hell were you having a run-in with Miller?*
>
> **Wylder:** *I think Dex should explain.*

My fingers flew across the screen.

> **Me:** *Mav, don't call Brae hot, or I'll make your phone say, "I have a defective sphincter" every time you get a text.*
>
> **Maverick:** *Harsh, dude. She okay?*
>
> **Me:** *Cora and Holly are with her. They brought dinner.*
>
> **Kol:** *Family meeting. At the ranch. Now.*
>
> **Maverick:** *Shit. He used the f-word.*

Family meetings were reserved for emergencies. Like when we found out a journalist was sniffing around town trying to write the dozenth tell-all book about our father's reign of terror. Or when Waylon told us he had cancer. Or when Kol found out he had a daughter.

No one rejected a family meeting. Not even Orion, who was noticeably absent in our back-and-forth.

Me: *I don't have my car.*

Maverick: *I got you. Be there in ten.*

It took him more like fifteen, but he finally showed. And that was Mav. He might do things in his own time and way, but he always came through.

As I climbed into his truck, I glanced at Cabin Two. I swore I caught the flash of blond hair through the window, but maybe it was just my imagination. She'd be okay. I told myself that over and over. Cora and Holly were with her. Yeti was there. It was broad daylight. It would be fine.

"Dude, are you having a stroke or something?" Mav asked. "Or are you trying to move that house with your mind?"

I shot him a dirty look as he peeled out of the drive. "I need to be back before dark."

He grinned. "So you can watch over the hot, little badass?"

"Stop calling her that," I ground out.

Mav's grin only widened. "You like her."

"I'm not ten, asshole."

"You sure act like it. She makes you grumpy. It pisses you the hell off that you like her."

I scowled at the road in front of us. "Drop me by the station. That's where my car is. I don't want you driving me home."

"That hurts, D-man. But I know it's only because I see the truth."

The pisser of it all was that he was right. But I wasn't about to tell him that.

Mav pulled up behind my car, and I hopped out, but as I did, he rolled down the passenger window. "Why does this feel like I'm dropping you off walk-of-shame style?"

I turned to scowl at my brother but didn't get a word out before a new voice cut through the air.

"Probably because anyone you're dropping off *is* doing a walk of shame."

I looked over toward the sidewalk, a genuine smile rising to my lips. "Aster Carrington, as I live and breathe."

Her glower aimed at my brother melted into something much warmer as she turned to me. "So good to see you, Dex."

I strode toward Aster, taking her in. She wore jeans paired with cowboy boots I knew saw some actual use on her grandfather's ranch. A white, billowy blouse revealed a turquoise necklace at her throat. Everything about her was designed to put her clients at ease. The boots said she was one of them. The rest said she was professional but not pretentious.

I pulled her into a quick hug. "How are you?"

"She's jealous she's not the one climbing out of my truck," Mav called.

Aster released me and flipped him off without even looking in his direction. "I'm good."

I had no idea what the hell had happened between them. Mav wouldn't say. But just before they went off to college, they'd had a falling out. Before then, they'd been thick as thieves, practically attached at the hip after we moved here. There were times I thought Aster was the only one who could truly get Mav to open up. But that wasn't the case anymore.

"How's Brae?" Aster cut into my thoughts. "Cora texted. I'm heading over there now. I just had to finish up with a client."

"How do you and Holly know her?" I asked the question I hadn't at the cabins.

"Compass," Aster said in a one-word answer. "It's a support group for those with missing loved ones. I volunteer time as a facilitator."

An ache settled in my gut. So many went without answers. Those my brothers and I could help. And those we couldn't, not without working locally and exposing exactly what we were doing in the shadows.

"It's really nice that you do that," I said softly.

She shrugged. "I know what it's like. Camilla might've only been gone for a month, but it felt like a lifetime. I want to help if I can."

Aster's twin sister had taken off in high school, scaring her family half to death. As it turned out, she'd taken off to LA and got caught up in the rougher side of things. Thanks to a private investigator, her parents found her and got her into rehab.

"Well, they're lucky to have you."

Aster's smile widened, making her pale-blue eyes shimmer. "Thanks. It's good to see you. Let's have a proper catch-up. Maybe we can get dinner with Brae or something. I'll text."

"What about me, Ice Queen?" Mav called.

"You're not invited, Satan," she shot back, taking off down the block.

I shook my head, turning back to Mav. "What the hell happened between you two?"

Hurt flashed across Maverick's expression so fast I almost missed it. But he covered it with a grin. "You know, fancy-ass family. Probably just got too cool for me."

But that wasn't Aster. *Something* had happened. I just wasn't sure what.

Mav didn't give me a chance to ask a follow-up. He peeled out, heading for the ranch. I scowled after him but got behind the wheel and followed.

I kept an eye on my speedometer, knowing I'd be on the radar after today. Miller would love nothing more than to give me a speeding ticket. It made the trip out to Twisted Oak Ranch seem even longer, but I finally hit the Bigfoot gate and then the tree house. Vehicles for everyone but Orion were already there.

Steeling myself, I shut off my engine and climbed out. As I walked up the front walkway, I went over my argument, every point I had for us to help Brae. Because she deserved it.

I was so caught up in planning my presentation that I nearly missed it. Only the sound of a bell jangling saved me.

Out of the corner of my eye, a flash of black-and-white fur barreled toward me. At the last second, I dodged, jumping up onto the porch. "Jesus, Pepper."

The goat made a quick one-eighty, running back toward me and headbutting my thigh.

"Ow, hell. That's gonna leave a mark, Pep."

"It's her love language," Uncle Waylon called from the screen door.

"Her love language is violence? Leaving bruises? Breaking bones?"

He let out a sound of derision, then opened the door and let Lucy the Irish wolfhound out. "When'd you get such a tender sensibility? DC changed you."

Lucy headed straight for me, rounding Pepper up and off the porch.

"Not wanting to get beat up just trying to get to the door makes me tender?" I clipped.

Waylon shrugged. "You said it, not me."

I shook my head, giving Lucy a good scratch. "You've got my back, my sweet girl."

She leaned into me for more affection.

As I straightened, it was to find Waylon watching me. Concern swirled in his brown eyes. He might not show it in typical ways, but he was always there for us. When we came to live here, traumatized and scared out of our minds, he'd moved at our speed. And he'd done everything he could to build a sense of safety. It had worked for most of us.

It wasn't that we didn't carry scars. We did. But the injuries had healed.

For everyone except Orion.

"Come on in. I got chicken tacos in the slow cooker," Waylon said, giving me a slap on the back.

"How many salsas and hot sauces?" I asked, knowing that, for him, the tacos were just a facilitator for the "good stuff."

He opened the screen door and held it for me. "Didn't have proper time to prepare. Only a dozen."

I chuckled, heading inside just as the clocks started going off. I passed one on the wall that shot a Bigfoot out like a cuckoo bird. The jerky motion nearly had me stumbling back a step. "Your clocks are violent, just like your damn goat," I muttered.

Waylon only laughed.

"Took you long enough," Mav called from the kitchen, where he was dishing up a plate of tacos.

"Some of us prefer not to give the law enforcement in this town another reason to hate us," I shot back.

Kol glowered at me from his spot at the kitchen table. "You're the only one flaring that up."

If it hadn't already been clear, I now knew I had a battle on my hands. "Sorry. I thought we were trying to help people. My mistake."

"Hold it," Waylon said. "Dex, get food. Kol, hold off on the full assault until Orion is here. Don't want to have to listen to this shit twice."

Wylder pinched the bridge of his nose in true eldest-brother fatigue. "Me either."

I snagged a plate, filling it with tortillas, chicken that had been slow-cooking for hours, and some lettuce, beans, and sour cream.

"Sour cream's for suckers who can't handle the heat," Mav jibed as he took a seat.

I just scowled at him as I pulled out a chair, catching sight of Skylar playing in the yard with Tink. The mini-Highland cow wore a feather boa and a tiara while Skylar wore a tutu with ski goggles and had a Nerf gun strapped to her back.

"Not everyone needs a meal to be a gut-rotting competition."

"Told you DC turned him soft," Waylon grumbled.

Wylder chuckled. "You know there's only one way to solve this."

I groaned, my stomach already regretting what I was about to do. "Hit me."

"Tier three, two, or one?" Wylder's hand hovered over the array of hot sauces in the center of the table like he was Vanna White.

Mav let out a hoot. "He's gonna be feeling this one, ladies and gents."

"I'd do anything to get you all to shut up," I shot back.

Wylder's fingers slowed over the hot sauces on one end of the grouping. "He's never gone above a level one in tier one. What will he attempt today?"

I met my brother's gaze. "Give me a level two."

A grin spread across Wylder's face. "Might I suggest Hellfire hot sauce, made with reaper peppers and black garlic?"

My stomach churned, but I held out my plate, not losing Wylder's gaze.

He just grinned wider, uncapped the bottle, and shook some out over one of my tacos. Mav's hand shot out, tipping Wylder's elbow and spilling more hot sauce over my food.

I glared at him.

He only shrugged. "Just gotta make sure you get the true flavor."

"I'm gonna put hot sauce in your mouthwash, you asswipe."

Maverick barked out a laugh. "You could try. Now, eat up, brother bear."

I glared down at the tacos but wrapped up the one with the Hellfire on it. *Jesus*. What kind of a name was that?

The second I bit down, I knew. The fires of hell erupted in my mouth, making my eyes flare wide and then instantly fill with tears.

"Fuck, he's already crying," Mav said, laughter in his voice.

Wylder winced, shaking his head. "Should've eased back in."

But I wasn't about to give in. I kept right on chewing, swallowing, then taking another bite. I ate the taco in three. But the fire did not subside. It got worse, in fact. "What the hell was that?" I croaked.

Waylon leaned back in his chair, his hand resting on his overalls-clad chest. "That's my personal favorite. Though they've got one with ghost peppers that gets you good."

"What do you think, Dex?" Wylder asked. "Want to go for ghost peppers next?"

I flipped him off, taking a bite of my hot sauce–free taco heaped with sour cream. The dairy helped take the edge off the worst of the burn. "You're all trying to kill me."

The screen door at the front of the house slammed, and I took a swig of the beer Wylder handed me from the fridge. Good God, I was out of hot sauce shape.

Orion's broad frame filled the entryway to the kitchen, and if I'd thought Kol's welcome had been cold, it had nothing on Orion's. He glared at me for a long beat.

"A little dramatic, even for you, Rion," Mav chided.

That glare moved to Maverick, who remained unaffected.

"Get some grub," Waylon ordered in a way that didn't put too much weight behind it.

Our great-uncle was the only person Orion listened to, and even then, it wasn't all the time. But now, Orion moved to plate a few tacos.

"Dex just downed some Hellfire," Wylder said, lifting his root beer. "You want to challenge for the night's supremacy?"

Orion jerked back his chair and simply shook his head in a rough decline.

"All right, Kol," Waylon began. "You called this family meeting."

Kol straightened in his chair. "I called it because Dex is putting us all at risk."

I stiffened, the heat of the hot sauce and my anger swirling together. "*You're* not involved. You made that clear. And that's fine, but you don't get to control what I do."

That was always Kol's way. He thought that if he was in charge of everything we all did or didn't do, he could make us safe. But his way wasn't always our way. And he didn't get that.

Kol's jaw clenched, the muscle along it rippling. "I'm trying to keep you from being an idiot. This already got dropped on our doorstep. The sheriff's department flooded Wylder's bar today."

"Yeah, because some sick fuck is tormenting Brae. Called her from her missing friend's phone or a cloned number and did some heavy-breathing shit. That's why the cops were there," I bit out.

Waylon muttered a curse. "They track it?"

I let out a breath, trying to calm my anger. "It was off before they could."

Wylder took a swig of his root beer. "Means they know what they're doing to a certain degree."

"Maybe," I hedged. "Anyone who's seen a thriller movie probably knows that."

"But I assume you tried to turn the phone back on remotely," Maverick added.

He knew me and my moves too well.

"I couldn't, which means the SIM card or battery's out of the device."

Wylder scrubbed a hand over his face. "A lot of trouble just to mess with someone."

It was. And that had my gut churning. Because someone who got pleasure from causing that sort of pain was not the kind of person I wanted aware of Brae's existence.

"I'm sorry for her," Kol said, his voice dropping. "I'll help you put in a security system at her house. Talk to Roger about making sure she's on the drive-by list. But we can't get involved. It's too risky."

"Like I said, *you* don't have to. But I make my own choices," I clipped. "And Mav and Wylder want to help, too."

Kol's gaze jumped around the table. "Seriously?"

Wylder winced. "She's a good person. Been through hell. And she doesn't have anyone."

"You don't know her," Kol shot back. "This could all be a manipulation."

My eyes narrowed on Kol. "You can't fake a missing person case like this. You know that."

Orion's hands lifted, finally giving in to the signing that was his last resort. *"We don't trust anyone outside the family."*

"*You* don't," I shot back, being harsher with him than I had been since we were kids. "I don't want to live like that anymore."

And for the first time, I realized that was true. I was so tired of looking at everyone with suspicion. It made life so damn depressing. And it kept us from helping people who needed it. People like Brae.

Waylon cleared his throat. "We can help without letting her know about the side project."

The side project being the Hourglass Network: our volunteer missing persons assistance. The website no one knew was attached to us. The network we'd put together in the shadows because time was slipping through fingers for so many.

"Doesn't matter," Kol gritted out. "It still gets us on Miller's radar. We need that like a hole in the head. He's made life hard enough for us just because of who our father was."

Orion bristled at the word *father*, his fingers fisting so tightly I worried he'd dislocate a knuckle. The muscles in his forearms rippled as tension radiated through him in waves.

Miller had made his opinion of the Archer brothers crystal-clear a number of times, but it was the touchiest for Kol. When he applied to be a Forest Service investigator, Miller had made sure his superiors knew every twisted detail about what we'd come from. Thankfully, Kol's bosses hadn't been supreme assholes and still gave him the job. But it exposed Kol in a way he hated.

"She doesn't have *anyone*," I said quietly. "Imagine if we didn't have each other to get through what we have."

Sympathy swept across Wylder's face, and he gripped his root beer tighter.

"Her parents kicked her out when she wouldn't put her baby up for adoption. The kid's dad isn't in the picture. Nova was the only person who was there for her, and then she disappeared almost in front of Brae's eyes. That should turn someone dark. Make them look at every single person with suspicion."

"But it didn't," Mav surmised. "I could see that much. She's like sunshine."

No, it was more than that. She wasn't just the sun. She was the sun*rise*. Even though darkness had claimed her for a time, she still rose. Every damn day.

My fingers flexed and clenched. "She does everything humanly possible to give her son an amazing life. She trained a dog to help search for lost people. She uprooted her whole life to look for her missing friend. She's fighting with everything she's got but doing it alone. I'm not going to let her."

"Me either," Wylder said quietly. "I get why you don't want to be involved, Kol. But I don't have the same risks as you."

A muscle fluttered in Kol's cheek. "I'm all Skylar has."

I knew he felt that weight like a hundred-ton stone on his

shoulders. He had no room for missteps or fuckups. He felt like he was already failing as a father and didn't have room for any other mistakes. It was a toxic mix of him blaming himself for not being there when everything went down with our dad and the bullshit Sky's mom had filled his head with.

His fingers gripped the edge of the table. "But Brae shouldn't have to do this alone. No one should."

Everyone was quiet for a long moment, but I could feel Orion stewing from across the table, his anger and annoyance mounting. I did my best to ignore it. Instead, I focused on the concession from Kol. It was as much of a win as I figured we'd get from him.

"We keep it aboveboard," Wylder said.

"You mean we keep him on the boring shit," Mav cut in.

I jabbed him with an elbow. "If there are risks on this one, I'll take them. I'm the one who brought her in. I carry the liabilities."

Because there were always risks. My less-than-legal walks through firewalls and security software to start. But there was more on the rare occasion we were on the scene. Potential trespassing, breaking and entering, theft. All of them were sometimes necessary to figure out what had happened to someone who'd vanished.

Orion shoved back his chair and stood, glowering at me. His hands lifted in quick, staccato beats. *"I hope you aren't putting your entire family at risk because you want to fuck her."*

And with that, he stormed out, the screen door slamming in his wake.

My fingers fisted, and I was glad my brother had left. Because if he hadn't, I likely would've decked him.

Waylon cleared his throat. "I want to meet her. Bring her for dinner. Think she likes three-pepper chili?"

Jesus.

I hoped Brae was as strong as I thought because she'd need it to get through a dinner with my family.

CHAPTER TWENTY-TWO
Braedyn

"Please, nectar of the gods, be kind to me today," I whispered as I bent, leaning my head against my coffee maker and breathing deeply.

Early-morning sun cascaded through the glass back doors. Hopefully, that would help, too. Because tossing and turning the entire night certainly hadn't.

As the coffee machine began to hum, I straightened. My back ached from the various uncomfortable positions I'd tried last night, and my palms and knees were still sore from the glass shards. If Nova were here, she'd try to talk me into one of her pretzel stretches and maybe a little meditation.

But she wasn't here.

I swiped my phone off the counter and opened my one and only social media app. I'd been slacking on posting since the move, but when I hadn't been able to sleep last night, I'd finally uploaded a new shot.

This one was Yeti running through a field with wildflowers springing up around her and Mount Lupine in the distance. My caption read, *Sometimes playtime is just as important as training time.*

There were a bunch of comments. Some familiar handles and others not.

> **PDustan88:** *Let me know how the HRD training is going. We want to work on that next.*
>
> **PugsNMugs:** *Look at that happy baby!*
>
> **NorCal27:** *Is this outside Starlight Grove? You should check out Three Creeks Canyon. Less populated but it's a stunner.*

My throat constricted, making it hard to breathe. The one thing I hadn't gathered the strength to do was revisit the scene of the crime. I knew I needed to, but every time I thought about it, my blood turned cold.

The feeling only intensified when I saw the next two comments.

> **V.Fab33:** *I remember what playtime is your favorite.*
>
> **FabeVic23:** *Wonder what made for the change of locales. Missing someone?*

I gripped my phone tighter as my stomach roiled. Vincent was a prick of epic proportions. And why? Because I hadn't signed his stupid NDA? Because I'd had the baby? Why did he care? It wasn't like I'd come after his family's billions. Other than Nova, I hadn't told a soul who Owen's father was.

But even all these years later, Vincent knew how to get under my skin. He knew that having sex for the first time had been a big deal to me. Just like he knew how much Nova meant to me. And his keeping tabs meant he knew she was missing. Now, he got to rub that in.

I slammed my phone on the counter, not even bothering to block the latest handles. He'd just create new ones. Instead, I grabbed my cup of coffee and whistled softly for Yeti. She was off her dog bed and at my side in an instant.

"Want to play?" I asked.

Her big booty plonked to the floor, and she panted happily.

A soft laugh left my throat. One I needed. "All right, little lady. Let's do this."

It had been a minute since we'd trained, but I knew Yeti would be back in the saddle quickly. Heading to the laundry room, I grabbed a set of Owen's pajamas. I put the shirt in one bag and the shorts in another, then headed outside with Yeti on my heels.

"*Assis. Couché.*" The French command asked for Yeti to sit and then lie down. I pointed her toward the house. "Cover your eyes." Yeti put her paws over her snout.

I grinned and headed into the backyard. The scents of the creek would help make the game fun. Dragging the pajama shirt as I went, I walked down about thirty yards and found the perfect hiding spot in the tall grass by the water. Then I walked back, spreading my scent trail in a nonsensical pattern.

This would be a good exercise with my scent trail, Owen's old ones from playing, and the new one I'd just laid. I couldn't help the smile that teased my lips.

"Is that dog covering its eyes?" A voice cut into my reverie.

Yeti's head snapped up, instantly on alert, but she didn't move from her spot as Dex crossed between our yards.

God, he looked good. Too good. Especially when I knew I was raggedy, in tattered shorts and a tank with my feet in knockoff Uggs from Target. Dex was anything but a mess as he walked toward me, dark jeans straining against thick thighs and a T-shirt that read *Hacking. Because punching people is frowned on* that was the kind of worn you knew would be incredibly soft.

My fingers twitched at my sides. God, I needed to get a grip. Or laid. Probably the latter since it had been exactly eight years and nine months. But that's what happened when you were a single parent with serious trust issues when it came to men.

Dex quirked a brow behind those damn tortoiseshell glasses.

"*À l>aise*," I said to Yeti, telling her to be at ease.

Dex shook his head. "French at seven in the morning feels unfair."

"If it helps, I only know about a dozen commands in French. The rest are plain ole English."

"So boring," Dex said with a grin. His gaze shifted to Yeti. "What was she doing?"

"We were going to do a training exercise. Want to help?"

He sent a suspicious look my way. "Are my balls at risk?"

A laugh bubbled out of me, and it felt so damn good. "Your balls are safe. You'll just be a good distraction. A new person."

"Okay," Dex agreed, but he still eyed Yeti a little warily.

"*Viens*, Yeti." The moment I spoke the words, Yeti bounded off the back deck and came toward me.

She wiggled with excitement, her whole body wagging. It made sense. She was still young. Calm would come with time and practice. I gave the hand signal for sit, and that big booty plonked down again despite her eagerness.

Bending, I opened the second bag for her to sniff. Yeti's nose twitched as she took in the scent, and her muscles quivered. She was ready for the game.

I glanced up to find dark-hazel eyes fixed on me. "Do me a favor and walk around. No rhyme or reason. It'll confuse the scent trail."

Dex frowned a touch but nodded, walking toward the water.

I closed the Ziploc bag with the pajama shorts. "Find."

Yeti didn't wait. She bounded forward, her nose pointed toward the ground. Her gaze snapped up for a moment as Dex crossed her path, and I thought she might seek him out, attention winning out over the game. But she didn't.

Her nose dropped back down, sniffing as she followed the track.

"She's certainly focused," Dex remarked, watching her as I followed behind.

"You can train dogs to search by trails, scents that are on the ground or in the air particles left behind all around us. We've somewhat mastered the first but haven't started on the second," I explained.

"Looks pretty damn impressive to me."

Yeti took a wrong turn, likely distracted by an older Owen scent. But it wasn't long before she corrected and found the trail I'd left minutes ago. A few seconds later, she let out three sharp barks.

I grinned. "That's her alert that she's found our missing victim."

Crossing to Yeti, I gave her an enthusiastic rubdown and a treat for her efforts. "*Va jouer*."

"What's that command?" Dex asked.

Yeti bounded through the yard in answer.

"Go play," I said, chuckling as she rolled in the grass.

I picked up the pajama shirt and headed toward Dex.

"Pretty damn impressive."

The grit coating his voice sent pleasant shivers across my skin, and I couldn't stop myself from looking up into those shadowy eyes. "We try."

Dex searched my face, his hand lifting and fingers ghosting beneath my eyes. "You've got shadows."

I swallowed, my throat catching on the action as his fingers stilled on my face. I wanted to soak in the feel of that connection, the warmth and rough realness embedded in the tips of his fingers. "Not my best night," I whispered.

His expression transformed then—to the familiar scowl that made me want to laugh now. Because I knew what was behind it. Caring. I'd never met someone who got so cranky for the best of reasons.

"Mr. Dex, why do you look like you're sucking on a lemon?" a new voice cut in.

I startled away from Dex at the sound of my son's presence, turning to find him standing on the back deck in robot pajamas, his glasses askew.

Yeti raced toward her best friend, elated at his presence as Dex searched for the right words.

"Your mom didn't get enough sleep," he finally answered honestly.

Owen's green gaze turned to me. "Uh-oh, big trouble." He glanced back at Dex. "You gonna ground her? One night, I stayed up playing my video game, and she grounded me."

Dex's lips twitched. "I'm definitely thinking about it."

I made a sound of protest.

Dex just arched a brow. "I think it's fair. Can't have you crashing on us."

It was my turn to scowl. "Maybe I'm gonna ground you."

"What's the cause?"

Being too damn gorgeous too early in the morning was what I wanted to say. "Interference in morning training" was what I reached for instead. Pathetically.

A grin tugged at Dex's lips. "You asked me to interfere."

"Only after you butted in."

"You welcomed that butting."

"You're the worst," I grumbled.

"Only because you're the worstest."

"What are you two talking about?" Owen cut in.

Wasn't that the million-dollar question?

Dex changed the subject. "How about I make you guys breakfast?"

Surprise sparked through me. "You cook?"

He looked a little insulted at my doubt. "I'll have you know that my great-uncle Waylon is an amazing cook, so I learned from the best. I might not do it often, but I have the skills."

One corner of my mouth tugged up. "What do you think, O? Should we risk our stomachs and let Dex make us breakfast?"

A huge grin broke out over Owen's face. "Definitely. If it's bad, we can just feed it to Yeti."

Dex's jaw dropped. "You doubt me?"

Owen giggled. "I gotta taste-test first."

"Fair enough. Give me two minutes, and I'll be back. Hellion, you got flour, eggs, and milk?"

"I do." My smile tugged wider. "I also have the number for poison control."

Dex made a motion like he'd just been stabbed in the heart. "You two are brutal."

"The brutalest," Owen called as Dex headed back for his place.

"Come on, team. In we go," I ordered Owen and Yeti.

We filed back into the house, and I coaxed Owen into getting dressed and brushing his teeth as he peppered me with questions about Dex. None of which I had the answer to.

It was bizarre how I only knew a handful of things about the man, yet I felt more seen by him than anyone else in years. It was as if we saw through to the core of each other, to what made us who we were. The rest of us didn't matter.

An alarm bell rang in my head as a warning of *DANGER* flashed. I shoved it down. Dex hadn't made a single move in my direction, so worrying that I might feel a pull too strongly in *his* was silly. Breakfast, especially after what had happened yesterday, was just a simple kindness.

A knock sounded on the front door.

"I've got it!" Owen yelled, tearing out of the bathroom and leaving the water running.

"Do not open that door," I warned as I shut off the water and righted his toothpaste.

"We know it's him," Owen said, exasperation filling his voice.

I started toward the door. "We do not know, and until we are one hundred percent certain, doors do not open in this house."

My son's face scrunched like he tasted something bad. It was likely a response to the seriousness in my tone. But the fact that an unknown someone had called me from Nova's phone meant we needed to take extra care. I tried to remind myself that I was number one in Nova's favorites list on her phone. Maybe someone had simply found her phone and called the number. I could've freaked them out by the way I answered.

But something told me that wasn't the case.

Steeling myself, I peeked through the window at the top of the door.

Dex.

Looking far too good. I ran a hand over my wild waves and knew it was no use. They wouldn't be tamed anytime soon.

"It's him. You can open the door." I stepped back as Owen rolled his eyes.

"Of course it's him, bruh."

"You keep rolling your eyes like that, and they're gonna get stuck," I muttered.

Owen grinned and opened the door. "Sorry, Mom had to do seventy million safety checks before she let me open the door."

Dex's gaze flicked to me. "Seventy million, huh?"

"Maybe more," Owen amended.

Dex stepped in, carrying a grocery bag and a duffel. "Sounds like she loves you a whole lot."

Owen's nose wrinkled. "I guess."

I pinched that nose. "Then stop acting like you smelled something bad."

He laughed and wiggled away from me. "I just don't need the mushy stuff, bro."

I made the same stabbing motion Dex had earlier and clutched my heart. "No mushy. And I'm a mom, not a bro."

Dex chuckled. "They grow up fast."

Too damn fast. As I straightened, I took in the bags again. "You moving in and didn't tell me?"

"You could totally sleep over," Owen offered. "No one sleeps in that third bedroom."

No one did because it was Nova's room. Her headquarters. And when I got her back, it was where she'd live. I had to believe that.

Dex must've seen my bristling because he swooped in. "I'm more of a camping-in-the-backyard guy."

"I loooooove camping," Owen cheered. "I used to go with my Cub Scout troop, and it was the best. Mom, do you think there's one here?"

"I know there is. Already got you set up for the fall."

Owen did a little half jump and started for the kitchen. "That's gonna be dope."

"Is dope a thing again?" Dex whispered, leaning toward me conspiratorially.

My mouth curved. "Apparently."

But as I spoke, I inhaled. Damn it, that was a mistake. Dex's scent wrapped around me—clean, like a soft wind after a hard rain, cedar and sandalwood mixing together but so light it made you strain for another hit.

Hell. Dex had turned me into some sort of animal, wanting to roll around in that scent and rub against him for a little more.

Our eyes locked. Close. Too close. The kind of nearness that meant I could feel the heat rolling off him in waves. His gaze dropped to my mouth as if he were memorizing the shape.

Yeti scrambled between us, breaking the spell. *All the dog cookies for her.*

I cleared my throat, putting some distance between us. "You never said what the bags were for."

Dex eyed the newly formed space but didn't comment. Instead, he lifted the grocery bag. "Pancake necessities." He raised the duffel. "Gear for your new alarm system."

My jaw went slack.

"That's bussin'," Owen called as we entered the kitchen. "Are you putting it in? Can I help?"

Dex deposited the duffel in a corner of the kitchen and the grocery bag on the counter. "You can totally help. We'll have a lot of sensors to put in."

"Excuse me, but shouldn't you be *asking* if I want a system?" I cut in.

"Bruh, it's gonna be awesome. We can play James Bond. You got any lasers in there?" Owen asked, peering into the bag.

"No lasers. And this was all approved by Blaze. He wants some outside cameras to catch the kids having keggers without him."

I wanted to laugh, but my head was swimming. "You should've asked *me*."

Dex moved into my space, that scent teasing again. "You're right. Hellion, can I put in an alarm system at your house? You'll be able to check who's at the door with a camera, and you and Owen will be extra safe."

His eyes met mine on that last sentiment, giving voice to unspoken words. Because someone out there wanted to scare me.

"Fine."

Owen cheered the moment the word was out of my mouth. "Can you teach me how to break an alarm?"

Dex grinned. "I could, but I think your mom might ground me."

"Dexter Archer. If you teach my kid to become a hacker, there will be H-E-double hockey sticks to pay."

"Bruh," Owen muttered. "You know I can spell, right?"

I turned to him. "No hacking."

He grinned widely, exposing the tiny gap between his front teeth. "Who, me? I'd never."

I turned to Dex, pointing a finger at him. "The worst. You are the absolute worst."

Laughter radiated from Dex, lighting the air around us. I wasn't sure I'd ever heard him laugh like that. Like he *meant* it.

"I'll make it up to you with pancakes. Deal?"

"Fine," I grumbled. "What can I do?"

Dex took me by the shoulders. The moment those rough palms curved around my bare skin, every part of me came alive. I wanted to push into his touch, feel more of it. It was as if I'd been in some half-numb state, and one touch had snapped me free.

"You can sit and drink your coffee," Dex commanded, guiding me toward a chair at the kitchen table. "You've had enough on your plate for a bit."

He bent as he spoke the words, his face close to mine. His gaze dropped to my lips again, sliding over them like he'd dragged his thumb across one. I sucked in a breath.

Yeti let out a loud, demanding bark, and Dex jerked upright, taking a huge step back.

"Yeti's big mad. Did you feed her yet?" Owen asked, oblivious to the moment between Dex and me.

I cleared my throat. "No. I haven't. You want to do that, bud?"

"On it," Owen said, full of energy at the fun of a new guest.

"Then you can be my kitchen assistant," Dex instructed as he set my coffee in front of me.

Owen poured two cups of food into Yeti's bowl. "I need a more bad booty name than *assistant*."

Dex chuckled as he washed his hands and started prepping ingredients. "Okay. How about *second-in-command*?"

"Better."

The two of them chattered away as they prepped breakfast, and I tried to think of the last time someone had cooked for me. A stabbing sensation lanced my chest.

Nova.

She wasn't one to prepare breakfasts, but she was one hell of a dinner chef. And she loved trying new cuisines. Everything from Thai to Indian to Greek. And she was the only one who could get Owen to try those adventurous foods. Because she made it fun.

Since she'd disappeared, I'd cooked every single meal other than the odd treat of Owen and me eating out. I'd cleaned every dish. I'd carried the weight of it all on my shoulders. And I was so damn tired, I felt like I could sleep for a month.

I jolted as a plate slid in front of me—a stack of two pancakes that obviously had things mixed into the batter. The stack was rimmed with an artful array of strawberries and a healthy dose of whipped cream on top.

"Your breakfast. Need anything else to drink?" Dex asked, his voice dipping low.

I saw that he'd already gotten milk for Owen, who was carrying his plate to the table.

"I'm good," I croaked. "What are these?"

Dex slid into the chair between me and Owen as if he belonged there, as if he *fit*. "Strawberry Oreo pancakes. My specialty."

My eyes flared. The combination sounded heavenly and sinful all at once, the perfect balance.

"Go on," he encouraged. "I need to know if I passed the test."

I cut a small bite, dipping it into the whipped cream and sliding it into my mouth. I couldn't help my eyes closing as I chewed. Flavors exploded on my tongue, different levels of sweetness all balancing each other out. I let out a humming noise without thinking, and when my eyes popped open, I found Dex watching me intently.

"Good?" he asked.

There was a hint of boyish uncertainty in the question. Something that made Dex all the more real.

"Best thing I've ever tasted," I whispered.

Pure pride bloomed in Dex's expression as if I'd told him he'd successfully launched an expedition to Mars or cured cancer.

"Ermygod." Owen struggled to speak around a mouthful of food. "Best ever!"

Dex chuckled as a beep sounded and then another. He slid his phone out, grimacing.

"What?" I asked, concern taking hold.

"My brother," he grumbled.

"Which one?"

"Orion."

Something about his expression said there was a story there. Then, a smile split his face as his fingers moved across the screen.

"Is everything okay?" I asked hesitantly because Dex's expression said it both was and wasn't.

His grin just widened as he lowered the phone, so I got a glimpse of the screen. "I changed his ringtone to the *Hannah Montana* song."

"You stole his phone?"

"Please," Dex said, offended. "I hacked it."

"Can we change Mom's?" Owen asked hopefully. "She hated that 'Baby Shark' song. That would be awesome."

I shouldn't have, but I stole a glance at the screen.

> **Orion:** *Change it back. Every time I try, it instantly reverts.*
>
> **Dex:** *Stop being a dick about Brae, and I'll fix it.*
>
> **Orion:** *We don't know if we can trust her.*

Anxiety ignited, spreading through me like wildfire. Had they fought? Over me? Why?

> **Maverick:** *Says the guy who guards his property with bear traps.*
>
> **Wylder:** *And exploding food dye balloons.*
>
> **Orion:** *Want to be able to track anyone who comes onto my property uninvited.*
>
> **Wylder:** *Jesus.*

The phone dinged again, and Dex jerked it upright, out of my line of sight. Guilt swamped me. Spying was wrong. Eavesdropping?

Whatever the hell I'd just done. But another wave of guilt hit at the fact that Dex had been fighting with one of his brothers over me.

"Did I do something to make him mad?" I asked.

Dex's gaze lifted as he winced. "It's not you. He doesn't trust anyone. And he doesn't love that I'm"—he glanced at Owen for a moment—"breaking rules to help you."

I tugged my lip between my teeth. "I'm sorry."

"It's not on you," Dex pressed. "I want to help. I've got an auto-search running on the phone. If it turns on again, we'll get a location. And I'm chasing down other leads as well."

He was doing everything he could to help, even though it was risky and caused strife with his family. "Thank you," I whispered. Because I wasn't going to argue with him helping. I *needed* him. But I also wouldn't ignore the fact that it cost him.

Dex's phone dinged again. As he read whatever was on the screen, his expression turned guarded, unreadable. Then his jaw dropped. "Oh fuck."

"That's a bad one, Mr. Dex. Gonna have extra chores for *sure*," Owen warned.

"What? What's wrong?" I pressed.

Dex's gaze flicked up to my face. "My brother…Orion. He wants to meet you. He wants you to come to family dinner."

Another wave of nerves hit. "And that's a bad thing?"

"Well, it's not good."

CHAPTER TWENTY-THREE
Braedyn

THE LATE-MORNING SUN SOAKED THE BACKYARD AS OWEN AND Yeti raced around the space. Owen had lost interest in the alarm project about an hour in. He might have had some serious hero worship when it came to Dex, but he still only had the attention span of an eight-year-old.

My thumb scrolled over the comments on the photo I'd posted last night, and I hit hide on Vincent's two douchebag contributions. I wouldn't have to look at them, and he would think I was simply ignoring him. A win-win in my book. Because if there was one thing an egomaniac hated, it was being ignored.

"What'd that phone ever do to you?"

My head jerked up at the sound of Dex's voice. "What is it with you and sneaking up on people?"

Dex frowned. "You need to be more aware of your surroundings."

"Maybe I just need to stop befriending black-hat stalkers."

His lips twitched. "Your friendly, neighborhood, *gray*-hat stalker is happy to report your system is up and running. Open the app."

"That was fast." I toggled to the app Dex had helped me download and set up an account for.

"It's not that large of a space," Dex said by way of explanation as he sat next to me on the steps. He leaned in closer to tap on the camera icon. As he did, that scent wafted toward me. It was sunbaked now, as if the cedar and sandalwood had lain beneath the rays for hours. "Here are your four different cameras."

"Isn't that a little overkill?"

Dex's gaze lifted to mine from behind those glasses. "Given everything going on, I don't think so."

My mouth flattened into a hard line. "Yeah, maybe not."

"Sorry." His voice dropped on the single word. "I don't want to bring back bad memories, but I want you to be safe."

I nodded, swallowing hard. "Safe is good. Show me what I need to know."

He walked me through how to make the cameras change directions, how the motion alerts worked, and how to arm and disarm the system with my phone.

"Pretty sure I could launch my house like a rocket now."

One corner of Dex's mouth kicked up. "Not quite, but it's a solid system. I get my gear from one of the best."

I had a feeling Blaze wasn't paying for that gear. "You didn't have to do this," I said softly.

"No, I didn't."

My gaze lifted, seeking Dex's. His answer was so unexpected. So...*him*. Honest and to the point but not exactly living in the land of politeness and half-truths.

He laid a hand over mine on the deck, his fingers not curling around mine but covering them. Steady pressure. Heat. The kind that trailed up my arm and invaded the rest of me. The kind that had me wondering what it would feel like to have all of Dex pinning me down, taking me, filling—*shit*.

I did everything I could to force the images from my head. What the hell was wrong with me?

"I did it because I wanted to. Because you have every right to feel safe in your home. Because no one should get messed with the way you were yesterday—especially after everything you've been through."

There was something in the way he said those words. Something that had my eyes lifting again, playing with fire. "You say that like you know what it feels like."

Dex's hand didn't leave mine. It stayed—that steady covering. I wasn't sure I'd ever had something like that. And he didn't look away from me as he spoke. "My mom. She disappeared when I was ten. And after everything came out about my dad, lots of people messed with us in all the ways."

I didn't speak, didn't breathe. All I could imagine was a boy not much older than Owen wondering where his mother had gone.

"Some people wanted us to think we were the spawn of Satan. Others wanted to jerk us around with reports of seeing Mom alive or dead. And I think some genuinely thought they were helping."

God, I couldn't imagine living through all that. The weight of it. The torment.

"You were twelve when they found out about your father?" I asked softly.

Dex's throat worked as he struggled to swallow. "Yeah. Sixth grade. Before that, my biggest problem was Leigh Friedman breaking up with me on the playground in front of all my friends."

"That bitch," I muttered.

He let out a soft chuckle that didn't quite ring true but said he appreciated my efforts to lighten his load. "Everything changed. It wasn't just that we all suddenly wondered if our dad had something to do with our mom's disappearance—"

"Did he?" My stomach cramped just thinking about the possibility.

Dex shrugged, the movement making me all the more aware of his hand over mine. The steady pressure. The heat. He looked out at the water, at Owen and Yeti racing in circles in front of it. "We still don't know. He either killed her, or she knew what she was doing when she disappeared. All we know is investigators never found her body with the others."

Everything in me twisted like a tight coil of rope that might explode outward with one wrong move. I wasn't sure which was worse:

knowing your mother had been killed and stolen from you or knowing she chose to walk away, leaving you with a monster.

"I'm sorry," I whispered, then shook my head. "No. I hate when people say that. I *am* sorry, but I'm also pissed off and sad and grieving for the twelve-year-old boy who never should've been leveled with all of this."

Dex's fingers moved then, curling around mine and squeezing. "I'm partial to your anger, Hellion. Makes your eyes burn with gold fire."

My breath hitched. "I find my mad pretty damn easily."

His mouth curved the barest amount. "Means something, you lighting that righteous fury for me. But I made it through. I'm okay."

"Are you?" The question spilled out before I could stop it.

Surprise and a hint of admiration lit Dex's expression. "I'm okay, and I'm not. It changed me. Changed all of us. And we've each dealt in our own way."

"And your way?"

Dex's jaw moved back and forth, locking and unlocking. Somehow, I knew answering this would cost him. "I needed to understand how he hid. How all the monsters hid. I needed to put together the pieces. So I started looking."

"On the internet," I surmised.

"In the dark places the internet hides."

My stomach roiled, knowing just from my bits of research what all the dark web housed. Graphic pornography and things that couldn't be classified with a word that constituted consent. Illegal offerings of every kind. Human trafficking. The worst humanity had to offer.

"When did you start?" Because I needed to know that piece, too.

"Started dabbling around age thirteen, knew what I was doing by sixteen, arrested by twenty-one for hacking into the FBI's files to help a friend look into their missing brother."

"Too young to know about that kind of darkness."

Dex's eyes found mine again. "Brae, I *lived* with that kind of darkness. It raised me. I may not have known it at the time, but it doesn't change the truth."

I didn't have anything to say to that. Not at first. "Makes it even more of a miracle that you turned out like you did."

"You don't know—"

It was my turn to squeeze Dex's hand. I flipped mine over so we were palm-to-palm and put all my strength behind the motion. "I know. I know that you decided to help me, even though it puts you at risk, even though it pisses off at least one of your brothers."

"Two," he admitted.

"Even though it pisses off *two* of your brothers. I know that you held me together when I was shattering like that glass on the floor. I know you made me pancakes because you saw how tired I was. And I know that you answered every single one of my kid's questions, even though he had fifty million. I know you're good, Dex."

His hand spasmed around mine as if my words were a physical blow. "People can hide their true natures."

"They can," I agreed. I'd seen it up close and personal with Vincent.

"Maybe I'm hiding who I really am from you."

He didn't know how much that terrified me. Not that he'd turn out to be a serial killer but that he would stop showing up. "You could be. And that's why I don't lean. But it won't change that I believe in your good."

"You not leaning is why I had to force my pancakes on you," Dex teased, the slightest lightness entering his tone.

"It's not easy for me to accept help when I've had it yanked out from under me so many times."

"But you're doing it."

"I'm doing it." I let out a long breath. "We all have a choice."

"I guess we do." Dex's gaze traced my face. "You're braver than me."

I scoffed. "I highly doubt that."

"Your bravery stops me in my damn tracks. You face everything. You don't look away. You don't give up. You keep fighting."

My eyes burned. Because I wanted to believe I was all of that. "Sometimes, I'm so damn tired of fighting."

Empathy washed over Dex's face. "You just need some reinforcements. I've got you covered."

God, that scared the hell out of me, but I wanted it so badly I could taste it. "Tell me about who I'm going to meet at this family dinner."

He was quiet for a moment before giving in to my subject change. "Well, you know Wylder, my sober brother who owns the bar. He's the eldest."

My brows lifted. "I didn't know he didn't drink."

"Not a drop. And I'm not speaking out of school. He's pretty open with that journey and his involvement in the program."

"Good for him. That's a tough road."

Dex nodded slightly. "Like I said, we all had our ways of coping, and some of them were more destructive than others."

A heaviness settled over me, like one of those coverings they gave you when you got an X-ray. A lead blanket. Because I couldn't imagine the stew of damage these brothers had had to deal with.

"We do what we can to get by. We keep going," I said quietly.

"We do." Dex swallowed. "Kol, the second oldest, turned inward. Guilt. Feels like he should've been there. Should've seen something. Protected us. Honestly, I think the surprise of finding out he had a daughter saved him."

The war found me again, the one where sadness and hope battled. "Skylar seems like she could light anyone's world."

"That little princess has us all wrapped around her fingers. She sort of centered things. Gave us all a focus outside ourselves."

"I get that." My gaze found Owen, who was now lying in the grass with Yeti, yammering away as if the dog could understand every word. "It cures the self-pity in a snap, gives you instant perspective."

"It does. And damn, they're amazing to watch grow."

"They are." My gaze flicked to Dex.

"What about her mom? In the picture?" I asked.

A different sort of shadow passed across Dex's face as his jaw turned to granite. "No. Not in the picture."

There was a story there, but it wasn't Dex's to tell.

I gave him an out. "What about Maverick?"

That tension eased—the way Maverick's presence seemed to do. One corner of Dex's mouth kicked up. "Youngest brother. Hell on wheels. Always looking for the next adrenaline high. Extreme sports, risky jobs. Anything he can get his hands on."

I grinned. "He seems like a character."

"That's one word for it."

A soft laugh escaped, and Dex turned, staring at my mouth as if trying to memorize the sound.

I forced my gaze away from the temptation—too much. "And Orion?"

I felt the change in Dex more than I saw it. His hand stiffened under mine before he pulled it away. I missed the contact and steady pressure almost immediately. But I welcomed it, too. It was a reminder that even Dex would go away. I couldn't lose sight of that.

"Middle brother. Everything that happened…it was the hardest on him."

I shifted, forcing myself to take Dex in again, to make myself accept the pieces of him he was willing to give. But when I saw his face, everything that was so focused inward melted away. Because what I saw there was pure and utter agony.

The emotion was so strong and sharp it forced me to suck in air. I wanted to reach for him again. To tell him I was there. But I stopped myself.

Instead, I simply waited. For whatever Dex wanted to lay at my feet.

"Orion saved us. When Mav and I found things we shouldn't have. When our father caught us. It was Orion who saved us. He got a gun from our father's stash and shot him. Killed him. And that cost him everything."

My heart hammered in my ears, creating a sort of whooshing sound that was difficult to hear through.

"Everything was so fucked," Dex croaked. "Cops came. They took Orion away. Think they went at him pretty hard. At least until they realized who my father really was and saw the trophies. Until they found the women's bodies buried in the orchard. Thirty-six. But they think there may be more."

My body jolted. Every revelation a blow. But it was nothing compared to what Dex had faced. The blows he'd been dealt.

"After those days in custody, Orion stopped speaking. It was like his words had been turned into weapons against him, and he refused to risk it anymore. He used to write to communicate, and he learned to sign—but only to our family. Now...it's just less and less."

God, everything in me hurt. My heart ached for Orion—for all of the Archer brothers.

"But he texted you today." I couldn't help trying to give Dex a sliver of hope.

The corners of his mouth lifted in a sad smile. "Maybe pissing him off is the key."

"It makes sense...that he doesn't trust easily."

"I don't think any of us do. That's what happens when someone so close to you turns. It makes you think anyone could. Or worse, that the ability is in you."

I stared at Dex for a long moment. "You're worried you'll turn out like your father."

It wasn't a question, but Dex answered it anyway. "His DNA runs through me. I can't help wondering if there's that urge in me. But I deal. I face it. I fucking despise guns, but I learned how to use every type I could get my hands on. More, I became a damn good shot. Got even better when I had access to some of the FBI's training facilities."

My tongue stuck to the roof of my mouth as I struggled to swallow. "You're not going to turn."

Dex stared back at me, the green in those hazel eyes darkening to nearly black behind his glasses. "You don't know that. I've learned a lot working beside profilers. Sometimes, living with that sort of darkness taints you."

"And sometimes it makes you seek the light. Makes you fuel it. Dex, you light the dark places."

He didn't move his gaze from my face for a long moment. "You really believe that."

"I *know* that." I might not have known Dex long, but I saw how he moved through the world. The way he helped when he had everything to lose and nothing to gain.

"We still haven't talked about Waylon."

Confusion bloomed at the abrupt turn in the conversation. But then I saw it for what it was—a deep need to steer away from the heaviness. "Tell me about him."

"Great-uncle on my dad's side. The only family who stepped forward to take us in. Has a ranch where he raises alpacas, rare sheep, goats, and even a few yaks."

My mouth curved. "Owen is going to flip when he gets to see that."

Dex chuckled, and the sound came out a little rusty, like he hadn't made it in a long time. In reality, he was simply shaking off the heaviness of what he'd shared. "He's a character. Amazing cook. Incredible and eccentric clockmaker. And a Bigfoot enthusiast."

Owen's head popped up in the grass, sending Yeti scrambling up. "Did you say Bigfoot?"

Dex grinned, his gaze connecting with Owen's. "I did. You like Bigfoot stories?"

Owen sent him a massive gap-toothed smile. "Tell him, Mom."

Dex's gaze moved to me, a hint of confusion in it.

I pressed my lips together to hide my grin. "In this house, we are Bigfoot believers. Why do you think our dog is named Yeti?"

Dex groaned, letting his head fall back. "Never mind. You can't come to dinner. You and Waylon will be way too much."

"Hey," I clipped. "The truth is out there. It's not my fault you don't want to believe."

CHAPTER TWENTY-FOUR
Dex

I LIFTED THE CAN OF LIGHTNING ENERGY TO MY MOUTH AND took a swig of the lukewarm liquid. My grimace was almost instantaneous. An ice-cold Lightning? Perfect deliciousness. A lukewarm Lightning? Disgusting.

I downed it anyway. I needed the energy, the pure caffeine. Because my vision was starting to go a little hazy.

My computer monitors taunted me as I leaned back in my chair and took off my glasses, setting them on the desk in front of me. I rubbed my eyes and hoped like hell the action would soothe the headache I had thrumming.

Cracking my neck, I slid my glasses back on. My gaze instantly flicked to the windows and Cabin Two.

Empty.

Just like it had been all day. Because Brae was at work and Owen was at camp. Nothing out of the ordinary had occurred over the last four days. And we'd settled into a routine of sorts.

I'd find some excuse to wander over. Sometimes, with food. Other times, with a new video game for Owen. Occasionally, to talk over the case with Brae.

The case that was currently making me want to pull my goddamned hair out. Because none of it made any sense. It was like Nova had been snatched off the trail by aliens. Waylon and Mav would have a field day with that idea.

Thankfully, someone in the sheriff's department had requested the camera footage from the state. I wasn't sure anyone had actually been through it, but the request had gotten a four-hour window of footage saved to a backup server with security that was a joke.

I'd tracked down all the vehicles I'd seen on the road-condition cameras, and every single driver had a reason to be there—and none of them were to kidnap someone off a trail.

I scowled at the screen as if it were personally responsible for dead end after dead end. An email notification dinged, and I switched over to that tab. A new message sat in my inbox from a familiar name.

Travis Moore.

The subject line simply said: *Background.*

I clicked on the email, quickly scanned the text, and noticed the attachment.

You did not get this from me. But I hope to hell it helps. Miller's still old-school and doesn't put everything in our digital files.

A buzz lit beneath my skin, the start of the high that came from digging up new information. Usually, it hit when I was breaking into a system like I'd done with the sheriff's department. But that hadn't even been a challenge. Their system was pathetic.

This was different. A gift. And it was a hell of a risk for Travis to take. If he got caught, he'd lose his job for sure.

The moment my security software scanned the attachment, I hit download. A second later, images that Trav had clearly taken on his phone filled my screen. It was the paper file on Nova's case.

I already had some of the information. Like the fact that the only fingerprints found on Nova's water bottle were hers and Brae's. But there was information I didn't have. Like the disturbances in the dirt where Brae had said the women were right before Nova disappeared.

The report was from the county crime lab and was done by a forensic tech named Olivia Bishop. Her analysis suggested a struggle of some sort. Possibly drag marks. At the bottom, there was a note from Sheriff Miller. *Likely animal attack.*

Except the report noted there was no blood on the scene. It was incredibly rare for a cougar or something of a similar size to take on a human simply standing on a trail. If they were running? Sure. The predator instinct could kick in. And I guessed if a female cougar had young in the area, it might've attacked.

But there would be blood. Larger drag marks that would continue through the underbrush. And eventually, a body. There was none of that. And it suggested that Nova had either walked out on her own two feet or had been carried.

I kept flipping through report after report. I slowed as I came to a written request for the K-9 team a county over to do a search. Roger had written it up and submitted it to Miller. But the bottom had a stamp that read *DENIED* and a note beneath.

Insufficient evidence to suggest the use of a K-9 unit would be beneficial. —Sheriff Ezra Miller

What in the actual fuck? A K-9 unit should've been one of the *first* calls. When scents were fresh and there were trails to follow. Hell, if we could've had Kol out there, he would've found something. I knew it.

A knock sounded on my cabin door, jolting me out of my spiral. I quickly locked my computer screens and opened the camera app on my phone. One of the last people I expected stood on my front steps.

I shoved back from my desk and stood, heading for the door. As I opened it, Kol looked up. He took me in for a moment. "Who pissed in your Cheerios?"

"Sheriff Miller," I muttered.

Kol's expression instantly went alert. "He pay you a visit?"

"No, but a little angel dropped Nova's entire case file in my lap, and Miller was, at best, negligent."

Understanding bloomed over Kol's face. "Show me."

Those two words brought instant relief. "That mean you're in?"

He grimaced. "I told you I was, didn't I?"

"That agreement was reluctant at best."

Kol's mouth thinned, making his dark scruff twitch. "I've been looking into things on my side."

Everything in me went wired. "You find something?"

As part of the investigative arm of the Forest Service, Kol typically covered cases involving poaching or growing pot illegally on national forest land, with the occasional missing person or accidental death.

"After you show me the case file," Kol ordered.

"God, being older than me makes you fucking bossy."

"Not bossy," Kol muttered. "The boss. There's a difference."

I rolled my eyes but led him toward my workspace.

Kol's face twisted in disgust. "You're living like a teenager who never leaves his room."

I followed his line of sight, taking in the crushed energy drink cans, snack wrappers, and other detritus. It was a little cluttered. A cheese puff or two might've even gotten lost on my desk.

"I've been working," I grumbled.

Kol arched a brow. "Have you felt sunshine on your face in the past seventy-two hours?"

"Yes," I clipped. I'd felt it as I walked over with dinner to put on Brae's grill. And I'd felt it when she smiled at me. And Brae's sunshine? That was a hell of a lot brighter. It was like baking on a beach for hours but feeling it from the inside.

"Fucking hell. You've been spending time with her."

I glared at my brother. "She's my neighbor. We're talking about the case."

"Sure," he snapped.

"We're friends." Why did that feel like a lie? Maybe because all I could think about was what it would feel like to run my fingers over those tanned thighs. Or what her moans would sound like as I took her. How it would feel to—

"It better *just* be friends," Kol muttered. "Now, show me the damn case file."

Grumpy bastard. I unlocked my computer using the two-factor security: my fingerprint and a password. No one who didn't have both would ever be able to break in.

Shoving my chair to the side, I let Kol scan the documents. The longer he read, the more thunderous his expression grew.

"What a goddamned waste of space," Kol growled.

He took his responsibilities, his oaths, and his *word* seriously. And he had no respect for people who didn't.

"It's fucking lazy for sure."

Kol scrubbed a hand over his face. "I wonder if it's the tourist factor. It's no secret that he's not a fan of the people who flood our town in the summer. Takes cases affecting locals way more seriously."

"Maybe." I stared at the screen. "But at this point, I would think it would be easier to throw everything he has at this. It would be less of a headache than having me and Brae breathing down his neck."

"But he's stubborn as hell and doesn't want to be proven wrong. He'd have to eat crow. And there *have* been instances of tourists getting swept away in the river or falling prey to animal attacks."

Miller's refusal to eat crow rang true. "Heaven forbid he be wrong about *anything*," I grumbled.

Kol scoffed. "God, I hate assholes like him."

So did I. Even more so because of the bullshit he put my brothers and me through. "Tell me what you dug up."

Kol straightened, going into report mode. "Talked to my boss."

Of course, he had. Kol didn't like taking unofficial paths.

"When I brought her what we had, she was concerned enough to let me add the case to my load. Nova and Brae might've been on state land when Nova disappeared, but that trail crosses over into national forest land about half a mile later. There's cause."

I grinned at my brother. This was his version of a hug and an *I love you*. "You know, you're kind of a master at getting the system on our side."

He scowled. "It's reasonable."

"It's also going to piss Miller off."

"That's just a bonus. For me and for Sherri."

Sherri was the head honcho at Kol's outpost. And I knew she wasn't a fan of Miller's douchebag ways.

I studied my brother for a long moment. "This means you'll be on their radar."

Kol held my stare. "Sometimes, it's worth it."

And *that* was the ultimate gift: Kol putting himself on the line because I asked.

"Thank you."

"Shut up," Kol muttered.

"Appreciate you."

"Fuck off."

"You're the bestest brother around."

Kol's lips twitched. "I'm telling that to the chat."

I chuckled. "Fair. They should have to work harder to take that crown."

Kol just shook his head.

"Now that the case is on your desk officially, you find anything?" I asked.

Any hints of humor slid from Kol's face.

I stiffened, knowing that look. It was the bad-news look. "What?"

"There have been about two dozen missing persons cases in Juniper County and the two surrounding counties in the past four years. But they're spread out enough that it wouldn't flag anything for one singular law enforcement outfit. About half of those occurred in and around parks and on public land. A woman who went missing from her campsite with friends. A man who was fishing with buddies went for a piss break and never came back. A couple more who weren't simply hikers who got lost."

"Too similar for comfort," I surmised.

"Too similar for comfort," he agreed.

Dread pooled low in my gut like liquid metal sloshing around and settling in. "You think someone's taking them."

A muscle fluttered along Kol's jaw. "I do."

CHAPTER TWENTY-FIVE
Braedyn

COUNTRY ROCK WOVE THROUGH THE AIR AT THE PERFECT VOLUME. Wylder must've learned what that decibel was over the years, pinpointing exactly what number to turn it to so you had sound to fill the silences but could still talk over it.

I slid two plates onto a booth table in the corner, one that gave patrons the perfect vantage point of the entire place. "Reuben with sweet potato fries and a double cheeseburger with curly fries."

Roger slid the Reuben closer to him. "You mean Trav's daily heart attack on a plate?"

"Like a Reuben's the picture of health," Travis shot back.

"Hey, look at these sweet potato fries. So much healthier than those curly fries."

I shook my head. "I could swap out both your fries for house salads," I offered.

Travis pulled his plate even closer, wrapping an arm around it. "Pry my fries from my cold, dead hands."

I held up both hands. "I surrender. No fries will be harmed."

Roger chuckled. "Smart move. Trav's real territorial over his food. Ask him what he did to the deputy who stole his leftovers."

I turned back to the man with brown hair and hints of auburn undertones. "Travis...what do you have to say for yourself?"

He lifted a fry. "I have to say that you don't steal the leftovers that were getting me through my day. Otherwise, you just might end up with hot sauce in your coffee."

"And all over your lunch," Roger added.

"Travis," I said, fighting a laugh.

He shrugged. "Justice."

"You two are warriors for it," I agreed. "Which is maybe why you've been in here for lunch every day this week. You checking up on me?"

Before this week, they'd come in for food exactly once. This week, I could've set my watch by their arrival.

Roger sent me a cocky grin. "Maybe we just come to chat up the pretty waitress."

I let out an amused scoff. "Sure you do."

Travis leaned back against the booth. "Anything out of the ordinary?"

I shook my head. Now that I'd had a few days to recover from the shock of the call, I wished for another one. I would handle it so differently. I'd be calm. I'd ask to speak to Nova. I'd keep whoever it was on the line until Dex's high-tech software could trace it.

He'd installed some sort of trap-and-trace app on my phone. I only had to open the app and hit a button to record the call and track the location. *If* I could keep the person on the line for long enough.

"That's good," Travis encouraged.

"Maybe. I just...I want answers. Who was it? Why call now after all this time?"

Travis and Roger shared a look.

"What?" I demanded.

Roger cleared his throat. "I wonder if they know you're here. If they know you're looking into things."

A chill skittered over my skin, but I stiffened my spine. "If someone took Nova, I hope they know I'm looking for them. I hope they know I'm coming for them. And that I won't stop until she's home."

A bell dinged, followed by Fiona's shouted words. "Order up."

"I gotta get that," I muttered, turning away before they could respond. But as I headed for the pass-through window, I felt eyes on me. As I glanced around, I came to terms with the fact that it was only my imagination. Everyone was fixed on their own business: conversations, phones, a book.

I let out a long breath as I grabbed two plates and headed for the couple in town for a hiking trip. It took everything in me not to warn them to stick together and not wander off alone. Instead, I told them to have a great time and deposited their burgers and fries.

A new but familiar face greeted me from another table as I moved to take the newcomer's order. "Jack, right?"

I was piss-poor at connecting faces and names, but I always remembered stories. Especially ones people shared at our Compass meetings. Jack's wife had gone missing six months ago. Went out for groceries and never came back.

He gave me a swift nod. "Nice to see you again, Brae."

"You, too. Can I get you something to drink?"

"Coke would be great," he said, drumming oil-stained fingers on the table.

"Coming right up."

Before I could turn, Jack's voice cut in again. "You have any more trouble?"

I stiffened slightly.

"Holly told me," he explained. "Word usually makes it around the group when someone has something happen—good or bad."

I shoved down the hint of annoyance that flickered. It wasn't gossip. Not really. It was community. I was just so damned used to going it alone.

"Nothing else. I wish there had been."

Jack's throat worked as he swallowed. "I get that. There was a reported sighting of my Cynthia over the border into Oregon. Keyed me up for months. Every time someone knocked on the door or my phone rang."

Empathy washed through me, along with a trickle of guilt at my earlier annoyance. This was the gift of being around people who'd been through it. They understood like no one else.

"I'm sorry. Sometimes, hope is pure torture. But we have to hold on anyway."

Grief washed through Jack's dark eyes. "Truer words were never spoken."

I gave him a quick squeeze on the shoulder. "I'll get you that Coke." And I would get him dessert on me.

Weaving my way through the tables, I sidled up to the bar.

"Whatcha need?" Wylder asked as he typed away on his phone, a pastime I found him frequently locked into. I wasn't sure if he was a dedicated Wordle player or had some secret pen pal. But it never affected his work. He had a sixth sense for when someone needed something.

"Coke."

Wylder shoved his phone into his pocket and scooped some ice into a glass. "Everything good?"

He asked the same question every day.

"Well, between you and your spidey-sense, Travis and Roger's stakeouts, Cora and Fiona's buddy system, and Aidan's glares at anyone who gets too close, I think I'm pretty well covered."

Wylder chuckled. "You are officially one of us. Welcome."

That hit me square in the chest. I didn't think I'd ever had a sense of true belonging like that. The accounting office I'd worked in before had been very official with boundaries. People didn't share much about their personal lives, and no one knew my story beyond me having a son.

Everything in Starlight Grove was so…different. People knew your business. Occasionally, they used it for wrong, like those who threw the Archer brothers' father in their faces. But mostly, they used it for good. To look out. To help.

"It's taking some getting used to," I admitted.

Wylder slid the Coke across the bar. "You will. But you might want to brace for family dinner. The Archers? We can be…a lot."

A hint of anxiety flitted through me. "Well, help a girl out. What are you guys into? Besides clockmaking and Bigfoot."

Wylder barked out a laugh. "Dex really has given you the inside scoop."

"Just bits and pieces, and mostly about Waylon. What about the rest of you? Hobbies? Family traditions? Help me show up armed to win everyone over."

"Hot sauce."

My brows pulled together. "Hot sauce is your family tradition?"

Wylder grinned. "A family rite of passage. A blood oath."

"Okay?" I said with a laugh.

"Come to dinner with an iron stomach because if someone pulls out Waylon's arsenal of hot sauces, there's no turning back. Everyone will give their all to best the others."

"I guess that's one way to bond," I surmised.

"You know it."

I took the Coke off the bar. "Bigfoot and hot sauce. I'll make sure I'm ready."

"Good luck and godspeed," Wylder called after me.

"Stop trying to scare me off," I tossed over my shoulder. "You and Dex both."

Only laughter followed me.

I dropped the Coke off with Jack and took his order before heading to the hostess and a group of familiar faces—two I didn't expect to see. I knew they both had jobs that probably didn't provide long lunch periods.

"Hey," I greeted the duo Cora was chatting with. Holly wore her hair pulled back in a loose braid and had paired it with a business-casual outfit appropriate for the local bank she worked at. And Aster wore a chic yet casual outfit with Western accents that spoke of life on a ranch.

"What are you guys doing here?" I asked.

The three of them shared a look, but it was Aster who spoke. "We wanted to check on you. Make sure all's okay."

"And we wanted cheeseburgers," Cora added with a twitch of her lips, attempting to inject a little levity into the moment.

Holly reached out a hand, resting it on my arm. "We're here for you. Whatever you need."

My eyes burned like they'd been dunked in acid for some sort of science experiment. "That's really kind." My voice took on a raspy edge I struggled to clear. "I'm good. No more calls. No nothing."

Aster studied me for a moment, something about her seeming to see a little more than the rest of them did. "You're wishing they'd call again."

I shrugged. "I'd handle it differently now. Play it smarter."

"Maybe they will," Cora offered. "Trav said they're looking into it."

"Speaking of, your fiancé's threatening to unalive anyone who looks twice at his french fries."

Cora's green eyes lit, and a hint of pink hit her cheeks. "Do not come between him and his food, trust me."

Holly let out a soft chuckle. "Head over heels."

"The kind of love we all deserve," Aster said softly.

Holly scoffed. "Not sure that's in the cards for most of us."

I'd learned during the dinner at my house that Holly and her husband had divorced after they lost their son. That kind of thing either had you leaning on each other or tearing each other apart. For Holly and John, it had been the latter.

Aster reached out and rubbed her shoulder. "Never give up the dream."

Holly's lips simply pressed into a hard line.

And that was my cue. "Booth or table?"

Aster grinned, knowing exactly what I was doing. "Booth all the way."

I led them to the open spot next to Travis and Roger so they could all chat. Taking their orders, I lost myself in the rhythm of the lunch rush. Running orders, cleaning tables, ringing folks up. Before I knew it, four in the afternoon hit, and it was time for me to clock out.

Wylder glanced up from mixing a cocktail as I grabbed my Bigfoot tote bag from the cabinet that housed our personal items.

"You out?" he asked.

"Yup. Gotta get Owen."

"Give me a sec, and I'll walk you out."

"I'm good," I assured him, pulling a tiny, silver cylinder out of my pocket. "Have pepper spray, will travel."

Wylder grinned. "Remind me not to piss you off."

"Oh, don't worry, I will."

With a wave to Aidan and Cora and a shouted farewell to Fiona in the kitchen, I headed out into the back parking lot—if it could even be called that. It was only eight spaces, shared between the Boot and the art gallery next door. But it was nice not to have to fight the tourist crush for street parking.

Beeping my locks, I slid in and started the engine, then maneuvered my way out of the small lot and toward the street. Flipping on my blinker, I turned in the direction of the rec center. But as I did, my heart stopped.

It was just a flash. Reddish-brown hair. Green eyes so like my son's flashing as he glanced over his shoulder.

Vincent.

I blinked a few times, trying to clear my vision. And in those precious moments, the man turned the corner.

Panic lit through me as I glanced around. A truck pulled out of a parking spot ahead, and I rushed toward it. I barely had the key out of the ignition before I was running, trying to find the man. As I rounded the corner, all I saw were tourists milling about and peeking in shops.

I hurried through them, searching, trying to see if the man had been real or just a figment of my imagination. I checked the three tourist shops and one of the many art galleries. Nothing.

Maybe I'd imagined it. Stress. The comments on my posted photo. The call from Nova's phone. The past was being dredged up left and right. It made sense that my mind would conjure the other main source of tension in my life.

A man with the same build and auburn hair as Vincent stepped out of a gallery. It was very much not Vincent. All the air left my lungs on a whoosh. *Just my imagination.*

Even if he was still watching my life from afar.

CHAPTER TWENTY-SIX
Dex

I MOVED THROUGH THE TREE HOUSE'S KITCHEN, FILING AWAY catalogues of clock parts, books on Bigfoot, and notices and bills I hoped like hell Waylon had paid. He needed a keeper. Not just an assistant but someone who followed the man around and reminded him that he'd started eighty-seven projects that still needed finishing.

A half-assembled cuckoo clock stared up at me from the kitchen table. Tools were scattered around it, along with a drawing. The little creature that was designed to pop out every hour on the hour was a shaggy billy goat. I just shook my head and carefully put everything into a cabinet housing a fire extinguisher, half a bottle of bubbles, a statue of Bigfoot, and a book on alien abductions.

I sighed and shoved the clock pieces in as carefully as possible.

"What are you doing with all my stuff?" Waylon barked as he sauntered in, Tink on his heels.

"Oh, no," I said the moment I caught sight of the mini-Highland cow. "Get Tink out of here. I just mopped."

"I'm sorry," Maverick called as he followed Tink in, Wylder behind him. "Did you just say you *mopped*?"

I stiffened, glaring at my brother and the cow next to him. "This place was a disaster. There was crap everywhere and hoofprints on the damn floor."

Waylon glowered in my direction. "I have an organizational system. Now, I'm not going to be able to find anything."

I arched a brow. "Oh really? Tell me where the Bigfoot statue is."

"Which one?" Waylon shot back.

Wylder chuckled. "He does have a point."

"The one that has *BELIEVE* carved into its stomach," I challenged.

Waylon frowned, drumming his fingers over his barrel chest. "I know I just saw it. I need to oil the wood, so I brought it into the kitchen."

"Because everyone oils their Bigfoot statues in the kitchen," Mav said, fighting a laugh.

"I'm still trying to get over the shock of Dex cleaning," Wylder cut in.

My spine snapped straight. "Hey, I can clean."

Maverick smirked. "Your new house going to get this treatment?"

"I'll have you know that I just got the site plan from the builder and am close enough to your cabin that I'll just dump my trash on your front porch," I shot back.

Mav snorted. "Your nest of snack wrappers and energy drink corpses will probably be petrified before you follow through on that threat."

"You sound like fucking Kol," I grumbled.

Mav stiffened and pointed a finger at me. "You take that back."

Wylder barked out a laugh. "You've done it now."

For our wildest brother, being compared to our most risk-averse one was the highest insult.

I grinned at Maverick. "I'm just callin' 'em like I see 'em."

The glare he sent my way should've had me taking a step back. But I didn't.

Mav lunged, but before he could reach me, Tink let out the deepest moo, charging between us as if she wanted to break up the fight. The only problem was, Maverick was moving too quickly to stop himself. He tumbled over the top of Tink and did a sort of flip that landed him on the floor.

Tink let out a surprised grunt as Mav hit the hardwood with an *oomph*.

Everyone was silent for a moment, and then we burst out laughing—everyone but Maverick.

"I'm gonna get you for this," he breathed, launching to his feet.

I darted around the kitchen table, keeping it between us as a barrier. "Hey, I didn't make you flip. That's all Tink." I shot a smile her way. "Good cow. I take it back. You can come into the kitchen anytime."

Mav lunged one way and then the other before making a break for it and running full speed around the table, chasing me.

But he came up short when Kol stepped into the kitchen and caught him by the back of his shirt.

"What the he—heck are you two doing?" Kol clipped.

His last-minute switch of hell to heck told me my niece was near.

"I'm trying to remove Dex's head from his body," Mav snarled.

Skylar stepped into the kitchen, her hair in high pigtails with glittery bows. She wore a tutu, combat boots, and a shirt that read *I'm just here for the snacks*. "Uncle Mav, that's grounding-worthy for sure."

Kol sent Maverick a pointed look that silently said, *Don't you dare be a bad example for my kid*.

Mav straightened, dusting himself off. "Dex started it. He said something really mean."

Skylar gaped up at me, her jaw dropping. "Uncle Dex, what did you say?"

I bit back my chuckle. "That Mav sounded like your dad."

Kol released his hold on Maverick, scowling at him. "Seriously?"

Mav just shrugged. "I'm not the rules-and-regs type. What can I say?"

"Sky, why don't you take Tink outside?" Kol suggested.

"Aw, man, you always make me miss the good stuff," she grumbled. "Come on, Tinky."

The cow immediately moved in her direction. She grabbed Tink's cheeks, getting right up close until they were nose to nose. "Who's the prettiest girl in the world? Who's the bestest cow? You, that's who." Then she led the cow out the back door and into the yard without looking back.

"This world does not deserve that tiny human," Wylder muttered.

"No, it doesn't," I agreed. "But she'll make it a better place."

Kol watched his daughter for a moment as she called for Pepper, and the three of them took off across the yard, Lucy rising from her spot on the deck to follow.

I couldn't imagine having the weight of raising a human being on your shoulders. Making sure they were safe, cared for. That they were growing up healthy in mind and body. Every choice you made had to feel like it weighed a million pounds. But Kol was doing it. And amazingly well. So was Brae.

Kol finally forced his gaze away from the back doors. "Who's going to tell me what the hell is really going on?"

Wylder's lips twitched. "It all started because Dex was cleaning."

Surprise lit Kol's features. "This Dex?"

"You guys are all assholes. You make it sound like I'm a pig."

The room went silent. And then they all laughed.

Waylon slapped me on the back. "Only when you get in the zone. That computer fries your brain, and nothing else exists."

"I think the hot, little badass breaks through that hacking haze," Mav chimed in.

I scowled in his direction. "Stop calling her that."

Mav's grin only widened. "Awwww, our Little Dex has a crush."

"Shut up."

"What are you, eight?" Mav shot back.

"No, but you are," I clipped.

Kol went stock-still. "You told me you two were friends."

"We are."

That familiar muscle began fluttering in his jaw. "Tell me you're not getting involved with someone whose case we're working."

Maverick and Wylder groaned, knowing a familiar lecture was about to commence.

"It's against every rule in the book," Kol ground out.

"For *law enforcement*. Which none of us is."

Kol's jaw ground back and forth. "I am."

"Then you can keep whatever boundaries you want to."

"You *do* like her," Kol surmised.

I shifted uncomfortably, tendrils of panic wrapping around me. "I told you, she's a good person."

Wylder let out a low whistle. "For Dex, that might as well be an engagement ring."

"Oh, fuck off."

Maverick rubbed his hands together like a kid on Christmas morning or some cartoon villain. "I can't *wait* to watch this go down."

"I am going to set the photo of you running from the pond, screaming as you shucked your shorts because you had a leech on your ass, as your lock screen. Hell, I'll put it on all the computers at the fire station, too."

Mav's eyes narrowed. "You're lucky I'm very secure with my body and have no problem with that."

"I dunno," Wylder muttered. "You were pretty gangly back then."

"And his ass was as white as snow," I said with a chuckle.

Mav didn't wait; he lunged, pulling me into a headlock and attempting to give me the world's worst noogie. I retaliated by punching at his kidney.

"Ow, shit. I hit my side on a landing the other day," Mav bit out.

I sent another blow. "Then let me go, you foot-licking asswipe."

A throat cleared. "Are we interrupting something?" Brae asked, amusement wrapping around each word. "The front door was open."

"Duuuuude, are you guys wrestling? I wanna tap in. Who's your favorite wrestler? Mine's Wild Side. He's the freaking dopest." Owen bounced up and down as the words tumbled out of his mouth.

At the sight of a kid, Mav released me. "You must be Owen. Heard a lot about you."

Owen just grinned. "Which brother are you?"

Mav chuckled. "I'm Maverick, the youngest." He sent Brae a smirk. "And the most handsome."

I smacked him upside the head as I straightened. "Stop pulling that sh—shinola."

Owen rolled his eyes. "I've heard the s-word before."

Brae wrapped an arm around his shoulders while she balanced a platter with the other. "And we know not to repeat it, right?"

"Bro, I'm not dumb. I don't want you to take my Switch."

Wylder chuckled. "Smart man. I'm Wylder."

"My mom works for you, right?" Owen asked.

"She does, and she fixed all my records for my accountant."

Owen beamed. "She's real good with that math stuff. Just don't ask her to do any computer stuff."

"Hey," Brae cut in, affronted.

Owen giggled as he tipped his head back to look at his mom. "You're good at other stuff. Like comic cookies." He glanced at me. "They're not boobie cookies, but they're bussin.'"

Kol frowned. "What are boobie cookies?"

CHAPTER TWENTY-SEVEN
Braedyn

HEAT HIT MY CHEEKS HARD AND FAST, AND I WANTED TO CRAWL into a hole just a little bit. It didn't take a genius to figure out that Kol was the second brother unsure about me. And I had a feeling *boobie cookies* wouldn't win him over.

"Yeah. And how do I get some?" Maverick cut in.

"Sorry," Owen said easily. "Boobie cookies are only for Mr. Dex."

Maverick turned to Dex, a mischievous grin on his face. "Only for you, huh? Lucky dog."

Dex sent his brother a glare that would've had me peeing my pants. Maverick just grinned wider.

"I, uh, like making creative cookies. My friend Nova calls them comic cookies. I'll make them for any occasion," I cut in.

Maverick's amused gaze moved back to me. "And what was the occasion for boobie cookies?"

My face was so hot I could've baked another set of boobie cookies on it. "There was a little cabin snafu the day we moved to Starlight Grove, and I walked in on Dex coming out of the shower."

Wylder fought a laugh. "You mean he thought you were breaking in, and your dog thought he was a threat, and a towel was lost in the process?"

"That's the gist of it. Anyone want a Bigfoot cookie?" I shoved the plate into the middle of the group, praying for a change in subject.

A big, broad man wearing Carhartt overalls brightened. "Did you say Bigfoot?"

A smile finally found my lips. "I did. There are also cookies in the form of hot sauce bottles, peppers, and a few clocks. Wylder told me some family interests."

"Bigfoot is all Waylon," Kol grumbled.

I glanced over at the towering man. "You don't believe?"

"You *do*?"

I straightened, squaring my shoulders. "The human race evolved from apes. Is it that much of a stretch to think there's a species out there that evolved differently? Plus, it's fun."

Waylon bit into a cookie and pointed the other half at me. "I like her."

Kol scoffed. "Won over in two seconds by Bigfoot."

"Did you hear about the sighting in the town a couple miles outside of Anchorage?" I asked.

Waylon nodded enthusiastically. "That video was wild."

"Videos can be doctored," Dex reminded us.

I sent him an annoyed look. "Don't be a buzzkill."

Waylon barked out a laugh. "Okay, I *really* like her."

"Bruh, is that a cow?" Owen asked, walking toward the back doors.

"That's Tink," Waylon informed him.

Owen shook his head in wonder. "A tree growing out of your freaking house and shaggy cows in your backyard? This place is doing the most."

"Doing the most?" Wylder asked, confused.

One corner of my mouth kicked up. "He means it's cool."

"Doing the most," Mav muttered. "I gotta keep up on my slang."

Dex clapped him on the back. "Good luck with that."

The sound of a screen door smacking against the frame sent everyone but me and Owen on alert. Dex moved in an instant, positioning himself next to me but also between me and Owen and the sound.

Confusion swept through me as heavy footsteps sounded. Then, a new figure stepped into the entryway to the kitchen. He filled more of the frame than the other Archer brothers would've. His shoulders were a bit broader, and his height topped them all by an inch or so. But he had the same hazel eyes—though maybe a little darker, the deep green snuffing out most of the gold.

And those eyes were pointed at me with suspicion.

I swallowed hard, assuming this was Orion. Some people would've been scared of someone that size glaring at them like they'd stolen their last Twinkie. But all I could think about was what Dex had shared. Orion's story and what he'd been through.

Instead of seeing the slightly scary man in front of me, I saw a boy. One who'd given everything to protect his brothers.

I lifted my hands to sign as I spoke. "Hi, Orion. It's nice to meet you."

Surprise washed across Orion's features, but he didn't say a word or even make a move to sign.

My hands lowered. "I looked up how to sign a few things, but I don't know much. Sorry."

Dex's hand found the small of my back, the heat of his palm bleeding into me. "It's nice you made the effort."

"It is," Wylder agreed, sending Orion a pointed look.

"I think it's really dope you talk with your hands. I wanna learn. Mom said me and her could take classes," Owen cut in, showing zero fear.

God, I loved my kid. He was the absolute best.

Orion's gaze traveled to Owen, curiosity there. But still, he said nothing.

Owen didn't seem to mind.

"Well," Waylon cut in, "brisket's been cooking for the past day, and it should be ready. Mashed potatoes and rolls are in the warmer." He sent Dex a chastising look. "Unless Cleany McGee over here moved them."

I tipped my head back to look at Dex in question.

He sighed. "Rolls and mashed potatoes in the oven make sense. I didn't move them."

Waylon just let out a *harumph*. "Let's eat."

It took a second for everyone to find their spots, Kol calling Skylar in from outside. She and Owen instantly began chattering about camp, and it helped to ease a little of the tension in the room. But I didn't miss that Orion sat directly opposite me, in a spot that gave him an easy exit out the back or front doors. I couldn't help wondering if that was intentional.

Skylar glanced up at him, pausing her animated conversation with Owen. "Can you teach us how to booby-trap a water balloon with food dye? There's a real meanie at camp who could use it."

"Absolutely not," Kol cut in.

There was the barest twitch to Orion's lips as his hands began to move in reply.

Dex leaned closer to me. "Orion told her that he has her covered."

I stifled a giggle as Kol glared at his brother. I was just glad that angry stare wasn't directed at me.

"So, Brae," Waylon said, handing me a gorgeous salad the glaring brother had made. "You moved from Oakland?"

I nodded as I dished some up for Owen and me. "Yes. I lived there for a little over eight years, but I grew up in Rhode Island. On the beach."

"Big difference, Rhode Island to Oakland and Oakland to Starlight Grove," Wylder suggested.

"It is," I agreed.

"But Starlight Grove is the best, right?" Skylar asked. "We got mountains and rivers and lakes. And soooooo many animals."

I grinned at the little girl. "It's definitely winning me over day by day. And if I get to meet some of your alpacas, I think it'll take the lead for sure."

"You have alpacas?" Owen all but shrieked.

Skylar giggled. "I can show you after dinner. We can bring them treats."

"What do alpacas like for treats?" I asked, curious.

Skylar leaned back in her seat, pulling up a mental list. "They're a lot like horses. They like carrots and apples. But they also love bananas, watermelon, and pumpkin."

"There are some watermelon cubes in the fridge for ya, Little Princess," Waylon told her.

"Thanks, Grampa Way Way," she said, reaching for a roll.

"What did you do in Oakland?" Kol cut into the conversation. His question didn't feel the same as Waylon's or Wylder's. His felt a little more like an interrogation. But if it meant he'd stop giving Dex a hard time, I'd take it.

I lifted my plate so Waylon could put some brisket on it. "I worked for a small accounting firm as a receptionist and then their office manager. It's how I learned bookkeeping."

Wylder broke off a piece of his roll. "And thank God you did because I never want to look at QuickBooks again."

The corner of my lips tipped up. "I don't mind it. I actually kind of like it. There's always an exact answer, no gray areas."

Wylder chewed thoughtfully. "I get that."

Maverick shook his head. "No way. The gray is where all the fun is."

Kol let out a grunt. "Of course you think that."

"Sorry, black-and-white boy, some of us like to live a little," Maverick shot back.

"And by living a little, you mean nearly breaking your neck at every chance?" Kol argued.

Maverick shrugged. "At least I'm *living*."

There was something there. A bite to the accusation. And I sensed it was a low blow.

Kol stiffened in his seat, divots carved into his cheeks from how hard he was clenching his jaw.

Shit. This had the potential to go bad. So I said the first thing that popped into my head.

"I hear you guys like hot sauce competitions."

CHAPTER TWENTY-EIGHT
Dex

THE ENTIRE KITCHEN WENT QUIET, BUT I HAD TO FIGHT A LAUGH. Barely an hour with my family, and Brae already had a sixth sense for when things were about to tip into the danger zone.

"What?" she pressed. "Is that not true?"

Wylder set down his root beer. "We do, but it's not something I would recommend you partake in unless you've got an iron gut."

Brae shoved her chair back, crossing to where she'd dropped her tote bag with the little Bigfoot on the corner. *Jesus.* She and Waylon were a match made in heaven.

She crossed back to the table and began depositing hot sauce bottles across the center. "I did some research and found a few things. My gift to the group. Did you know there's a little gourmet shop two towns over that has a whole wall of hot sauce?"

Orion had barely taken his eyes off her since his arrival. And it wasn't in an interested way. It was in a looking-for-evidence way. He wanted to prove that she was the enemy combatant he hoped she was.

It annoyed the hell out of me.

As if he could feel my glower, his gaze flicked to me for the barest moment. I fought the urge to bare my teeth at him or flip him off. But his focus was already back on the woman next to me.

"What do you say?" Brae asked. "Hot sauce challenge?"

Maverick let out a hoot. "Will you marry me, Little Badass? You had me at boobie cookies and hot sauce."

Brae laughed. "I already know I can't keep up with you."

"Damn," Mav muttered. "A heartbreaker on top of it. Mad respect."

I turned my glare from Orion to Maverick.

He lifted both hands in surrender. "Yeah, yeah. No looky, no touchy."

"How about you try shutty uppy?" I suggested.

"That's an almost swear," Skylar informed. "It's not nice to tell people to shut up."

My lips twitched. "Noted, Little Princess."

Skylar turned to Brae, lowering her voice to a comically conspiratorial tone. "Kick their booties. They're always bragging about how many peppers they can handle."

Brae slid back into her chair and leaned across Owen to deliver a whisper of her own. "I'm representing girl power tonight."

She held out a fist, and Sky grinned as she bumped it.

I leaned back, taking in Brae as she straightened. "You really think you can take everyone at this table?"

A sly smile spread across her face. "Oh, I'm gonna smoke you."

Mav let out a hoot. "Let's get this party started, ladies and gents. What did you bring as the offering, Little Badass?"

Brae made a Vanna White move across the hot sauces. "I bring you the burn-your-mouths-off collection from Five Fire Farms outside the Bay Area. One of my personal favorites. I was very pleased to see it here."

A trickle of awareness slid through me. "You like hot sauce."

Her damn perfect lips twitched. "I might have a taste for it."

"Goddamn. She's a badass. She's hot. And she likes to eat fire." Mav laid his head on the table. "I'm done for. No one will ever compete."

Brae laughed, and the sound wrapped around me like ghosted fingertips. I wanted to lean into it. Bury my face in the sound.

"Why do I have a feeling you're never hurting for company?" Brae challenged.

Maverick straightened, waggling his eyebrows. "Who, me? I'm one hundred percent a lonely boy."

Wylder scoffed. "Tell that to the women always bugging me to know when you're coming into the bar."

"Hey," he shot back. "I can't help it if the ladies want what they can't have."

"Enough," Waylon muttered. "I wanna try these Five Fire Farms." He reached for the bottle with only one chili pepper. "We start out easy."

The bottle went around the table, skipping over the kids. Each of us put a little on some brisket or potatoes and chowed down.

"Hoo," Wylder breathed. "Even the mild's got a kick."

"Come on, boss. You can't hang?" Brae challenged.

"Oh, I can hang," Wylder shot back as he reached for the two-chili pepper sauce.

That one had me paying attention, the heat building in my gut and mouth. But as I looked over at Brae, she looked like she was just eating fucking ice cream. She flipped a strand of blond hair over her shoulder, and I wanted to slide my fingers through it. Grip the wavy locks as I tipped her head back and took her mouth. As I undid every damn button down the center of her pale-pink sundress.

"I can barely taste it," Brae said easily. "What about you, Kol?"

My brother grimaced at her. "You taste it."

She shrugged. "Let's see about number three."

She poured a few shakes onto a bite of mashed potatoes and swallowed it down. "Okay. Now, we're talking."

Kol grabbed the bottle from her hand, doubling the amount on his own potatoes as if trying to make a point. As he swallowed, sweat broke out on his brow and his eyes went wide.

Maverick burst out laughing. "Someone's talking a big game but can't follow through."

"Remember, Daddy," Skylar began. "It's okay to lose to a girl. We're all equal."

Wylder snickered. "Yeah, it's okay to lose to someone about a third of your size."

Orion snatched the bottle, trying it himself. He was more stoic about his reaction, but his cheeks turned bright red and he started to pant like Lucy did on a hot summer day. He reached for his water.

"I wouldn't," Brae warned. "I hear water makes it worse."

Orion glared at her and then reached across the table for Skylar's milk, taking a swig and making his niece giggle.

"If Rion had to do milk, I'm out." Wylder gave the table two knocks.

Sky let out a cheer. "One down, Miss Brae!"

Wylder shook his head. "That hurts, Little Princess."

She just grinned at him. "Sometimes, girls gotta stick together."

Waylon and I survived that round, but when Mav tried the three-chili pepper sauce, he shot out of his chair, running for the sink. He stuck his head under the faucet, trying to wash out his mouth. "What was that?" he spluttered. "Three chilis grown in hell?"

Brae laughed as she held out a hand for Skylar, who slapped it.

"Bruh, that's a little embarrassing," Owen told Mav.

Orion's lips twitched at the comment—the first tiny fissure in his shields.

"God, these kids are freaking harsh," Mav muttered.

"Try living with one," Kol shot back.

"On to four," Waylon said, grabbing the bottle and trying the sauce. He let out a garbled sound before knocking twice on the table. "That's my hard limit," he croaked.

I grinned as I took the bottle. I thought about trying to best Brae, but my mouth was still on fire from the last round, and I was having too much fun watching her trounce everyone. I knocked twice on the table and handed her the bottle. "Too much for me."

Brae's brow arched. "You sure about that, Buttercup?"

"I preferred Bird Poop Boy," Wylder cut in.

Brae chuckled. "He can be both."

I leaned back in my chair. "My stomach is going to thank me for this choice tomorrow."

Brae sprinkled a few drops on her potatoes and took a nice-sized bite. Pink hit her cheeks this time, but no sweat broke out, and she didn't even reach for a drink after. She simply offered the bottle to Orion across the table.

He studied her for a long moment before taking the bottle and shaking out several drops over his meat. He took a bite. The moment the brisket hit his tongue, his eyes went wide as saucers. Orion was out of his chair in a flash, running for the trash and spitting out the bite.

"Flag on the play!" Mav hollered. "Disqualified."

Brae grinned as Skylar cheered. "What do you think, Kol? Got what it takes?" Brae asked.

He glowered at her, which only made Brae smile wider. Kol snagged the bottle from where Orion was sitting and shook out two drops onto his potatoes. Lifting the bite to his mouth, he paused, his hand trembling.

Finally, he dropped the fork to the plate. "Sh—" He halted what he was about to say. "I can't do it."

Skylar leapt from her chair, dancing around the room. "Girls rule, boys drool! Girls rule, boys drool!"

Owen grinned up at Brae. "Pretty bussin', bruh."

Brae flicked her hair over her shoulder in an exaggerated motion, sending a faint red-currant scent my way. "That's my trophy right there."

I reached over, unable to stop myself from touching her, even though I knew it was the last thing I should do. But everything about her drew me in. That scent. The way her eyes lit in victory. How her mouth curved in that taunting bow. My hand slid under that fall of hair, and I squeezed the back of her neck, relishing the feel of her silky skin as the pads of my fingers ghosted over her pulse point. "You did good, Hellion."

Golden eyes found mine, flashing with something I couldn't identify. "Thanks, Buttercup. I like your family."

"You gotta tell me how Buttercup came about," Wylder said as he struggled not to laugh.

I tried to glare at Brae, but it was more of a twitching smile. "Thanks for that."

Brae beamed up at me as she answered Wylder. "He was soooooo very sunshiney when I first met him, Buttercup was the only name that fit."

Kol let out a sound that was a cross between a scoff and a snort.

"Hey," I shot back at him. "You're the grumpiest a-hole around, so I don't think you have room to judge."

"A-hole still counts as a swear, Uncle Dex," Sky cut in.

I shook my head. "Noted, Little Princess."

Mav leaned back in his chair. "Buttercup works for me."

"Don't even think about it," I warned, then turned to Brae. "Do you see what you've done?"

She just shrugged. "Sorry, not sorry. You kind of deserve it."

I couldn't help but laugh. And as I glanced around the table, I knew she'd made more progress than I'd thought possible. Kol looked at her with grudging respect. Orion with something less than hatred. And Waylon? He was sunk.

It was enough to get started.

"All right," Waylon said, rolling out a map over the kitchen table where dinner had once been. Skylar had offered to show Owen the animals, giving the adults time to talk about what we needed to.

I helped Waylon flatten the edges, using the hot sauce bottles from the earlier battle as weights.

"This map is gorgeous," Brae said almost reverently, her fingers ghosting over the paper. "It's like art."

There was a shift in the air, and I knew where it was coming from.

"Orion made it," I told her.

He worked in an infinite number of styles and mediums, but he always made something that took your breath away. This map in particular was a blend of watercolor and ink. The watercolors captured mountains, rivers, and forests, while the ink was there for roads, trails, and markers.

Brae looked up and toward my middle brother. "It's amazing. I can't believe you did all this."

She was good with him. Never pushed him to respond but still made him a part of the conversation. The few people Orion was forced to come into contact with outside the family could be weird. Some asked question after question as if they could force him to speak. Others looked at him with pity. Some thought he was stupid. And still more would practically scream at him as if he were hard of hearing.

Brae treated him like everyone else. She didn't take it easy on him by giving him a hot sauce win he would've hated. But she wasn't pushy either. She just let him be who he needed to be.

Orion's throat worked as he swallowed, and his hands lifted to sign.

"He says thank you," I translated.

Brae beamed like she'd won the lotto and gotten a visit from royalty all at the same time. "You're welcome." Her gaze dipped to the map, instantly going serious. "This was the trailhead we hiked out of." Her slender finger dragged along the route. "And this is where I went off the trail. Where Nova disappeared."

There was a heaviness to her last statement. Guilt.

I couldn't keep myself from touching her, even though I knew I shouldn't. I slid a hand over her shoulder and squeezed, feeling the heat of her skin bloom against my palm. Scalding, just like the hellion she was. "It's not your fault."

"Maybe, maybe not. The outcome's the same either way."

I hated that she carried that weight. Because it was the kind of heaviness that could drown a person.

Kol cleared his throat. "They bring in search and rescue when it happened?"

Brae nodded. "Yes, but not until almost two days later. And it had rained."

Kol muttered a curse.

"Idiots," Wylder grumbled.

And I knew why. The older the scene, the less likely a trail someone left is undisturbed—harder for anyone to track.

Brae's mouth thinned. "I learned through training Yeti for search just how detrimental that time was. But then, I didn't know just how much we'd lost."

"It's not our only resource," I assured her. "Let me walk you through what we'll do, how we'll tackle it."

Orion's eyes flashed, that hazel that was darker than the rest of ours lightening for a moment. I knew he didn't want me sharing a damn thing about how we worked. I kept talking anyway.

"Waylon and Kol have tracking covered. At least in the physical realm," I explained. "They know their stuff."

"I used to know my stuff," Waylon muttered. "This whippersnapper has surpassed me."

I didn't miss the look of pride on Kol's face at Waylon's words. Each of us shared a unique bond with Waylon, and for Kol, it was all about being out in nature and learning how to read it.

Maverick slapped me on the shoulder. "This nerd keeps his tracking to the interwebs."

"You keep calling me a nerd, and you're gonna feel just how far the *interwebs* stretch," I warned.

Mav just grinned. "I provide a medic's eye and help Orion with the geographic profiling."

Brae's expression brightened. "I've been reading up about that. You can look at areas of similar crimes to analyze where a perpetrator is likely to live or work. The only problem is we only have one crime. I haven't found anything else that I can be sure is linked."

The room went silent.

She stiffened. Her fingers locked around the table, and her knuckles bleached white. "What aren't you telling me?"

Kol stepped forward. "I asked my boss to add Nova's case to my workload. It's close enough to national forest land that we've got due cause."

Brae's eyes went glassy, but she still forced herself to meet Kol's eyes. "Thank you."

"If something happened that's not accidental, we need to know what."

"And you found something?" Brae pushed.

Kol gripped the back of his neck. "When looking into her case and searching similar circumstances, I discovered a few cases that could be considered like crimes."

Brae's breaths came quicker now. "You think someone's taking people."

Kol lifted a shoulder and then dropped it. "I don't know."

"I come in and profile the victims," Wylder said softly. "See what they might have in common."

Brae's gaze came to me. "I showed you the similar cases I found. You'll fill them in?"

I nodded. "I'll make sure they have everything they need."

She scanned the room. "You all have pretty established roles. Like you've done this before."

No one said a word. Because that wasn't something any of us could give her. Not yet, anyway.

Her gaze dropped. "No-go zone. Got it."

"You need to come to terms with one thing." Kol's voice was quiet, but it held an edge, grit. "You may not get the outcome to this you want."

My hand fisted at my side, trying to keep myself from decking my brother right then and there. She didn't need to be reminded of that fact.

Brae twisted her fingers in the threads of a friendship bracelet on her wrist. "I'd know if she was gone. I'd feel it."

Kol shook his head. "Sometimes, our mind plays tricks, and hope can be a dirty liar. Before we go down this road, you need to make sure you want the answers. No matter what."

Brae's chin jutted out, defiance sliding over her features. "I'm already walking that road. You just need to decide if you're gonna help me."

Hellion through and through.

He jerked his head in a nod. "We'll help. Right, boys?"

Waylon patted his stomach. "She had me at Bigfoot cookies."

"She had me at giving Miller a verbal smackdown," Wylder said with a smile.

"It was really the badass hotness for me," Mav added, darting out of my path as I tried to punch him in the gut.

I straightened, looking down at Brae. She'd had me since she'd called me Bird Poop Boy in a bar full of people. "You know I've got your back."

We all turned to Orion. His jaw was hard as granite, the muscle along it fluttering. Finally, his hands lifted. *"I hope this isn't a huge fucking mistake."*

I hoped so, too. Because there was an infinite number of ways it could all go sideways. And if it did? That weight would be on me. One more failure to add to the load.

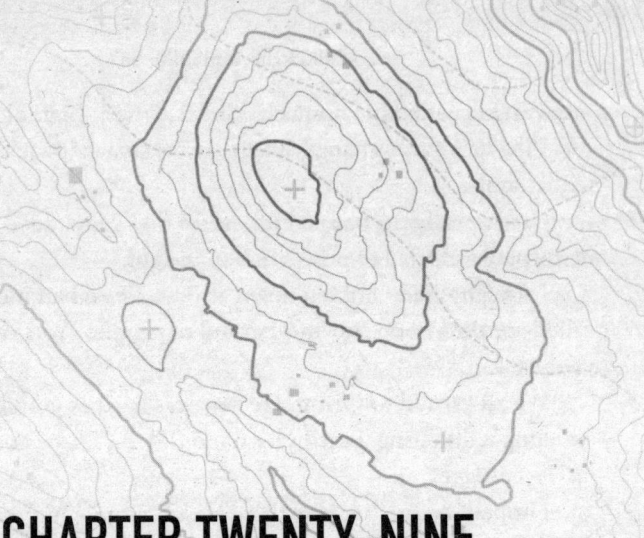

CHAPTER TWENTY-NINE
Braedyn

I LEANED BACK, BRACING MY PALMS ON MY BACK DECK, AND tipped my face to the sky as my mind swirled around all the information I'd gathered tonight. It was one of those crystal-clear nights—the kind where you could trace every star in the sky.

I wondered if this corner of the world had a disproportionate number of those nights like they had a disproportionate number of missing people. People who had vanished, leaving their loved ones spinning, wondering what the hell had happened, never able to move on.

A flash sailed across the sky, making me suck in a breath. Shooting star. I closed my eyes and wished.

Please, let me find Nova. Please, let her be okay.

There were days I was so certain she'd walk through my door. Days where I was sure I'd get a call from law enforcement telling me they'd found her and that everything was okay.

But as the days passed, turning to months and then a year, those days of certainty came less often.

Kol's words echoed in my head. *"Before we go down this road, you need to make sure you want the answers. No matter what."*

Part of me didn't want to walk the road, but I didn't have a choice. I needed to. For Nova. And for me.

Grass rustled in the direction of Dex's house, but I didn't reach for my pepper spray. Somehow, I knew it was him. And that was seriously messed up. How did I know someone's energy after knowing them for only a handful of weeks?

"You shouldn't be sitting out here alone." Dex's voice rumbled through the dark like a pissed-off freight train.

"I heard you coming," I said, not taking my eyes off the sky.

"I wanted you to hear me."

"Stalker."

"Hellion."

My mouth curved. "I like looking up at the stars. Didn't get this in Oakland. Not even in Rhode Island. It's clearer here."

Dex lowered himself onto the step next to me, so close his thigh brushed mine, making the material of my sundress skate across my skin. I had to fight not to lean into the sensation.

"It's pretty damn gorgeous," he said, the words almost a sigh. "Missed it when I was in DC."

"I bet." Now that I knew what it was like to be surrounded by this kind of beauty all the time, I wasn't sure I could go back. "But it's more than the stars' beauty. It's Nova. She's somewhere out there. Under the same sky. Looking up makes me feel…not so far away from her."

Even in moments when it felt like that comforting sky might vanish before my eyes like she had or when it felt like a chasm separated us, I still held tight. I trusted that I would find her, even across a vanishing sky. And somehow, having Dex next to me, looking up at the same sky helped me believe that all the more.

He was quiet for a moment, and then his hand covered mine. The move was the same as he'd done before, his palm pressing down, steady pressure and heat. But this time, he wove his fingers through mine. He created a tapestry that made me believe we were stronger together.

Panic flared somewhere deep, but I shoved it down and breathed. In and out. Over and over as I counted the stars until the panic ebbed.

"I used to think that about my mom," Dex said softly. "Even when

I thought she'd left us by choice. I'd think how she was out there, looking up at the same moon. How could we be that far apart when we were under the same moon?"

My fingers tightened around his. "That makes it so much harder. Not knowing if she chose to leave."

Dex swallowed, his throat working before he spoke. "Exactly. Those what-ifs. Did she throw us all away, or was she ripped from us?"

I traced the length of his pinky finger as if all the ridges and lines could tell me the story of his life. "I hate that for you."

He stared out at the shadowy horizon. "She wouldn't even know me now. And that kills. Either way, I would be a stranger to her."

God, did I ever understand that, how the mind twisted stolen time and molded us into something we'd never been before.

"Sometimes, I wonder if Nova would even recognize me walking down the street. It's like I'm two entirely different people. The one who ended up frozen in time when she disappeared and the one irrevocably changed by her disappearance. And that last one...that one is so night and day from who I used to be."

Dex squeezed my fingers, his callused skin skating over mine. "She'd know you. There's no way she wouldn't. I'd recognize you blindfolded and in the dark. Because you *glow*, Hellion."

His words were a brand—pleasure and pain because they were a claiming. One that terrified me to want so badly.

"I want to believe that. That she could see me in the dark."

"She can," Dex rasped. "You're a goddamned miracle. Pain changes us. Grief. Trauma. It's all a sculptor's knife. But you let it change you for the better."

I looked at him through the darkness, the starlight and faint glow of the kitchen lights illuminating his face: the hard angle of his jaw covered in scruff, the way the green in his eyes seemed like endless pools I could get lost in. "You didn't know me before."

"Don't have to. I know that losing your friend—your family—could've turned you bitter. Instead, it had you looking for the good, claiming it. Just like you keep looking for those stars you share with her." Dex's gaze held mine captive. "You're not like me. You didn't stop living."

"You live," I argued.

He shrugged. "A half-life. Never putting myself in a position where someone could pull the rug out."

I could see what he meant. He had friends but no one truly *close* other than his brothers. He didn't talk about what he was feeling. This might've been the most he'd ever shared in that respect. Which only made it more of a gift.

Gripping Dex's hand, I stood.

"What are you doing?" he asked, his brows pulling together.

"We're living." I tugged Dex to his feet and pulled out my phone, hitting my music app and letting the soft instrumentals fill the air around us.

Dex's mouth pursed. "Not much of a dancer, Hellion."

I tugged him toward me. "Then I'll lead."

My arms looped around his neck, and I started to sway. Dex frowned, but his arms finally came around me, his hands resting low on my back. "Why do I feel like I'm at a fifth-grade dance right now?" he grumbled.

I couldn't help but laugh. "Live a little, Buttercup. We've got stars and music, and we're *alive*."

The last was the greatest gift of all.

Dex pulled me closer. Everything about him had a slightly deceptive air—not in a bad way, a surprising one. Like how that tall body was finely honed muscle beneath humorous hacker shirts and tortoiseshell glasses. How beneath that sometimes scowly mask was a depth of emotion. But most of all, how every contact lit a buzz in me I'd never experienced before.

His thumb swept back and forth over the cotton of my sundress. I swore I could feel the texture of his fingertips, the swirls of calluses and life.

Then he shocked me with that same deceptive nature, grabbing my arm and spinning me out, then back again. I hit his chest with a certain power, the kind that had the air leaving my lungs and my gaze snapping up to his face. "You're full of surprises, aren't you?"

Dex's mouth twisted into a beautiful grin full of mischief. "You said we should live."

"We should." My heart hammered, giving me away as it beat against his chest.

His gaze dropped to my mouth, stilling there as if he were memorizing every line and curve. And I swore I could taste him, even now, as his face hovered above mine. Mint and a bite of something. Chocolate from dessert, maybe?

I leaned harder against him, tempting fate, ignoring every warning sign. Because I wanted to know that potent combination. Wanted to burn everything about Dex into all my senses.

He lifted a hand between us, his thumb tracing my bottom lip and then skating over my cheek to the column of my neck, stopping on my pulse point. "Feel that life here. Like butterfly wings. Wonder if that butterfly would take flight if I kissed you."

My lips parted as I sucked in a breath, and I knew my pulse gave away my answer.

"You want me to kiss you, Hellion? Want me to drown in your taste? You want to *live*?"

I didn't answer with words. Instead, I lived. I pushed up on my tiptoes, closing the distance between us. The moment my mouth connected with Dex's, he lost any questions and took.

His hand stayed at my throat while the other sank into my hair. His fingers fisted, asking me to open for him, to give more. I did. And I'd been right about the mint and chocolate. But there was also something more.

Dex's tongue stroked in, and as cedar and sandalwood swirled around me, I swore I could taste them, too, in the best ways. It was as if everything about Dex was bleeding into me.

I stretched up, pressing myself harder against him, searching for more. That buzz was back. Stronger than before. Dex Archer was the most potent kind of drug, and after one kiss, I knew I'd be addicted.

And then the latch of the door sounded.

Dex moved so fast he resembled one of the heroes in Owen's favorite cartoons, shoving me back and stepping between me and the noise.

"Moooom," Owen muttered sleepily through the dark. "Yeti puked, and it made me puke, too."

Like a bucket of ice water, his words crashed over me as Dex's stance changed. A different sort of tension slid through him. I braced for him to run. To text me later and tell me the kiss was a mistake. Instead, he surprised me.

"Good thing you've got me," Dex said, stepping forward to ruffle Owen's hair as Yeti wandered out the back door. She looked completely unconcerned about the pukefest she'd instigated, which I was sure was courtesy of the extra three treats I'd caught Owen feeding her.

"I am an excellent puke cleaner-upper," Dex continued. "One time, Mav had the stomach flu so bad I swear I could catch it on the fly."

"Gross," Owen muttered. "But awesome."

Dex laughed, his gaze finding me. "I'll handle cleanup. You get the kiddo."

I struggled to get my mouth to obey because it suddenly wasn't just me. I didn't have to balance getting ginger ale and Pepto into Owen while attempting to clean the mess at the same time. I had help. That panic was back, but I shoved it down.

"Ginger ale for the puke king?" I asked.

Owen sent me a wan smile. "Just none of the pink stuff."

I chuckled. "Let's take it a little at a time."

And I told myself to do the same thing.

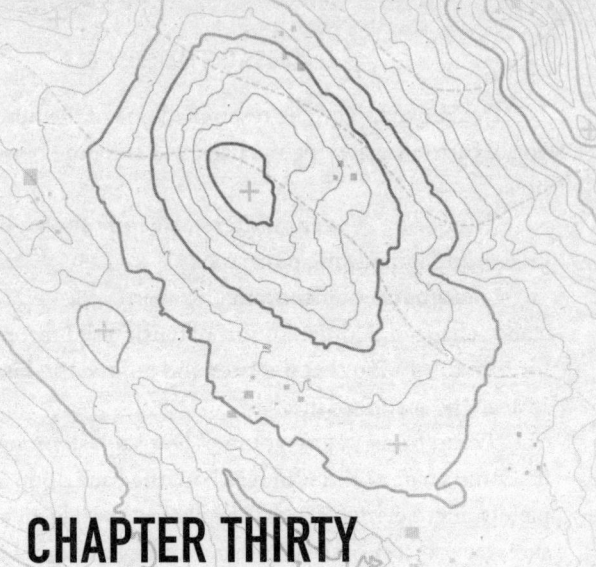

CHAPTER THIRTY
Braedyn

THE BUZZ AND WHIR OF THE COFFEE MACHINE CUT THROUGH the morning sounds of the rest of the house: Owen getting ready for camp, Yeti following behind as he ran between rooms in a nonsensical pattern.

Both seemed perfectly fine after their barf-a-palooza last night. But I was not.

I wasn't fine because I'd kissed Dex Archer. I wasn't fine because I wanted to kiss him again, even though I knew it was the worst idea known to man. I wasn't fine because Dex had kept his distance from me while helping me clean up the mess and get Owen back to bed.

It was as if he didn't want to risk coming within touching distance. As if he worried I would jump him. And, honestly, he *should* have been worried.

The moment the coffee stopped, I poured it over ice, mixed in some creamer, and started guzzling. I needed every ounce of caffeine.

Because sleep had been fitful at best. Every time I dropped into deep unconsciousness, Dex was there. His hands. His tongue. His big body pinning me down.

My eyes popped open. "Not today, Satan," I muttered, then drank more coffee. Because coffee could fix anything. Coffee was my only hope.

"Mom! How do I look? I totally got the drip, right?" Owen skidded to a stop, Yeti on his heels. He was wearing a brightly colored Pac-Man T-shirt and shorts that were equally blinding but definitely clashed with the shirt. He had on his Converse that he'd drawn video game controllers, computers, a Bigfoot, and candy on. But somehow, all the chaos worked.

"My kid, I don't know what drip means, but you are cool as heck."

Owen grinned up at me. "Cool as heck? You might as well say I'm the biggest nerd in nerdville."

"Hey," I clipped, affronted. "Cool as heck is the ultimate compliment."

"Sure, bruh," Owen muttered, but a smile still stretched across his face.

I drilled a finger into his side, making him squeal with laughter. "Did you pack a swimsuit and towel in your bag?"

"Shoot!" He took off running, Yeti letting out a bark and racing behind him.

I couldn't help but laugh. Gathering up my coffee and tote bag, I headed for the front door. It was a miracle if we loaded up in two goes. It was usually three. Four on a rough day. Things were always forgotten. My sunglasses. Owen's Switch. Whatever item one of us couldn't live without that day.

Pulling my phone out of my pocket, I disarmed the alarm. I was still getting used to that. But safe was better than sorry. I unlocked the door and stepped outside.

The barest flutter of white caught my attention—a piece of paper lying on the porch. But something held it in place.

A necklace.

A necklace I recognized.

My heart hammered, rattling against my ribs, forcing my pulse into the danger zone. Blood roared in my ears as I bent, trying to see.

A gold heart locket.

One that looked old. One that had unique star engravings—the same ones I'd seen at the Rose Bowl flea market. The ones I'd haggled over, getting the stall's owner to come down to fifty-six dollars.

It had still been a stretch for me, but I had known Nova would love it. And she had. So much that she'd worn it every single day.

But here it was. On my front steps.

And there was dried blood smeared across the pendant and caked in the chain.

And then I saw the note.

HOW MUCH DO YOU MISS ME?

The lettering was big and blocky. The kind that told you nothing about the person who wrote it. But the words told me everything.

The world went hazy around me, as if a film had dropped over my eyes. I stumbled back, struggling to reach for the door. My coffee slipped from my grip, falling to the front porch and spilling onto the wood, narrowly missing the note.

There wasn't time to clean it up. My gaze jumped around, searching the trees that framed the large gravel area in front of the cabins. Was someone watching? Waiting?

I fumbled for the doorknob, finally getting it to turn. I stumbled into the house, and my phone clattered to the hardwood. It was all I could do to throw the lock.

Nova's necklace. Blood. The note.

My legs gave way, and I fell to the floor.

Some part of me was aware of Yeti's arrival. Owen's.

"Mom?"

I heard the fear in his voice, but I couldn't get myself to answer.

"What happened? Are you sick? Mom?" Owen pressed, anxiety bleeding into his tone.

I opened my mouth, but no words came out.

Owen swiped my phone off the floor, holding it up to my face to unlock it. And then he was tapping on the screen.

"Dex?" he asked, his voice higher than normal. "Something's wrong with my mom. We need you."

I tried to lift my hand to tell Owen I was okay. But my arms were cramped so tightly I couldn't move. They hurt. Every breath was a shallow stab, and black dots danced across my vision.

Don't pass out. Don't pass out.

A pounding sounded. "Owen, it's me. Unlock the door."

Dex's familiar voice skated over me. But it didn't help ease me. My breaths still came in short, brutal stabs.

Owen scrambled toward the door, unlocking it and throwing it open.

Yeti moved to his side and got between me and Dex. She let out a low growl.

"Yeti," Dex said, his voice low. "You know me. I gotta help your person, okay?"

Yeti didn't move for a moment. Then Dex crouched low, holding out a hand.

"He's a friend, Yeti," Owen said.

My dog eased, and Dex didn't wait. He was in front of me in a flash. Rough hands cupped my face. "It's me. I'm right here. Talk to me."

All I could do was keep breathing, trying to grab hold of those short, sharp pants.

Dex grabbed one of my hands and placed it on his chest. "Breathe with me, okay? Follow me. In, two, three. Out, two, three."

I tried. Tried to follow. But the best I could get to was two.

"You're doing it, Hellion. Nice and easy. Follow me." Dex kept leading my breaths. Finally, I reached three. Then he extended it to four. Finally, five.

My hands and arms started to unlock. The tingling in my fingers and toes began to subside.

"That's my girl," Dex whispered. "That's my fucking girl. She'll battle back from hell if she has to."

His praise was like a balm to flesh that had been ravaged.

"Nova," I croaked, loud enough that only he could hear.

Dex stiffened, instantly on alert. "O, can you get some water for your mom?"

He looked unsure for a moment and then nodded, running for the kitchen.

"What happened?" Dex pressed.

He'd probably missed the note amid the dropped coffee and trying to get to me.

"Necklace outside. It's Nova's. There's blood," I rasped, my brain still not quite functioning on all cylinders.

Dex's entire form vibrated with silent fury.

But I could only think about all the horrible possibilities that blood could mean. Nova hurt. Nova tortured. Nova dead.

CHAPTER THIRTY-ONE
Dex

THE CABIN SWIRLED WITH PEOPLE NOW, MAKING THE SPACE FEEL infinitely smaller. The sheriff's department. A couple of crime scene techs from the county. And my whole family, minus Orion. Mav had taken Owen and Yeti into my yard to play. He'd gone begrudgingly, knowing something distinctly not good was up. But Mav had distracted him by pulling out some Nerf guns from his truck. I had no idea why the hell my brother had them. But he did, and I was grateful.

Waylon ambled into the living room with a camp mug that read *Drink coffee, then find Bigfoot*. "You've got quite the mug collection. I picked my favorite." He grinned at Brae as he set the mug down. "Chamomile tea with some spiced honey. My own blend."

Brae sent him an unsteady smile. "This going to burn my mouth off?"

Waylon let out a guffaw. "I know you're made of way stronger stuff than this tea."

She was. Brae was made of pure steel—the kind that still managed to lock a door despite nearly passing out from a panic attack. The kind that pulled it together to assure her kid she was okay, even though everything in her was breaking.

"Thank you." She wrapped her hands around the mug and held it to her. There was a blanket draped over her lap, but despite that, the tea, and the already eighty-degree weather, she shivered.

I fucking hated that. It stoked the rage I'd shoved down deep. I wanted to find whoever had done this and ruin them. No, more than ruin them. I wanted to *hurt* them. My father's genes were alive and well in me. I'd always known it, but this was a brutal reminder.

"You want anything to eat?" Wylder asked, worry etched into his face.

Brae shook her head. "Thank you, but I don't think I could stomach much right now."

My hands fisted at my sides, and a heavy palm landed on my shoulder. Kol. He squeezed hard. "She's safe," he whispered. "Breathe through it."

Always looking out for us. Always knowing when one of us was hitting our limit.

Heavy footsteps sounded behind me. Two sets. I turned to see Roger and Travis heading our way. Both had a serious set to their features, but Roger's anger broke through a little more.

He stepped forward, clearing his throat. "How are you feeling, B?"

I tried to swallow down the annoyance at the fact that he'd given her a nickname of sorts. Because I didn't have a right to that emotion. I didn't have a right to anything when it came to Brae.

"Much better," she lied. "I'm sorry...sorry about being such a mess when you got here."

"Don't you dare apologize," Travis ordered. "This would be too much for anyone."

"He's right," Roger agreed. "You need to cut yourself a little slack."

Waylon patted her shoulder. "You'll be back up to fighting strength in no time."

"Do you think you're ready to walk us through what happened?" Roger asked.

"You don't have to if you need some time," I bit out, sounding more than a little pissed off. I was usually better at masking, hiding the rage that lived inside me. But not today. Not when someone was messing with Brae, threatening her, scaring the hell out of her.

Roger sent me a shut-the-hell-up look.

"I'd rather get it over with," Brae said quietly.

I hovered a few feet from the couch, but I wanted to go to her. Touch her. Sit next to her. Pull her onto my lap and cradle her to me. But I didn't. Because I couldn't be trusted. Not when there was this much darkness swirling inside me.

Roger pulled out his phone. "Is it okay if I record?"

Brae nodded woodenly. "Sure."

An elbow hit me square in the gut, and I turned to glower at Wylder. "What?" I hissed.

He inclined his head toward Brae. "Be there for her, asshole."

His words were only whispers, but each one hit like a carefully placed blow. I didn't respond. Couldn't. Because going to Brae now felt as risky as tangling with a grizzly.

"Then I will," Wylder clipped, starting toward her.

Some otherworldly force spurred me into action. I rounded Wylder, giving him his own elbow to the gut but a hell of a lot harder than the one he'd given me, and crossed to the couch.

Wylder doubled over, coughing. Waylon thumped his back. "You okay there?"

"Peachy," Wylder wheezed.

I lowered myself to the couch and instantly regretted it. Brae's scent wrapped around me—red currant and something I couldn't quite put my finger on. Maybe it was just the magic created when that scent came into contact with her skin. Heady and drugging, pulling me under.

Just like it had last night. When I'd lost all control and kissed her. Even though she deserved so much better than me, I hadn't been able to stop myself.

My back teeth gnashed together as I reached for Brae's empty hand. I wove my fingers through hers, trying to be a steady, grounding point and fighting to keep the rage from my grip.

Brae's golden eyes flicked up to mine. There were endless questions there, ones I had no answers to.

Roger cleared his throat, a hint of annoyance in his expression. I got it. He likely thought I'd keep her from sharing everything, from having to speak about anything that would cause her pain. But the truth was, I needed all the same information he did.

"Ready?" he asked, his voice far more gentle than his stare.

Brae nodded.

"Walk us through what happened."

Brae gripped my hand like a lifeline. Only I knew it wasn't a lifeline she should count on. She swallowed hard, her delicate throat working with the motion. "Normal day. I was getting ready to take Owen to camp and then head to work. I wanted to take my stuff to the car so I could help Owen with his."

Her fingers tightened around mine. "I wasn't thinking about anything other than how many trips it would take to get everything. And then I opened the door and saw it."

A slight tremble took root in Brae, and I couldn't help but move closer, pressing my body against hers, giving her something to lean on.

"What did you see?" Travis asked softly.

"I... It was...the necklace I gave Nova for Christmas five years ago. It's an antique. The etchings are unique—these little stars carved into it. She wore it every day. It's in every photo. Every memory. She loved it. And it was there. With blood. And that note." Brae's body shook harder.

Fuck this.

I pulled my hand from hers and wrapped an arm around her, pulling her against me as I took her empty hand with my other.

"Did you see anyone? Anything out of the norm?" Roger asked.

Brae shook her head. "I didn't see a thing."

"I'm going through the footage," Kol said, staring down at his phone as he stood opposite the couch. "Dex put cameras on all four sides of the house, including one over the door."

At my cabin, I had motion alerts. Anytime something moved within camera range, I got a notification. But Brae hadn't wanted that. She hadn't wanted to be woken at all hours because a bunny hopped by. I didn't mind that. Sleep came fitfully for me these days anyway.

Roger's gaze flicked to Kol's cell. "You'll send that to us, right?"

Even though Roger and Kol were on the same team, things got a little dicey with interagency overlap. It was a delicate dance.

"Already sent to your and Trav's emails," Kol said, not looking up.

Roger eased a fraction and turned back to Brae. "Has anything else out of the ordinary happened recently? Other than the phone call you received?"

"No, I...I can't think of anything."

Roger's lips thinned. "We've got techs going over the front porch. The gravel makes it impossible to look for tire treads, but we'll keep at it. We're gonna find this son of a bitch, B. I promise."

My grip on Brae's hand tightened reflexively.

"Nova," Brae said softly. "We need to find Nova."

Everything inside me twisted. It was the same sort of feeling that had taken hold that day all those years ago when I told Maverick we should sneak into Dad's workshop. The day I realized who he really was. Because the phone call, the necklace with the dried, caked blood... none of that told us Nova was alive. It only told us that something bad had happened to her.

A flicker of movement caught my eye, Kol's spine going ramrod straight as his expression turned thunderous.

"What?" I demanded.

"They're on the camera footage," he gritted out.

But the frustration and fury bleeding into Kol's words didn't speak of getting an ID on someone.

"I want to see," Brae demanded. There was no waver in her voice now, only pure steel.

Kol shook his head. "Brae—"

"Show me," she demanded.

A muscle fluttered in Kol's cheek, but he flipped the phone around.

We all leaned in to watch as he hit Play. There was nothing at first. Just the low light of the sconce that stood next to the door. But then a shadow flickered over the steps.

I braced as a figure moved into frame. Hooded. Baggy black sweatshirt and dark work pants that made it difficult to make out the person's size. They slid the note and necklace out of their pocket with hands covered in leather gloves. They arranged it, then rearranged it, making sure it was just so.

And then they looked up at the camera.

Like they knew exactly where it was. And it wasn't the hood of their sweatshirt covering their head. It was a mask—one of those terrifying burlap masks with black eyes and a mouth, and *X*'s crossing all of them.

The figure's head cocked one way and then the other, an animalistic quality to it. And then they lifted a hand and fucking waved.

Brae sucked in a sharp breath as she gripped my hand like a vise.

"They're fucking taunting her," Wylder snarled.

"He knew exactly where the camera was," Roger noted.

I shook my head. I wanted that to be a clue, but I knew better. "There are cameras all the way around this house, and they aren't exactly hidden. One casing at a distance and they'd know."

"He's got a point," Travis muttered, but the frustration in his voice was clear. "Then we look for other identifiers. Where'd he get that mask? Anything unique about his shoes?"

Wylder shook his head. "Might not even be a he."

Travis's face scrunched. "You think that's a woman?"

"I think we don't know. The clothes are baggy. They hide any real data of size or shape. We can't close any possibilities off until we know for sure," Wylder explained.

I forced myself to keep breathing, to not let all of this send me into a downward spiral I'd never come back from. My fingers tightened around Brae's shoulder. "I need to make a call."

Her gaze flicked up to mine. Her face had gone unnaturally pale, and the last thing I wanted to do was leave her. But it was to keep her and Owen safe. That was the only thing that could've pulled me from her at that moment.

"I'll be fine," she said hoarsely.

Such a goddamned lie. But she was lying to try to make it easier on me.

I forced my fingers to uncurl from her shoulder and release her hand. But it hurt so bad it was like peeling my flesh from my bones.

I didn't look at Brae as I stood. Instead, I looked at Kol. "Send that clip to Anson."

He jerked his head in a nod.

"Wait just a damn minute," Roger clipped, squaring his shoulders. "Who the hell is Anson? You can't bring random people into an ongoing investigation."

"He's not random," I growled. "He was one of the best profilers the BAU has ever seen. And he's going to give us insight into this bastard. So back the fuck off."

I didn't wait for a response. If Roger wanted to turn this into a pissing contest, fine. I'd just go around him.

Stalking outside, I let the back door slam. I could see Mav and Owen in the distance. They ran and whooped and shot off Nerf guns as Yeti tried to snatch the darts out of the air.

I pulled my phone from my pocket as I watched them, hitting Anson's name in my contacts. It rang four times before he answered, and I heard sawing in the background, meaning he was on a jobsite. "Dex, how the hell are you?"

There was a warmth to his tone that had never been there before. Not until he met his fiancée. Rhodes had turned my broody best friend's world upside down in the best possible way.

"Need your help." My voice had gone emotionless. It was the only way I could function at the moment, when memories were battling for supremacy.

The sawing grew fainter in the background of the call. "Talk to me."

"Got a neighbor here, new to Starlight Grove. Moved up here because her friend went missing a year ago while they were hiking the canyon. She always thought it was foul play. Local law enforcement didn't agree."

"And let me guess, they dawdled because of it," Anson surmised.

"Some resources were extended, some leads investigated, but the sheriff shuffled it off to the cold case files the minute they hit a year out. Now, my neighbor's getting threats. A call from her friend's phone with heavy breathing. Just got a bloody necklace that belonged to the friend with a note that read *How much do you miss me?*"

Anson cursed. "Blood fresh or dry?"

"Dry."

Anson was quiet for a long moment, and I knew he was thinking the same thing I was: The chances of Nova being alive were slim to none. And if she *was* alive, what had she lived through?

"Send me everything," Anson clipped. "You need me in person?"

Hell, he was a good friend. Willing to drive a good four and a half hours from Sparrow Falls, Oregon, at the drop of a hat. "Not yet. Just need your brain."

"You got it. Wylder working the victim profile?" Anson asked. He'd talked with my brother a handful of times as Wylder honed his skills. Two psych nerds going down rabbit holes.

"Yeah, he's pulling things together."

"I'll call him to get his take, too," Anson said.

"Thanks," I rasped. It was all I could say.

"How many times you get my ass out of a sling the past couple of years?"

He wasn't wrong. Anson and his now family had run into more than their fair share of trouble in Sparrow Falls. But they'd made it through. And that gave me hope that Brae would, too.

"You know I'm happy to break into any internet hidey-holes for you."

Anson chuckled. "Good to have the gray hat on my side."

He might think I was a blend of the light and the dark, but I was feeling a hell of a lot darker lately. "I'll check in later when I've sent everything over."

"Dex?"

"Yeah?"

"Watch your fuckin' back, okay? I really don't want you getting dead."

One corner of my mouth kicked up. "I'll do my best."

Anson hung up without a goodbye, like he always did, and I headed back inside. It was only to find a blustering Sheriff Miller in the middle of the living room.

"Why the hell are there civilians at my crime scene?" he snarled. "All of you get the hell out of here."

Waylon's chest puffed as he straightened his shoulders. "Oh no you don't. She's got no family around these parts, so I'm stepping in. Brae's my family now. So back off, you blowhard."

Miller's face turned tomato red. "You can't just make someone your family."

"The hell I can't. Family isn't always blood. Sometimes, it's a choice and showing up time and again. You'd know that if anyone but your blood kin could stand being in the same room with you for more than five minutes," Waylon snapped.

"He's gonna get himself arrested," Wylder mumbled.

"You watch your tone with me, you—"

"Hey, Sheriff," a younger officer cut in at the door. "Just got a call that the Lerners' cows got loose again. They're blocking traffic on the highway."

"Goddammit," Miller swore, glaring at all of us. But he stalked out the front door to deal with his new crisis.

"He's a no-show, no-answer on the radio for hours and then shows up just to throw his weight around," Travis muttered.

Waylon let out a huff. "Sounds just like the asswipe."

Brae looked up at Waylon, her eyes glittering. She hadn't let a single tear fall since I'd gotten to the cabin. Her voice and body had trembled, but she'd never given in to the tears until now.

"No one..." She swallowed and tried again. "No one has ever claimed me before. I never...I never felt like I belonged. Not with anyone but Nova."

Fuck me. Brae sliced me to the bone: with her pain, her bravery, her pure honesty. And I couldn't hold myself back from her.

I moved right to the spot I'd vacated, wrapping an arm around her shoulders again and pulling her into my side. "We're claiming you, Hellion. You belong with us now."

And, God, I wanted her as more than family. I wanted all of her. And it fucking terrified me.

CHAPTER THIRTY-TWO
Braedyn

I STRAIGHTENED FROM THE COUCH, TAKING A MOMENT TO TWIST and crack my back. There'd been far too much sitting today, and my back was paying the price.

Owen looked up from his spot on the floor, where he was currently using Yeti as a bean bag chair. "You should do some of Supernova's stretches."

An innocent suggestion and a brutal blow all at once. But he wasn't wrong. And it was a gift that he still remembered. Nova used to talk him into doing all sorts of yoga poses with her. She'd make up funny names that would make him giggle.

"Gonna downward dog with me?" I challenged.

"Naw, bruh. I'm cozy."

A soft laugh left my lips, and I held on to the vibrations and warmth. Because I would need it.

At least all the law enforcement people had left. Wylder had finally gone into the Boot to check on things after leaving Fiona in charge that morning. Waylon had to go feed the alpacas and goats, and Maverick had offered to help. Kol took off to work on submitting all the recent discoveries via a mountain of paperwork. But Dex? Dex had stayed.

It both surprised me and didn't. But that was Dex—all sorts of opposites and juxtapositions. He'd gone back and forth between taking calls and playing with Owen. He'd made us amazing BLTs for lunch, even though I'd only managed to swallow a quarter of mine.

As if responding to the lack of food, my stomach growled.

Owen laughed, his eyes on his video game. "Your stomach sounds like a monster."

I bent over and tickled his sides. "The stomach monster's gonna get you."

He twisted and squealed. "Don't make me lose!"

"Heaven forbid a life be lost on the planes of fantastical battle."

Owen righted himself as I stopped tickling and punched a few keys. "You're lucky I've got Superman reflexes."

"I guess I am." I looked out onto the back deck. Dex paced with his phone pressed to his ear. The sun was hanging low in the sky now, casting him in a golden glow he was made for. He tugged off his glasses and pinched the bridge of his nose, wincing like a headache was brewing. Then he straightened, shoving his glasses back into place and looking like nothing was wrong at all.

The sun slipped a little deeper into the horizon, and a shiver ran through me as the image of the masked man flashed in my mind. We had an alarm. Dex was right next door. Roger had promised there would be drive-bys.

But still, I didn't feel safe in my own home. And that pissed me the hell off.

It was nearly impossible to hold on to the mad when I was this tired, though. It was a bone-deep weariness completely at odds with the fact that I'd spent most of the day on the couch.

Movement caught my attention, and the back door swung open. "What're you thinking about so hard over there?" Dex asked as he strode across the space.

"Just summoning the energy to make dinner," I said with a half smile.

Dex instantly shook his head. "You don't have to worry about that."

"You already made lunch. You don't have to make dinner, too," I argued.

"I'm not." Dex's words had a finality to them.

My brow scrunched. "Well, it's not appearing out of thin air."

A knock sounded on the door, and Dex grinned. "You sure about that?"

He strode to the front door, peeking through the window before opening it and stepping aside. "Perfect timing."

A parade of Archers filed inside. Skylar led the charge, racing in and dropping to the floor next to Owen. "We missed you at camp. Is this Yeti? She's the cutest." Skylar instantly wrapped her arms around my dog's neck and shoved her face into her fur. "Dad, can we get a dog?"

"You already have a Highland cow and a goat. And there's Lucy, too," Kol said, shuffling in and setting a towel-covered baking dish on the island that separated the living area from the kitchen.

"They're Grampa Way Way's. I need a dog of my own," Skylar argued.

Kol sent me a cantankerous look. "I'm blaming you for this."

My mouth made the barest curve as if remembering I could, in fact, smile. "If you get one, I'll help you train it."

"See, Daddy? It's perfect," Skylar cried.

"Every girl needs a dog." Waylon shuffled in with a massive aluminum container, and Maverick followed, holding a pot.

Wylder brought up the rear, carrying another baking dish. "It's good security. You loooove that."

Kol scowled at his family. "You're ganging up on me."

"Hey, I didn't say a word," Mav argued. "I'll just send you adoption links."

Wylder chuckled. "Send 'em to Sky. Then he'll never stand a chance."

All the brothers and Waylon deposited their various dishes on the island.

"What is all this?" I asked.

"Comfort food," Waylon answered instantly. "After a hard day, you need comfort food. We've got fried chicken, mashed potatoes, homemade mac and cheese, rolls from scratch, and green bean casserole."

My nose stung as I worked to keep the tears from my eyes. They brought me a whole dinner. Waylon had probably been working on it since he left my house around lunchtime. Because he cared. And they all showed up, so I wasn't alone.

Before I could say a word, another knock sounded. Dex frowned, and I knew it was because he wasn't expecting anyone else. He'd shared that Orion almost never left ranch property.

Dex crossed to the door, peeking out before opening it. "Hey, Jimmy," he greeted. "What's up?"

"Orion sent in an order for a chocolate cake. Paid me thirty bucks to deliver it here," a youngish voice said from the doorway.

"Thanks, man."

"No problem. I'm saving for new wheels, so I'm never saying no to thirty."

"Good luck with that," Dex said, a smile in his voice.

"Thanks. You guys have a good night."

"You, too." Dex closed the door and headed back to the living room. "I guess we have dessert, too."

Wylder grinned at the box and then at me. "From Orion, that might as well be a hug."

It felt like one. "Thank you," I croaked. I cast a quick glance in Owen's direction to see him teaching Skylar his game, completely oblivious to the rest of us. "I didn't want to admit I was still a little unsteady at the idea of being alone."

Dex's mouth thinned into a hard line. "You're not alone, and you're not going to be alone. I'm gonna sleep on the couch until they catch this bastard."

My eyes popped comically wide. "You're what?"

Maverick slapped Dex on the back. "You might want to ask the lady first. Otherwise, it's known as breaking and entering."

Dex sent him a scowl before turning back to me. "You're gonna feel safe, Hellion."

"O-okay then." I'd just have to come to terms with the mountain-man/professor/hacker guy sleeping on my couch. Just like I'd have to live with the temptation of those lips hovering over mine—their heat and their promise. But what was one more sleepless night?

"I talked to the camp director," Kol broke in. "Let her know what was going on so they're extra careful."

I'd been planning to do that at drop-off tomorrow, but now I didn't have to. It hit me then they were all showing up in their own ways. In ways my parents never had. In ways Nova and I had tried to be for each other as much as we could. And for the first time in forever, I wondered if this was what family felt like.

CHAPTER THIRTY-THREE
Braedyn

I STOOD IN THE DOORWAY WATCHING OWEN'S CHEST RISE AND fall, his face completely slack in truly deep sleep. My lips twitched. My boy always ended up at an angle across the bed. It didn't matter that he had plenty of room to stretch out in a straight line; he always sprawled.

The blond lock of hair curling across his forehead fluttered with one of his deep exhales. He was safe. And he'd asked remarkably few questions for a kid who always had a million. I'd ended up telling him that someone had played a mean joke and scared me but that everything was okay now.

It wasn't altogether *un*true. Someone was playing with me. It was just far more twisted than I'd ever let my son know. I stared at him for just a moment longer. God, I wanted to preserve this—the innocence Owen carried with him now. But I knew it wouldn't last forever. Because the world was a balance of sweet and suck, and nothing would change that.

Closing my eyes, I shut the door, hoping my boy would hold on to the sweet. As I stepped deeper into the hallway, I heard the shower running. Everything in me stilled. Dex, in my shower.

Images flooded my brain that I had no business seeing, even in my imagination. I forced myself into the primary bedroom and shut the door behind me. "Your best friend is still missing, and there's a monster out there leaving sick trophies behind. Maybe don't think about your hot, unhinged neighbor in your shower...naked."

I scrubbed a hand over my face and hurried toward the dresser. I needed a task. Focusing on getting ready for bed seemed like the best option, one where I didn't have to hear the fall of the water against a tub or flesh.

"Think about something else. Anything else." I recited every French command I'd taught Yeti as I brushed my teeth and washed my face. I started all over again as I pulled on my coziest pajamas.

Even though it was getting into the eighties during the day, the mountain air turned cold every night. I loved it. I'd sleep with my window cracked and let that brisk air sweep through.

I stilled. I couldn't do that anymore. Not now. Instead of that scaring me, it pissed me the hell off that someone would steal my simple pleasures on top of everything else.

Then I spotted the skylight. It was something that looked like it had been added to the cabin later. Maybe in the eighties. And there was a crank to open it.

I climbed up onto the chest at the end of my bed and stretched up onto my tiptoes. I could just reach. Gripping it as best I could, I tried to turn it. Nothing.

A grunt escaped my lips as I threw more of my weight into it. The chest shifted slightly beneath me, and I let out a startled sound.

A second later, my door flew open, and a shirtless Dex was striding inside, fury lighting the gold in those hazel eyes. The fury quickly turned to confusion, but my arms were already windmilling, my balance knocked clean out from under me.

Dex moved in a flash, making it to me just as I tumbled. I hit his chest with an *oomph*, the air knocked straight from my lungs.

"What the hell were you thinking?" he barked.

"Shhh, you'll wake Owen. And what the hell were you doing barging into my room without knocking?"

"I heard sounds of a struggle."

I glared up at him, annoyed with everything. His helpfulness; his warm, hard body pressed against mine; the fact that he made me *want* for the first time in almost a decade. "I groaned. That's hardly a struggle. What if I'd been indulging in some self-care?"

Those hazel eyes lost all darkness and lit with sparks and swirls. "Hellion, you do that when we're under the same roof, and we're gonna have problems."

My jaw went slack. "You aren't serious."

"Deadly," Dex growled. He set me on my feet, his hands fisting and unfisting, making the ink across his chest ripple. His phoenix tattoo was stunning, intricate and delicate but powerful, too. Ash floated all around the creature as it took flight, its wings stretching out and reaching to the tips of Dex's shoulders.

And then I realized there was text woven through it. Names on feathers. Kol. Wylder. Orion. Maverick. All of them. Dex and his brothers, rising out of the ashes.

"Braedyn," Dex rasped. "I can't. I shouldn't have kissed you last night. Shouldn't have let myself go there."

Stinging hurt swept through me at the thought that last night's stolen moments were a mistake. Not that I hadn't experienced some flickers of doubt myself, it was just that…I didn't want those moments to be a mistake.

My gaze lifted to Dex's face, but his expression stopped me dead because there was pure torture there.

"I'm trying with everything I have not to go there," he croaked.

"Why?" The question was out of my mouth before I could consider the wisdom of it.

"It's not because I don't want to, Hellion. If I let my baser half have its way, I'd pin you to that mattress and not let you up for days."

My mouth went dry, and I pressed my thighs together as my skin started to tingle.

"Fuck," Dex muttered. "Don't do that. I can't take much more."

"Sorry?" A war of confusion swept through me.

"I'm looking out for you. My head is a fucked-up place. And you don't need that in your life. Not in that way. I'll be your friend. Owen's friend. I'll have your back. But that's all I can give."

Why did that hurt so badly? Why did it hurt when I knew he was right? The last thing I needed was the risk another relationship brought. Yet I couldn't handle him closing that door. "Don't you think I should decide what's best for me? You might have your demons, but they've made you beautiful, just like you said mine have done to me."

"Don't." The word was part plea, part demand.

"I'm not going to beg. I'm worth a hell of a lot more than that. But I'm not going to say that I don't think you're making a mistake."

Pain streaked across Dex's expression. "Don't look at me like that. It's what's best. For both of us."

I lifted my chin, a little fight, a bit of risk winding its way back. "That's what you say."

Dex's dark eyes flashed. "Hellion, you don't want the darkness that lives in me anywhere near you."

And with that, he strode from the room.

Leaving me standing there, heart breaking for the man who thought he was bad simply for where he came from. There was no greater lie than that.

I tiptoed out of my room and toward the kitchen, the early rays of sun just peeking over the forest and coming in through the back windows lighting my way. I'd been up for hours, sleep barely finding me last night. My body and mind were at war. My body only wanted one thing: for Dex's resolve to snap like a twig. All my mind could think about and see was the image of his face, ravaged by guilt over something he wasn't.

It hadn't been a restful night, to say the least. Thankfully, my coffee machine was fairly quiet. I'd make two cups and down them on the back deck until everyone was awake. But the moment I hit the kitchen, a voice cut through the dark.

"Come get your fucking dog," Dex grumbled. At least, it sounded like him, but his voice was muffled.

I crossed into the living room and flipped on a lamp. It was just enough light to see that Yeti had found a new bed. And that bed was Dex.

She was stretched out on top of him, her head burrowed next to his, and her fur practically suffocating him.

A sound of strangled amusement burst out of me.

"It's not funny."

My lips twitched. "She likes you."

Even beneath the pile of fur, I could see Dex's scowl. "How much does she weigh? Two fifty?"

"I'll have you know she's only one hundred and forty-two pounds."

Dex grunted. "Light as a feather. Now, will you get her off me?"

Yeti let out a contented sigh.

"She seems like she's having a great time."

A growl left Dex's lips. Yeti seemed to enjoy the sound because she lifted her head and licked Dex's cheek.

"Seriously?" he snarled.

I couldn't hold in my laughter this time. "I think she's in love."

"I think it's a stalker situation," Dex shot back.

I laughed as I hauled a disappointed Yeti off Dex. "Come on, girl. Gotta know when he's just not that into you." And boy, did I feel that after last night.

Yeti only sent a longing look in Dex's direction.

"She scares me," Dex muttered as he rose, running a hand through artfully rumpled hair and reaching for those damn glasses. I had to get out of here.

"She should scare you," I muttered as I led Yeti to the backyard.

By the time I got back inside, Owen was up, battering Dex with endless questions, which Dex was barely managing one-word answers to.

I grinned at him. "Not a morning person?"

"Stop smiling," he grumbled, shoving a mug of coffee at me. "There's nothing to smile about."

My grin only widened. "I don't know. I kind of like watching your feathers get ruffled."

"You're a sadist," Dex clipped.

I leaned back against the counter. "Probably."

He just glared back at me through glasses askew in a rumpled T-shirt that read *My other computer is your computer*.

God, I liked messing with him too much.

And for that reason alone, I turned to the fridge. "You know, I got you those life-threatening energy drinks you love so much the other day. You don't have to lower yourself to drinking coffee with the rest of us."

Surprise lit in Dex's dark-hazel eyes as I straightened and handed him one of the slim cans. "You got me Lightning."

The reverence he said that with almost made me laugh. "You sound like I just got you the Hope Diamond or tickets to the World Series."

His fingers brushed mine as he took the can, making a shiver skate over my skin in a dangerous way. "Might as well have gotten me a Jeter rookie card," he mumbled as he cracked open the can and took a swig.

I couldn't watch as he drank. Not those lips hugging the can or the way the corded muscles of his neck worked as he swallowed.

Nope. Nope. Nope.

Instead, I moved straight to the stove and started breakfast as Owen chattered at Dex. As the caffeine started to take effect, Dex became more responsive. By the time I set a scramble, toast, and fruit on the table, they were deep in a discussion about computers, which I only understood every fifth word of.

But there was something about the normalcy of it. The kind I'd never really had. Because even when we had Nova, she was out the door at the crack of dawn for morning yoga classes. This was new. And I liked it too much.

"All right," I said, rising to clear plates. "Get your backpack, O. We gotta get rolling."

"Aw, man," he muttered. "I wanna hang with Dex today."

Dex grinned as he stood, stilling my motion. "I am the coolest option, obviously. But we can hang tonight. I'm working on building a new computer. You can help."

Owen's eyes went wide. "Seriously?"

"Seriously."

Owen let out a wild banshee cry and raced to his room.

Dex took the plates from me, his fingers brushing mine. My gaze lifted, colliding with his before his dropped to my mouth. "You cook. I clean."

I cleared my throat. "Seems fair enough." I crossed to the junk drawer and pulled out the extra key to my cabin, anything for some distance. Anything to not smell that cedar-and-sandalwood scent. "In case you need to get in here while I'm gone."

Dex's mouth thinned, but he took it. "You want me to follow you to camp and work? Or drop you both off?"

God, that was nice. Too nice. I shook my head. "I'm good."

The hard line of Dex's mouth didn't shift. "Text me when you get there and when you head home."

I tried not to shift uncomfortably. "I'll be home right after work. Owen has a playdate after camp."

"Good." The single word sounded more like a grunt, and I rolled my eyes.

"See you later, Buttercup," I called as I grabbed my bag and ushered Owen out of the house.

The first lunch-goers at the hostess stand were a welcome sight because I'd already scrubbed every table, organized all the condiment bottles, and refilled every salt and pepper shaker. There was nothing left for me to do, which meant my mind was spinning.

I moved to head for the hostess stand, but Cora swooped in and guided the couple to their table. My face fell.

A chuckle sounded to my right. "Why do you look like someone just stole your puppy?" Wylder asked.

I sent a scowl in his direction. "I like to stay busy. Is that a crime?"

Fiona patted my shoulder as she passed behind me. "Yeah, Wylder, you'd think you'd appreciate someone here to work." She sent a pointed look at Aidan, who was leaning against the bar, scrolling on his phone.

"Hey," Aidan said, affronted. "I got no customers."

Wylder's gaze narrowed on him. "Then hit the stockroom. That's been on your task list for two weeks."

Aidan flicked Fiona a scathing look. "There will be payback."

The woman with gray sprinkled liberally through her dark hair cackled. "You don't scare me, pipsqueak."

"I gotta work on my mad-dog look," Aidan grumbled as he headed for the stockroom.

Two familiar faces appeared at the hostess stand, and I started in that direction. "I got 'em."

Aster's hair hung in loose waves that framed her face, and she wore jeans and an antique belt buckle paired with a blouse covered in pale-blue flowers. Holly had her blond hair swept back into a high bun, a few wisps falling free.

Holly didn't wait, just crossed into my space and pulled me into a hug. "Are you okay? I wanted to come over last night, but Cora said the Archers had you covered. You know you can come stay with me anytime."

It wasn't the first offer I'd gotten. Cora had suggested that Owen and I stay in her small apartment over the coffee shop, telling me she could stay with Travis in his cabin outside of town. The fact that she was willing to take me in despite her lack of space said everything about who she was and the community I found myself a part of.

"You're always welcome at mine, too. We've got a few guesthouses on the ranch also," Aster said. She was trying to keep her expression easy, but I saw the concern bleeding through.

"Thank you. Both of you. That means more than you could know. But I'm good. Dex said he'd stay at my place until all of this was over."

Both women were silent for a moment, and then Aster let out a little squeal. The sound was a burst of happiness after a trying few weeks. "You know crises can bring people together."

My cheeks heated. "It's not like that."

"Mm-hmm," Cora said with a smirk as she walked up to our group. "I bet it's not like that at all. Because a man just loves to sleep on a lumpy couch away from his nice, comfortable bed."

Aster's pale-blue eyes twinkled. "Who said he's sleeping on the couch?"

"He is!" I squeaked. "He's just being nice."

"Nice is a good start," Cora suggested.

"Just be careful," Holly warned, looking truly concerned.

Annoyance flashed through me. "Dex is an incredible man who's turned his life upside down to make me feel safe. But you can rest assured, he only sees me as a friend."

Holly's lips pursed, but she didn't say anything.

Aster frowned. "What do you mean?"

I couldn't help but stiffen. "He just won't go there. I don't think with anyone."

Sympathy washed over Aster's face. "He's carrying a hell of a weight."

"Dr. Carrington, reporting for duty," Cora quipped.

Aster sent her a quelling look. "We could all do with a little therapy in our lives. It helps us dig into who and why we are. Helps us figure out how to live better, healthier, happier."

Cora held up her arms in an X. "No, thank you. Stay out of my head, please."

I chuckled. "I'm pretty sure she's a shrink, not a mind reader."

"Thank God," Cora mumbled. "Because you do not want to know about the dream I had about Chris Hemsworth the other night."

Aster choked on a laugh. "Don't tell Travis."

Cora looked thoughtful for a moment. "I wonder if I could order him a Thor costume on the internet."

"Who's wearing a Thor costume?" Maverick's voice cut in. "You know, I have impeccable biceps."

Aster instantly stiffened, her face transforming into a hard mask. "I think you're confusing biceps for your inflated ego."

"Ouch, Ice Queen. You're feeling extra spicy today, aren't you?" Mav shot back.

"You're acting extra moronic today, so what do you expect, Satan?"

Maverick moved, wrapping an arm around me and pulling me in front of him. "Protect me from the mean lady, Little Badass."

I swore I saw a flicker of pain as Aster zeroed in on Maverick's arm around me. But she quickly covered it, squaring her shoulders. "Running scared, just like always."

I ducked out of Maverick's hold, giving him a little shove. "Do you need something, or are you just trying to start trouble?"

"Hey, I'm the innocent party here. Just stopping by to see my brother on the way to the base."

I pointed toward the bar. "Wylder's in that direction, if you haven't noticed."

Mav let out a huff. "I can see when I'm not wanted." He dipped his head. "Cora. Holly. Ice Queen."

Cora stifled a giggle, but Aster just flipped him off as Holly shook her head.

That only made Maverick grin as he headed for the bar.

The moment he was out of earshot, I turned to Aster. "What the hell is the deal with you two?"

Cora let out a low whistle.

But Aster just shook her head. "It's a long story."

I bet. "I've got time."

Her lips thinned. "Let's just say there are some things you can't forgive."

But there wasn't just anger in Aster's pale-blue eyes. There was soul-deep pain. And that left me with one question.

What the hell had happened between those two?

CHAPTER THIRTY-FOUR
Dex

I PULLED MY 4RUNNER INTO THE TRAILHEAD PARKING LOT NEXT to Kol's truck. He had something laid out over the hood and barely looked up as I pulled in. I swore he had otherworldly senses sometimes. It was like he knew the specific hum of my engine or the way my tires crunched on the gravel.

Turning off the engine, I slid out and crossed to my brother. I could see now that he had one of Orion's maps on the hood and was marking things off in pencil.

"Orion's working on an incident-specific map for us, but this is what we've got in the meantime," Kol muttered.

I knew what *incident-specific* meant: Any and all information that pertained to Nova's disappearance. Orion built one for every missing persons case we dealt with. It wasn't just things pertaining to the missing either. Similar cases were also noted. Crimes with any chance of a link to ours. Suspects' residences and places of employment.

Orion created intricate, layered maps that he scanned on a massive scanner, and I put them into our team app. We could layer each of Orion's findings as we needed. And he said it helped him with the geographic profiling of the case.

"You want to hike out and get a feel for the scene?" I asked.

Kol finally looked up. "Yeah."

As he rolled up the map and put it back in his truck, I grabbed my lightweight pack from my SUV. It wasn't as if we'd be going far, but you never knew what you'd come across. And the Archer brothers were always prepared. Well, all of us but Mav.

My pack held a satellite phone, a first-aid kit, water, energy bars, bear spray, and a SIG P226. I hated carrying it. Hated the weight it added to my pack. Despised having any sort of gun in my presence at all.

But sometimes you had to face the fear. It was why I'd mastered shooting every type of gun I could get my hands on. Why I knew how to disarm them all in a matter of seconds. Why I'd made sure I understood everything about them.

Because with that knowledge, the gun lost its power. Or at least that was what I'd hoped would happen. But every time I fired one, a flash of memory hit.

Orion squeezing the trigger. The shock on Dad's face as he stumbled back. The knife clattering from his hand. So much blood.

"You good?" Kol's voice cut into the memories.

I tightened the straps on my pack. "Yup."

It was a lie, and we both knew it. But Kol didn't push. He never did. He simply adjusted his own pack and started for the trail.

Normally, I'd take a second to appreciate the fresh air, the way the trees made an almost tunnel over the path, and the smattering of wildflowers in full bloom. But not today. Today, my head was focused on a missing woman…and on Brae—even if I tried to point it anywhere else.

"How were Brae and Owen this morning?" Kol asked, bringing me right back to the place I was trying to avoid.

But I had to appreciate that his question was a hell of a turnaround from refusing to help and cursing me for wanting to. But I didn't mention it. That would just turn Kol into a grizzly with a thorn in his paw. "Good. Kids are resilient, man. Owen was chatting my head off about backdoors into mainframes and remote access tools."

Kol chuckled as he scanned his surroundings, always looking for the things I couldn't see. "Please, do not get that kid arrested for hacking at age eight."

My lips twitched. "Who, me?"

"Jesus," Kol muttered.

I laughed.

"And Brae's holding up?" Kol pressed.

God, he was good. Cantankerous and guarded, but once you got behind his walls, Kol would protect you with everything he had. And Brae and Owen were starting to crack those shields.

"She's holding it together but trying to hide how much this fucks her up."

"How could it not?" Kol said, his voice low. "Whoever's doing this is seriously twisted."

The words had my heart picking up speed to that anxious, fluttering beat. I had the ridiculous urge to turn around and drive into town just to check on Brae. *She's fine.* I spoke the words silently, over and over, until I finally pulled out my phone.

Barely any bars, but I managed to get off a text.

> **Me:** *All good?*
>
> **Wylder:** *Besides Mav ruffling Aster's feathers and nearly getting an iced tea poured on his head? Just peachy.*
>
> **Me:** *What the hell is wrong with him?*
>
> **Wylder:** *Maybe he's a masochist.*
>
> **Me:** *Or he just likes Aster's brand of pain.*
>
> **Wylder:** *Maybe.*
>
> **Me:** *Brae's good?*

Pressing for info on her specifically was telling, and I knew it, but I wouldn't be able to focus if I didn't ask. And I needed my brain pointed in one direction—one that wasn't Brae-centric.

> **Wylder:** *Your girl's good. I got her back.*

Your girl. Fuck me, that sounded way too good. I shoved the sensation down, locking it away with the stew of emotions I never let myself truly feel—nothing too bad but nothing too good either. I needed to live in the stable middle.

"This is it," Kol called, looking down at his GPS.

That pulled my head out of my ass and into the present where it needed to be.

Kol pulled out his phone and selected Nova's bio in our casefile app. It had a handful of photos of her, along with height, weight, and identifying features. Kol always wanted that information fresh because he said it impacted the trail someone might leave behind.

"Brae said she went off the trail toward the water to get a photo of the wildflowers. That's gotta be here." I could just make out the pops of peach poppies through the trees. The little bed of them grew in the one patch of unfiltered sunlight a ways up from the riverbank.

It made sense. Poppies needed plenty of sun to grow, and it was rare to find them in forested areas. But these had found a way.

"Let's find her trail first." Kol shoved his phone into his pocket and headed for the break in the brush.

A year after the incident, there wouldn't be anything Brae left behind. There'd been rain, snow, and sun in heavy rotation since then. Wildlife would've tracked through. Possibly people, too.

But there were still things Kol would see—stuff the rest of us would miss. He'd told me once that it was like his mind saw all the infinite possibilities and then narrowed them down based on likelihood, as if he were constantly running a math equation.

Kol crouched low before stepping off the path. He cocked his head one way and then the other, taking it all in. He pointed in one direction. "Underbrush is broken down through here. My guess is that more than one person was lured off the trail by the wildflowers."

Kol led the way, taking note of some broken branches and trampled earth. We spotted a few slide marks that told us how easy it would've been for Brae to slip. And if Nova had wandered off trail, too, she might've fallen into the river. But it didn't explain her water bottle in the parking lot or someone having her phone and necklace. It didn't explain the dried blood.

And it wasn't logical. If Nova moved off trail toward the river, she would've followed Brae. And Brae would've heard her.

After studying where the makeshift trail came to an end, we turned around and headed back up the embankment. But as we did, I heard a muttered curse.

Kol's hand went to the butt of his gun as he put a finger to his lips. He moved stealthily up the trail, then frowned. "Sheriff Miller?"

The man whirled around, his hand going to the butt of his weapon as well, as his mustache twitched wildly. "Jesus, Kol. Make a little noise, would ya?"

Kol frowned as we stepped out onto the trail. "What are you doing out here?"

Miller's eyes shifted to the side in that cagey way of his, and I thought he'd tell us to get lost or something more colorful. But he didn't. Instead, he sighed and scrubbed a hand over his face. "I fucked up."

I stiffened, bracing for whatever was to come.

"I thought she was just a flighty tourist, in over her head, and got herself killed. I was wrong. So I'm trying to start from the beginning," Miller muttered. "Wanted to walk the trail they did to get a feel."

The same thing we were doing. Because Miller had good skills behind the assholishness. He just needed to be motivated to use them.

"We're doing the same," Kol said gruffly.

Miller jerked his head in a nod. "Let me know if you come up with anything helpful. I gotta get back to the station."

He headed down the trail toward the parking area without another word. I turned to Kol. "What the hell was that? Did Miller grow a heart?"

Kol watched the sheriff go. "I guess miracles do happen."

Setting the grocery bags on Brae's kitchen counter, I slid an earbud into one ear and then hit Anson's name in my contacts.

"About time," he answered.

"Nice to talk to you, too," I grumbled.

"Where were you?"

"Grocery shopping. Are you my jealous husband now?" I sniped.

Anson chuckled. "I think I've got all I can handle with Rhodes."

His soon-to-be wife was certainly a handful, and there was a reason he'd nicknamed her Reckless. But she also lit his whole world.

I started pulling out ingredients for a make-your-own-pizza night. It had been one of my favorites growing up—one of the few memories of my mom I clung to. She made a scoreboard, marking us all on presentation, flavor, and creativity. Now, I'd give that to Owen.

"You have a chance to look at everything?" I asked.

"Going through it all a third time now." Anson's brain and Kol's brain worked in similar ways but on completely different planes.

Kol looked at the physical, nature. Anson looked at the human mind. But they both saw patterns and trails the rest of us missed.

"And?" I pressed.

"I'm not sure."

I could hear the frustration in Anson's voice. It was something I rarely had to identify with him because he always had it all figured out. I placed the dough in the fridge and straightened. "Talk it out. What's holding you up?"

"The victims. There are zero common threads if you look at local missing persons cases."

I frowned but kept unpacking bags: veggies, pepperoni, hot peppers, olives. "Could one or two of them be skewing the profile?"

One incorrect victim in a pool could send you in a completely wrong direction. A few could be a disaster.

"Maybe," Anson muttered. "But even if I removed all the males, there's not a through line with the women. Different ages, races, and hair and eye color. Usually, a serial offender has a type."

"Crimes of opportunity?" I pulled out the pizza sauce and set it on the counter.

"Maybe. But they'd need a hell of a lot of patience. Typically, that wanes, too. The unsub gets more reckless."

"Isn't that what they're doing now? Calling Brae from Nova's phone? Leaving the necklace and note? That's escalation."

"I guess you do listen to what I try to teach you," Anson said, a hint of humor in his voice.

I scowled down at my phone. "Fuck off."

"You're right. That make you feel better?"

"No. No, it doesn't."

Anson sobered. "We'll figure out who's doing this. I had a thought. But it's a risk."

I straightened, setting down the pack of ricotta. "Tell me."

"You have that friend who does the podcast. *Sounds Like Serial*."

In my work with missing persons, my path had crossed with a true crime podcaster on a mission to give a voice to the forgotten. Ridley Sawyer fought for victims and their families with everything she had.

"What about her?" I asked.

"I wonder if she could do an episode on the case. You know how she does those one-offs between her deep dives."

"Didn't know you were a fanboy. Want me to get you an autograph?"

"I'm trying to help your ornery ass," Anson griped.

"I know. I know. It's not a bad idea. Could flush out new information."

Anson was silent for a moment.

I stilled, a weight settling deep. "That's not why you want me to do it."

"I think it could spook the unsub, or they could like the attention and want more, do something to get it."

"You're trying to get them to make a mistake," I surmised.

"Yes. But you'd have to keep a close eye on Brae, make sure she doesn't become a target."

My back molars ground together. "I'll think about it."

"That's your polite way of saying get fucked."

I scrubbed a hand over my face. "I'll think about it. And thank you for looking at all this."

"I'll keep looking. Maybe I'll find something new."

"Yeah. Appreciate it."

Anson hung up before I could thank him again. He hated gratitude. But when I looked at my phone, I frowned.

It was almost five. Owen had a playdate, so Brae should've been home forty-five minutes ago.

A sick feeling slid through me. I called her phone. It rang and rang before going to voicemail. I tried again. Same thing.

All I could think was one thing.

Escalation.

CHAPTER THIRTY-FIVE
Braedyn

HOLLY GRINNED OVER AT ME AS SHE SWUNG HER TOTE, WHICH was some sort of hybrid between a basket and a bag. "I'm so glad you said yes."

"I'm so glad you asked. I used to go to the Oakland farmers' market every Saturday but haven't gotten it together to find one here." As we turned a corner onto one of the side streets in Starlight Grove, my lips parted in a soft gasp.

"Pretty adorable, huh?" Holly asked.

"Understatement." But I didn't look at her. I couldn't. I was too busy taking in all the amazing stalls. The market was smaller than the ones I frequented in Oakland, but it made up for that in charm. And the variety was incredible.

A beekeeper's stand with honey and honey-infused products. A few more traditional farms. A bread stand that smelled heavenly. One that specialized in cupcakes.

This was just what I needed: an afternoon with a new friend. I'd checked on Owen before shoving my phone into the recesses of my bag where it wouldn't taunt me. Because Vincent was getting frustrated with my lack of response, maybe even angry.

When I hadn't been able to sleep last night, I'd posted a photo of Mount Lupine and Yeti in the distance. It was a ways away from the cabin, but the first comment had popped up.

VF2099: *Starlight Grove. Interesting.*

Most wouldn't have read it as a threat, but I knew the subtext. *I know where you are.* Unease trickled through me, but I reminded myself that he'd never once done anything other than dropping a harassing threat by comment or email. He simply wanted me to know he saw all my failings.

VicFab42: *Must be hard to lose everything.*

Anger surged at the memory. He likely mocked the idea of every hardship we had to endure. And why? I hadn't asked him for a single thing. Instead, I'd scrimped and saved, always putting Owen's needs first and working myself to the bone. But we'd made it.

A gentle hand touched my forearm. "Are you okay?"

I startled slightly but let out a breath, realizing it was just Holly. "Sorry. I was in another world."

Her brows pulled together. Holly had at least ten years on me, but you'd never know it if it weren't for the few wisps of gray threaded through the blond at her temples. "Worrying about Nova?"

Guilt swirled because I hadn't been. That's where my mind should've been focused. Instead, it had been selfishly focused inward. "My ex, actually. Just being a douchebag of epic proportions."

A hint of surprise found Holly's green eyes. "Is he involved in your and Owen's lives?"

I shook my head. "No. By his own choice. But he sends messages every now and then. And they're asshole-ish."

Her mouth thinned into a hard line. "Neither of you deserve that."

"Owen doesn't know," I assured her as we moved into a farmer's stall and mulled over the produce.

"But you do. Have you tried blocking him?"

I went for some fresh arugula and heirloom tomatoes, a meal pulling together in my mind. "He just starts new accounts. I've realized simply hiding the comments and ignoring him annoys him the most."

Holly chuckled at that. "Men and their egos."

I grinned. "The ultimate weakness." I moved to the cheese stand next door and eyed some burrata. "What about your ex? Are things amicable?"

She lifted a shoulder and then dropped it as she picked up a pecorino. "It's a silent fury. Like we're both so mad that the other couldn't be what we needed."

"I'm sorry," I said softly.

"We couldn't recover. Losing our boy. It was too much. There was so much rage. Mostly at ourselves, but the occasional explosions at each other were more than we could take."

I reached over and took Holly's hand, squeezing it gently. She still wore a wedding band on her finger. Even after the years that had passed. I didn't have words to comfort her, but I had my presence.

Holly squeezed my hand in return and then straightened. "You know what we need?"

I arched a brow. "A shot?"

She laughed, light and airy, as if we hadn't just delved into such heavy topics. "Cupcakes."

I grinned back at her. "I'm in."

My SUV bumped over the gravel road as I made the turn toward Creekside Cabins and the place that was now home. As I pulled to a stop in front of Cabin Two, I found Dex scowling at my vehicle, a phone pressed to his ear.

My stomach plummeted. I quickly shut off the engine, leaving my bag of produce in the passenger seat and hopping out.

"Yeah, she's here." Dex's eyes scanned me from head to toe. "She looks fine."

He seemed supremely annoyed with that fact.

"Thanks, Kol. Later." Dex shoved the phone into his pocket, his scowl deepening to a glare.

"What did I do?" I asked.

"Where the hell have you been?"

My eyes flared in surprise. "I was at the farmers' market. Do you have a thing against fresh tomatoes and cupcakes that look so fluffy they could fly away?"

"Why. The. Hell. Didn't. You. Pick. Up. Your. Phone?" Each word was forced out through gritted teeth as Dex jerked a hand through his hair.

Oh crap.

I shifted, a flicker of guilt sliding through me.

"Yeah," Dex bit out. "That little device people try to reach you on."

I lifted my chin. "I didn't know I had a keeper."

"You have someone who's looking out for you. And it'd be nice if you didn't scare the hell out of them. Or told them you would be an hour later than you thought."

I bristled at the demand. It felt too similar to commands of the past.

Get rid of it. I'm not going to have a bastard as a son, and I'm sure as hell not marrying you.

Get out of town. We don't need to be publicly humiliated that our daughter's a whore.

You need to give the baby up. Then maybe you'll have a chance at an honorable life.

I'd been told to do this or that so many times. Ordered around like I didn't have a mind of my own. A glare slid over my features. "I've been taking care of myself for a long time, Dex. And I wasn't aware I had to report my location to you twenty-four-seven."

Those dark-hazel eyes flashed. "I don't know if you remember, but some maniac left a bloody fucking necklace on your doorstep. And a note that most would consider threatening."

"I didn't forget," I hissed. "I live with it every moment of the day, playing it over and over."

"Then act like you remember it," Dex clipped.

"I'm not used to people needing to know where I am, all right?"

That only seemed to make Dex madder. "People care about you, Brae. *I* care about you."

Shit. My actual name. No Hellion, just Brae. And that stung. But the words that followed were the most painful bomb. He *cared*. And he'd spat the words like grenades.

"Why do you sound so mad about it?" I challenged.

"Because I am," he snapped.

Those fathomless eyes tracked over my face, some unreadable emotion there.

"Fuck it," he growled. And then he was on me, closing the distance in four long strides. There was no hesitation, no worry about what it might mean.

Dex's hands slid through my hair with a forcefulness that had a wave of shivers cascading over my skin—the kind that meant all of me was paying attention. Those strong, thick fingers tightened in the strands, tugging my head back.

"Tell me to stop," Dex gritted out, his eyes going stormy—the kind of storm that threatened to leave wreckage in its wake.

"What if I don't want you to?"

"Hellion." The word was pure warning.

"Burn it out, Dex. Burn it all out."

It was all he needed. Dex took my mouth like a man starved. There was no easing into the kiss. It was nothing like the stolen, tender moments of before. There was only sharp demand and desperate need. And God, I needed it. To let out some of what had been stewing inside me: the good, the bad, the fear, the hope.

There was so much there that I never gave voice to. That was stewing and swirling. That I carried alone.

I gave it all to Dex now.

I poured everything I had into the kiss, giving as good as I got. Our tongues twisted and twirled, battling for supremacy. Dex's free hand cupped my ass, lifting me. My legs encircled his waist on instinct, clamping around him and holding on, letting out more of everything I held inside.

I pressed myself harder against him, rocking, needing the friction.

He groaned into my mouth as he turned and carried me toward the house. But he didn't lose my mouth even once.

Dex fumbled with the door handle, maneuvering us inside. My hands sank into his hair, tugging silently, begging for more but not being able to give words to what that *more* was.

We knocked into a wall, sending a painting crashing to the floor as Dex stumbled with me into the living room. I only gripped his hair harder, hoping the painting hadn't been damaged but not exactly worrying about what kind of dent that could put in my savings.

Yeti let out a bark, and Dex's head twisted in her direction. "Bed," he ordered, sending my dog running for her place in my bedroom.

Dex's hand slipped from my hair, moving to my blouse, beneath it. My nipples pebbled against the lace of my bralette. It was almost painful, the way they strained for him. His mouth, his touch.

My legs tightened around Dex's waist as he tugged at the shirt. I lifted my arms, trying to help, and he sent the fabric sailing to the floor. His eyes went hooded as they zeroed in on my breasts.

"So fucking pretty. Taut, little nipples. Dusky pink and goddamn perfect." Dex's head bent, his mouth closing around one peak through the thin lace. He sucked deep, and I lost all sense of space and time.

My back arched as a soft mewl left my lips. Dex sucked harder, and then his teeth grazed the tight bud. I let out a whimper as a flush of wet heat gathered between my legs.

My breaths turned to quick pants. A buzz lit beneath my skin, and my gaze went a little fuzzy.

"Taste like red currant and vanilla. Could live on that taste and nothing else," Dex whispered against my skin.

I struggled for sanity, to right myself, but I didn't want to.

Dex lowered me to the couch—the same one he'd slept on the night before. As he straightened, his gaze zeroed in on my rib cage—the tattoo there. The phoenix. Delicate yet infinitely powerful.

There were no ashes in my tattoo, simply a creature taking flight after crossing through from the other side. Dex's throat worked as he swallowed and then traced the outline with featherlight fingertips. "It's like you understood me before we even met."

Fear tried to take root, but I shoved it down, pushed it out. I reached up, grabbing for Dex. I needed to let it out…into him. The desperate edge was back, the need to lose myself and everything that held me down.

Dex broke away for a moment, tugging his tee over his head and tossing it to the floor. His phoenix stared back at me—the one that could hold me captive. The one that taunted me with a bond both Dex and I were terrified of but couldn't ignore.

It was too tempting not to touch. My fingers ran over his chest, through the dusting of hair that only made the tattoo feel more real. As if the creature could take flight and swallow me whole.

But I wanted it to. I wanted to lose myself in all that was Dex.

His fingers found the button of my jeans, and I felt the first hesitation, the slight panic bleeding through the haze of need. It was as if Dex read it before I did.

"Stop?" he asked. There was no annoyance or anger. So unlike Vincent, who didn't care what I wanted. He'd thought he had rights to me anytime he wanted.

"I haven't…not since Owen was born. And my body…it's…" I didn't know how to put words to the fears and insecurities.

Dex's face softened as his fingers deftly unbuttoned my jeans. They were the kind that came up to my belly button. The kind that hid the marks and scars.

Dex's fingers skimmed just under the waistband. Back and forth. Featherlight. "You're changed because you brought life into the world. Can't think of anything more beautiful than that."

My mouth went dry as I struggled to swallow. "Dex."

He peeled down one side of my jeans, revealing the streaks along my belly and hip. They'd turned from deep red to the palest white over the years. But against my golden skin, they stood out clear as day.

"Phoenix wings," Dex whispered as he dropped to his knees. His lips hovered over the changed flesh, and then he skimmed across the marks as he spoke. "Carried you through battle and the aftermath. Carried your boy and carried you. Most beautiful sight of all."

Everything burned. Like I was turning into the very creature Dex spoke of.

My fingers clutched at his shoulders. Broad. Strong. And adorned with the wings he described on me.

"Tell me you want this. Tell me you need it, consequences be damned."

My breaths came quicker now. Fast, sharp pants as black dots danced in front of my vision. "I want everything," I rasped. Because I was greedy when it came to Dex Archer. I didn't want just his fingers or his mouth. I needed to know how it felt to have him moving inside me, stretching me, taking everything he had to give.

"Never heard anything sweeter," Dex growled. "And I'm going to give it to you. I want to hear those throaty, little moans as you shatter. I want to *feel* them."

My thighs clenched on instinct as more wetness gathered. More heat. More need.

"Not yet, baby." Dex ran his knuckles along the seam of my jeans. I nearly came apart right there. Sparks danced through me as the black spots intensified. He made the move again. "Soon."

And then, Dex's fingers were in the band of my jeans and boy shorts. He yanked them down in a move so smooth I would've thought it impossible. He lifted one leg out and then the other.

"So damn beautiful, spread out for me." Dex adjusted his glasses, and I moved to try to close my legs, but Dex was in the way. His gaze snapped to my face. "Don't steal this from me. This work of art. Perfect pussy and phoenix wings."

My breaths tripped and tangled, but I didn't try to close my legs again.

Dex grinned. "That's my girl. Giving me all I want. Giving you all you need."

A single finger slid through my wet heat, and my hips arched up to meet him as my jaw opened in a silent plea.

Dex's fingers swiped over me again, two this time, as his other hand trailed up between my breasts to collar my throat. But it didn't stay there. It slid to the side, to my pulse point.

Those two fingers slowly thrust inside me, and I couldn't hold back my moan.

"Don't come." The words were an order and a plea. "The first time you come, I'm gonna feel you flutter on my cock, wanna feel every ounce of fire. We're gonna fly together."

My inner walls clamped down on Dex's fingers as they swirled inside me.

I shuddered as he stretched me. "I can't—I—"

"You can," Dex ordered. "I can feel you here." His fingers swirled again. "And I can feel you here." His hand pressed to the side of my throat. "We're going to walk right up to that breaking point. We're gonna feel it all."

I clamped down on those fingers inside me, my whole body shuddering this time.

"You're close. Almost ready for me."

My hips lifted, rising to meet Dex's fingers. They felt so damn good but were so far from what I wanted. I let out a sound of frustration.

"In a hurry, Hellion?"

I fought the urge to bare my teeth at him. "Yes."

A low, throaty chuckle left Dex and skated over my skin. "Not quite yet." His fingers thrust deeper this time, rotating and curling, pressing on a spot that had light flickering over my vision.

"Now, you're there," Dex growled, his hand clamping over my throat. I could feel my pulse hammering against the pressure of his palm.

And then it was all gone. The grip of him at my throat. Those beautiful fingers moving inside me.

I let out a sound of protest that had Dex chuckling again. Then he made a tsking sound. "Patience."

This time, I growled at him, but the sound halted in my throat as Dex's fingers went to the button of his jeans. He kicked off one boot and then the other as he deftly unbuttoned his pants.

He searched for something. His wallet, I realized. A small foil packet.

My throat went dry, and my eyes burned as they zeroed in on the packet.

"Always gonna make sure you're safe," Dex rasped as he shucked his pants.

He didn't know what that meant to me. With my one and only partner being someone who never thought about my safety and well-being, this meant everything.

Dex rolled the condom onto his thick length, and my mouth went dry for a different reason, my thighs pressing together. It was nearly more than I could take.

And then he was back, that big body covering mine, my legs hooking around him. Dex searched my eyes. "Yes?"

"Yes," I breathed.

He didn't wait. He slid inside me on one long glide, hissing as his hazel eyes flashed. My head tipped back against the couch, my body arching, meeting him there.

It was almost more than I could take. Pressure. Heat. That stretch.

Dex's body quivered. With restraint, I realized. Holding himself back. Another gift. Suffering to give me time to adjust, to ease into him.

The sting melted to only heat as Dex's hand slid over my throat, finding that pulse point again. Staying there. He read the beat of my body and didn't move until he felt some change.

As every ounce of discomfort left me and just as desperation edged in, Dex began to move. He kicked off the rhythm, the dance, but I found him there. My body met his, letting his thrusts deepen, claiming all of me.

Dex let out a low moan as he sank into me. "Everything I could've dreamed of."

My fingers tightened on his shoulders, digging in as he picked up the pace. "More."

Those dark eyes flashed. "Told you I'd give you whatever you needed."

Dex thrust into me with more power this time, a strength that was almost otherworldly. One hand braced above my head, the other on my throat. "Show me how you fly. Let me feel you."

Everything went hazy as my entire body vibrated. Power and heat. Pressure and that final spark.

"Fingers on your clit," Dex barked. "Now."

I didn't think. I listened. A single circle around that bundle of nerves, and I was lost. Splintering in a way that was beautiful and painful all at once as Dex arched into me again, releasing. And I felt it all. I came apart with a force I'd never known. One I knew would change everything.

CHAPTER THIRTY-SIX
Dex

THE STEADY BEAT OF BRAE'S HEART THUMPED AGAINST MINE. Calmer now. More relaxed. It was like we'd done battle, said things in a shared language without saying a single word.

My fingers trailed over her back, tracing an invisible design. A clock, I realized. There was something to that—the steady tick of time, the thing it felt we were racing against in so many ways. Because what would happen when my lease was up at the end of the summer? Designs might be underway for my house at the ranch, but I sure as hell wouldn't be living next door. What would happen when we found the asshole messing with Brae? The one who'd hurt Nova?

I breathed out those worries and kept tracing the clock—the one I'd built with Waylon all those years ago. The one he'd used to get me talking, sharing. He was wise that way.

And just like then, I started talking now. "I was scared. Scared something had happened to you."

Brae lifted her head and looked at me for a moment with those golden eyes before settling back into the crook of my neck. "I'm sorry. It was dumb. I'm not used to checking in with anyone other than Owen. Not since…"

Her voice trailed off, but I knew what she meant. Not since Nova disappeared.

Brae cleared her throat. "I'd checked on Owen right before I went to the farmers' market, so I didn't think about someone else trying to get ahold of me."

I traced the intricate antique hands of the invisible clock, the pieces salvaged from one ruined piece but given new life. "I don't want to be scared for someone."

Shame washed over me as I spoke the words aloud. But they were one of my deepest truths. The ones I never gave voice to. "I was furious that you made me care."

Brae's palm pressed against the wing of my tattoo. "I get that fear. Mine's different, but it lives in me. Caring about someone who will disappear."

My breaths started coming quicker. I barely finished an exhale before my body was trying to suck in air all over again. The muscles in my forearms started to tighten painfully as if curling in on each other. Images flashed in my mind. All the what-ifs. All the things swirling around Brae.

"Hey," she bit out, her voice a stinging slap as she moved to straddle me, framing my face with her hands. "Dex. Look at me. Just like you taught me. Breathe with me."

She lifted my hand to her chest, laying it over the delicate lace of her bra, the only thing covering her. "You're with me," she commanded.

Pure truth. I was with her, and it scared the hell out of me. I sucked in a pained breath as Brae's chest rose. I exhaled, feeling like I was expelling shards of glass from my lungs instead of air.

"With me." Brae pressed my palm harder against her chest. "Look at me. Breathe with me."

The next breath was a little less painful, but I still had to battle for it. Brae didn't rush me. In and out. Over and over.

My lungs slowly unlocked, and there was no pain, only the residual ache of a panic attack—the ache that came from overusing muscles.

Brae's thumbs stroked my stubbled cheeks. "There he is."

She came into clearer view then: her phoenix on her rib cage, the wings fluttering over her lower belly and hips. Beauty and power. Fighting for me.

"You terrify me."

One corner of Brae's mouth kicked up. "I'm going to take that as a compliment."

I barked out a laugh that sounded like I'd just smoked a pack of cigarettes. "You would, Hellion."

Her smile came easier, but there was a tinge of sadness. "I don't know if I'll ever fully trust again. And I know why. Vincent, my ex, bailing on Owen...on me when I wouldn't get an abortion. My parents tossing me to the curb. Nova vanishing." Her voice cracked on the last sentence. "They all left. Even if Nova didn't have a choice. It marked me. Changed me. Made it hard for me to lean. I don't know if I'll ever be ready for a true partnership again."

"I told myself I'd never get married. Never have a family. That I wouldn't risk becoming what my father was and destroying the people I loved most."

Grief flooded Brae's face. Her grip tightened on my cheeks. "You will never become him."

"You don't know—"

"I do." Brae leaned in, getting right up in my face. "I know because of who you show up to be, even on your worst day."

"Hellion—"

"Be logical," she snapped. "I've studied the psychology of killers. You hurt defenseless animals and like it?"

My face screwed up. "No."

"You have a thing for setting fires?"

I knew the signs she was listing off. A sort of checklist I'd heard from profilers at the BAU.

"Do you?" she pressed.

"No," I clipped.

"I know you care about others, have empathy for them, because you're helping me, even when it gets you into trouble."

I didn't say a word in response.

Brae let out a huff of annoyance. "And I sure as hell know you harbor zero superficial charm. There's a scowl twisting your lips so often I wonder if you even know how to smile."

"Hey." I jackknifed into a sitting position, bringing us face-to-face. "I'll have you know I was damn cheery before you came along. My friends and family would say the same."

Brae stared at me and then burst out laughing. The sound was so fucking beautiful, and I felt it as much as I heard it. It invaded me.

"What?" I clipped, fighting off the takeover.

Her golden eyes danced and glistened. "Buttercup, you got grumpy because you like me."

"Shut up," I grumbled.

Brae's smile only widened. "You *really* like me."

I snapped my mouth closed because I more than liked her and I fucking knew it. She owned me.

The laugh was back. "Who would've thought this was my vengeance for you breaking into my cabin?"

I glared back at her. "The threat of pepper spray and that damn dog almost taking my balls wasn't enough?"

Brae just beamed. "Never enough. You being forced into liking me and being all scowly about it is, though."

"You're never going to let me live this down now, are you?"

"Nope," she said, popping the *p*.

The sound of tires on gravel had us both turning to the front windows and peeking through gauzy curtains.

"Oh shit," Brae squealed, hopping off me and causing me to utter a pained curse.

"Now, my balls are on the revenge list, too."

"That's Aster's truck. Owen's home!" she hissed like we were in a library.

It took a second for the words to hit. But when they did, I cursed again and leapt from the couch.

We scrambled for clothes, tossing each other the other's jeans as we dressed in some haphazard dance. A knock sounded on the door.

"Fuck, fuck, fuck!" Brae swore.

"Now that's not polite," I teased.

Yeti let out a bark, running from the back room toward the door.

"Coming!" Brae called as she buttoned her jeans.

"No, you aren't, but you were earlier."

The look she scalded me with should've fried me on the spot, but I just laughed as I pulled on my tee, and Brae rushed to the door.

She hauled it open, out of breath. "Owen. Hi."

He looked up at his mom, a little confused at her higher-pitched tone.

"Thanks for dropping him off, Aster," she went on.

She did a head-to-toe sweep of Brae and tried to fight a knowing smile. "No problem."

"Mom, why's that painting on the floor? And, Dex, your shirt's on inside out," Owen said as he stepped inside.

Aster choked on a laugh. "You just let me know anytime you need a little afternoon…break."

"Aster," I warned.

"Hey," she shot back. "I'm just looking out for a sister."

"Get in your rig," I ordered, shaking my head as I spotted her nephew, Eli, watching us in the doorway. "Or I'll tell Mav you asked for him to stop by."

She glared at me. "You do that, make sure to tell him I shoot trespassers."

"I think he'd risk the bullet," I called as she walked away.

Brae just shook her head. "You're a troublemaker."

I leaned in, dangerously close. "You have no idea."

CHAPTER THIRTY-SEVEN
Braedyn

OWEN WOULD NOT STOP TALKING ABOUT DEX AND HIS INSIDE-out shirt. He thought it was *hilarious*. He wanted to know if he'd had it on that way the whole day, why no one had told him, if he was trying to start a new trend.

And every time Owen brought it up, Dex would look at me and wink. The bastard.

Even the next day, Owen didn't let it drop. "At least you have your shirt on the right way now," he called to Dex as he got out and headed to camp.

Dex choked on a laugh as he gave my son a thumbs-up and winked at me. *Again*.

"It's not funny," I hissed from my spot in the passenger seat.

Dex navigated my SUV away from the rec center and toward town, a cocky-as-hell grin twisting his lips. "I mean, it's a little funny. Owen thought there might've been an earthquake he missed."

My lips thinned. Thankfully, Owen's mind hadn't gone to the truth of the situation—not that it would at his age, but the paranoia was real. "You're real freaking lucky the only one who truly knows is Aster."

A low chuckle left Dex's lips. "Aster does have friends."

A curse slipped free, and Dex only laughed more. But anxiety dug its icy claws into my sides, making it harder to breathe.

"Hey," Dex said softly, reaching over and laying a hand over mine. That steady pressure. That heat.

I wanted to lean into both. I wanted to trust that they'd always be there when I needed them. But I didn't trust anyone, myself most of all. Because no one I bet on had stayed. God, I felt like the worst kind of human, even thinking that about Nova.

None of it was her fault. Not in the slightest. Yet I still felt the sting of betrayal. The agony of losing her.

Dex swung into one of the parking spots behind the Boot and shut off the engine. But he didn't move his hand from mine. His fingers didn't slide through mine. He didn't push for more. He simply showed me he was there. "Talk to me."

"What are we doing?" The whisper was a cannon in the SUV, echoing around and bouncing off every surface. "I have a son—one growing incredibly fond of you."

Owen had started copying everything Dex did, down to asking me to buy him some hacker T-shirts. He was the first man he'd ever really had in his life on a consistent basis. And it scared the hell out of me to think what might happen if this all blew up.

"You think I'll bail on Owen?" Dex challenged.

"I think if I piss you off or become someone you don't like very much, it'll be hard for you *not* to do that."

His perfect mouth thinned. "I don't bail. Your kid is cool as hell. I like teaching him about computers and listening to his endless questions. His mind works different than mine, and I learn just as much from him. He's amazing and deserves all the people who care about him in his life."

Crap. Crap. Crap.

My nose stung. "He's the best."

Dex squeezed my hand. "He is. But I don't think this is really about him."

My heart thudded against my rib cage in that pulsing two-toned beat. "You don't want a family. I can't trust a soul. That's a recipe for disaster."

A muscle popped in Dex's cheek. "Maybe."

I looked up into those shadowy eyes. "How's it not?"

His gaze held mine for a long moment as if he, too, were looking for answers. "Maybe we figure out how to do both."

My heart picked up speed. Fear and hope spurred the beats along like a rider pressing their heels into a horse's flanks. "I don't want to force you into something you don't want."

"Never said I didn't want it. Said I wasn't ever going to reach for it."

That racing heart of mine shattered then for the man who wanted but never let himself take. Living a half-life all this time. "Dex." His name was more breath than word.

"I think we take it one day at a time. You don't want Owen to know? I get that. We'll figure it out. Otherwise, one day at a time."

I swallowed, trying to clear the fear still clinging to my insides. "One day at a time."

"That's my girl." Dex leaned over and brushed his lips feather-light against mine.

It was the first time he'd kissed me since the incident yesterday. And this one felt more real somehow. Not a heated moment where we'd lost control but a choice.

"I have to go to work," I whispered against his lips.

Dex's fingers slid into my hair. "I know the boss. I can get you a day off."

I laughed, the sound ping-ponging between us. "I'm not leaving Wylder in the lurch."

"Yeah, yeah, you're all responsible." Dex released me, climbing out of the car. I followed his movements, and he beeped the locks and tossed me the keys. "Wanna pick me up at the cabins on your way to get Owen?"

Dex was planning on meeting up with Kol to go over the case. He wasn't sharing much—not yet. But they were focused, and that meant something.

"Sure, just tell me where you'll be."

"Probably back at the cabins by then, but I'll let you know if I'm somewhere else."

I nodded, starting toward the front of the building. Dex fell into step beside me. He didn't take my hand. Instead, he placed his palm on the small of my back.

The heat of it scalded my skin through my T-shirt, which was adorned with the words *The Boot*. His thumb traced the spot where my back and hip met as if he'd memorized where those stretch marks were.

Phoenix wings.

The words echoed in my head like the most beautiful sort of brand.

A door slammed, jolting me out of my swirling thoughts.

"Dexter Archer," a woman called out.

Dex's hand was gone from my back, a grin stretching his face as he strode toward her. "Ever Devereux."

Ever.

God, even her name was cool. And the rest of her was, too. She wore scuffed-up combat boots and dark jeans. A worn and faded tee with layered necklaces, and she had delicate tattoos on her fingers.

Dex pulled her into a hard hug, lifting her off the ground. I wanted to die a little. I hadn't seen him greet *anyone* like this before. Not a single soul. Certainly not me.

He released the woman, setting her on her feet and stepping back. He turned to me and read my face in a single breath. And then the asshole laughed.

He *laughed*.

I glowered at him, mentally vowing vengeance. Something that locked him out of every tech device he owned. His beloved hot sauce in his coffee. Shaving cream in his Oreos.

Dex moved to my side. "Brae, this is Ever. She grew up with us in Connecticut. She and Orion were high school sweethearts."

You could've knocked me over with a feather. *Orion had a first love?* I guessed everyone did, but I couldn't picture it. But what I could see clear as day were those words hitting Ever.

The first blow was a jab. *She grew up with us.* The second was a sucker punch to the kidneys. *Orion.* The third blow was a knockout. *High school sweethearts.*

But I knew in an instant that Ever was a fighter because she pulled herself together after the death blow. She straightened, tugging her mouth into a smile. "It's nice to meet you."

"You, too." And I meant it. Because I suddenly felt for her. She knew loss. And that was a club that bonded, even if none of us wanted to be a part of it.

"What are you doing here?" Dex asked.

Ever's mouth twisted into a lopsided grin. "On my break. You know I had to check in."

A hint of pain washed over Dex's face, but he covered it. "Ever works for Medicine For Humanity. Where were you this time?"

"Cameroon," Ever said, tugging on the hem of her tee. "Got to see some gorillas."

"That's really incredible," I said.

Her blue-green eyes softened. "Not a bad gig." She turned to Dex, pausing for a moment before speaking again. "How is he?"

The words were whispered, but each one was like a knife to the chest. Because they were full of longing and pain.

Dex's fingers twitched at his side as if he wanted to reach for something or maybe put his fist through a wall. "He's okay."

Ever's fingers tightened in the hem of her tee. The movements were so similar. Maybe because they were spurred on by the same pain. But she didn't say a word, just stared at Dex.

He sighed and scrubbed a hand through his hair. "He's communicating less. On his own more."

Ever's head turned, the breeze picking up her hair and making it look a little wild. "I'm gonna go talk to Wy. Good to see you, Dex. Maybe we can get coffee before I head out."

"You got it. Where you headed to next?" he asked, trying to steer them away from the hard and into the normal.

"Haiti. I've never been."

"Always an adventure for you."

"Always." Ever sent him a sad smile before turning to me. "Give this one hell. He deserves it. He shaved my Barbie's head when I was eight."

"You stole my best baseball card," Dex shot back.

"You didn't have a right to it. You're a freaking Yankees fan," Ever said, disgusted.

"The Mets," Dex muttered. "Who picks a losing team?"

Ever pointed a finger at him. "We have heart, and that's something you can't buy."

Dex just laughed as she headed inside, then turned to me.

"I like her," I said.

Dex's lips twitched. "You didn't at first."

I let out a soft huff. "I was annoyed."

"Jealous."

"*Annoyed.*"

Dex pulled me to him. "I kind of like you jealous."

"Now *you're* annoying."

He laughed, brushing some hair from my face. "Nothing to be jealous of there. Not even close."

I knew that now. It had only taken about five seconds to realize it. "What's the story?"

Dex's gaze traced my face. "They loved each other. A *real* kind of love. The kind you knew could go the distance, even when they were only fifteen."

"What happened?" I whispered.

Dex's jaw worked back and forth as he searched for the words. "After Orion saved us, he broke up with her. But she never gave up. She wrote letters. Sent emails. Called. Even now, all this time later, every time she gets a break from her job, she comes here. He never sees her. But she comes anyway."

God, that killed me. For both of them. It was as if Orion had shoved away every good thing in his life—Ever, any true connection—by staying tucked away on the ranch and silencing himself. If he just let himself—

"Don't even think about it, Hellion."

My gaze flicked up to Dex's face. "What?"

"I see those wheels turning. Do not try to play matchmaker."

"I'm not." I totally was.

"Bullshit. But you can't. I think it would be too much for Orion. He can't handle it."

My shoulders slumped. "Okay."

Dex's lips brushed my temple. "You take care today. Text me if you're running late."

I stepped out of his hold and gave him a salute. "I don't know, though. Pissed-off sex kind of has its benefits."

"Hellion…"

"See you later, Buttercup."

I arched my back, feeling a few bones pop.

"I heard that one from clear over here," Roger muttered over the bar as he bent over a burger.

"Long day," I admitted. We were officially in peak tourist season—at least according to Wylder. And I felt it. More families. And more families meant more kids, who tended to be loud. There was a steady drumbeat behind my eyes as a result.

"Amen to that," Roger mumbled around a bite of cheeseburger.

I set down the freshly rolled silverware. "You okay?"

There were dark circles under Roger's blue eyes, and his scruff was thicker.

He took a sip of his beer, swallowing the bite of burger. "Just a lot going on."

I leaned into the bar. "Meaning you and Travis are working my case in addition to whatever else is on your desk."

Roger's lips twitched. "Maybe."

"I heard via Kol that the sheriff's department is putting officers back on the case. Shouldn't that mean it's no longer side work?"

Roger scowled. "Miller gave it to some green-behind-the-ears deputy. Said he'll be overseeing the case personally. Wants to give the kid 'real-world experience.' But the deputy wasn't even here when Nova went missing."

A fresh wave of annoyance flooded me. "Every time I think he's pulling his head out of his ass, he proves me wrong."

Roger lifted his beer. "Try working for him for a decade."

"I can't imagine." My gaze flicked to the clock on the wall. "I'm out. You need a refill before I take off?"

Roger shook his head. "I'm all good. Take care of yourself."

"You get some sleep," I ordered.

"Yes, ma'am," he said with a grin.

I rolled my eyes and grabbed my tote bag. "I'm off," I called to Wylder and Fiona.

"See you, honey pie," Fiona called as she wiped down a table.

"You want me to walk you out?" Wylder offered.

"All good. See you tomorrow."

I headed down the back hall and out into the sunshine. I breathed deeply, taking in the fresh air—the best thing after a long day.

Beeping the locks, I headed for my SUV. As I reached for the door, footsteps sounded behind me. I turned, and the whole world fell away.

Tall. Leanly muscled. Reddish-brown hair. His face had a few lines in it now, but those green eyes were just the same. And they were the mirror image of my son's.

"Hello, Braedyn."

CHAPTER THIRTY-EIGHT
Braedyn

Everything in me froze. My muscles locked. My lungs seized. The space between Vincent and me felt like a mile and a breath all at once.

He smiled. The one I remembered. The one that used to make me stupid. Now, it only had revulsion sweeping through me.

But it also made me realize one thing: maybe I *had* seen him downtown last week.

"It's so good to see you," he murmured.

The way he smiled, the way the skin crinkled around his eyes, the way warmth infused his words… I almost believed him.

But that was Vincent. Charming and enchanting one minute, and cruel and selfish the next.

Breathe, Brae. Just breathe.

I straightened, calling on all my strength. I'd endured more than pampered Vincent could ever fathom, and that meant he didn't stand a chance against me. "I wish I could say the same."

Vincent chuckled. "Looks like you've found a little more fire. Gotta say, it looks good on you. Way better than the simpering girl from the wrong side of the tracks."

It was funny how you could see things more clearly with distance, recognize patterns you never saw before. Like how Vincent's compliments always seemed to come with an insult. Raising you up and cutting you down all at once.

And the wrong side of the tracks for him could be someone who had millions instead of billions. My parents might've been judgmental assholes, but they worked hard for the home they owned in a community they built deep roots in. But I guessed that was part of being family: I could judge them, but Vincent sure as hell couldn't.

"Hate to see you breathing commoners' air. Maybe you should go back to your compound."

One corner of Vincent's mouth kicked up. "Gotta handle some business first."

I stiffened, my blood turning cold. "What do you want?"

"Well, Braedyn, you made a real mess of things."

My fists clenched at my sides as rage built, but I knew better than to play into Vincent's hand. So I waited. He had no patience. Too eager to get what he wanted or inflict some sort of pain.

"You just had to go around blabbing to any news outlet that would listen."

I frowned. *News outlet?* And then it dawned. "The articles about Nova?"

"Ding, ding, ding. She's not as stupid as she looks, folks."

My skin bristled as I fought the urge to pop him one in his perfect nose.

"You fucked up. Because one of those articles got reprinted in *The Harbor Gazette*," Vincent went on, the hints of anger bleeding into his tone.

Confusion swirled as I tried to figure out why Vincent would give one damn about an article covering Nova's disappearance. She meant nothing to him. He'd constantly demeaned her in front of me and suggested I find new friends.

"'Nova is the kindest, most giving soul you'll ever meet. She gave up everything to help me raise my son when I was doing it on my own.'" Vincent snarled the words, spitting them out like bullets.

I recognized them then. It was an interview I'd done ahead of the one-year anniversary of Nova's disappearance with a paper in Redding, California. I never thought about Vincent reading it. The words weren't a dig at him. They were the truth—one I shared to show who Nova was. How generous. How amazing.

"My fucking brother read that article and started putting two and two together."

Oh shit.

"My family doesn't like bastards, Braedyn."

My spine snapped straight. "Don't you ever call *my* son that ugly word. Say it again, and I'll make you regret it."

Vincent made a tsking noise. "Now, now, Braedyn. Threats are just uncalled for. Is this the sort of example you're setting for my son?"

"He's not yours," I gritted out. "He's nothing of yours. You didn't raise him. You didn't even make him. I'm convinced because he has none of your ugliness."

"Watch your mouth," Vincent growled.

"You stay the hell away from us. Crawl back into your pompous, pampered hole and never come back."

"Oh, I'm not going anywhere. Because my parents want to meet their grandson. And lucky for you, they're willing to pay. If you sign over custody now, they'll make sure you live in whatever luxury this hovel of a town can provide."

I saw red. I'd never really understood the phrase before, but I understood it now. A filmy, ruby haze settled over my vision. "First, you want me to 'get rid' of your son, then you want to pay me to deny he exists, and now you want to *buy* Owen off me? He's a human being. He's not for sale."

Vincent let out a huff. "Don't be so dramatic. Money makes the world go 'round. And like you've made such a good life for him? Living in dangerous neighborhoods with hand-me-down clothes and never having the things he wants."

Every word was a knife to the gut. Because so many of them were true. "Get out of here. Or the next article your family sees will be the one about how the Fabers try to buy children."

Vincent moved so fast, I didn't have a prayer of dodging him. He grabbed my wrist so hard I let out a gasp of pain. "Listen to me, you little cunt, you are going to shut your fucking mouth and do as you're told. If my parents want their bastard grandchild, then they're going to get him."

Pain burned in my wrist, but it was nothing compared to the terror racing through me.

Vincent grabbed my arm harder, shaking me. "Do. You. Understand?"

The panic shifted to anger, overtaking the fear. The fingers of my free hand slipped into my jeans pocket and closed around my tiny pepper spray. I tugged it free, flipping the cap and taking aim at Vincent's eyes. I sprayed.

The howl that left his mouth was like a high-pitched animal cry. His hold on my wrist dropped away as he pawed at his eyes. I didn't wait. I brought my knee up, connecting directly with his balls before shoving him back.

Vincent crumpled to the pavement, rocking in pain.

"*That's* what you get for touching a woman without her permission. Stay the hell away from me. And stay the hell away from Owen. Or you'll get a lot worse than pepper spray."

I hurried into my SUV, my hand shaking as I dropped the key fob and pepper spray into the cupholder and took the wheel. Putting the vehicle in drive, I peeled out of the parking lot. The second I hit Mountain View Way, I forced myself to ease off the gas.

"You're safe. You're safe. You're safe."

I spoke the words over and over to myself. But I wasn't sure that was true. Physically, maybe. But as my wrist throbbed, I wasn't even sure of that.

A fresh wave of panic sliced through me as I thought about Owen. The little boy I'd shielded from everything to do with his father. Now that I'd refused the offer of money, I had no doubt Vincent would take me to court. And he'd use his family's name, resources, and power to sway any judge we got.

"Breathe. Just breathe."

I remembered what it felt like to feel Dex's chest rise and fall under my hand. *"Breathe with me."*

My eyes stung, but my breathing slowed. And my heart warred with itself. Because I could see the beauty of Dex and me in that one phrase. *Breathe with me.* The way we said it to each other when we needed it because we understood. The panic. The fear. The source might be different, but the pain was the same.

I knew I was falling. Because of the understanding. Because of some pull I couldn't name.

And that scared the hell out of me, too.

But I kept breathing. All the way back to the cabins. But as I made that final turn toward home, I caught sight of Dex striding down his front steps. His forearms rippled with the force of him fisting his hands, and his expression had gone thunderous.

Something was wrong. Very wrong.

I didn't even pull the SUV into a spot. I didn't turn off the engine. I threw it in park. "What? What happened?"

Panic coursed through me. Something was wrong. Nova? If it were about Owen, the call would've come to me. But I still found myself checking my phone's screen, letting out a shaky breath when I saw no missed calls.

And then words I never would've expected spilled out of Dex's mouth. "The camp. They can't find Skylar. She's missing."

CHAPTER THIRTY-NINE
Dex

MY PULSE THRUMMED IN MY EARS AS WE DROVE A GOOD TEN miles over the speed limit. Yeti leaned against one of the doors and let out a bark as Brae made a hard turn. Yeti probably thought it was a game.

But all I could hear was Kol. *"I need you. It's Sky."* His voice cracked on her name as if breaking. But it was *Kol* who was breaking. And the rest of us would shatter right along with him if anything had happened to that little princess. Sometimes, it felt like Skylar was the only light in our worlds.

Brae swerved into the lot, pulling right up into a fire lane but not giving a damn. She threw it in park and leapt out.

"You can't park there," a counselor yelled.

I sent the boy no older than twenty a look that likely had him pissing himself.

"N-never mind," he stammered.

But Brae was already running toward Owen, who stood next to the camp director and a stone-faced Kol. And Owen was crying.

Brae ran faster, spurring me into action. The moment she reached him, she sank to her knees and pulled him to her. "Hey, hey. What's going on?"

Owen let loose a sob. "Max was picking on me again. He shoved me down and broke my glasses. Sky got real mad and chased him toward the woods, but then they didn't come back, and I don't know where they are."

The words were a jumble of tripping syllables, but I could make out the gist. "How long ago?" I gripped Kol's shoulder as I asked, trying to keep my voice even.

"Forty minutes," Kol ground out.

I understood his fury. He'd called me less than ten minutes ago, right after the camp had called him, which meant they had stood around with their thumbs up their asses for half an hour before calling anyone.

I glared at the director. "That was real fuckin' stupid."

"Language," the woman snapped.

"That's the last thing you should be worried about," Kol snarled. "Maybe you should be worried about my daughter. Who you *lost*."

The woman paled as if finally realizing just how bad this was. "I'll call the sheriff."

"You do that," Kol sneered. The last person he trusted was Sheriff Miller.

Brae pulled back from Owen but kept hold of his shoulders. "It's going to be okay, O."

"You gotta find her, Mom!" Owen was frantic now. "She was trying to help me. I got her lost, and now no one can find her. But you can, right? You'll find her. She's my best friend."

I knew Owen's words had to jab straight into Brae's heart. She struggled to keep her composure. "We're gonna find her. Do you think you can be really brave while I help Kol and Dex look?"

Owen sniffed, his cheeks streaked with tears. "I-I can be brave."

A woman I didn't recognize stepped forward. "Jude and I can stay with him." She tried to smile. "I've even got some video games for emergencies."

"Thank you," Brae whispered, but she didn't step away from Owen right away. "He's not allowed to go home with anyone but me."

The woman nodded, understanding it would be hard to leave your child with anyone when another was missing. "Of course. There are lots of us here, and I'll look after him like my own."

Brae swallowed hard. "Thank you." Standing, she finally released Owen and looked at Kol. "Do you have anything in your SUV of Skylar's? A sweatshirt? A stuffed animal? Something with her scent."

Kol's throat worked as he struggled to swallow. "I've got a jacket. She wore it last night when we went to feed the cows."

"Perfect. You have an evidence bag I can use?" Brae asked.

Kol's face went white.

She reached out and touched his arm. "I just need a clean bag so my scent doesn't get mixed with Skylar's. That's all."

"Yeah, I got one." The words were coated in grit and pain.

My brother never showed emotion. Not like this. And the fact that he was now killed something in me.

"Grab me the bag, but don't touch the jacket," Brae ordered, heading to the SUV.

I was fast on her heels as she crossed to the back of the vehicle. "What can I do?"

I heard the emptiness in my voice, the fact that I had turned everything off. But I didn't have a choice. If I let my emotions take hold now, I'd be useless.

"You can get a first-aid kit from one of the counselors and a few bottles of water." Brae opened her back hatch. "I should've kept a ready pack. We haven't done any volunteer searches here yet."

I reached out and squeezed her shoulder. "I can get us the supplies."

"Yeah," Brae whispered.

"She's going to be okay. They probably just got turned around." I said the words as much for myself as for Brae.

Her head lifted, taking in the surrounding forests. "It'd be easy to do."

"Of course." I gave her arm one more squeeze and turned to the kid acting as parking officer earlier. "You got a first-aid kit? Water?"

He nodded, going pale again.

"Get me both."

The kid took off running, and I grabbed the empty backpack from the trunk as Brae let Yeti out of the back seat.

"*Au pied*," Brae commanded, and Yeti instantly came to her side, body quivering.

I slammed the hatch closed just as the kid came running back with my requested supplies. "Thanks," I said, shoving them into my pack. "Ready."

Brae was already moving, crossing to Kol, who was holding out a plastic bag. As she carefully used it to retrieve the jacket, I slid on the pack. "You want to go with us or split up?" I asked my brother.

Kol looked torn, but his mind found the answer as he glanced out at the forest. "Split up. We'll cover more ground. Waylon, Mav, and Wylder are on their way. They'll help."

And we'd find her. There was no other option.

"Stay in touch," I ordered, pulling out my phone to make sure I had service. There were plenty of areas around Starlight Grove that were spotty at best, but thankfully, we were close enough to town to have a good number of bars here.

"Got it." Kol was already off, heading for a break in the trees and looking for clues only he could see.

Brae held the bag open for Yeti, who sniffed eagerly. "Find Skylar. Find."

Yeti took one more sniff and then bolted toward the playground, circling the swing set with her nose to the ground. Brae gave Owen an encouraging smile as he watched. A second later, Yeti was taking off toward the trees.

"What if Yeti gets lost?" I asked as we picked up to a jog and followed.

"She's got a GPS tracker on her collar so I can locate her. And she's pretty good about waiting for me to catch up periodically."

I held back a branch for Brae to pass. "And you? What if you get turned around?"

"Maps on my phone, and I usually carry a GPS device."

"Tell me you never do this kind of shit on your own," I growled.

"I don't. Not searches. Training, sure."

The idea of Brae wandering around in the woods with only Yeti for company scared the hell out of me.

We moved deeper into the woods to find Yeti circling an especially thick patch of underbrush. Brae leaned down, studying it. "Look."

I bent, catching sight of pink fibers that looked like they could've come from a T-shirt.

"Mark these coordinates down." Brae read them off as I typed them into a note on my phone.

"Good girl, Yeti. Find Skylar," Brae encouraged.

The dog dropped her nose to the ground again. She wove an imperfect pattern that had me wondering just what had happened out in these woods. Then she picked up speed.

"It's stronger now, the scent." Hope surged in Brae's voice. "The way Yeti's picking up the pace, it's easier for her to follow now."

We started jogging, trying to keep up with the dog. The only sounds were the birds overhead and our feet hitting the forest floor.

And then I heard it. A pained yell.

My whole being turned to lead, but I didn't let that stop me. As Yeti took off, so did I. She raced ahead, able to dodge and weave more quickly than I could. But I had sheer panic on my side.

Yeti let out a couple of sharp barks that I knew had to be an alert.

As I rounded a tight set of trees, I came upon a sight I never would've expected. Skylar was atop a *much* larger boy's back, her blond pigtails caked with dirt and leaves, more dirt smeared on her cheek, and she had the boy in some sort of choke hold.

"Say you're sorry," she demanded, pure fury in her voice.

The boy's eyes were wide as he caught sight of me. "Help me! She's crazy!"

"That's not nice either. Now, you gotta say sorry twice." Sky gripped him harder, her face stormy.

I felt Brae pull up short next to me and let out a strangled sound of surprise.

I shook my head, scrubbing a hand over my jaw as relief swept through me. "Hey, Little Princess. You wanna let him go?"

"No," she snarled. "Sometimes, a lesson's gotta be learned, and I'm gonna be his teacher."

Brae gripped my arm, pressing her face into it to keep from laughing.

That was a phrase right out of Waylon's playbook if I'd ever heard one.

"Sky, he's gonna have consequences, don't you worry. But you don't want to get in trouble, too."

Her hazel gaze flicked up to me, the first sign of uncertainty there. "You promise? He hurt Owen. And we don't hurt. That's rule one."

God, my niece was the best. Pink T-shirt that read *Don't make me get my uncle*, combat boots, and rainbow shorts. Pure ferocity adorned her face.

"I promise you'll have your vengeance, Little Princess."

With one last squeeze, she leapt off the boy and brushed herself off. Then she went straight for Yeti, giving her all the scratches.

But I didn't take my eyes off the little pissant who'd hurt Owen and gotten Skylar lost. I stalked toward him, offering him a hand to help him stand. But I didn't let go when he was on his feet. I gripped his hand firmly and got right in his face.

"If you *ever* come at Owen again, I'll let Sky do her worst, and I'll make sure every secret you have is posted to your Snapchat weekly. I can do it. I used to hack computers for the FBI."

The boy paled.

"You get me?" I snarled.

He nodded in a staccato beat.

"Good. Now, start walking," I ordered.

A grin spread across Brae's face as the terrified bully passed her. "Buttercup, did you just threaten a ten-year-old for my kid?"

I shrugged. "Worth it."

Her expression went soft around the edges. "I think that's the nicest thing anyone's ever done for me."

CHAPTER FORTY
Braedyn

SKYLAR SKIPPED AHEAD OF US, CHATTERING TO YETI AS IF THE dog could understand each and every word she spoke. She was completely oblivious to the fact that we'd all been scared out of our minds for her. Though maybe that was the best thing. A gentle yet strong word from Kol about not running into the woods might be all that was needed.

And bully Max was so embarrassed and possibly still terrified about Dex's threats that I was starting to feel bad for him. He trudged along between Skylar and us, his head bowed, staring at his shoes.

But the moment we broke through the tree line, Kol was running at his daughter full tilt. Suddenly, the amusement of how we'd found the two kids was gone, and I was reminded of everything that had been at stake. Memories of the search after Nova's disappearance flashed in my mind. How much I wished for this sort of reunion.

Skylar giggled as her dad lifted her into the air and held her to him. But it was the way Kol's body shook with silent sobs that had me almost breaking on the spot.

"Daddy?" Skylar asked, confused. "What's wrong?"

"Nothing, baby. Nothing now." He held her for a long time, and I knew he was coming to terms with being faced with his worst nightmares only to make it out the other side.

Dex's arm slid around my shoulders, pulling me to him as he brushed his lips across my temple. "We're going to find you answers, too."

Him knowing where my mind had gone—to Nova, always to Nova—was a gift. But I couldn't help noticing that he hadn't promised me a happy ending like Kol had gotten.

Kol's hazel gaze lifted to me. "Thank you," he croaked. "Anything you need. Anything at all. It's yours. You found my girl."

"You don't need to say that," I rasped. "I'm happy to help."

"I'm saying it anyway." Kol's eyes burned with something. Fear, I realized. And I understood it. A pressure came with being a single parent. Every decision was on your shoulders. And when something went awry, it could only be your fault. The weight was always heavier because you carried it alone.

"All I need is for you to take that girl out for a milkshake and have some time just the two of you," I whispered.

"I wasn't lost, Daddy. Just had some business to attend to." Skylar glared at Max, whose head was still hung low.

Kol pulled back. "Some business to attend to?"

I got the sense he would've laughed if he hadn't just been terrified out of his mind.

"Yeah, Max owes Owen an apology," Skylar huffed.

Max's cheeks heated, but before he could say a word, a woman started calling for him—his mother, I guessed. And she did *not* look happy.

Kol pinned his daughter with a hard stare. "Then you tell a camp counselor. You don't chase someone into the woods."

Skylar let out a huff. "Sometimes, you gotta stick up for what's right."

Kol's mouth thinned. "We'll talk about this at home." His gaze flicked to me. "Thank you again. And Yeti, too."

"You're welcome."

Kol was already pulling his phone out of his pocket as he shifted

Sky in his arms. "I need to call Mav, Wylder, and Waylon. Let them know they can go back to work."

As Kol carried his daughter toward the parking lot, Owen came running over to them, still holding his broken glasses. Kol set Skylar down, and Owen engulfed her in a huge hug, but Kol didn't take his eyes off his daughter for a second. It was as though he feared Sky would disappear again if he blinked.

"He blames himself," Dex said quietly.

My gaze flicked to him. "For Skylar getting lost?"

Dex shook his head. "For what happened to my brothers and me. He was supposed to be home that day. Mav and I wanted him to play soccer with us, but he took his girlfriend out instead. He was seventeen, and girlfriends were a hell of a lot more exciting than little brothers. Came home to cop cars. Dad dead. Orion in cuffs. Me traumatized. Wylder trying to handle the cops and find a lawyer for Orion. Maverick rushed to the ER. He feels like he failed us."

I watched a tortured expression play over Kol's face. Another failure in his book. *Hell.* "It wasn't his to take on. Only one person is responsible, and that's your father."

"I know that. But we carry the scars anyway. And the ones carved with guilt are always deeper."

My gaze flicked up to Dex's face as he watched his brother and niece. His words, the way he spoke them, told me there was more to the story. There was more to whatever Dex carried and the scars he bore.

Owen released Skylar and came running at me. Yeti let out a bark as Owen launched himself at me. I caught him with an *oomph* and stumbled back a few steps. But Dex stepped right in to steady me—to steady us.

"You found her," he whispered.

"We found her," I echoed.

"She had ole Max in a choke hold," Dex informed Owen.

Owen's eyes went wide as he slid down me so he could stand. "Seriously?"

"Seriously. I don't think he'll bother you again," Dex assured him.

Owen glanced over to where Max was clearly being lectured by his mother. "He always makes fun of me. My glasses."

Dex's mouth thinned. "Sometimes, people can't handle anything that's different, but it doesn't say anything about you. It only says something about him."

Owen looked down at his broken glasses. "I wish I wasn't different."

Dex crouched low so he was at eye level with Owen. "Different is a superpower. It means you notice things others don't. And getting picked on just means you know what it feels like and can look out for others who might be going through the same thing."

"I bet no one ever made fun of you," Owen muttered.

"You'd be wrong about that." Dex dipped his head to meet Owen's gaze. "Growing up, my teeth were really crooked, and then I had to wear braces. A few kids called me Beaver Teeth."

Owen's face scrunched up. "Harsh."

"Yeah. It wasn't fun. And then, in high school, kids thought I was weird for spending so much time working on computers. Called me Hard Drive."

"Computers are cool," Owen argued.

"I think so, too. And I'm really glad I didn't let them scare me out of working with them, or I wouldn't have found what I love to do."

"Glasses aren't cool, though."

Dex arched a brow. "Excuse me?" He tweaked his own glasses. "I think they're bussin.'"

A giggle bubbled up and out of Owen. "I don't think you should say bussin.'"

"Okay, fine, they're dead-ass cool."

Owen's gaze flicked to me to see if I'd call Dex on the swear. "I guess yours are," he mumbled.

"Maybe you just need to find a pair that really fits who you are. Then you'll wear them with pride," Dex suggested.

"Maybe," Owen muttered. "Do you think? Would you, um, help me look for them? The glasses?"

Dex grinned, his whole face lighting up as he held out a fist for a bump. "We're on a style mission."

A throat cleared, and we all looked at a red-faced Max. "I, uh, I'm real sorry, Owen. I shouldn't have pushed you." He swallowed. "We're going to pay for your new glasses."

The woman behind him cleared her throat again. "I mean, I am. My mom will pay for them now, but I gotta work it off with chores."

The woman nodded. "I'm so sorry. There have been some things going on at home that have Max acting out. It's not an excuse. We'll be talking them through. But I'm just sorry Owen was an outlet."

I squeezed Owen's shoulder. "What do you think?"

"Apology accepted," Owen mumbled, but he still didn't look completely convinced.

"Thank you," I told Max's mom.

She nodded, laying a hand on her son's shoulder. Max cast a quick, panicked look at Dex. "You'll tell Skylar I said sorry? I don't want her to jump me again. She's tiny, but she's really freaking strong."

Dex choked on a laugh. "I'll tell her. As long as you're nice to everyone at camp, I think you're safe."

Relief swept over Max's features as he and his mom walked away.

Owen looked up at Dex in awe. "What did you and Sky do?"

Dex just grinned as he patted Owen's shoulder. "We got your back. Always."

CHAPTER FORTY-ONE
Braedyn

I PULLED THE OVERSIZED SWEATSHIRT OVER MY HEAD, BURROWING into the softness. It didn't matter that I'd turned the water to scalding hot. Or that, even though it was dark outside, the sunbaked earth was still hovering at about seventy degrees. I couldn't get warm.

A shiver raced through me. "Get it together," I whispered.

Skylar was fine. Home with her dad. Perfectly safe. Owen was, too. Dex had found a temporary fix for his glasses with superglue and a tool he used in building his computers. We were okay. For now.

But even as that thought entered my head, Vincent's face flashed in my mind. His threats echoed in my ears. And that fear—fear I'd tamped down to focus on finding Skylar—started to swirl all over again. It was only compounded by the reminder that while we'd found Skylar safe and sound, Nova was still missing. And we were no closer to finding her.

Stepping out of my room, I padded down the hallway in my slippers toward the sounds of battle.

"No way, bruh. I'm gonna smash you," Owen cheered.

"Prepare to eat ice sword," Dex shot back.

A soft smile tipped my lips as I turned the corner to find them sitting on pillows in front of the TV. Dex had brought over his gaming system, and they were now *both* eight, apparently. Their bodies leaned one way and then another as they trash-talked. They threw everything into their attacks and defenses, their arms flailing as they punched buttons on their controllers.

The game took place in some sort of fantasy land. Dex's character looked like a troll while Owen's...I couldn't identify. But the creature had wings and a thorny sword.

Suddenly, Owen's character leapt into the air, executing a spin kick and then stabbing Dex's troll through the heart.

"Yes!" Owen cheered as he jumped up, much the way his character had, minus the kick. "Victory is mine!" He raced around the room.

Yeti barked and darted after him, loving this sort of game.

Dex groaned, flopping back onto the floor, hands clutching his chest. "Downed by the winged beast in the prime of my troll life."

Owen laughed, reaching out a hand to pull Dex to his feet. "I'd say there's always next time, but I'm never gonna let you win."

Dex moved fast, tugging Owen into a playful headlock and giving him a noogie. "What was that about never letting me win?"

Owen cackled with laughter as he struggled to get free. "I'll never surrender."

I watched from the entryway as they teased and tumbled, and realized Owen had never had this. The kind of male camaraderie with play-fighting and battling on the fields of imagination. I tried to meet Owen in his interests: Nerf battles, the occasional video game. But this was different. Another frequency. One I hadn't been able to give him.

Dex lifted Owen into the air and threw him onto the couch in an exaggerated body slam. The move was so slow, I knew there was great care in it. But Owen howled with laughter, playing the part of demolished wrestler.

"Victory is mine!" Dex cheered, taking Owen's earlier words.

"Watch your back, troll man. I'm coming for you," Owen vowed.

Dex laughed, his gaze finally catching on me. "The princess has emerged. Or should I say the hellion?"

One corner of my mouth kicked up. "The hellion has come to take this bat boy to bed."

"Aw, man," Owen complained.

"Hey," Dex said, drilling a finger into his side. "The sooner you sleep, the sooner we get a rematch."

Owen considered that for a moment and then nodded, standing from the couch. "Gonna brush my teeth."

I gaped at Dex, my jaw fully hanging open as Owen headed for the bathroom. "Did you seriously just get my kid to start his bedtime routine with only *one* protest?"

Dex's lips twitched. "I'm getting that this isn't usually the case."

I let out an annoyed huff. "I get at least half a dozen battles. Sometimes, the full dozen. 'I need a snack. One more story. I'm thirsty. I think I need to pee again. Does Yeti need to go out? She looks like she does.'"

A low chuckle left Dex's mouth, and he crossed to me. He dragged a finger across my bottom lip, along my jaw, then down my neck to my pulse point. "All you need is the video game rematch method."

My breath hitched as he stroked my pulse point. "I'll keep that in mind."

Dex kept stroking my neck, circling the point that gave me away. "You've got shadows in your eyes, Hellion. The gold isn't burning as bright."

I swallowed, knowing he felt the movement. I needed to tell him about Vincent, about the threats, about everything. I just couldn't find the words.

"I know today had to bring up Nova," Dex said softly.

He wasn't wrong there. It was that, too. It was everything. It felt like the whole world was bearing down on me.

Pain streaked across his face, and something else…fear maybe? "I have something else we can try."

"What?" I straightened instantly, but Dex didn't lose his contact with my throat.

"I have a friend who has a podcast. It covers cold cases. She's in the middle of one right now, but she'll do a high-level overview of other cases each week. Open up a tip line in case someone has information but has been too scared to come forward."

"Yes." He hadn't even asked a question, but I was answering anyway. "The more eyes and ears, the better." I'd tried reaching out to a few podcasts over the past year, but none of them had bitten on covering Nova's case.

Dex's mouth thinned. "It could piss the unsub off. I talked to a profiler friend of mine, and Anson said it could make them so mad they'll lash out and make a mistake."

My heart beat a little faster. He meant I could be at risk. That whoever was messing with me could take it further. "I have to try," I whispered.

"Okay," Dex rasped, his thumb stroking my pulse point again. "I'll call."

I pulled my knees up to my chest, hugging them tightly as Dex set his laptop on the coffee table in front of the couch. "I can't believe she wanted to talk now. Isn't that a little fast?"

Nerves churned in my belly. I hated going back there. Hated revisiting everything. But Nova was worth it. Every time.

"Ridley said it was actually perfect timing. She's waiting for an open records request to come through," Dex explained.

I froze. "Wait. Ridley? As in Ridley Sawyer? As in the *Sounds Like Serial* podcast?" I squeaked.

Dex's brows rose. "You've heard of it?"

"Anyone who's ever listened to a single true crime podcast has probably heard of it. They've got millions of downloads and nearly as many followers."

Dex's lips twitched. "A little bit of a fangirl?"

My cheeks heated. "I followed a case she did a few years ago. Missing teenager in Minnesota."

Dex sobered. "I remember that one."

It hadn't had a happy ending, but Ridley had brought the family closure.

"How do you know her?" I asked.

Dex's mouth twisted into a grin. "I heard the podcast. Could tell she was doing it to help people, not to make a buck. So I offered my services."

My jaw dropped. "You hack for her."

"I can neither confirm nor deny."

I shook my head. "Hacker with a heart of gold."

"Don't ruin my rep," Dex muttered.

An alert sounded, and then a woman filled the screen. She was stunning, her blond hair piled high in a messy bun that somehow managed to look artful and chic. She wore a yoga top with crisscrossed straps that revealed tanned skin and toned arms.

Her eyes lit, and a huge smile split her face. "Dex."

"Hey, Rids. It's good to see you," Dex greeted. The familiarity had a niggle of *something* eating at me.

"You, too. It's been way too long. You need to come over to Shady Cove now that you're back in NorCal."

"Are you even home?" Dex challenged.

Ridley's berry lips twitched. "Not at the moment, but I will be soon."

"Damn soon," a deep voice said as a man with dark hair and scruff dipped into the screen. He slid a mug with a tea tag hanging out in front of Ridley and kissed the top of her head.

Ridley looked up at him, and her whole face transformed as if he were her sun, moon, and stars all at once. "Thanks, Law Man." She tugged him to her for a quick kiss.

The hard lines of his face softened the barest amount. "Give 'em hell, Chaos."

And then he was gone, sliding out of what I could tell was some sort of van.

Ridley turned to me, her cheeks flushed. "Sorry about that. And for not introducing myself. I'm Ridley."

"Hi," I squeaked. "I'm Brae."

Dex chuckled low, and I elbowed him hard in the stomach.

"It's nice to meet you, Brae." Ridley's expression sobered. "I'm so sorry to hear about your friend. I'll do whatever I can to help. I'll record a breakdown of the case after I've finished going through all the materials Dex sent over, but I always think it helps to hear from the missing's loved ones. It makes people want to help."

My mouth went dry, but I managed a nod. "That makes sense."

Dex took my hand, his fingers sliding through mine. Ridley didn't miss the movement. A soft smile curved her mouth, but she didn't say anything.

"If there's anything more you need, just let us know," Dex offered.

"Will do." Ridley reached for her mouse, moving it around and seeming to do things to her computer. "Brae, will you say something so I can test levels?"

I cleared my throat. "Testing, one, two, three. Isn't that what they do in the movies?"

Ridley laughed, and the sound was breezy. Effortless. As if she made it all the time—even though she'd been through hell. She'd lost her twin sister the night before their college graduation. I knew that much just from following the show.

"You're official now. And perfectly in range," Ridley said. "You ready?"

She met my gaze through the camera and held it. She didn't look away, even when I didn't speak at first. She kept holding that focus as if to tell me she was here with me, no matter what.

"I'm ready," I croaked.

Dex squeezed my hand, telling me he was there, too.

"All right. Let's do this." Ridley moved her mouse again, clicking something on the screen. "Brae, you've been friends with Nova almost all your life."

I nodded, then immediately realized no one would see it. "Yes." I swallowed. "Since preschool. But our bond was really cemented in the third grade. A boy was picking on both of us, and we teamed up for revenge."

Ridley grinned. "Sounds like my kind of friend."

"She's the best friend you could ask for. Nova is like walking sunshine.

But the kind set aflame because she's so fierce. She's the friend who always has your back. Your first call when something goes right or wrong. Your biggest cheerleader and always a safe place to land."

Ridley's gaze went a little misty. "Sounds more like you're sisters."

Warmth spread through me, knowing Ridley got it. "We are." An image of Vincent popped into my head, his face twisted in anger at what I'd shared about his lack of presence in his son's life. But I wouldn't be silenced. He didn't get to steal Nova's gifts just because it made him look bad.

I sucked in a breath, knowing I had to tell Dex about the encounter after this, knowing I needed to make plans. But first, I needed to show up for Nova the way she'd shown up for me countless times.

"Our bond is one of the greatest gifts I've ever been given. When I got pregnant at nineteen and didn't have anyone to help me, Nova stepped in. She helped me start over. She helped raise my beautiful son. She's our family, and we'll do anything to bring her home."

"She sounds like an amazing woman," Ridley whispered.

"She is," I croaked.

Ridley asked more gently guiding questions: about Nova, about the time she'd been gone, the disappearance itself. And then she ended with one final question. "If you could say one thing to Nova right now, what would it be?"

"I love you," I rasped. "I love you, and I miss you, and I've never stopped looking. Not for a single day. You aren't forgotten."

"No, she isn't," Ridley said firmly. "And the *Sounds Like Serial* family is going to make sure her name and face are spread wide. We're going to try to help you find some answers."

"Thank you," I whispered.

Ridley nodded, moving to click more things on the screen. "You were great. I know it takes a lot out of you, so make Dex feed you a snack and then try to sleep as much as possible tonight."

"I've got ice cream in the freezer," Dex assured her.

"That's perfect." Ridley smiled and then turned back to me. "Have Dex give you my number. Text or call anytime. I'm always here, even if you just need to talk to someone who's been there."

"That's really kind. Thank you."

"I wish I could do more. If no progress has been made by the time I wrap up this case, I can head to you guys next. Do a deep dive on Nova's disappearance."

God, she was so kind. Because I knew what she really wanted to do was go home after her current case.

I gripped Dex's hand harder. "That means more than I can say."

"Happy to help." Ridley glanced over her shoulder. "I'd better go before Law Man gets hangry. No one wants that."

A soft chuckle left my lips. "Have a good night."

"You, too." Her gaze flicked to Dex. "Take care of yourself, and don't get arrested."

Dex laughed. "I'll do my best."

With a wave, Dex clicked out of the video chat and closed his screen. Then he turned to face me. "How do you feel?"

"A little wrung out. But good, too. Like I'm actually doing something. She has a different demographic than the other media I've gotten coverage from. Maybe it'll shake something loose."

"It might," Dex agreed. His lips fluttered slightly as if he were fighting a grin.

"What?"

His beautiful mouth found a full smile. "You were jealous. When she got on the call. Weren't you?"

I let out a huff. "She's gorgeous. And she's all *it's been way too long*. I was a little annoyed. That's all."

Dex's laugh was full-out this time. "Jealous…twice."

"Whatever," I grumbled, even though he had a point.

Dex leaned in and brushed his mouth over mine. "You're cute when you're jealous."

I shoved him. "You're annoying."

As I pulled my arm back, Dex's face went thunderous. It took my brain a second to register the expression and then I was so damn confused as to why it was there. But Dex caught my forearm, stilling my movements as his gaze zeroed in on my wrist.

"Why. The. Hell. Are. There. Fingerprint. Bruises. On. Your. Wrist?"

CHAPTER FORTY-TWO
Dex

Fury pulsed through me like waves of lava destroying everything in its path. But I couldn't take my eyes off the marks on Brae's wrist. I could see it as clear as day. Slashes of bruising that meant someone had gripped her so hard they'd burst blood vessels beneath the skin.

"Breathe."

Some part of me heard Brae's voice through the haze of rage, but it wasn't cutting it back. Not nearly enough. Someone had hurt her. Touched her with the intent to harm. And I wanted to kill them.

That thought should've snapped me out of it. The urge for violence should've terrified me. But it didn't. Because I wanted agony for whoever had done this.

"Dex. I'm fine. I'm perfectly all right." Brae took my other hand and placed it over her chest. "Breathe with me."

The contact, the feel of her heart beating beneath my palm…it helped. She was alive. Breathing. Safe.

My gaze cut to her golden one. "Who?" I demanded.

Brae winced, biting her lower lip.

"Tell me," I gritted out.

"Don't you growl at me," Brae snapped. "I'm not telling you anything until you dial it back a few notches."

That fire. It calmed even more than her touch, her heartbeat. Because her fire reminded me just how strong Brae was.

"I'm not growling at you. I'm growling at whoever fucking dared to put their hands on you."

She let out a soft huff of air. "That's a little better. Would it help if I told you I pepper-sprayed him in the eyes and kneed him in the junk?"

My brows almost hit my hairline. Had a customer gotten rough with her? Wylder would've called me if someone had. But maybe he hadn't seen. "What the hell happened?"

Brae shifted, peeling my hand from her arm and tugging the sweatshirt down so the bruises were out of sight. "Vincent showed up after my shift when I was getting into my car."

Everything in me froze. "Vincent the douchebag ex? That Vincent?"

"One and the same."

"Why?" I snarled.

Brae pulled at a thread on the couch's seam. "I guess the newspaper from the town I grew up in reprinted an interview I did with a paper out here. Talking about Nova. Her case. I mentioned how she helped me raise Owen after everyone in my life bailed on me."

"Like you did tonight," I surmised.

She nodded. "Vincent's brother saw the article, put two and two together, and told their parents. The Fabers want their grandson. He offered me money to sign over custody of Owen. I didn't react well."

Dread pooled, spreading from my gut and into my limbs. "Do you think he's going to take you to court?"

"I don't know," Brae whispered. "But I need to find a lawyer just in case. I was going to tell you when I got home, but then Sky was missing. And then the interview with Ridley and—"

"Hey." I scooped up Brae and cradled her to me. "I'm not mad at you. I'm fucking furious at him. You didn't do anything wrong."

Brae burrowed into me, and something about her leaning on

me—something she rarely did without a fight—struck me right in the goddamned heart.

"I'm scared," Brae whispered, her eyes filling. "They have endless resources. They have more money than God. What if they try to take Owen?"

"He's not going anywhere," I gritted out. "Not going to happen."

Brae's hands fisted in my shirt. "He's all I have left. I can't lose him, too."

That organ that kept me alive, the one beating at a ragged pace, shattered then. She'd been through so much: people deserting her when she needed them the most, having her only support system ripped away, and now this… Life was so fucking unfair.

But that's where I came in. I could balance those scales. At least when it came to Vincent. I would find every fucking skeleton in his closet. He wouldn't be able to litter a gum wrapper without me knowing it. And I would make him pay.

"You're not going to lose Owen. We won't let that happen," I vowed.

"We?" Brae asked, her voice starting to slur.

She'd been through too much today, and the adrenaline was finally leaving her system.

I pushed to my feet, cradling Brae against me, her red-currant scent wrapping around me. "We, Hellion. You're not in this alone. And in case it's been lost on you, it's not just me who has your back. You've won over the Archers one by one. We've *all* got your back."

"Not Orion," Brae said sleepily as I carried her into her bedroom.

"He did send you cake. I think that's a pretty good start."

Brae's mouth curved as her eyes fluttered shut. "That cake was really good."

"It was." I carefully laid her on the mattress, pulling off her slippers and then tucking the covers around her.

"Dex?" she mumbled.

"Yeah, Hellion?"

"Will you stay with me?"

Fuck me. She'd never asked that before.

"Yeah. I'll stay. Just give me a second to check the doors and turn off the lights. Okay?"

Her eyes were still closed, but little lines appeared between her brows. "You'll come back?"

A knife to the goddamned chest. And then I made a promise I knew I shouldn't. But I did anyway. "I'll always come back, Hellion. As long as you want me to."

"Okay, Buttercup." And then her whole body went slack, and her breathing deepened. She was asleep.

I couldn't move. Not at first. Because walking away felt like a betrayal. Even when I knew I'd return.

A thought of the douchebag finally spurred me into action. I moved as fast and quietly as possible, checking every door and window and the alarm system, then shut off the lights and moved for the weapon I needed.

I snatched my laptop from the coffee table and strode back toward the bedroom. Brae lay curled on her side, deep breaths fluttering the hair that had fallen across her face. I eased onto the bed, careful not to wake her.

As soon as I settled, I pulled my phone out of my pocket. I brought up my brothers' group chat and started typing.

> **Me:** *How do you feel about a revenge mission?*
>
> *Maverick changed the group name to 50 Shades of Slay.*
>
> **Maverick:** *We ride at dawn. Who we fuckin' with?*

I shook my head, wanting to laugh but not being able to get there. Mav didn't need to know the why, just the who, because he trusted me not to ask for help unless the cause was just. And that kind of trust was a gift.

> **Kol:** *Change it back. What's up, Dex?*
>
> **Maverick:** *You change it back, Gramps. Oh, wait, you still have an AOL email and pay your bills through the mail.*
>
> **Wylder:** *Mav, not the time.*

> *Wylder changed the group name to Hot Sauce and Hot Goss.*
>
> **Wylder:** *What's going on?*
>
> **Me:** *Brae's asshole ex showed outside the Boot this afternoon. Put fucking bruises on her arm and wants to take Owen. I want him buried.*
>
> **Orion:** *Name.*

Oh, hell. If Orion was in, Vincent was a dead man walking. But I didn't give a single fuck. He'd earned what was about to come his way.

> **Me:** *Vincent Faber. Wealthy family from Rhode Island.*
>
> **Kol:** *Want me to tail him? I've got off tomorrow. I can put in some man-hours while Skylar is at camp.*
>
> **Maverick:** *You're letting her go back?*
>
> **Kol:** *Waylon and Blaze are joining the counselor ranks.*
>
> **Wylder:** *Sweet baby Jesus. They have no idea what they're in for.*
>
> **Kol:** *Tail?*

Kol was coming through with his vow to have Brae's back, and it felt damn good to know my brother was on her side. They all were.

> **Me:** *Please. Send me everything. I'm going to hit the digital trail. See what I can find. But Brae needs a lawyer. Anyone know someone good?*
>
> **Orion:** *I might. Give me a day.*
>
> **Maverick:** *I'm sorry, YOU know someone? You never leave Twisted Oak Ranch, and you don't talk.*
>
> *Orion sent Mav a middle finger emoji.*
>
> **Maverick:** *That's uncalled for. I was just curious.*
>
> **Me:** *You're just an asshole, you mean. Thanks, Rion. Let me know what you find.*

Wylder: *You're going to bury him, aren't you?*

Me: *I'm going to ruin everything good in his life and expose every dirty little secret he has. And after he's dead and buried, I'm going to set that grave on fucking fire.*

Maverick: *God, I love it when you're on a vengeance streak.*

Maverick changed the name of the group to 50 Shades of Slay.

Kol: *MAVERICK.*

Maverick: *Peace out, bitches. I got a douchebag to fuck with.*

And fuck with him, he would. Just like the rest of my brothers would do their parts.

At the end of the day, Vincent Faber would never breathe easy again. Just like he deserved.

CHAPTER FORTY-THREE
Braedyn

I MOVED THE RAG ACROSS THE ALREADY-CLEAN BAR TOP, BUT IT was the only thing I could think to do. I'd already done the books, filled the condiment bottles, straightened the stockroom, readied the tables, and rolled the remaining silverware. Anything to keep from worrying: about Owen at camp, about Vincent, about Nova.

There was so much swirling in my head that it made me move at hyperspeed in an effort to escape it all. But it still swirled. Pressing down and trying to drown me.

Wylder shifted behind the bar, his gaze zeroing in on my hand. No, not my hand, my wrist.

I said a few mental curses and pulled the sleeve of my blouse down. I'd thought the lightweight top would hide my bruises, but the billowy sleeve was too easily pushed up.

"Are you sure you're up for working today?" Wylder asked, his voice so gentle.

"I'm good. I promise. And if you try to send me home, I'll just climb the walls."

His lips twitched. "I get that. I'll hope for a busy-as-hell day then."

I bowed to him, hands in prayer position. "Thank you, kind sir."

"Who's bowing to this fool?" Fiona asked as she strode over. "The last thing we need is any more power going to his head."

Wylder's lips twitched. "Come on, we all know you're the one really in charge."

She tapped her nose and then made a sign that she was watching him. "How you holdin' up, honey?"

There was something about Fiona's honeys. They always felt so damn warm and comforting. "Doing good," I lied. But it also wasn't a lie. Because despite everything that was swirling, I *was* okay. And I had Dex to thank for that.

"Glad to hear it," Fiona said with a clap.

"And she's lookin' good, too," Aidan called from his spot at the end of the bar where he was grabbing silverware.

Wylder scowled at him. "Rules."

Aidan held up both hands. "Hey, I'm just stating the obvious."

"Thank you, Aidan. You are looking pretty damn good yourself."

He gave an elaborate bow. "New jeans. They do great things for my ass."

I laughed, but Wylder just shook his head. "Want to open us up, Brae?" he asked.

God, did I ever. I needed all the distractions today. "On it, boss."

I headed for the front doors, unlocking them just before the big clock on the wall hit eleven. As I opened one wide, a man stepped up. I braced for a moment and then breathed a sigh of relief as I took in Jack, the man from Compass, whose wife had disappeared.

He saw me tense and took a step back. It was a kind gesture, one that acknowledged his sheer size and potential to be intimidating. "Sorry to startle you. I'm early," he said sheepishly.

I sent him a warm smile. "I'm jumpy lately. It's not your fault."

His face hardened. "I'm so sorry for everything that's been going on. Anything I can do to help?"

The offer warmed me the same way Fiona's honeys did. "I wish there were, but I don't think so. Actually, you can come in and order some food because being busy helps."

One corner of Jack's mouth kicked up. "That, I can do. Not sure what I'd do without this place and the diner."

My stomach twisted as I put the pieces together. "Hard to eat alone?"

Because I got it. Even though I had Owen, Nova's spot at our kitchen table was always glaringly empty.

Jack nodded as he followed me toward a booth. "House feels so damn empty. And I never have been much of a cook. Cynthia was the best. She loved trying new recipes, getting all fancy. Every time I try to make something in her kitchen, I just…"

His words trailed off, but I squeezed his arm, finishing for him. "It's just too hard. I get it."

Jack's throat worked as he swallowed. "I know you do."

"I may not be able to fix this, but I can get you fed. Want something to drink while you look at the menu?"

"A Coke and a water would be great."

I headed for the bar to give Wylder the order, but I was already brainstorming ways to bring Jack into the fold. He needed a community, a family. Maybe I could host a barbeque, have everyone from Compass and the Archers at my cabin.

"Excuse me?"

I turned at the voice, taking in the stunning woman opposite me. She had deep-brown eyes that mirrored the tones of her skin, hair that hung in a curly halo around her face, and an outfit that looked like some mix of ranch life and a Paris runway.

"Hi," I greeted. "Looking for a table?"

I hadn't seen her around before, and she didn't scream *tourist*. They were usually wearing some form of outdoor gear.

"Actually, I'm looking for Braedyn Winslow."

I stiffened, a million panicked thoughts running through my mind. But I forced myself to square my shoulders and face whatever was coming. Maybe she was here to serve me with papers. My mouth went dry. "I'm Braedyn."

The woman's smile widened, making lines deepen around her mouth and telling me she made the movement often. "Wonderful to meet you. I'm Maren Robinson. Your new attorney. If you'd like me to be."

My mouth went slack as I stared back at her. "I'm sorry, you're what?"

"Your new attorney."

I felt heat at my side and glanced over to see Wylder. There was an expression of suspicion lining his face. "Did Dex hire you?" he asked.

Maren shook her head. "No, Orion Archer did. He said he's a friend of Ms. Winslow's and that he wanted to help."

"A friend?" Wylder choked out, his eyes bugging.

Maren looked between the two of us. "Is that not true?"

"No, no, it is. We just… Orion doesn't usually…" I struggled to explain.

"Orion doesn't usually deal with people if he has any way of avoiding it," Wylder finished for me.

Maren nodded slowly but still seemed a little confused. "Well, he contacted me via email. Told me what was going on. And it just so happens, I don't love manipulative assholes and specialize in family law. I can send you my credentials—"

"Already got them pulled up," Wylder said, studying his phone. "Harvard Law." His eyes went wide. "Jesus, you clerked for a Supreme Court judge?"

Maren's lips twitched. "It was an experience."

Wylder glanced up at me. "She's a certified baddie."

Good. That was good. But it also wasn't. "Ms. Robinson—"

"Please, call me Maren."

"Maren," I amended, my palms going sweaty. "I don't want to waste your time. You might be too expensive for what I can—"

"Oh, my fees have already been covered. Orion paid the retainer."

A mixture of emotions swirled through me. Warmth, shame, hope. "He did?"

"He did," Maren said with a soft smile.

Wylder scrubbed a hand over his face. "That's as good a seal of approval as I've ever seen."

It felt like a hug from the brother who could barely stand to be in the same room as me—even more than the chocolate cake.

"I'll pay him back," I whispered. "It might take me a while, but I'll pay him back."

Wylder reached over and squeezed my hand. "Don't lessen his gift. Let him do this for you. I think it's good. It's the first time in years he's reached out."

My stomach twisted, but I understood. I didn't want to belittle his gift. Taking a deep breath, I turned to Maren. "Okay, what do we do first?"

"You give me everything you have on Vincent Faber. And then I bury him." There was joy on Maren's face. And I knew then that she was a warrior for justice.

I just hoped it was enough.

CHAPTER FORTY-FOUR
Dex

MY EYES ACHED, AND I TIPPED MY GLASSES UP TO RUB THEM. Reaching for the tiny bottle next to my computer, I deposited a few drops of solution into each eye. It did nothing.

I knew why. I'd slept for maybe two hours last night and was running on Lightning Energy drinks and Kit Kat bars. But I was making progress. I might've hit a dead end when it came to Nova, but I hadn't with Vincent. I'd found a handful of things that said he had secrets.

Old Vinny boy hadn't been very smart. He thought his last name and billions would protect him, but it wouldn't. And I'd found endless bookings with an escort service that catered to darker desires. And there was something about his latest business dealings that had me wondering if they were completely legal.

But I needed more time. There wasn't enough yet to get Vincent to back off—or better yet, send him to prison. Because Brae deserved to breathe easy and not have this asshole breathing down her neck.

But I'd seen the rich and powerful slip through the system before. And I wasn't about to let Vincent do that. To be assured of his destruction, I needed more. Unfortunately, he was hiding that proof somewhere. I just needed to locate it.

Cracking my neck, I glanced out the window and stiffened. Brae's SUV was back. I checked the clock on my computer screen and cursed. It was already five. I couldn't sworn it had been noon just a second ago.

I shoved my chair back and swiped up my phone. It only took me a matter of seconds to reach Brae's cabin. She'd given me the extra key, but I still knocked. I didn't want to scare her, and I sure as hell didn't want to risk her pepper-spray wrath.

Voices sounded inside, along with a happy bark from Yeti. The dog had gone from hating me to loving me a little too much. My neck hurt because she'd taken to lying on my head during the night, and the nearly one-hundred-fifty-pound dog was not good for my spinal health.

The door swung open, and Owen grinned up at me through the glasses I'd superglued. "We saw you on the camera app, so I got to open the door."

"Pretty damn cool. Have you—?"

My words were cut off by the massive furry beast that slammed into me. Her paws went around my neck as she attacked me in some sort of hug, peppering slobbery kisses all over my face.

"Help," I choked out. "I'm being attacked."

Owen burst out laughing. "Mom! Yeti's strangling Dex."

Footsteps sounded as I struggled to get free of the dog. Instead, I got a mouthful of fur.

"Yeti, down," Brae commanded.

The dog hesitated for a single moment and then leapt off me, all four paws landing on the floor.

My face screwed up as I picked dog hair out of my mouth. "What the hell was that?"

Brae struggled not to laugh. "I told you. I think she has a crush on you."

I scowled. "She's not my type."

Brae lost hold of her laughter then. She crouched down to rub Yeti. "It's okay, girl. I've been there."

"Maybe we need to get her a friend," Owen suggested hopefully. "We could get her a puppy."

Brae pushed to her feet, shaking her head. "There is no time or space for a new puppy in this house."

"Aw, man," Owen complained.

I ruffled his hair. "You can always go hang out at the ranch. There are a bazillion animals there."

Owen considered that. "I do like those alpacas. They spit."

Brae pinched the bridge of her nose. "Boys."

"The spitting's cool, bruh," I said, fighting laughter.

"Yeah, bro," Owen echoed.

"Well, how do you feel about a trip to see the spitting alpacas now?" Brae suggested.

"Let's go," Owen said, bouncing on the balls of his feet.

I studied her for a moment. "Any reason you want to go?"

She shifted for a moment. "I made something for Orion."

Oh shit.

I scrubbed a hand over my jaw. "Orion doesn't do well with gifts or gratitude."

"Too bad," Brae clipped. "I'm giving him both anyway."

I grinned. My hellion had a take-no-shit fire, and I absolutely loved it. "All right, then."

"Really?" she asked hopefully.

"Really." My grin widened. "We just have to make sure we avoid the bear traps and exploding dye balloons."

Brae's jaw went slack. "I'm sorry, did you say bear traps?"

"I wanna see a bear trap," Owen cut in. "I bet that could snap your leg in two. Totally boss."

Well, she couldn't say I hadn't warned her.

Brae cradled the tin of cookies to her chest as I navigated my SUV toward Orion's house. We'd dropped Owen with Kol and Sky, so he could go see the spitting alpacas, but he made us promise to tell him if one of the bear traps took off someone's leg.

Brae's fingers drummed over the tin in a rapid, nonsensical beat.

"What kind did you make him?" I asked.

The corners of Brae's mouth tipped up. "I don't know him as well, so it was harder. But I did maps. A few bottles of hot sauce. Legal scales. And a no-trespassing sign."

I barked out a laugh at the last one. "Oh, the irony."

"I thought it was appropriate."

My gaze flicked over to her before returning to the ranch road. "He hasn't done anything like this in…I don't even know how long. It's the first time he's come out of his protective shell in his own way."

Brae gripped the tin tighter, her tapping halting. "I'll never be able to repay him. To thank him. Maren is already filing paperwork to make the restraining order permanent and working on making my sole custody official."

My tongue stuck to the roof of my mouth as I struggled to swallow. "Sometimes the giving, the act of kindness, is reward enough for the giver. Sometimes, it's the miracle. It gives you purpose. Helps you keep fighting."

Brae looked at me as I pulled up to the fence and stopped. "You sound like you know from experience."

I wanted to tell her. To give her that one other piece of me—the one I didn't share with anyone. "You aren't the first person we've helped with a missing persons case."

Surprise lit in those golden eyes but then understanding. "Who else?"

"About a dozen across the country. Started with a case I had at the FBI. Someone who didn't fit the profile the BAU was building. Their eighteen-year-old daughter went missing, but it wasn't because of the killer the FBI was tracking. Her family wasn't going to get answers. She would have fallen through the cracks."

"So you helped," Brae surmised.

"I told my brothers about the case. It was in Idaho, not that far away. We all started adding our take on the case. Kol, the terrain and paths she could've taken from the college campus where she disappeared. Orion, building the map with all the points we had flagged for the case. Wylder, creating a sort of profile but for the victim, not the perpetrator. And Mav helped with Kol's tracking, filling in the missing pieces on her medical records and made Orion's map into a geographical profile."

I let out a breath, realizing I'd been holding it through the tumble of truth. "It just worked. We all had something to bring to the table."

"Did you find her?" Brae asked softly.

"We did." Sorrow swept through me at the reminder. "There was a guy she was seeing. Older. Not on a great path. They got into a fight. He got violent. She hit her head at just the right angle for death to be instant. He panicked and buried her in a forest behind his fraternity house."

Pain swirled in Brae's eyes. "So young. So much life ahead of her."

"Tragic on every level."

Those golden eyes found mine. "But you gave her family, friends, and everyone who loved her closure. That's a gift. Even if they didn't get a happy ending. There are no more questions. They can start to heal."

I knew Brae wanted that for herself. Worried she wouldn't get her own happy ending. And with as much time as had passed, closure and giving Nova peace were likely the best Brae could hope for.

I slid my fingers through hers. "It helped me to give that closure to them."

Brae studied me, putting the pieces together like she always did. "Because of your father?"

Shifting in my seat, I turned to face her. She was like the sun, warmth and hope and acceptance. I didn't want to hide from that as I spoke my truth; I wanted to bask in it. And it was then that I realized I didn't fear telling her. I didn't worry she'd suddenly turn off that light. I knew she'd meet me in the darkness.

"My father stole these women's lives—stole them from all the people who loved them. He left their families and friends with endless questions for years, wondering if the worst had happened. Maybe because it was the same with my mom, I kept thinking about being stuck in the in-between. Not knowing whether to hope or to lay to rest."

"It's purgatory," Brae whispered, understanding the way so few could.

"Exactly." The word was a pained rasp. "I wanted to end their purgatory. And it helped, giving someone closure. I wanted to do it again."

"So you found another case."

I nodded. "I found another case. And that led us to a different one. We just kept at it. Now, we have a website where people can submit information to get our help. We can't help everyone, but we try. We just do it anonymously."

Brae frowned. "Why anonymously?"

My lips twisted in a mix of grimace and grin. "You don't think the media would have a field day if they found out the sons of Edmond Archer, the most prolific serial killer of the past two decades, ran some sort of vigilante missing persons group? They'd twist it like they twist everything. And all those eyes would be on us."

"But—"

I didn't let her get the sentiment out, whatever her argument would be. "We skirt what's legal, Brae. If anyone finds out, Kol could lose his job. I could get arrested. And I don't have a safety net from the bureau now."

Understanding swept over her expression, and her fingers squeezed mine. "Thank you. For telling me. It's safe with me. I promise."

A little of the tension bled out of me. "I know it is." And for the first time since my world had been turned upside down, I realized I trusted someone who wasn't one of my brothers or Waylon. I'd given Brae all the ammunition she needed to end me. And she simply held it close like it was a treasure instead of a weapon.

"It's why your brothers didn't want to help me at first—because I know who you are."

Brae didn't miss a trick.

I grinned at her. "They're helping now, aren't they?"

Brae laughed softly. "They are. And I need to thank the one it cost the most."

I loved that she got that, too. That Orion carried the heaviest weight of all of us. That reaching out for him cost more. But he was doing it anyway.

Three words danced in my brain as I stared back at Brae. Three words that had the power to change everything. But I swallowed them down. Because they scared the hell out of me, and I knew they'd send Brae running for the hills.

"Let's try to avoid some bear traps, okay?" I said instead.

She grinned back at me. "Don't lose a foot."

"I'll do my best."

We climbed out of the SUV, and I took in my brother's house—the one he'd built with the help of Waylon, Blaze, and the rest of their small crew. He'd slowly added on over the years, but he'd done it in a way that was seamless.

It had rough wood so dark it toed the line between brown and black. Weather had aged it in a way that gave the house character but also carried a rough warning. A porch wrapped around the entire house, and I knew it was where Orion spent most of his evenings.

The house itself was on one of the farthest edges of our property, right on the border of our ranch and the land that belonged to Aster's grandfather. Out here, only animals and trees surrounded Orion. Just how he liked it.

"It's beautiful," Brae breathed as she took in the structure. "And those horses."

"That's Aster's grandfather's ranch," I explained.

"They're beautiful. Peaceful."

"That's why he likes it out here."

"I would, too," Brae said wistfully.

A flash of an image sparked in my mind. A house set on a meadow not far from here. Owen and Yeti running around a yard. Brae and I on a porch swing. It felt so real I could taste it. And then it was gone again. But I already knew I'd be telling the architect to add a porch swing to our designs.

I cleared my throat. "Come on."

Brae glanced up at the sudden roughness in my voice but didn't say a word. Instead, she followed me up the path. I pointed out little booby traps along the way. A trip wire that would have a sound grenade detonating. A hole in the walkway covered by false stones. And a bear trap covered by shrubs just beneath the porch in case someone tried to scale it.

Each revelation had Brae's eyes growing wider. "You weren't kidding."

"No, I was not."

Brae swallowed hard as we reached the porch steps. "Can I leave these on the porch, or will something explode in my face?"

"As long as you avoid the third stair, you're good."

"This place is a lawsuit waiting to happen," she muttered as she deposited the tin on the top step.

Just as she did, the front door swung open and a hulking figure filled the space. Orion glowered at both of us, but Brae wasn't deterred. She beamed up at him. "I made you thank-you cookies. You're a little hard to bake for, but I did my best."

Orion stayed silent but eyed the cookies, and I swore there was the slightest twitch to his lips.

"Thank you for sending me Maren. She's amazing. She's already filing paperwork or motions or whatever the legal jargon is. Thank you."

The scowl was back on Orion's face. He turned to me, signing. *"I'm working on Nova's map."*

"How's it going?" I asked, then turned to Brae. "He's working on the case map for Nova."

Orion's hands began to move again, and I spoke his signs aloud so Brae could understand. "I've mapped out as many possible routes as I can think of. Does Brae remember hearing anything? A vehicle, a horse?"

Brae worried the corner of her lip as she clasped her hands in front of her, shaking her head. "I don't think so. But that day...it's fuzzy now. Like I've thought about it so much, I've worn out the memory."

Orion frowned, his gaze dropping to the floorboards in front of him. I could almost see his thoughts whirling as if running through endless possibilities in his mind. He looked up again, his hands moving.

"What about vehicles in the parking lot when you arrived?" I translated.

"There were three. A beige SUV with Nevada plates. A green Subaru. And a silver pickup. I don't remember plates on the other two, so they were probably California, but I can't be sure. I've played those moments over and over in my head, but that's all I can remember." Frustration laced Brae's tone as if she were kicking herself for what she couldn't see.

Orion's hands moved again, and I gave voice to his words. "Anything out of place on the trail? Anything at all?"

Brae bit her lip harder and shook her head. "It's fuzzy. I don't—I can't see it all."

I wrapped an arm around her and pulled her to my side. "Hey, it's not your fault. It's trauma. More may come with time." My lips brushed over her temple.

Orion tracked my movements with his gaze, locking on the signs of affection, and I swore there was a hint of longing in his eyes. But whatever the flicker of emotion was, he covered it quickly. *"She should talk to Aster."*

"Not a bad idea," I said.

"What?" Brae asked, looking up at me.

"Aster. She might have an idea for how to recover more accurate memories."

Brae straightened against me. "Anything. I'll do anything."

And that scared me most of all. Because if Brae got reckless, whoever this monster was could take advantage. And they could do anything.

CHAPTER FORTY-FIVE
Braedyn

THE BUZZ OF CONVERSATION FILLED THE CAVERNOUS BAR SPACE. The Boot didn't open for another two hours, but there were almost a dozen people gathered around tables Aidan had pulled together. *All here for me.*

Holly sat chatting with Fiona, a stack of papers in front of her, along with a notepad. Aidan flirted mercilessly with Aster, whose head tipped back in a laugh as Roger chuckled. Wylder and Kol moved around the tables, refilling coffees. Travis said something to Cora that made her blush and giggle. The only people we were still waiting on were Maverick and Waylon.

Dex leaned into my side. "You okay?"

I nodded, swallowing down the emotions that left a heaviness in my throat. "It's just. A lot. Everyone showing up like this. Taking time off work and rearranging schedules."

"Hellion. You've got people who care."

A burn lit along my sternum, spreading up and out. "I'm starting to see that."

"Scares the hell out of you, doesn't it?"

My gaze flicked up to his dark-hazel eyes. So much swirled there. "When you don't have anyone, there's less to lose."

Dex wrapped his arms around me, and I pressed my face to his chest, burrowing in. His lips ghosted over my hair. "You're just going to have to get used to us sticking around."

A war of feeling erupted, battling it out over my mind and body. Hope and fear. Love and loss. I didn't know what to grab ahold of.

Breathing deeply, I tried to rest in the knowledge that all of these people were here because they wanted to help. I released Dex and pulled myself from his hold to face the chattering group. My gaze hitched on Roger's, and I didn't miss the flicker of hurt, but he covered it quickly with a grin.

Guilt swirled low in my belly. He'd asked me out no less than half a dozen times, and I'd always said no. Said I wasn't ready. And it hadn't been a lie. Apparently, it only took the right person to change that.

"I come bearing breakfast," Maverick boomed, carrying in a massive box of food as Waylon lumbered in behind him with another, then Blaze with yet another.

My eyes went wide. "You think we have an army?"

Mav sent me a wink. "Gotta feed this muscle mass, Little Badass."

Aster let out a scoff as she took a sip of her coffee.

"Don't be jealous now, Ice Queen. I brought you your favorite breakfast burrito with *mild* salsa." He rolled his eyes at the word *mild*.

Aster stiffened, her body going ramrod straight. "Can't say I'm really a fan of those anymore."

"Oh, really?" Mav challenged, sliding a to-go box in front of her. "Is that why Sally said you get it at least two mornings a week?"

Aster's cheeks flushed, and her pale-blue eyes flashed. "Maybe I just don't like it from you, Satan."

"Guess I could let you starve to death." He started to take the box away, but Aster jerked it from his hands.

"Go sit on a cactus," she muttered.

Mav's lips twitched. "Never knew you were into ass play. Kinky, I like it."

The look Aster leveled him with should've fried him on the spot, but Maverick just grinned.

Kol let out a whistle. "Enough of Mav's bullshit. Let's get spread this out and get to work. We don't have long."

Maverick gave his brother a mock salute as he set down his box and began pulling things out. Waylon and Blaze followed suit.

Blaze beamed at me as he unloaded donuts and pastries of every kind. "The Little Dude treating you well?"

My cheeks heated. "I'm very lucky to have him as a neighbor."

"Your very friendly neighbor," Dex said, voice pitched low.

Blaze let out a hoot. "Love to see it. You want a donut or a bear claw?"

Dex held out a hand. "You didn't make those, right?"

Blaze rolled his eyes. "I'm not wasting any of Lolli's recipes on you."

"Lolli?" I asked, confused.

Dex just shook his head and scrubbed a hand over his jaw. "The grandmother of some friends of mine. She has an affinity for *special* brownies and other creations. I never should've introduced her to Blaze."

My landlord just snickered. "She's my sister from another mister. The universe would've brought us together no matter what. We're here to open minds and chakras."

"Oh, Jesus," Dex muttered. "More like you're here to have us all seeing pink elephants in tutus for a week."

"Okay, let's sit and begin," Kol called.

"Who put you in charge?" Mav asked, scowling.

"I did," I said, cutting off a potential battle for dominance.

Maverick turned to me. "I'm hurt, Little Badass."

I grinned at him. "If you were in charge, this meeting would take twenty years and end in shots."

Waylon guffawed as he slid into a chair. "She knows you well already."

"Okay, let's run through updates first. I've shared the list of similar cases in the area," Kol continued. "If this is a single unsub, they're smart. Moving across county, town, and jurisdictional lines just enough that it didn't flag law enforcement right off."

"Same with the victim profile," Wylder added. "There's a wide variety. Men and women. Different ages, races, risk levels."

"Crimes of opportunity?" Aster inquired, tapping away on her phone screen.

"Possibly," Wylder said.

Dex leaned forward. "It could be multiple unsubs. Or maybe there was something the victims did, someplace they all went that tripped something in a single unsub and made them targets."

A shiver tracked down my spine. Kol had pulled four cases in the area over the last two years. Had one person taken them all? Hurt them? Killed them?

The further we got into things, the more my hope dwindled. And God, that hurt like hell.

Fingers wove through mine, squeezing. My gaze found Dex's as different members of our group added to the case, each bringing what they had to offer.

"I'm right here." Dex mouthed the reassurance.

But I couldn't help wondering...for how long? I squeezed his hand as if that could keep him here.

"Brae?"

Aster's voice had me snapping out of my different sort of fear. "Sorry," I said quickly. "What did you say?"

She sent me a soft smile. "Just that you wanted to work on some memory recall?"

I nodded. "That day. It's gotten a little fuzzy. I wondered if there's something I can do to sharpen the memories."

"That's totally normal," Aster assured me. "You went through a serious trauma. There are a few things that might help. Guided meditation. Journaling. But the thing that might help most is going back to the scene. The problem is, it can also be a huge trigger. You need to take care around that and only do it if you're ready."

My whole body stiffened, and my fingers constricted around Dex's. "I...I keep planning on going but then never see it through."

Empathy washed over Aster's face. "You don't have to if you're not there yet."

"I'll go with you whenever you're ready," Cora offered kindly.

"Me, too," Holly chimed in.

Dex's thumb stroked back and forth across my hand. I just kept breathing.

"I've wanted to go back. I've said I would since I moved here. But I still just...haven't," I admitted. And with those words came a wash of shame. I said I was here to find her, to fight for her, but I hadn't done the one thing that might actually shake something loose.

"There's no rush," Aster assured me. "We can go anytime you're ready."

But there was a rush. Nova. She'd been out there alone for so long. Whether she was living through hell or no longer breathing, she was alone. And I couldn't stand that. She'd been the one to make sure I never was. I had to do the same for her.

"Saturday?" I croaked.

Dex leaned into me, his lips hovering at my temple. "We're with you. You're not alone."

That almost scared me more. Because I had so much more to lose.

My back ached, and my feet throbbed, but I'd never been more grateful for the distraction. We'd been slammed for most of the day with tourists and locals alike, and now that things had slowed to a trickle as we hit half past two, I almost wished it would start all over again. I'd take exhausted and hurting over being alone with my thoughts.

A flash of movement caught my eye at the hostess stand. I grinned as I crossed to Travis. "Twice in one day? What'd I do to deserve that?"

He chuckled. "You can thank Roger's ravenous appetite. I called in a to-go order."

"I'll go check on that for you."

"Brae."

I stopped, turning back to face Travis. I saw it then, the concern, the worry.

"Are you okay? The meeting this morning...it was a lot."

God, he was a good human. I had somehow ended up surrounded by them here. Stumbled my way into a family—the kind that would order takeout just for an excuse to check up on me.

"I'm all right. I promise."

Travis just stared me down.

I let out a long breath. "This has been hard. And the deeper we dig, the more hope I lose."

Worry streaked across his face. "Brae..."

"I know. I know the chances of her being alive are slim. I think I'm finally coming to terms with that. But I don't want her to be alone. I need to find her. To put her to rest." Tears brimmed in my eyes, but I quickly swiped them away.

"Well, well. What do we have here?" a gruff voice asked.

I looked up to see Sheriff Miller ambling in, an annoyed look on his face.

"Sheriff," Travis greeted, stiffening on the single word.

"Making social calls on duty?" he asked.

"No, sir," Travis ground out. "Rog and I are on lunch. I'm just picking it up."

"Must be paying you too much if you can get takeout all the time."

God, every time I thought Miller might be turning a corner, he proved otherwise.

"Can I help you with something, Sheriff?" I asked, trying to rescue Travis.

"Came to see if you'd gotten any other calls, threats, anything suspicious," Miller muttered.

Surprise lit through me, and I could see it in Travis's eyes, as well. "No. I haven't. It's been pretty quiet."

Miller's lips thinned. "All right. You call me if anything pops up."

"Sure. Um, thank you."

He jerked his head in a nod and headed for the door. "Just doin' my job."

"For the first time in a decade," Travis muttered.

I tried to stifle my laugh as I made a beeline for the kitchen to grab his food. When I got back, Travis was still staring at the spot where the sheriff had been.

"Here you go."

He jolted slightly. "Thanks, Brae. You let me know if you need anything."

"I will. Thank you for everything. You and Cora both."

"Anytime."

As he left, I moved to wipe down tables and refill condiments, anything to keep busy. Aidan had left for the day, so it was only Wylder and me. He'd hold down the fort alone until the evening crew came in. Sometimes, I didn't know how he did it. He worked over twelve-hour shifts most days. But he never seemed tired and never complained.

A shadow fell over the table I was clearing, making me straighten to offer help. But the word died on my lips as I caught sight of angry, green eyes. Vincent was dressed in his usual preppy fare: khakis, a polo shirt, loafers that probably cost as much as my car, and a watch I knew cost more than the cabin I lived in.

"You never know when to shut your fucking mouth," he snarled.

I stiffened as movement caught my eye: Wylder, rounding the bar as he shoved his phone into his pocket.

I wasn't alone. I was safe. And Vincent Faber didn't get to make me cower. "I would've thought the pepper spray and busted balls would've made you smarter."

Redness crept up Vincent's throat. "That podcast has *millions* of subscribers. You throw *my* business all over it. You spread your bullshit lies."

"Get a grip. I never mentioned you, an ex, nothing. But it doesn't surprise me that you can make anything about you."

"You said you were raising a son alone. The son my fucking family has realized is mine."

I grinned, the action sharkish. "What's the matter, Vincent? Mommy and Daddy realize you're a waste of space who blows through their money and doesn't do anything worthwhile?"

Vincent moved so fast I wouldn't have been able to stop him. But Wylder did. The moment Vincent's hand rose to strike, Wylder caught it at the wrist. "I wouldn't do that if I were you."

Vincent snarled and ripped his hand free. "The hacker felon's degenerate brother. How lovely. Isn't it risky for a drunk to be working in a bar?"

Everything in me tensed as if lead filled my muscles. He knew who Dex was. Wylder. He knew their histories. This was more than keeping tabs on an ex and your kid. This was gathering ammunition.

"Get out," I spat.

"Gonna second that request," Wylder said coolly. "Got the right to refuse service to anyone, and if you don't go, I have no problem removing you forcibly."

"I'll sue you so fast your head will spin," Vincent threatened. "I'll own this bar and tear it to the ground just for shits and giggles."

"Oh, you could try," Wylder agreed. "But I think you'll find the law around here doesn't take too kindly to you richy-rich types thinking they can mess with the locals. And they sure as hell don't take too kindly to people *stalking* their residents."

A muscle fluttered wildly along Vincent's jaw. "I'm not stalking anybody. I'm checking in on what's *mine*." His gaze flicked to me, raking over my body in a way that had me wanting to shower and vomit all at once. "You thought you could leave *me*. Disobey *my orders*. I own you, Braedyn. And you better come to heel."

"What. Did. You. Say?"

The new voice was familiar, but it vibrated with a fury I'd never heard before.

As my gaze lifted, I saw that fury was a living, breathing thing. And it engulfed Dex.

CHAPTER FORTY-SIX
Dex

I DID EVERYTHING I COULD TO MAKE SURE I NEVER BECAME MY father. I meditated. I gave back. I *never* let my temper get the best of me.

And part of that last piece was never letting more people in—not beyond the surface level that meant I would lose it if someone hurt them or something happened to them. But that had all been blown to hell.

Because as I stared back at the piece of shit trying to dominate Brae, to reduce her to property, I knew I had the ability to kill. That alone should've snapped me out of it, but it didn't. It only stoked the fire living inside me—one my father had laid the kindling for.

The dipshit douchebag whirled, no awareness of when someone else was present. Someone else who could end him in a matter of seconds. It would be far too easy.

The moment Vincent registered who I was, his eyes widened a fraction. Then true fury lit his features. "So this is who she's spreading her legs for now. A felon with a serial killer for a father. The courts are going to *love* that. They'll be begging me to take my bastard boy."

I prowled toward the man. There was nothing and no one but

him. The person I wanted to end, wipe from this earth once and for all. "You're right, and you're wrong, Vinny. I can call you Vinny, right?"

Heat bloomed over the asshole's face. "You can call me *sir*, you trailer trash."

A low chuckle left my lips, but it wasn't a light sound. It was pure darkness. "Well, Vinny. You're wrong that I'm a felon. Never did time. Worked for the FBI instead. And I can produce half a dozen high-level agents who would love to tell a judge what an upstanding citizen I am."

A sound of derision left Vincent's lips.

"But you're right that my father was a serial killer. He did things that would give you nightmares for the rest of your pathetic life. And he made me. He *raised* me. So you better think long and hard before you mess with two people who mean something to me."

Fear flooded the weasel's expression. He realized he was alone with me and two people who would most certainly not have his back. But he doubled down, proving he was a moron in addition to being an asshole.

"You can't touch me. But I'm going to own you before this is done. I'll own this whole godforsaken town before this is over." Vincent's gaze flicked to Brae.

Just him looking at her was more than I could take—his gaze traveling over her skin, her face. But then he spoke. "And I'll take that boy of yours. You should be grateful. He'll have everything your pathetic ass could never give him."

My fist lashed out, connecting with his jaw in a vicious punch, one that had his head snapping back at an unnatural angle. Vincent went down like a ton of bricks. But it wasn't enough.

I moved lightning fast to grab and hit him again, but Wylder was faster. He grabbed me by the arm and hauled me back, trying to create distance.

"That's enough," Wylder bit out. "You got him. Got him good."

"It's not enough," I snarled, trying to get to Vincent, to hurt him worse.

Wylder cursed, struggling to keep me back as Vincent staggered to his feet.

"Gonna sue you," he spat, his voice slurring just a little.

I pushed harder against Wylder, but then Brae was there, filling my vision with all she was. Her beauty. Her understanding. Her worry.

She framed my face in her hands. "Dex. Look at me. Right at me. I'm safe. Okay?"

Those golden eyes broke through. "Hellion," I croaked.

"That's right. And I'm right here, okay?"

Vincent started spewing more bullshit, and my gaze moved to him.

Wylder cursed. "Get Dex to my office. I'll get rid of the asshole."

"Me," Brae commanded. "Look at me. Right here."

My gaze returned to her as if she owned it, owned me. Not in the way Vincent had spoken of, though. In a way that existed because I had given her that ownership. My body. My goddamned soul.

"That's it. With me," she praised.

Some part of me was aware of her guiding me to Wylder's office. Shutting the door and locking it behind us. Though I wasn't sure whether that was to keep me in or Vincent out.

Brae's hands were on my face. She lifted my glasses off and set them on the desk. And then those hands were back. So soft compared to my stubbled jaw, my skin that felt so rough and undeserving.

"Don't," I rasped.

Pain streaked across her face—pain I put there. It only strengthened my resolve. Because that's what I did. I inflicted hurt. Worse.

"Dex," she whispered.

"Don't touch me. You shouldn't touch me."

"Why?" The word was so gentle, searching for understanding.

"I can hurt people. I'll hurt you. I have him in me, Brae. I have him in me." Each word was barbed and ripped from my throat, leaving me in bloody shreds.

A wash of empathy spread over Brae's face. She moved toward me, and I backed up, trying to ward her off, shield her, protect her. I hit the desk, nowhere else to go, and Brae was on me.

Those hands were back on my face, shaking me gently. "Dex. You aren't him. You're nothing like him. You use your power for good.

You protect. You help. You never turn away, even though it would be so easy."

"I wanted to kill him." The words were a whisper. A dark secret.

Brae's shoulders lifted and then fell. "So did I. You didn't."

"I could've." She needed to know. To see.

"Yes. You could've. Which means the fact that you didn't carries all the more weight."

She didn't understand. Didn't see. "You shouldn't be around me."

"I get to decide that. And I can't imagine anyone better to be around. Dex." Brae's voice hitched as if she were struggling with the words. "You gave me a family. You gave me one when I felt like I never really had that. You gave me a community."

I shook my head. "You gave it to yourself."

"Bullshit. You opened doors that were closed and locked. You gave my son someone to look up to. Someone to help him be proud of exactly who he is."

More fear flooded me. "He needs to stay away from me, too."

"No." The word was so final it jolted me. Brae's golden eyes flashed. "We're not going anywhere. I'm not going anywhere."

Her mouth met mine in a kiss that was more of an attack than anything else. Brae's tongue lashed against mine, making me instantly react, battle—as if my body could say everything my words were failing to convey.

My hand dove into her hair, pulling the strands, fisting them. Brae moaned into my mouth, arching against me instead of pulling away. My dick strained for attention, pressing hard against the zipper of my jeans. She owned me, all right, down to my goddamned balls. Everything in me came alive at her touch, her sounds.

Fucking hell.

Brae nipped my bottom lip and then took the kiss deeper. I growled into her mouth in response and palmed her breast through the cotton of her sundress. Her nipple pebbled against my hand as if it were dying to get to me, as if she would meet me anywhere I went.

She was consuming me—her taste, her touch. It was all-consuming. Burning me alive and drowning me all at once.

My hand left that perfect breast, the one that filled my hand and just a little more. It dove under her dress, finding the barest lace covering everything I wanted, covering my heaven and torturous hell.

"This is all you wear under these dresses?" I growled against Brae's lips.

She pulled back, golden eyes flashing in challenge. "If you had investigated before now, you would've known."

My fingers wrapped around the delicate lace. And I let the fury free so she could see. I ripped the lace from her in one brutal tear. Her whole body bowed, but she didn't break. My hellion met me in the fire. The inferno so dark that it terrified me.

But not her. Not Brae. She was right there.

Her fingers found the button of my jeans. They moved in jerky, staccato motions. Suddenly, my jeans were being shucked down my legs, and my cock was in her hand. She stroked me, up and down, squeezing gently toward the end of each thrust.

I groaned, my head tipping back, a bead of wetness bleeding from my tip. Even my goddamned dick bowed at her altar.

"Need you to let go, Dex. Let it all go. Pour it into me. Let me take it from you."

My head jerked up, gaze colliding with hers as my fingers dug into her hip. "I can't." But I wanted to. So damn badly. Wanted to lose myself in nothing but her.

"You can." Brae stroked harder, and I thrust into her fist as my fingers dipped between her thighs.

I felt the wetness, and my eyes fell closed. "Fucking weeping."

"For you," she whispered.

"I don't have a condom." That would stop it. Protect us both.

"I'm on the pill."

Fuck. Fuck. Fuck.

My hips arched into her, meeting her hand but wanting so much more. My eyes flew open. "Got checked," I ground out. Received all my results just yesterday. Nothing was keeping us apart now, and I knew I would break. No force of will could keep me from her now.

"Let it out, Dex. Release it all. Let me take it."

Those brave words from delicate lips were all it took. My hands moved to her waist as I kicked off my shoes and pants. I swore only the fury still burning snapped them free. I flipped our positions, pinning Brae to the desk.

But her legs encircled my waist, meeting me there like always, her eyes not moving from mine as my tip bumped her entrance. Her fingers dove into my hair, pulling it taut. As she pulled harder, I drove into her.

Brae's back arched, a moan leaving her lips as I slid in. The way she moved, the way she met me…so fucking beautiful. And goddamn, she gripped me like a vise. I pulled back, thrusting home again, deeper this time.

A buzz lit beneath my skin, a high that was only her.

Brae's head lifted as her fingers found my shoulders, gripping so hard her nails nearly pierced my skin, even through my tee. "Let go," she commanded.

As though she knew I was still holding some part of myself back. But not now. Not anymore.

I let go. I took her. Like the animal I was. Powering into her, over her.

Brae's legs trembled around me, and her mouth fell open. "More." The word was a plea.

I thrust impossibly deeper as she met me there, battled with me, for me. That buzz intensified, a tingle starting low on my spine. My fingers tightened in her hair as I took her. "Need you with me," I growled. "Always with me."

Her inner walls trembled, fluttering. "Almost."

"Get there." It was an order and a prayer. I needed it with her, not alone.

Brae's nails bit into my shoulders as her eyes flared, and she clamped down on my dick—waving pulses that set me free.

I arched into her, moved through the waves. Losing myself as I spilled into her. That last wall between us crumbled down. There was nothing left. She had all of me.

We rode out the waning waves together until I collapsed against her, against the desk, trying not to crush her but having nothing left.

Brae's hands found my cheeks as her eyes searched mine. "Even your rage is beautiful."

"Hellion," I croaked.

"Not scared of you, Dex. And I never will be. I *see* you, and it's nothing but endless beauty."

No more defenses, no more holding back. She had it all. Everything I had to give. I rested my forehead against hers, knowing I loved her, would always love her, and hoping like hell we could make it through whatever lay ahead.

CHAPTER FORTY-SEVEN
Braedyn

DEX REACHED OVER, HIS HAND LACING THROUGH MINE AS HIS other remained on the wheel. The contact was steady, grounding, just like the man himself. His falter two days ago had brought us closer, as if whatever barrier he'd put up between us had been demolished.

Neither of us had put that fact into words. We'd simply enjoyed being together. With Owen and Yeti. My dog had fallen head over heels for Dex. Literally. Every night, she ended up sleeping on top of his head like some sort of doggy halo as I cuddled into him. We'd been careful to set an alarm, so he was out of my room before Owen woke, but neither of us had wanted to sleep apart.

"What are you smiling about?" Dex asked as his gaze flicked from the road out of town to me.

"How much Yeti loves you."

Dex grunted. "You mean how she's trying to smother me in my sleep?"

I laughed. It was the last sound I thought I'd make on a day like today—one where I was returning to the spot where everything had fallen apart. But with Dex, it was somehow possible.

"I told you. She's got a crush," I argued.

"Last night, she jumped in the shower with me. That's just wrong."

"She was probably worried you were drowning."

"She's trying to get me to break my neck. Your dog is a secret assassin."

Another laugh bubbled out of me. "We gotta get you on one of those funny home video shows. Do they even still have those?"

"Don't you dare," Dex warned.

I just grinned.

His fingers tightened around mine. "How are you feeling?"

I wasn't sure I had an answer for that question. Not in its entirety. "I'm gonna make it through."

Truth. Because with Dex and so many people who cared about me, there was no way I wouldn't.

"You will. And I'm with you. The whole time."

"I know." And that was the ultimate gift. Not knowing that someone would fix everything in your life—because that was impossible—but knowing they would face whatever came with you, that you'd never be alone.

"Good." The word sounded more like a grunt than anything else.

My lips twitched. "You don't have to be grumpy about it."

"I'm grumpy that you have to go through what you're about to."

It was my turn to squeeze Dex's fingers. "We do hard things for the people we love. But that doesn't mean there isn't good mixed in, too. Good in the fact that Owen and Skylar are running wild on the ranch with Waylon and Wylder. Good in the call from Maren this morning that she got all our paperwork in before the courts closed yesterday and thinks we're going to wreck Vincent. Good in the fact that I have so many people showing up for me throughout all of this."

"Sunshine and pure grit. That's you, Hellion," Dex whispered softly.

"You make me braver," I admitted.

"Good."

I fought a smile at the second grunted word.

When Dex pulled into the familiar parking area, a handful of cars were already there. I saw Kol, Cora, and Aster standing in a small group off to the side. But the familiar boulder and array of trees, the map and trail sign had my heart picking up speed.

I'd thought about bringing Yeti with us, but the truth was, until we had a lead on where Nova might be, Yeti wouldn't be helpful. Today was about remembering. Going back to the worst day of my life.

Dex leaned over as he turned off the engine, his lips brushing against my temple. "I'm with you."

I let out a steadying breath and climbed out of the SUV.

Aster looked up and sent me a gentle smile. "How are you doing?"

"I'm okay." And that was true.

Cora moved to give me a quick hug. "Holly wanted to be here, but her kitchen sink sprung a leak, and she had to wait for the plumber."

"Bummer. Leaks are no fun." I was secretly glad she hadn't been able to make it. Four people were enough. And they were all people I could settle around and didn't feel I needed to put up a front with.

"Hey, Little Badass," Kol greeted.

"Not you, too," Dex complained.

Kol's lips twitched. "Hey, it fits her."

Cora grinned. "I agree."

I turned to Aster, clasping my hands together in front of me and squeezing as hard as I could. "Where do we start?"

She nodded, understanding that I needed to get moving or I never would. "Let's go back to that day. Start out as you did."

My mouth suddenly felt dry, and my fingers began to tingle. But then I felt a hand on my lower back. "You're not alone."

I wasn't. I knew it down to my bones. And Nova wouldn't be much longer either.

Crossing to the SUV where Dex had left our day packs, I hoisted one onto my back. "We parked in that spot there." I pointed to an empty one. "There were three other vehicles in the lot. A beige SUV, a green Subaru, and a silver pickup."

"Did you see anyone on the path?" Kol asked.

"A couple. Mid-thirties, maybe. They had a dog. A border collie."

Kol nodded, making a note.

Aster moved in closer to me, adjusting her pack and looking at home in hiking boots, khaki shorts, and a workout tank. "Let's key into Nova. Picture her—what she was wearing, how her hair was, every detail you can remember."

Pain—so much at having to call up her memory. I didn't do it often because the price was so great. As if drawing her in my mind meant carving her into my very flesh.

"She went to Goodwill before our trip to kit herself out. Bought a whole outfit. It had a purple theme. Tan shorts with purple and pink stitching. A purple tank with flowers right along here." My fingers ghosted along the hem of my shirt as my vision blurred. "A purple bandana she wore as a headband, her hair up in a tangled bun. And the locket—"

My voice broke on the last word. The heart locket. The one I'd given her. The one now in the evidence locker at the sheriff's station. The one with the dried blood on it.

"Good," Aster said. "That's so good. Why don't we start walking? Let your mind wander. Let yourself see that day."

She made a motion for me to start out first. And it made sense. She didn't want herself or the rest of the group skewing my memories.

They came in flashes. Snippets of Nova tossing out jokes or shit-talking me along the way. Quick, five-second reels of places we'd stopped or things we'd seen.

As we moved farther and farther down the trail, my chest grew tighter. Because we were getting to the spot. I saw it from a different angle now, but that same peachy-pink hue of the poppies peeked through the trees.

"Here," I croaked. "Here is where we stopped. I went to see those flowers and then…and then she was gone."

Something sounded—not from behind me, where the rest of the group was—but from the trees to my left.

I frowned, looking through the forest. And then it got louder.

My blood turned to ice. Freezing so instantly, it burned like frostbite.

My name. Over and over. My name in Nova's voice.

I was running toward the sound before I could consider the wisdom of it. Toward Nova. Even as I heard Dex shouting from behind me to stop. Even as I heard thundering footsteps. I pushed harder, my muscles aching as I stretched them to their breaking point.

Brambles and branches slapped at my arms and legs, tore at my skin, but I didn't give a damn. I needed to get to Nova.

A flash of something. Color, maybe? Purple?

I moved toward it and then stopped dead. A purple tank soiled and caked with blood. Shorts you could barely see the stitching on. And a body. Head slumped forward. Limbs unnaturally askew. Hair covering the woman's face.

I did the only thing I could. I screamed.

CHAPTER FORTY-EIGHT
Dex

THE SCREAM SPLIT THE TREES, IGNITING A FEAR IN MY VEINS. My lungs burned as I leapt over a fallen log and raced toward the sound: the eerie voice that seemed just a bit drugged. The piercing cry.

I skidded to a halt just as Brae came into view and hauled her against me to shield her from whatever threatened her. And then I saw it. The body. Unmoving. Limp.

Kol broke through the trees, gun at his side. The weapon was pointed toward the ground but still ready to do whatever needed to be done at a moment's notice.

He caught sight of me and Brae...and then the body. He lifted the gun, sweeping the surrounding trees as he moved toward the fallen form.

Brae still screamed, that strange voice coming through in the pockets where she sucked in air. It was Brae's name. Over and over. Desperate and begging.

Kol bent, pulling back the hair, and then stilled. "It's a fucking dummy. It's fake."

Fury lit through me, burning everything in its wake. But still, I kept hold of Brae. I rocked her back and forth. "It's not her. It's not Nova."

The screaming stopped, hitched into a garbled sob. "Not her?"

Brae's voice was completely raw, ravaged, and pained.

"It's not her. It's fake." But it looked so damn real. Not like a regular mannequin but an actual lifelike human replica of some sort.

Brae's name was still being chanted over and over. "Find that fucking speaker," I barked out.

Kol pulled a pair of gloves from his pocket and donned them, moving the mannequin and tugging something from beside it: a portable speaker connected to some sort of recorder. He pressed a button, and the sound cut off.

Nothing but wind in the trees now. No birdcalls or other animal sounds. Brae had likely startled them with her screaming.

I held her to me and kept rocking her back and forth. She trembled against me, her legs finally giving way. I caught her and lowered us to the forest floor, cradling her so she wouldn't see the grisly mannequin. It didn't matter that it was fake. It was too close to the real thing.

"It's her clothes. Her voice," Brae croaked.

I stiffened, my muscles turning to cement as she continued. "Her shorts, her shirt. Nova. That was Nova saying my name."

My gaze lifted to find Kol's. What in the actual hell was happening?

Brae sat huddled on the couch, staring at nothing, Yeti curled next to her. The blankness on her face scared the hell out of me as I watched her from outside. I didn't want her to hear the conversation I was about to have.

"Did you get the photos?" I asked into my phone, pacing across the back deck barefoot.

The sound of Anson tapping his keyboard came over the line. "I'm looking at them now."

"They think it's Nova's actual clothes. Her voice. It'll take a week or two for DNA testing to come back on the blood on the shirt."

It wasn't an amount of blood that necessarily meant death, but it could if the wound hadn't been treated. And there was no way to know when the voice had been recorded. Yesterday? A year ago? And what the hell was the point?

"Whoever this is, they get off on emotional torture," Anson surmised.

"Tell me something I don't fucking know," I clipped.

Anson shifted, making the chair he was sitting in squeak. "Are you holding it together?"

"No." There was no point in bullshitting him. He'd know.

Anson was quiet for a long moment, likely thinking over his approach. "All you can do is hold on. And make sure you're holding on to each other."

"I have to keep her safe." The words were guttural and came from my deepest parts—the ones I hid from everyone but Brae.

"I know. I understand that fear. It's gonna bring up a hell of a lot of stuff for you."

"I'm not here for a shrink session. I'm here for insights. Anything that will help us catch this fucker," I ground out.

Anson sighed. "All right. This is someone who likely enjoys various forms of torture. It's not just about the victim but all those in the victim's orbit. They likely relive the kill or violence when they get a reaction from a victim's loved one."

Dread pooled low, like oil spilling out and sliding through the ocean. "Is Nova dead?"

Anson went quiet again. "Likely. And if she's not, I don't want to think what she's been through."

More dread, a sick feeling.

"This isn't the unsub's first offense. If you're not finding any like crimes in the area, then they've been working up to this."

And they had to be close enough to watch us. They must have known what we were doing today, which meant they'd heard through the grapevine of people who sat at those tables at the Boot two days ago. The only problem was that each person at those tables could've told a dozen others, and those dozen...a dozen more. Gossip and small towns were like wildfire and a desert-dry forest.

"They knew where we would be, Anson."

"Gotta close the circle. Information to your family only. I know it sucks, but it's the way it's gotta be."

I scrubbed a hand over my jaw. "It's not just what we're sharing, though. The Juniper County Sheriff's Department isn't exactly locked down. The sheriff just started to believe something bad could've happened to Nova."

Anson muttered a curse. "Well, keep Brae's location, plans...all of that under wraps. She goes nowhere alone."

"That's a fuckin' given," I growled.

"And keep breathing. You need me to come down there?"

God, he was a good friend. One who had been through his own hell. But he and Rhodes had made it through. And she had helped heal him in ways I hadn't thought possible. Just like Brae was doing for me.

"You're doing everything you can from Sparrow Falls. But thank you. You offering means something."

"Just say the word and I'm there. And in the meantime, watch your back."

"You know I will." Needing eyes in the back of my head was more like it.

"Keep checking in."

"Talk soon." I hit End on the call and just stared inside for a moment.

Brae was still staring into space, and then I saw her shiver. Even though it was eighty-five degrees outside, and she was wrapped in blankets, she was cold.

Fucking hell.

I strode toward the back door and through it, taking a moment to flip the deadbolt and arm the alarm. I crossed the space in six long strides and crouched in front of Brae. My hands lifted to her face, trying to get her to focus.

"Brae," I whispered.

She blinked a few times, jolting from wherever her brain was, and then her teeth started chattering. "C-cold."

I didn't wait, just moved. Tossing off the pile of blankets, I gave Yeti the command to stay and lifted Brae into my arms. The dog watched as I cradled her to me, battling indecision. "*Reste*," I said again.

Yeti's head dropped back to the couch, but she was just as worried about Brae as I was.

My hellion. Tough as nails. A warrior. And she was shaking like a leaf as I strode toward the bathroom off the primary bedroom. It wasn't huge, but the shower was spacious enough. It was clear that Blaze had modernized with a new shower and vanity.

I lowered Brae's feet to the floor, but it killed me to let her go. As if I were ripping my skin from my own damn flesh. I framed her face with my hands and dropped my forehead to hers. "Gonna get you warm, okay? Just stay right here."

Tearing myself away from her, I moved to the shower and turned the water to hot. I was back to Brae in a matter of seconds, but it felt like a lifetime. "Is it okay if I undress you?"

Brae's teeth chattered, but she nodded in jerky motions.

I moved to the hem of her tank. "Arms up."

She lifted her limbs robotically, and as I gently tugged her tank and bra off, I noticed all sorts of scrapes on her arms and chest that must have come from running through the woods. A curse slipped free as I tossed the clothing to the floor and moved to the medicine cabinet. I should've noticed before. None of them were too deep, but that didn't mean they couldn't get infected.

Opening the cabinet, I found hydrogen peroxide and cotton swabs. I doused one and moved back to her. "This might sting a little, okay?"

She nodded again in that robotic movement.

But there was no reaction when I gently brushed the cotton over her skin. It was as if Brae felt nothing at all. And that killed me. She'd gone totally and completely numb, apart from the cold racking her.

I moved as swiftly and thoroughly as possible, disinfecting every scrape and scratch, cleaning away every sign of dirt. When I was done, my hands moved to the button on her waistband. "I'm going to get these shorts off now, all right?"

Brae swayed slightly but nodded again.

I pulled them down, not looking at parts of her body for too long, other than to judge any injuries. I shucked my own clothes and guided Brae into the shower as fast as I could.

Her body shook harder, more viciously. I maneuvered her under the spray, the water just shy of too hot. "Gonna get you warm, Hellion. Gonna get you strong."

A soft moan left Brae's lips. Not a sexual one. One of relief.

"That's it. That's my girl." My fingers ran through her hair as the water soaked the strands, turning them a darker shade of blond. I reached for the shampoo on the shelf and filled my palms, rubbing them together.

Turning Brae so she faced the water, I began to wash her hair. She leaned back into me, into my touch, humming as if reveling in the sensation.

The sound was a balm to my ravaged soul, to the worry and fear I'd been battling all day. I might not be able to fix this, but I could take care of her. I could do something to ease at least the slightest bit of pain.

My fingers dug into Brae's scalp, massaging. She let out another moan.

"Gonna rinse now, okay?"

Brae turned on her own this time, her eyes meeting mine as she stepped back under the spray, a little more aware.

My hands lifted, rinsing the suds from her strands.

"Feels good," she whispered.

I leaned in and pressed my lips to her forehead. "I'm glad."

I repeated the steps with the conditioner, coating every strand before rinsing again. When Brae met my gaze once more, I saw that more of her was there. But as the numbness faded, the pain swirled. Her golden eyes were heavy with it.

"Almost done," I promised.

"My hair tie," she rasped.

Frowning, I looked around and found it hanging from a hook.

"Need to put my hair up," she explained.

"I've got it," I assured her. I gathered that mountain of blond hair, squeezing the excess water from it and winding it into a sphere atop her head. I awkwardly wrapped the rubber band around it, finally getting it to stay.

"Thank you." Brae's voice was still raw, even after the tea and rest.

I pressed my lips to her temple. "I've got you."

I reached for the bodywash, and as I opened it, the scents of red currant and vanilla filled the shower. It wasn't quite Brae's scent but something that blended with whatever was uniquely her.

As I poured the bodywash into my palm, the scent grew. I slid soapy hands over her shoulders and down her arms, careful to make sure every scrape and scratch was cleaned all over again. My hands moved over her belly and up to palm her breasts.

Brae's breathing picked up, and I tried to ignore the familiar hitch. My dick didn't have any such reservations.

"Sorry," I muttered. "Ignore my dick."

Brae's mouth curved the barest amount. "Not his fault."

"He likes you a little too much."

She arched into my touch, eyes going hooded. "Dex?"

"Yes?" I croaked.

"Make me feel," Brae whispered. "Anything but the cold. Anything but the pain."

My chest constricted, my rib cage strangling my lungs. "I'm not sure that's—"

She cut off my sentence with a kiss, her tongue stroking in. It wasn't forceful like in Wylder's office. It was searching, pleading. And when she broke the kiss, her eyes held the same emotions. "Please. You're everything that isn't cold. You're warmth. You're fire. You're life."

My hand slid along her jaw, down to feel the pulse fluttering in her neck. "You're sure?"

And then Brae leveled me. "You're always what I need."

CHAPTER FORTY-NINE
Braedyn

Admitting I needed Dex should've terrified me. After everything I'd lost and all those who had *chosen* to walk away from me, the last thing I should've been doing was leaning. But here I was.

Because Dex was the only thing I needed in that moment. He was the opposite of coldness and pain. He was life and breath and heat.

My hand snaked out to stroke him. The feel of him in my palm, his response, made me feel powerful. And that helped, too.

Dex's eyes slowly closed, and a groan left his lips. "Hellion."

I studied him then, taking in how his head tipped back, exposing his throat. Those broad shoulders strung tight, the ink rippling over his chest. Then his head lifted as he straightened, and hazel eyes locked on mine.

Dex's hands slid along my jaw, his mouth meeting mine. The kiss was more than any before it. It wasn't the desperate need of the first moments we'd shared. It wasn't my demand to break through his defenses in Wylder's office. This one gave voice to words neither of us had been brave enough to speak aloud—but something I knew we both felt.

Stretching onto my tiptoes, I met Dex there, in the unspoken truths between us. I leaned into him, trusting he would catch me, but still not ready to speak the words.

Dex slid his hands lower, fingers gliding over my skin through the water. One stopped where my jaw met my neck, at that pulse point he favored.

"Why?" I whispered into the echoey shower.

Confusion twisted his features.

"Why do you always put your hand right there?" I asked.

Dex's thumb stroked my pulse point. "Your body will tell me things you're not ready to."

My heart took a tripping tumble.

His mouth curved. "It whispers your secrets to my fingertips."

And it did. It told him everything.

While that one hand stayed right at the spot that gave me away, the other traveled down. Lower and lower. Fingers ghosted over my center, and my eyes fluttered closed.

"Don't steal that beauty from me," Dex rasped. "Those Midas eyes. All gold fire."

My eyes flew open again, eager to give him what he wanted.

Dex stroked and teased. "Tell me how you feel."

My breaths came quicker. "Like I'm coming back to life."

Two fingers slid inside, swirling. "Good. Getting warmer?"

"Yes," I breathed.

"You want more?"

My hands moved to his shoulders, gripping them hard. "You. I want *you*."

Those dark-hazel eyes flashed brighter for the barest second, and then his fingers were gone from my body and neck, and he was lifting me, bracing me against the cool shower tile. But I didn't feel the cold.

Dex held me with one arm as he slid inside me, and it was everything I needed. The stretch, the heat. Him.

I arched into him, bracing my back harder against the wall as his hand found my throat again. I knew what he would feel there: my heart racing, my pulse fluttering like butterfly wings.

Dex took me in a tempo we'd never shared before, slowing as if he were memorizing everything about me from the inside out. As his thumb stroked my pulse point, it was almost too much for me to bear. The tenderness. The heat. The certainty.

"Tell me what you need, Brae. Faster? Deeper?"

"This," I croaked. "Just like this."

Each stroke drove inside me as everything about Dex imprinted itself on my bones. Not just this physical connection, but so much more.

My walls tightened around him, and tears gathered in my eyes. "Dex," I breathed.

"I'm with you. You aren't alone. You never will be."

He picked up his pace, finding it with me, that place where we took each other further. To the edge before spilling over into what was only ours.

"With me," Dex gasped. "With me."

I searched for it, finding it in Dex's eyes, in the feel of him moving inside me. It was a type of shattering I'd never experienced before. It started slow, growing and quickening until it turned into a wild fury. Light danced across my vision, but I held on to Dex—his body and his eyes—because I didn't want to lose him either.

The sound that came from Dex's throat was almost animalistic but so damn raw and real as he emptied himself into me and I took all he had to give. And as we rode out every wave together, no coldness remained in me. Because I wasn't alone. I had him.

Dex slowly slid from me, lowering me to the floor and bringing me under the spray. His hand found my neck again. "Want to feel you when I say this."

My heart hammered against my rib cage, fear and hope swirling in equal measure.

"You might not be ready. And that's okay. But I love you, Brae. I love your fierce hellion ways. I love your tender heart. I love how you make me feel more understood than anyone ever has. And more accepted. You said I gave you a home, but it's you. Because I've never felt okay in my own skin, so scared of what I could be—"

"Dex," I croaked.

"But you made me unafraid. For the first time in forever. You made me okay with who I am."

"Because it's beautiful," I whispered.

His thumb traced that pulse point. "You're beautiful. Not just your body but the way you live. The way you inspire others to live. And I love the wild boy you've raised to be such an amazing human."

My voice hitched. "He loves you."

His mouth curved. "I know he does."

I stared up at Dex, not moving, not even breathing. "I love you." The words were barely audible. Just above a whisper.

They hurt. They cost me. As love always should. Because I knew it meant that if anything happened to him, I'd carry those scars with me forever. But I wasn't going to run from this. Wouldn't hide. Because a life without Dex would be like living in the dark. And I wanted the sunrise.

Dex froze. "Say it again."

"I love you." Just a little louder.

Unshed tears glistened in his eyes. "I feel it. I feel it everywhere."

Then he kissed me, the same as before, but it meant more now because we'd spoken the words aloud and let our bodies give them a voice.

When he finally pulled back, he stroked a hand over my jaw. "Let me take care of my girl."

And he did.

Dex rinsed my body, keeping me under the spray as he dipped out to grab towels. He quickly dried himself and wrapped the terry cloth around his waist before moving to me. Shutting off the water, he guided me out and softly dried every inch of my body.

"I'm okay," I assured him.

He looked up from where he knelt at my feet. "Taking care of my girl. Because it's a fucking privilege. Don't steal that from me."

My mouth curved. "All right, then."

Dex wrapped me in the massive, fluffy robe I kept for the days I did leave-in hair treatments and painted my toes, then pulled out the stool from the corner and sat me on it. He fumbled around the bathroom looking for items, but I didn't ask what. There were no nerves about him looking through my things. There was only peace.

He finally pulled out a hair dryer, brush, and leave-in conditioner. Assembling the items, he gently tugged my hair down from its bun and smoothed the strands. He lifted the bottle from the counter and held it up. "Dime size, nickel, or quarter?"

My smile pulled wider. "Nickel."

Dex squeezed the exact right amount into his palm, then coated my hair, running his fingers through my strands and slowly detangling them. All of it felt like putting actions to his earlier words. It felt like love.

As the hair dryer flipped on and Dex meticulously dried every strand, that love buried itself deep. He reached for his glasses, studying my mane to make sure he hadn't missed any spots, then met my eyes in the mirror. "How'd I do?"

"I love you." It was the only thing I could say. The only thing I felt. No coldness, no pain, no fear. He'd burned them out. It didn't mean they wouldn't return or that I wouldn't have to face them, but I wouldn't be doing it alone.

Dex tipped my head back, his hand sliding down my throat. "Say it again so I can feel it."

"I love you."

"That's my fucking girl."

CHAPTER FIFTY
Braedyn

"ONE BREAKFAST BURRITO WITH JUNIOR HOT SAUCE AT YOUR service." Dex slid the plate in front of Owen with a flourish.

I arched a brow. "Hot sauce?"

The last thing I needed was to kill a bunch of taste buds in my kid's mouth before he even made it to third grade.

"*Junior* hot sauce. We're working on developing his palate for spice. Right, O?"

Owen chomped down on the breakfast burrito, nodding enthusiastically. "Ish the best."

Dex slid into the chair next to me as he deposited breakfast burritos on the table for us, too. "It's just pico de gallo. Stow your scowl, Hellion."

I sent a mock glare his way.

Dex only laughed. "For you, I brought the new five–chili pepper blend Waylon has decided to home brew. If you try it, you're taking your life in your hands."

"Challenge accepted." I dotted a few splashes on the end of my burrito and took a huge bite. I felt the heat almost instantly, but it also tasted damn good. "Is that...cinnamon?"

"Jesus." Dex shook his head. "You have a mouth of steel."

I grinned back at him. "Ask Kol when he wants to go head-to-head with me again."

"I think his stomach is still recovering from last time."

"Skylar's still talking about it," Owen said, taking a sip of juice.

"How are the glasses feeling?" I asked.

It had been two weeks since the incident off Tree Creeks Canyon trail—two weeks in which nothing else had happened. There had been no threats. No calls. Nothing. We were still waiting on the test results from the lab on the clothing. Apparently, there was a backlog.

Our ragtag team of investigators was still working on our own, and everyone was pitching in. The entire crew from Compass was helping me filter tips from the line Ridley had set up for the *Sounds Like Serial* episode, and Holly was running that ship with an iron fist. But I didn't mind. She had everything labeled, referenced, and cross-referenced.

Dex and his brothers were running down everything they could on Nova and all the similar missing persons cases. So far, nothing had brought a break in the case. But that didn't mean we stopped trying—or stopped *living*.

For the first time since Nova disappeared, I was finding balance. Maren was hard at work trying to secure my permanent sole custody of Owen. She said things were looking good, especially since I'd received a permanent restraining order for both Owen and me, and we hadn't seen a single sign of Vincent around town. We were safe.

My fingers fell to the worn threads of the friendship bracelet Nova had made me. It wasn't just dedication to finding Nova that I needed; it was dedication to *living*—for me and her.

So we were. Which meant family dinners at Twisted Oak Ranch; milkshake stops at the Grove Griddle; hikes with Yeti, Dex, and Owen; and new glasses for my boy.

Dex had kept his word and helped Owen find just the right pair for him. They were a deep blue with a design along the sides that reminded me of something you might find inside a computer. Instead of going for something that would help Owen blend in, he went for something that would make him stand out.

"They're good," Owen said, lifting his burrito. "And how's my drip now?"

I frowned, trying to see if he'd dropped part of his burrito.

Dex choked on a laugh. "He means he looks good. Gotta keep up with the times, Hellion."

My gaze narrowed on the man next to me. "Are you trying to say you're cooler than me?"

"You said it, not me."

I couldn't hold my glare. And God, I wanted to kiss him. We were easing Owen into little displays of affection, but we needed to have a conversation with him before things went any further. And it was time.

My fingers laced through Dex's under the table, squeezing. "Can we talk to you about something?" I asked Owen.

He instantly looked suspicious, then guilty. "Okay. I fed Yeti my broccoli at the table last night. But I really don't like it. And trust me, I paid the price because her farts were the worst, and I'm the one she hangs with after dinner."

Dex tried to cover his laughter with a cough, and Yeti lifted her head from her dog bed as if to say, *Did you seriously just throw me under the bus?*

I attempted to hide my smile but failed. "I wasn't talking about your not-so-stealthy broccoli move."

"You knew?" Owen demanded.

"Why do you think there weren't any brownies for dessert?"

"Aw, man. Why is chocolate always the price?"

I chuckled. "It's only fair. Balance is the key to life."

Owen studied me for a moment. "If it's not the broccoli, what is it?"

"Well, Dex and I wanted to tell you we've started seeing each other." *Seeing* felt like such a cop-out. It was so much more than that.

"He's sitting right there. I hope you see him," Owen muttered.

Dex's lips twitched. "Your mom means that we're a couple."

"Like boyfriend and girlfriend?" Owen asked.

Dex only grinned wider. "Just like that."

Owen's whole face scrunched. "Why the heck would you want to do that? Girls are gross."

"Hey," I clipped, affronted. "I'm sitting right here. And that is *not* very nice."

Owen shook his head. "Not moms. Moms are awesome. But girlfriends?" He shivered. "It's a total ick."

Dex's whole body shook as he tried to hold back his laughter. "Well, I'm gonna let you in on a secret. In a few years, you're gonna feel a whole lot different about that."

Owen shrugged, lifting his burrito. "It's your life."

I gaped at my kid as he went back to his breakfast and then turned to Dex. "Why did it just sound like he thinks you're ruining your life by dating me?"

Dex let his laughter free but leaned in and tugged my chair to him. "Don't worry, Hellion. I like a little life-ruining."

And then he kissed me. It wasn't over-the-top, just one of those nice and easy ones that felt like a lazy Sunday morning. It was my new favorite pastime, trying to identify all the different kinds of kisses Dex gave me. I constantly changed my mind about the top three. But today, this one led the pack.

"Sick," Owen complained. "And I don't mean the good kind."

I straightened. "Owen…"

"Hey, you guys can do whatever you want, but I'm trying to eat here."

I shook my head. "You might see some kissing."

Owen's nose wrinkled.

"But on the upside, I'll be around more for video game tournaments and pizza-making competitions," Dex offered.

Owen mulled that over. "I guess that's worth some gross kissing."

"I'm so glad," I said wanly.

Dex reached over and squeezed my neck, his thumb hovering over my pulse point. "Take the wins where you can get them, Hellion."

Owen watched us a little more thoughtfully as he toyed with the edge of his burrito. "Does this mean…like maybe one day…Dex would be my dad?"

My heart lurched, and then it was as if a phantom fist squeezed it hard. "It's a little early—"

"Anyone who gets to be your dad will be the luckiest guy in the world," Dex said, cutting me off. "If one day it's me? I'm gonna be over the moon and brag to all my brothers."

One corner of Owen's mouth kicked up. "I am pretty cool."

Dex reached over and ruffled Owen's hair. "The absolute coolest."

My heart melted on the spot.

"Hey, Brae," Wylder called over the throng of the bar. "Is there any way you can stay late today?"

There was pleading in Wylder's hazel eyes, and I knew why. We were slammed. There was some sort of tour group in town, and they'd decided the Boot was the place they needed to stop for a late lunch.

"Sure. Let me just text Dex." I slid my phone out of my back pocket to type out the message. Owen had a playdate with Skylar after camp. Apparently, friends who were girls were fine. It was just girlfriends that were gross. And I was still salty about it.

> **Me:** *Wylder needs me to stay a little late. That okay with you, bodyguard?*

Because even though all had been quiet, Dex was still driving me to and from work—and anywhere else I wanted to go. I appreciated his care, but I also didn't know how much longer we could keep this up. Especially when he'd started a white-hat consulting project for a large tech company.

> **Dex:** *Your body is definitely worth guarding.*

My mouth curved as my cheeks heated.

"Now that's a sexting smile," Aidan called as he passed with a tray.

"It is not," I shouted back.

"Sure, Delicious. Whatever you say."

I shook my head and went back to my phone.

Me: *You're getting me in trouble at work.*

Dex: *Good. I'm just wrapping up a piece of this project. Be there in about an hour, and I'll wait at the bar until you're ready.*

He'd taken to doing that, too. Just coming in thirty minutes or an hour before I got off to shoot the shit with his brother and the rest of the staff. But I'd feel his eyes on me from time to time, the warmth of them. It was our little routine, a slice of normalcy amid the mayhem. And I loved it.

Me: *See you soon.*

I ended the text with a kissy face emoji and went back to work. I chatted with the tourist group who was on a West Coast tour from Charlotte, North Carolina. And for the first time, I felt like a real local, sharing my favorite spots for shopping and eating. I bussed tables and slung food and knew I'd sleep like a baby tonight.

"B, baby," Aidan called from the other side of the bar.

"Yeah?"

"We're out of napkins. Can you grab them?"

"Sure thing," I hollered back.

I slid my tray onto the bar and turned for the back hallway. We were so packed, there was a line at the women's bathroom. But the hall cleared after that. I passed Wylder's office, a smile tipping my lips at the memories I had of the space, and headed for the stockroom.

But before I could reach for the doorknob, a hand landed on my shoulder. Just as it did, something sharp pricked my low back.

"Keep moving. Straight ahead. You look behind you, you make a sound, I'll punch this blade in your kidney and leave you bleeding out on the floor."

The world went a little fuzzy as adrenaline flooded my system. Panic, fear. That voice. I didn't need to look behind me to see who it was. I knew.

I'd heard it whisper countless pretty lies. I'd heard it sling subtle insults that made me doubt myself. I'd heard it make promises it never meant to keep. And I'd heard it say countless cruel things as he told me he wanted nothing to do with our child.

Vincent.

"Finally, she fucking listens. I guess I should've shown you some goddamned force years ago. Maybe you would've learned to obey."

He thought he could scare me, terrify me into following him out the back door so he could hurt me or worse. But he was wrong.

My gaze jumped around the hallway, looking for something, anything.

"What's the matter, Braedyn? Cat finally got your fucking tongue?"

I saw it then. The fire alarm. If I pulled it, people would come running toward the nearest exit, and at least half would head for this door. It wasn't a weapon, but it was something.

"Answer me, goddammit." Vincent pricked the knife into my side. Not deep but enough that I let out a pained yelp. "I guess she can speak. I like the sound of your pain better than your voice anyway."

"What do you want?" I croaked as I counted the steps to the fire alarm. Ten? Twelve?

"I'll tell you what I fucking want," he snarled. "I want you to go out that back door and sign away all your parental rights on that bastard boy."

Vincent had lost his grip on reality. He thought paperwork at knifepoint would hold up in court? But just the fact that he'd thought it had me worried. Or he could be lying.

"You shouldn't be here," I said, keeping my voice low and as gentle as possible. "You'll get in trouble. I have a restraining order—"

His hand fisted in my hair. "I fucking know you have a restraining order. The family lawyer told my parents, and they cut me off, you toxic little cunt."

I sucked in a pained breath.

"You thought you could leave *me*? You're nothing compared to me. I had to teach you a lesson. Remind you I was right there, watching. That you always belonged to me."

Fear rippled through me in hot waves. *This* was why he'd left those taunting messages and made those dozens of profiles to stalk me. Because I left?

"But you never learned. You gave birth to that bastard and tried to ruin my life. Well, you're not getting away with it. We're going to fix it. You're going to sign those papers, and my parents will welcome me right back into the fold when I give them their grandson."

"Hey, Little Badass," a voice called from behind us.

Crap, crap, crap. Maverick.

It wasn't that I didn't want help. I did. But Mav getting caught up in this wouldn't spell good things.

I didn't answer; I just kept walking as Vincent kept a hard grip on my shoulder.

"Brae, wait up!" There was no cheerful amusement in his voice now; there was only hardness. A command.

"Keep walking, or I'll gut him and then you," Vincent snarled.

"Stop!" Maverick yelled.

Vincent whirled me around, placing me in front of him and pointing the knife directly at my rib cage. "Back off. I know you think you're playing the hero, hotshot, but you'll only get her dead. And then how will you feel?"

Vincent knew *exactly* who Maverick was, down to his job and every button to press. That only added to the panic coursing through me.

Maverick's eyes always seemed lighter than his brothers', as if the mischief in them turned the gold brighter somehow. But now? Now, they were a stormy shade, the dark green almost engulfing the gold. "Let. Her. Go."

Vincent laughed, the sound ugly and cutting. "Now why would I want to do that?"

"Because if you take this any further, that precious, pampered life of yours is gonna get ruined."

It was then that I realized Mav knew exactly who Vincent was, too. Dex must've shown his brother a photo after Vincent showed up. Another line of defense.

Vincent scoffed and pressed the tip of the blade into my skin.

"There's something you should know, smoke eater. The kind of money my family has? It gets me out of *anything*."

And that's what he truly thought. That because of his parents' wealth, he could do anything he wanted. He could treat human beings like property or trash. None of it mattered.

Fury blazed through me, fueled by heartbreak, humiliation, endless sleepless nights, and questions from my son about why his dad didn't love him. I let all of that wash through me and remembered the self-defense class I'd taken at my local YMCA in Oakland.

I slammed my foot down on top of Vincent's. Those pathetic, little loafers didn't give him any sort of protection. He howled in pain, his body contorting. The blade sliced along my side, and white-hot pain burned, but I didn't let it stop me.

Whirling to face him, I brought my palm up in a strike that ended with a satisfying crunch. And then Vincent dropped like a marionette with its strings cut.

Maverick raced forward, kicked the knife away, and rolled Vincent to his stomach while yanking his hands behind his back.

"My nose! She broke my fucking nose!" Vincent wailed.

"Apparently, you didn't learn your lesson at the broken balls," I snapped.

"Hey, Little Badass. Enough with the trash talk. Call the cops," Maverick gritted out.

"Okay, okay." The cops. That was a good idea. Pain flared in my side, and when I touched it, my fingers came away coated in red.

Oh shit.

CHAPTER FIFTY-ONE
Dex

EVERYTHING IN ME HAD GONE NUMB—THE KIND OF NUMBNESS that caused a faint buzzing in your ears. It spread, entering my body and limbs, but it wasn't the vibration I'd grown used to around Brae. Nothing that made me feel alive. This was sheer panic and had everything in me turning off.

"Brae's fine."

That was how Wylder had started the call. But I knew something had happened. Brae wasn't truly okay.

I wound my way through the throng of tourists. There'd been no parking anywhere close, and now, so many people crowded the sidewalk that it was hard to navigate. Some whispered in groups, and snatches of their conversations hit my ears.

"...woman attacked..."

"He had a knife..."

"You would think it would be safe in a place like this."

I shut them out. Just like I ignored everything else, I pushed through everyone until I reached the entrance of the Boot. Various deputies and other officers were on the scene, even the fire department.

As I started for the entrance, a familiar, barrel-chested man stepped into my path, a smug look on his face. "This establishment is closed."

My hands fisted at my sides as my gaze picked out at least half a dozen pressure points that would drop this asshole to his knees. Probably not a good idea if I didn't want to get tased or shot. "I'm here for Brae."

Grady's smugness only intensified. "I'm afraid I can't let you through."

My fingers twitched at my sides, rolling into fists. My hold on the rage that lived inside me was tenuous at best.

"Stop being a fuckwit and let him through." Roger stepped out into the sunlight, glaring at Grady.

Grady's smug look turned to a scowl. "Law enforcement only."

"He's her boyfriend, and you know it. So stop trying to exert dominance just because no one wants to suck your dick," Roger snapped.

Red splotches appeared all over Grady's face. "You're gonna get what's coming to you one of these days."

"Can't wait," Roger called, giving Grady a little finger wave as he stalked off. "Come on. She's back here."

"Talk to me." My words were strangled at best, spoken through gritted teeth and a throat so tight it was a miracle any air made it through.

"Vincent Faber is now in custody, sitting in a cell at the station. He came up behind Brae and tried to get her to go with him. Used a knife as motivation."

The word *knife* had blazing ice blasting through my system, the kind of coldness that burned.

"Mav came up on them," Roger continued. "Vincent held her at knifepoint, but Brae broke his nose and likely a few toes for good measure. Got a fighter there."

I couldn't think about what a badass she was because it only reminded me that she'd had to defend herself in the first place. All I could manage to say was her name. "Brae."

"Got a bit of a cut," Roger said carefully. "Mav's tending to her right now."

I saw her then, a flash of blond hair as she sat, straddling one of the bar chairs so her front was to the wooden slats. Her Boot T-shirt was tucked up under her bra, her back and side exposed—a side that Mav was currently sewing to-fucking-gether.

Fury. Fear. Guilt. Shame. It all swirled together in an ugly stew. I hadn't been there. Brae had needed me, and I hadn't been there.

I stalked toward the woman who had somehow come to mean everything to me. I rounded Mav, coming to Brae's front and dropping to my knees. She was a little pale, but her eyes were bright. I couldn't stop myself from touching her, my hands lifting to those too-pale cheeks.

"Hellion."

"Hey," she whispered, forcing a wobbly smile.

I pressed my forehead to hers. "I'm so sorry."

"It's not yours to be sorry for." Her hands wrapped around my forearms, gripping tightly.

"I should've been here," I rasped.

"You're here now."

It wasn't enough. Not nearly enough. "I want to rip him limb from limb."

"Little Badass did a number on his nose if that helps," Mav said, pulling the medical-grade thread through Brae's side.

"Not good enough," I snarled.

Brae's fingers dug into my forearms. "Hey, I'm okay. Just a little cut. And this will get him out of my and Owen's lives forever."

"Already called Maren Robinson," Wylder said, his expression unreadable. "She's adding to the filing as we speak."

Guilt still swarmed that I hadn't done more already—more to end Vincent for good. But I'd been distracted by Nova's case and whoever had been taunting Brae, and missed the threat right in front of us.

"Honestly, I should thank the asshole," Brae muttered.

"Don't joke. Not about this." My forehead dropped to hers again. "I need you to be okay. Safe."

"I am," she whispered.

I felt her warm breath mixing with mine. Something about that soothed, as did the hint of red currant and vanilla that swirled around me. Brae was okay.

"And I'm all done," Mav said, forcing me to pull back from Brae, even though it was the last thing I wanted to do.

Mav taped a piece of gauze over the wound. "I put some antibiotic ointment on it. You'll want to wash around the wound twice daily, but try not to get the stitches wet. Replace the covering and reapply the ointment. I can get you everything you need."

Brae tugged her T-shirt down. "Thank you, Mav. I really didn't want to go to the hospital."

Mav held out his fist for a knuckle bump. "I got you covered, Little Badass. These should be able to come out in about a week."

They talked about wound care some more and what to look out for, but all I could do was stare at the blood soaking the pale pink shirt—Brae's blood. It spread over a good portion of the side.

My back teeth ground together.

Wylder cleared his throat. "Uh, Brae?"

She looked up at him in question.

He tossed her one of the tees that usually lived by the hostess stand. "May want to change into this so Dex's brain doesn't explode."

She looked from the new tee to the blood on the one she was wearing to me, understanding blooming. "I'm good, Buttercup. No need to kill someone with death-ray eyes."

"He. Hurt. You."

Brae's hands lifted to my cheeks. "And I'm still here. I hurt him back. I got away."

"And I dislocated his shoulder," Mav cut in helpfully.

Brae's mouth brushed mine. "I'm all good."

A throat cleared, making us pull apart. Roger stood there with a newly arrived Travis. And they both looked...furious.

I was on my feet in a flash, Brae rising behind me.

"What?" she asked. "What is it?"

Travis looked between us. "We found something in Vincent's hotel room."

I wrapped an arm around Brae's shoulders, pulling her gently to my side.

"There was a computer," Travis went on.

Of course there was. And I'd been all over that system, gathering as much dirt as possible on the douchebag. I'd be anonymously dropping the evidence in the Juniper County District Attorney's email as soon as possible to add some time to Vincent's sentence.

"It was a secondary one," Roger added, his gaze moving to me. He knew me too well. Knew I'd have already been in every system I could get my hands on. But I hadn't seen any signs of a secondary system. Vincent's email address was logged in four places. His phone, iPad, laptop, and work desktop. Nowhere else.

Travis shifted from one foot to the other. "It was one of those cheap deals. Not connected to the internet. More of a file server."

"What kind of files?" I gritted out.

Travis's focus flicked to me and then to the woman next to me. "Brae. It was all Brae."

CHAPTER FIFTY-TWO
Braedyn

TEN DAYS. IT HAD BEEN TEN DAYS SINCE VINCENT'S ARREST. TEN days since my world had been ripped apart yet again. But I hadn't felt it the way I had in the past.

Because I had the Archers. I had Waylon showing up with homemade dinner. Skylar taking me out to play with Tink and making Owen and me laugh until our sides ached. Mav checking my wound for infection on the regular and finally taking out my stitches yesterday. Wylder paying extra attention to me at the Boot and never letting me do anything alone. Kol offering to watch Owen when I had to meet with my lawyer and the Juniper County District Attorney. And Orion. Who supported me in his very Orion way. He sent a care package full of healing items and chocolate cake. Because, apparently, chocolate cake was Orion's love language.

And it wasn't just them. I had Roger and Travis keeping me updated on everything case-wise. Aster and Holly stopping by with flowers and regular check-ins. Aidan, Cora, and Fiona keeping an eye on me at work. Alma and Jack taking extra care at our Compass meeting.

I'd built a community. A home. And that eased the pain of everything. The heartbreak.

I pulled my SUV into the parking spot at the trailhead and stared at the sign: *Three Creeks Canyon Trail*.

My hands stayed on the wheel, foot on the brake, as I stared at the sign like it held all the answers just out of reach.

The problem was that law enforcement thought they had found their answers because Vincent's second laptop had a treasure trove of data—not just files on Owen and me but also on Nova, including photos of us from the moment we left Rhode Island.

No one knew for sure if Vincent had taken them or if he'd hired someone because he wasn't talking. His family had retained some high-powered criminal attorney out of New York, and he'd shut his client right up.

But that didn't stop law enforcement from going through every inch of that computer. They'd found files containing every article ever written about Nova's disappearance. Even some sheriff's department records he'd managed to get ahold of.

The state police and Sheriff Miller were circling him like buzzards. Travis and Roger had shared that there was more than a little talk about Vincent being behind Nova's disappearance.

Dex's profiler friend had said it was possible. From what he could put together of Vincent's makeup, he wouldn't want me to have anyone—no help from a single soul. He'd feel some sort of ownership over me and a need to punish me for not toeing the line. And while there were other missing persons cases, this could've been an outlier or exception.

But something niggled at me. I felt as if I was missing some tiny piece that would make it all make sense.

I stared harder at the sign, my vision going blurry. A car passed on the road behind me, making me blink and clear away the burn in my eyes.

Forcing my hand from the wheel, I turned off the engine. I couldn't shake the unsettled feeling. So I'd come back to where it all began. And I'd roped Aster and Dex into meeting me here. Just more proof of the amazing community I'd built—it just wasn't complete without Nova.

"Where are you?" I whispered into the nothingness around me. The burn was back in my eyes. "Are you gone?" Pain ripped at my heart. "I'll never give up on you, Supernova. Never."

And I wouldn't. Even if all that was left to find were bones, I wouldn't rest until those bones were at peace.

My phone dinged, and I swiped it up from the cupholder. I didn't usually have service up here, but one tiny bar was breaking through.

> **Dex:** *Running ten behind. The groomer wanted to put a bow on Yeti.*

My mouth curved as I imagined how that had gone over with Dex.

> **Me:** *Can't wait to see how adorable she looks.*

> **Dex:** *Stop. I'm burning that bow.*

I laughed, my fingers tapping on the screen.

> **Me:** *See you soon.*

> **Dex:** *Stay in the car unless Aster is with you.*

It meant something that he was still concerned. Still wanted me to be careful and use the buddy system. Because it meant he trusted my gut.

> **Me:** *I'll be the one in the Bigfoot T-shirt.*

> **Dex:** *Don't stop believing. Be there soon.*

God, I loved him. I loved him with everything I had in me. It was the kind of love that terrified you. But I was willing to live with the fear because there was such beauty on the other side of it.

A familiar truck pulled in two spots down, and Aster gave me a wave as she parked—yet again giving up one of her rare afternoons off. It was a gift. And so was her friendship.

I snatched my keys from the cupholder and got out of the SUV, sending her an authentic smile. One that said I was so grateful she was here, even though this was damn hard. "Thank you for coming."

Aster beeped her locks as she hoisted her pack over her shoulder. She looked like she'd done this a million times—and she probably had done it hundreds throughout her life. Her pale-blond hair was swept up in a ponytail, and she had a bandana tied around it like a headband.

That tiny detail reminded me so much of Nova. Maybe that was a good thing. Maybe it would help me unlock something new.

Aster's mouth curved, and her smile felt authentic, too. A little sad but also reassuring. "It's an honor that you wanted me to come. I'll help however I can."

"I feel really lucky to have met you," I croaked. "What brought me here is the worst possible pain, but I'm still grateful for the things that have come out of that hurt."

She closed the distance between us and pulled me into a quick hug. "That's the best we can hope for. That we're able to find the good amid the hard."

Releasing her, I tried to pull myself together. "Gonna claim all the good I can."

"Amen to that," Aster agreed.

"Dex will be here any minute. He was picking up Yeti from the groomer, and I think he might've gotten into it with her over a bow."

Aster arched a brow. "A bow?"

"Don't ask." I pressed a button on my key fob, and the back hatch of my SUV opened.

We were planning to do the full hike that Nova and I had done, hoping it would help me figure out what I was missing—or help me let go.

I tried to remember her now. The way she was that day. How her locket caught the sunlight. How her laugh sounded when it caught on the breeze. The way her pale-gray eyes glowed as she teased me. *"If I get poison ivy on my hoo-ha, my revenge will be vast, Braedyn Winslow."*

I heard the words as clear as day. And I laughed. Because my best friend—my sister—was freaking hilarious. I missed her so damn much. I would until I left this earth. But I would pay that price over and over for the gift of knowing and loving Nova Monroe. It was a beautiful sort of pain when you thought about it. The kind that was an honor to carry.

So I took that pain and held it close as I grabbed my backpack and set it next to the tire. I double-checked everything. Water. Granola bars. First-aid kit. Just in case, I pulled out the bear spray that worked just as well on humans as it did on animals.

The wind picked up, rustling the tree branches. Something else sounded. I thought it was Aster. Moving closer, maybe? It was the sound of footsteps crunching gravel.

I looked up, movement catching my eye. There was a flash of color, and then a figure stepped up behind Aster. I opened my mouth to scream, but it was too late. The butt of the gun came down hard on the back of Aster's head. It was as if she were a marionette, and someone had cut all her strings.

She crumpled to the ground. Not moving. I prayed she was still breathing.

I started forward, but the man made a tsking noise, stopping me in my tracks. It took me a second to recognize the face hidden beneath the ball cap. And then he leveled his gun directly at my head.

"You just couldn't leave well enough alone, could you?"

CHAPTER FIFTY-THREE
Braedyn

MY BRAIN STRUGGLED TO COMPUTE WHAT I WAS SEEING. The tan sheriff's department uniform. The ball cap pulled low. The gun that wasn't a service weapon. Because that was still secured in his gun belt.

"Sheriff Miller?" The words came out in a sort of wheeze, barely audible.

"I didn't want it to come to this. I didn't want to have to hurt you. But you won't fucking stop."

My breaths came quicker, short pants as if my ribs had tightened so badly around those organs that I couldn't take a full inhale.

My fingers started tingling, the sensation spreading up my forearms. I needed to breathe. If I didn't, I'd pass out, and everything would be over.

I forced a pained inhale, my gaze flying back to Aster. She still wasn't moving. But I didn't see any blood pooling. The only problem was that I didn't see her chest moving either.

"What did you do?" I whispered, my focus returning to the man in front of me.

Because more than anything, I needed to know the answer. It

didn't matter that he had a gun aimed at my head. I felt the truth at the tips of my fingers. I was so close to ending the torment I'd felt for the last year.

Miller's face screwed up. "*I* didn't do anything. Now drop the fucking bear spray."

Anger surged, burning out some of the fear and helping me breathe. "Doesn't look like you're doing nothing now."

"Watch your tone with me, you little bitch. You've been sticking your nose where it doesn't belong for a goddamned year, and it's time you learned your place." He closed the distance in three long strides. "Drop the spray and start walking."

I hesitated for a moment too long, and a shot pierced the air. I dropped to the ground, fear coursing through me.

"The next one goes through your femur. I hear that's painful."

I dropped the bear spray. It was no match for a bullet. But I had to think. I'd make him believe he had the upper hand, then make my move. I'd done it to Vincent, and he was younger and stronger.

Miller hoisted me up and shoved me toward the trail, making me stumble as I struggled to stay upright. My mouth went dry, and I shook out my hands, trying to clear the tingling sensation.

"Nova. Where is she?" It was the only question that mattered. The only *thing* that mattered. That and buying time until Dex arrived. Just five minutes. He would help Aster, and he would find me.

"I don't know," Miller ground out, shoving the barrel of the gun into my back.

"You have to." He *had* to. I was desperate now. The answers were so close I could almost see them.

"What I know is that you've brought more people to this corner of the forest than anyone has in years," Miller snarled.

Confusion swept through me. He was holding me at gunpoint because he didn't want me in these woods?

Miller gave me another shove when I slowed. "You know, this is one of the least popular trails up here. Most people go for the waterfall one or the Mount Lupine trail. But no, not you. You had to do Three Creeks Canyon."

"We didn't want touristy." I didn't know why I was explaining myself to him. But I remembered someone telling me that this trail was beautiful, a little quieter.

A slew of curses spilled from Miller. "Well, that was a dumb fucking idea."

"Why?"

The sound of the rushing river grew closer. Even though we were tipping into July, the water was still high, showing just how much snow the higher elevations had received last winter.

Miller gripped the back of my tee, giving me a little shake before shoving me forward again. "Because I'm getting paid more than a little money to make sure law enforcement stays the hell out of this forest."

The confusion was back. I tried to put the pieces together but couldn't.

"You know what grows great around here?" Miller went on. He didn't wait for my answer. "Weed. It might be legal now, but there's a limit to what the state will allow an individual to grow. And not everyone wants to play by those rules."

My mind swirled. I'd seen something on the news about stuff like this. Organized crime outfits using state or national land for their drug operations, hiding them in plain sight, so to speak.

Nausea swept through me, a truly sick feeling, as I turned to face the man with the gun. "You killed Nova because she stumbled onto your pot operation?"

Pain was there now, fighting for supremacy against the nausea. A human life. A person who made this world better—stolen for money and drugs.

"I told you. I didn't do a fucking thing," Miller clipped. "And I'm not about to ask those motherfuckers running the show what they did with her. But if you don't stop digging, they're gonna end our arrangement, and the only way they do that is with a bullet to the brain."

Panic gripped me in the kind of vise that locked my muscles and seized my lungs. "I'll stop," I croaked.

It was a lie, and Miller knew it. But I had to try. The image of

Owen's face swirled in my mind. I was his only parent. The only person on this earth he had left. I couldn't leave him. I wouldn't.

And Dex. A wave of memories hit me. The way those dark-hazel eyes sparked with gold as he laughed. The quiet way he explained computer skills to my son. The reverent look on his face when he spoke those three little words—the ones that meant everything to me.

"I know you won't." Miller shoved me forward. "You never stop. I hoped you would after that delusional ex of yours had all that stuff on his computer, but here you are again. I'm driving by, and there's your damn car. I can't risk it. Too much is at stake."

Panic washed through me. "Dex knows where I am. He's only a couple of minutes away. If I'm not here, it'll only bring more attention to the area."

Miller let out a scoff. "Not when they find your body in the river. They'll know I was right all along. It's easy for tourists to fall in and get dead. Or maybe they'll think you couldn't take it anymore, missing that friend you call a sister."

No. No. No. I wouldn't let that happen.

"I'm sorry, Brae. I didn't want it to come to this." Miller lifted his gun. "Step off the trail."

I saw where we were now. The same spot where Nova had disappeared.

"Depression can get the best of people," Miller went on. "And you've been through a lot lately. Your ex showing up and attacking you. Learning that he likely killed your best friend. All that guilt. It won't be a surprise when they find you downstream somewhere. Maybe you couldn't take any of it anymore."

Rage, fast and blazing, blasted through me. "No."

Miller's brown eyes flashed. "I can make this easy, or I can make this real fuckin' hard. I've got good aim. A little graze to the head, and the ME will just think the injuries were from getting bashed against the rocks."

"I'm not making this easy on you." I wasn't taking it lying down either. I'd done that too many times. Letting Vincent walk all over me.

Not telling my parents what I really thought of them and their judgmental ways. No more.

Because I'd found my strength along the way. And I'd built it. I'd made a home for Owen and me. I'd kept him safe and happy. I'd made a life I was proud of.

Miller lifted the gun a little higher. "Your choice."

The sound wasn't like I'd imagined. There was no rocketing blast. It was more of a pop. Like a balloon squeezed too tightly.

I didn't have time to brace for pain or try to dive out of the way. But agony didn't come, and neither did nothingness. Instead, Miller crumpled to the ground, blood spreading on his chest and turning his uniform a sickly shade of red.

My gaze jumped around, trying to see where the shot had come from. Movement caught my eye, and a figure emerged from the trees. All the air left my lungs on a whoosh.

I bent over, trying to catch my breath before finally straightening and taking in my rescuer. Tears of relief sprang to my eyes at the familiar face, the one that had always shown me kindness. "Thank you. I—"

His head cocked to the side slightly, the move so animalistic it halted my words. And then he lifted a gun.

Another shot rang out. The sound was different. Something hit me, like lightning striking me over and over, and I was suddenly on the ground.

The man stepped over me. "I'm sorry, Brae."

I blinked up at him. "Travis?" I rasped. And then everything went black.

CHAPTER FIFTY-FOUR
Dex

YETI SHOVED HER HEAD OUT THE WINDOW, A LOOK OF PURE glee on her face.

I chuckled, making the turn that would take me toward Three Creeks Canyon trailhead. "Enjoy that good hair day. And let me tell you, you smell a hell of a lot better."

Yeti let out a howl of happiness, chattering away into the wind.

A ring came through my SUV's speakers, and I took in the name on my vehicle's screen. I hit a button on my steering wheel. "Hey, Kol."

"Hey—what is that sound?"

"Yeti has her head out the car window, and she's very happy about it."

Kol grunted. "Are you some sort of over-the-top dog dad now?"

"Hey, Yeti and I have bonded." That bond might be comprised of her trying to crush my skull by sleeping on my head every night and suffocating me with her one-hundred-forty-two-pound love, but it was a bond nonetheless.

"Jesus," Kol muttered.

"You needed something?"

"Where are you?"

"I'm heading to the Three Creeks Canyon trailhead to meet Brae and Aster."

I swore I could feel the alertness through the phone. "What's going on?" Kol demanded.

I shifted in my seat, a little of the humor at Yeti's antics fleeing. "Something has been eating at Brae. She doesn't think Vincent killed Nova."

"Thank fuck," Kol muttered.

"I told you," Mav said in the background.

That same alertness that had found Kol settled into my muscles. "You don't either?"

"It just doesn't add up to me. Vincent was obsessed with Brae, some twisted need to think she was still under his thumb. And it got kicked up with all the interviews about Nova. But if he was jealous of Nova or wanted her out of the picture, why *then*? She'd been in Brae's life forever."

A sick feeling settled in my gut. Because if it wasn't Vincent...

"I'm about two minutes out. You want to meet us there?"

"We're about five minutes away," Kol said by way of answer.

I wasn't shocked. When Kol was on a case, he'd drive or walk the area over and over. He said the process was like looking at a puzzle from different angles. You never knew what might get kicked free. And he occasionally brought Maverick because while Kol knew tracking like no one else, Mav knew things the forest could tell you.

"See you in a few." I clicked off the call and took the final turn a little faster than I should've. Yeti pulled her head back into the SUV and gave me a dirty look. "Sorry, girl. Gotta get us to your mama."

The trailhead came into view, and a prickle of unease settled deep. There was no flash of blond hair. The only color came from Brae's maroon SUV and Aster's navy pickup.

I pulled in two spaces down from Brae's vehicle and was out of my vehicle in a flash. "Brae," I called, lifting my voice in something just short of a yell. The only answer was the wind whistling through the trees and the river in the distance.

Stalking toward the vehicle, I peeked inside. Nothing. I tested a door. Locked up tight.

Fear turned my blood colder with every step, every breath. My heart rate should've been ratcheting up with panic. But not me. Mine turned slower, frigid. Maybe it was the DNA that flowed through me.

But as I rounded the back bumper and caught sight of Brae's familiar pack, the one with the patch that read *Bigfoot Patrol*, my heart stopped altogether. Her brightly colored water bottle was shoved into a side pocket. And Brae was nowhere.

Blood pulsed in my ears in slow, brutal waves like ocean water crashing against rock, yet somehow my heart stopped at the same time.

A body. Blond hair spilled over a woman's face. Aster. Not Brae. And God, I was going to hell for the relief that coursed through me at that.

But I was already on the move, dropping to my knees as I brushed the hair out of Aster's face. I pressed my fingers to her neck, hoping for a pulse. Another wave of relief found me as I felt the flutter against my fingertips. I bent over her and felt soft breaths against my cheek. Unconscious but breathing.

Two doors slammed, and I whirled. I would've reached for my gun, but it was still in my damned SUV. My muscles unlocked at the sight of Kol and Maverick striding toward me.

"What happened?" Kol demanded.

"I don't know. Aster was on the ground. Brae's... She's...she's gone." The words cost me. Just speaking them out loud hurt—a brutal pain like knives being shoved under fingernails or an uppercut so vicious it splintered ribs and sent the shards into your heart.

Kol's expression went thunderous. But Maverick? He was frozen. He didn't blink. I didn't think he even breathed.

"Mav," I said, my voice low. "You got your bag?"

He still didn't move.

"Aster needs you, man," I pressed. He was the one with real medical training.

At my words, Maverick jolted like he'd been shocked. But it was only a matter of seconds before he was back with a kit.

I was instantly on my feet because I couldn't do anything else for Aster. It was Brae who needed me now. Just thinking her name was a physical blow, and I nearly staggered under its weight. "Kol," I croaked.

"Called for backup," he growled. "Now, get out of the damn scene."

I normally would've hit back at the order, but not now. Not when I knew why he'd issued it. I instantly moved back to where Kol was standing.

"Get our brothers," he muttered, but his gaze was already locked on the area around Brae's vehicle, tracing footprints and reading them as if they were a foreign language only he could translate. And maybe they were.

I was only partly aware of the text I sent to our chain. My phone buzzed in my hand.

> **Wylder:** *I'm on my way.*

One brother down.

> **Orion:** *Working the map.*

It was Orion-speak for saying he was following his own sort of lead.

"Aster's stable," Maverick said, his voice trembling slightly. "She's got a wound on the back of her head. Someone hit her with something. Rounded. Not sharp." With each new piece of information, his voice hardened.

A soft moan of pain sounded.

"Easy, Ice Queen. I've got you." Mav's voice had gone gentle again.

Kol gave the vehicle a wide berth as he circled it. "I see her. Moving around the SUV. She stops here." He pointed to a cluster of footprints in the dirt. "Someone else comes. Size indicates male. They move this way." He traced a path in the distance.

"Toward the trail," I growled.

Kol nodded. "The trail." His gaze flicked to my SUV. "You think you can work with the dog?"

My gaze moved to Yeti, watching us through the open window of my 4Runner, on alert. I wasn't sure, but I could try. "I need something with Brae's scent." I was already moving back to my SUV. "Evidence bag?"

Kol was moving then, too, grabbing something from his truck.

The coldness in me intensified as I took the bag from him, registering the word *EVIDENCE* in block letters, the orange seal. I didn't want to put anything of Brae's in a bag like this. But I didn't have a choice.

Opening her pack, I pulled out a sweatshirt, using the bag so I didn't touch it. The sweatshirt was a burst of color, with rainbow stripes so opposite to the darkness swirling inside me.

I moved to my SUV and let Yeti out. I didn't know all the fancy French commands, but I tried for English. "Come."

Yeti answered instantly, happily panting away. She had no idea what was wrong. That someone had Brae. My lungs constricted, but I bent down, trying to remember how my hellion had done it.

"Find Brae, Yeti. Find."

Yeti sniffed the open bag and let out a happy bark. Her nose dropped to the dirt as she ambled around. Finally, she caught the trail near the SUV. She circled it and then took off toward the trail.

"We'll keep you updated," Kol called to Maverick and then turned to me. "Let's go."

But I was already there.

Yeti moved quickly down the trail, her nose ghosting over the dirt path. Brae had explained to me once that Yeti was trained in trailing, a specific type of tracking. But she was starting to work with the dog on air tracking, where she didn't just follow a footstep path but scents in the air.

Yeti's progress faltered for a moment, and as I looked over her head, I saw why. That coldness in me turned to icy shards. Something had fallen across the path. *Someone.*

I was running before I consciously gave myself the command. As I did, I took in things in snapshots: a tan uniform, a male form—long and lean. A familiar face.

"Fucking hell," Kol muttered.

I crouched, pressing two fingers to Sheriff Miller's neck. I shook my head. "Gone."

There was no pulse, and his eyes were wide and unblinking. Emotions warred within me. Relief that it wasn't Brae. Fear that whoever likely had her was capable of cold-blooded murder.

Kol pulled out his phone, barking out information, likely to the sheriff's department and his own Forest Service agency contacts. But Yeti was still moving. She circled the area and then started off the trail, heading into the woods.

Her nose moved from the forest floor into the air, and she sniffed as if struggling, ambled a bit.

"Someone's carrying her," Kol clipped. "There are signs of a struggle, maybe someone falling on the path."

I locked down the fear that wanted to take hold and welcomed the fury instead. They wouldn't hurt her. I would tear them apart before they could.

Yeti caught something moving deeper into the trees. The brush grew thicker, the pines closer together, but the dog kept leading us on. Then she stopped, confused. But I saw it.

ATV tracks.

"Goddammit," Kol muttered, pulling out his phone again.

Mine let out a ding. A text flashed.

> **Orion:** *I think I see her. Through my binoculars. I'm a good three miles away. Between the ranch and where Three Creeks trail meets West Ridge trail. Cabin. Male suspect. She doesn't look conscious. Sending coordinates.*

It was the longest text I'd gotten from Orion in years. But I could only focus on one thing. *She doesn't look conscious.* Which meant she might not be breathing, alive.

I shoved the fear down again, harder this time, and locked it away. Then, I let the darkness free.

Kol looked up from his phone, clearly having read the same text. "We're about a mile from these coordinates. You and I move out? Or wait for backup?"

There was a reason to wait for our area's SWAT team or some kind of backup. But I couldn't. There was no way I would risk something happening to Brae while we sat around.

My gaze locked with my brother's. I knew what kind of risk I'd be putting Kol in, and I couldn't. "I'll go alone."

"The hell you will," Kol snarled. "You go with me, or you wait for SWAT."

I muttered a curse. "You and me. But I take point."

Kol jerked his head in a nod, then bent, pulling his backup weapon from an ankle holster. "You need it."

Everything in me recoiled. But this was for Brae.

I took the weapon, feeling the weight of it in my hand. The XD Sub-Compact 9mm was light but, at the same time, incredibly heavy. I checked the safety, the grip. I let myself feel the weight of something that could end a life. And then, I let the darkness take over. For Brae.

"Let's go."

CHAPTER FIFTY-FIVE
Braedyn

Everything hurt. Like I'd been shot with countless miniature bullets that had embedded themselves beneath my skin. But also like I'd run two marathons back-to-back. And I was not a runner.

The ATV bumped along a trail that didn't seem all that established, thankfully not going too fast. But every divot and ridge sent a fresh wave of pain through my system.

Breathe, Brae. Think.

I gave myself simple commands, knowing I needed to take stock of everything around me. My hands were bound in front of my face, the plastic zip ties digging into my skin, and I could feel something similar around my ankles. My memory of being put on the ATV was fuzzy. But one thing wasn't.

Travis.

I bit the inside of my cheek so hard I tasted blood. Travis was one of the few people willing to help me from the beginning. Kind. Caring. Dedicated to his job. I'd baked him fucking cookies.

My mind swirled, trying to put the pieces together. Was he part of the marijuana growing outfit? Something else? Something darker?

Nausea rolled through me, and I did my best not to empty the meager contents of my stomach along the dirt trail. My gaze flicked up to the man I thought I'd known. I couldn't see his face, but maybe that was for the best. It would've been a stranger's anyway.

Taking a deep breath, I threw all my weight toward the rear of the ATV, hoping the force would be enough to toss me clear off the vehicle and over the wheels—and just maybe enough to break the zip ties around my ankles.

Instead, I came up against different restraints. Ropes. Travis had tied me to the rack on the back of the ATV.

A low chuckle came from in front of me. It was hard to tell if it was even a laugh over the sound of the engine, but Travis's gaze flicked over his shoulder. And the look on his face...it was pure glee.

"You know, I had a feeling you'd be a fighter. That's gonna make it so much more fun. I've been gettin' a little tired of the lack of challenge lately. Haven't had a nice competitor since your bestie. But she lost that fight pretty damn quick."

The nausea was back, almost painful in its ferocity. Nova. He was the one. He took her.

I told myself to breathe, but it didn't do any good. My breaths tripped and tangled. *Nova*.

Her name played over and over in my mind. Tears burned my eyes as a sob clogged my throat, but I did everything I could to shove them down.

"How?" I croaked. I wasn't even sure he'd be able to hear me over the engine. But he did.

"Come on, Brae. You're smarter than that. I've been keeping tabs on you since the moment you moved to Starlight Grove. Having access to law enforcement databases and software, I could triangulate your cell phone's location anytime. And your boy toy taught me a few tricks without even knowing it."

Dex's hacking and computer prowess. It had put ideas in an already-twisted mind.

Travis slowed the ATV, the sound of the engine easing a bit. "Honestly, I should thank you. I knew I'd take you. I just needed an opportunity. Miller being an even dumber fuck made it all the more perfect. I get to blame his death and your disappearance on the pot ring. I was just waiting for someone to find out and get Miller's ass fired, but dead is better. Maybe I'll even run for sheriff."

My breaths came faster as I tried to play out possibilities in my mind. Dex would be at the trailhead by now. He would be looking for me. But I wasn't sure there'd be enough clues to point him in my direction.

The ATV slowed as an old but well-maintained cabin came into view. I remembered Cora mentioning that Travis lived in one of the few cabins on National Forest land that had been grandfathered in to still having inhabitants. Was this where he had Nova? How? Cora, Roger, Travis's friends and family—they would've known.

But Travis didn't stop at the house. He drove past it a hundred yards—maybe more—and *then* he slowed. The building looked like a large shed. The kind you'd maybe keep snow equipment or gardening gear in. Big enough to fit the ATV, but Travis shut off the engine and hopped off instead.

He rounded the vehicle so he was standing near my head, that damn grin still on his face. And then he pulled something from his pocket. The handle was black metal, but a gleaming silver blade popped from the housing when he pressed a button. "Welcome home, Brae."

I railed against the ropes, trying in vain to get free. Tears leaked from my eyes, though not from grief or even fear. From frustration.

Travis gripped me by the hair, lifting one of the tears with his thumb and licking it. "The taste of fear. There's nothing like it." His gaze narrowed on my face as he showed me the blade. "Tell me you'll be a good girl."

That nausea was back, but I forced myself to nod. In three quick flicks of his knife, Travis was hauling me to my feet. The zip ties around my wrists were still in place, but the ones around my ankles were gone. I rolled one foot and then the other, trying to revive the blood flow.

Travis gripped my hair again, pulling it so tightly I had to bite back a scream. "You even think about running, and I'll gut you like a prized buck. Alive or dead, you'll serve the same purpose for me. But alive would be so much more fun."

Icy tendrils of fear wrapped around me, but I did everything I could to battle them back. I thought of Owen, Dex, and the family I was building in Starlight Grove. *Breathe, Brae.*

"What purpose am I serving?" I rasped, my voice raw.

Travis's fingers tightened even more. "Do you know how boring it is working for the sheriff's department in this town?"

Confusion washed over me as I tried to put that piece in place.

"Don't get me wrong. I was fucking fascinated by Edmond Archer—all those women he stalked, tortured, killed—and being so close to that kind of power by befriending his sons. But it was Cora who really showed me what I was meant to do. When her mom went missing in high school, I thought…*this*. This was what I needed. To be in on the action, the search, the high of finding someone and holding their life in my hands."

The sickness roiling inside me intensified as the picture became a little clearer.

"But you know what's even better?" Travis's smile widened, entering into manic territory. "Working the case while knowing *exactly* where the person is. If they're dead or alive. Watching people scramble like ants, knowing I'm pulling all the strings."

Dead or alive. He'd hurt people. Killed them. *Nova.*

"I'll never forget the first one. Dumb bitch sniffling at a campsite parking lot. Got in a fight with her boyfriend and wanted a ride back to town." His creepy grin got even wider. "I offered to take her where she needed to go. Straight to a grave right over there." Travis pointed with his knife to a field with a mix of wildflowers and grasses.

I struggled not to vomit.

"I killed her, *and* I got to work the case. I got to watch her mother sob and her brother fall apart. I got to feel their pain, control it. Because *I* had all the answers. It was even better when Cora got involved with that little Compass crew." A low chuckle left Travis's lips, grating against my skin. "I got to hear all about their little sobfests. Even talked my way into attending a few meetings." He shook me hard. "A total fucking high!"

"Nova?" I croaked.

I needed to know. The truth. Finally.

Travis just laughed harder. "Wanna see where your bestie lived? Where she cried out for you when I told her you weren't looking? All those stupid articles. You didn't know she was right here for so long."

He dragged me by the hair toward the shed, my feet scrabbling in the dirt, trying to right myself. Travis hauled open the door, but there was nothing out of the norm. A space for the ATV, normal tools. And then I saw it. A door in the floor. One with a complicated, expensive-looking lock.

Travis bent, pressed his palm to it, and then threw it open. Dark. So dark I couldn't see a thing. And then Travis hit a switch on the wall. Fluorescent lights flickered on, bathing the space in a fake, blue glow.

Bile surged up my throat. Metal stairs led to a room of nightmares. The space was finished in the sort of material garage floors sometimes were. There was a hole in the floor that looked like a makeshift toilet and some sort of shower next to it. A stained mattress lay against one wall. And it smelled. But worse, there were chains with what looked like shackles.

"I tried keeping one alive before Nova. Alma from your little support group? Her daughter. But she had no fight. Starved herself to death before a month. But Nova…" Travis's hand tightened in my hair. "She wanted to live. And goddamn, it was fun. Using her phone and some stupid software to call you while I got to watch in the damn bar." Glee filled his voice. "Making her record the audio to put with the dummy. Priceless."

It took everything I had not to throw up or fall apart.

"Made it just over a year. You were so close yet so far."

Pain—unbearable, soul-crushing pain—swept through me. Nova. My Nova had been alive all this time. I'd almost gotten to her in time. But I'd failed her. It took everything I had not let my sob free. But I refused to give him that pleasure.

"Now, it's time for a new toy. Welcome to home sweet home, Brae," Travis singsonged.

The hell it was. Rage like I'd never known before spurred me into action. I hauled myself upright, barely feeling the pain in my scalp.

Surprise lit Travis's gaze, but my knee was already moving—that same skill I'd used on Vincent but with a hell of a lot more power. I hit true, my knee striking his groin with enough force that Travis's eyes went wide in pain and shock, and the knife clattered to the ground. He managed one brutal blow to my ribs as he went down, but it didn't matter; I was already running.

I had no idea where I was. I just knew I needed to find cover. I ran straight for the trees, pushing my muscles as hard as they would go. But they hurt, cramped so badly it stole my breath. It had to be the aftermath of the Taser shot, but I kept pushing.

Cursing sounded behind me, and a fresh wave of panic hit. I pushed harder, leaping over fallen logs and around brush. My skin burned where branches tore at my flesh, but I didn't stop.

The sound of the river hit my ears. I moved toward it as if it could save me. Closer and closer, the roaring water getting louder and louder. I'd take it for escape, even at the risk of drowning.

Fingers snagged in my shirt, hauling me back in a vicious jerk. "You're going to pay for disobeying me," Travis snarled. "I'm gonna kill you, and I'm gonna make it hurt."

CHAPTER FIFTY-SIX
Dex

IT DIDN'T MATTER THAT KOL AND I HAD JUST RUN A SOLID MILE, following the coordinates and a trail I knew wasn't on any map. It didn't matter that we'd pushed our bodies to the breaking point, Yeti at our sides. My body was still ice-cold. The eighty-something-degree weather didn't touch it. And I knew I wouldn't feel any warmth until I had Brae in my arms.

Yeti let out a soft whine, pulling up short as a cabin came into view.

"Wait," I clipped, bringing Kol to a stop. I turned to the dog, watching as she scented the air. "I think she has something."

Kol looked into the distance. "ATV's over there, but no one's around."

I held the bag out for Yeti to sniff. "Find Brae."

Yeti's nose twitched. She seemed to be following something in the air and led us toward the trees. Not exactly back the way we'd come but sort of.

Within a matter of minutes, she dropped her nose to the ground again.

"She's got a trail," I surmised.

Kol bent, picking up some threads that had caught on some brambles. "Someone's been through here."

I adjusted my grip on my weapon, the weight of it burning into me as we followed Yeti deeper into the forest. The sounds of the river built with each step, pounding against my eardrums.

And then everything stopped.

The world I'd known tipped on its axis because, standing on the bank of the river, was a man I'd known for half my life. A friend. Someone I fucking trusted. And he had a gun pressed to Brae's head.

Yeti let out a low growl as I dropped the scent bag and lifted my weapon—the one that felt like it carried the weight of the world.

"Stay." My command wasn't loud, but it held a finality that had the dog pulling up short. But still, her body quivered. She waited for a single command from me to let her loose on the monster who had Brae. On *Travis*.

"Fucking hell," Kol swore.

Travis's eyes flared at Yeti's growl, true panic swirling through the green depths as he caught sight of us. He yanked Brae in front of him, pressing the barrel of his gun to her temple. "You're a little early to the party, I'm afraid, boys."

"U.S. Forest Service," Kol stated. "Lower your weapon."

"Kol, come on now. No need to be official." Travis grinned at my brother, but sweat broke out over his brow. "We're all just having a little fun here."

"Fun?" I snarled, the darkness swirling and spreading as I held my gun steady in Travis's direction. There was only one problem: That was also where Brae was.

Her golden eyes were wide, and dirt was smudged across her face. Her blond hair was tangled, and brambles had gotten caught in it somewhere along the way. But amid it all, she was still so beautiful. Because she'd become my home, my resting place.

"You don't know the meaning of the word," Travis taunted, his creepy grin spreading wider. "You know, it really added something, you coming back here. And even before that, you were an influence on me, so I've really gotta thank you. Knowing what your dad did showed me I wasn't alone with my darkness, but it was your obsession with computers that added to my game. Helped me do things I never thought possible."

My face twisted as my gut roiled and guilt swirled. "What the hell are you talking about?"

"Every time I took someone, you gave me the gift of watching exactly what it did to the people around them. Their emails, their text messages, their phone calls. I knew it was possible to hack them because of you. I might not have your skills, but the internet provides a wealth of knowledge."

That coldness coursing through me burned now. It left scars I knew I'd never recover from.

"I got to feel every ounce of pain I dealt them. Every tear, every shred of fury."

Travis's hand fisted in Brae's hair, and she yelped. I could see she gave her all to swallow it quickly and not give him the satisfaction of the reaction. But I saw the pure joy on Travis's face—joy at causing others pain.

"You took Nova." I spoke the words I already knew were true.

Travis's grin widened. "Want to know where I buried her? Want to know how loud she screamed in the end? Begged for her life? How close you were to finding her? How recently she lost it all?"

Tears filled Brae's eyes, cresting her lids and spilling down her cheeks. And I wanted to kill him. For the first time, I knew for sure that I had darkness in me. The kind that lived in my father. Only I knew now, with the certainty Brae had given me, that it only came out in protection of those I loved. It came out in search of the light.

"Let Brae go," I growled.

Travis laughed. "Or what? You'll throw your gun at me? I know you won't shoot it. Your head's too much of a fucked-up place."

He knew because I'd shared that I hated guns when he offered to take me hunting in high school. He knew because I'd given him that knowledge, the weapon to use against me.

My gaze flicked to Kol. He didn't have the shot. Brae was fully blocking Travis in his line of sight.

I struggled to swallow as my eyes locked with Brae's tear-filled ones. And then she mouthed the words that meant more than even *I love you*, the words that meant everything because I knew what it cost her to give them.

"*I trust you.*"

My eyes closed, just for a moment. But I felt a lifetime in that smattering of seconds. Images of Brae. The infinite incarnations of her face. Laughing. Determined. Angry. Joyful. Coming apart. Telling me she loved me.

My eyes opened as Travis's taunts filled my ears, but I couldn't hear them. All I could hear were Brae's words. She might not have spoken them aloud, but my brain still formed the sounds. *I trust you.*

I fired.

CHAPTER FIFTY-SEVEN
Braedyn

I didn't look away from Dex—not at the weapon in his hand but at those dark-hazel eyes. The ones that had given me a gift I wasn't sure I'd ever find again. The gift of trusting.

Such peace came with that trust. I held tightly to that as the shot rang out.

It sounded different than before: louder, harsher. But I just gripped that peace and trust. And I didn't lose Dex's eyes.

The gun at my temple slipped, and someone fired a second shot. I couldn't tell if it was Dex or Travis.

The hand in my hair loosened as Travis stumbled backward toward the river. I whirled, pain flaring along my side. But I ignored it. I needed to see.

Travis's arms windmilled as blood bloomed on his shoulder, another patch on his chest. His eyes were wide, his face unnaturally pale, and then he fell. He hit the side of the embankment twice and then flew into the river. The rushing rapids grabbed his body, pulling it under, and then he was simply…gone.

Footsteps sounded behind me as Kol barked orders into his

phone. And then he was there. Dex. His hands framed my face, rough against soft, steady pressure and peace.

"Are you hurt? Are you okay? Tell me." The questions were a barrage of demands, but I answered him with only one thing.

My hands fisted in his tee as pain rocketed through my body, my heart breaking at knowing she was gone. My Nova was gone. But Dex was here. Holding on despite it all. Always my safest landing place. "I love you. I *trust* you." I couldn't hold back from telling him both, not when I knew we didn't get infinite chances to tell the people we loved the most important things.

Dex's hand slid down to the pulse point in my neck. "Tell me again."

My eyes burned, filling with tears. "I love you." And then the one last piece of myself I could finally give him. "I trust you."

His lips brushed featherlight over mine. "You made me want to reach for things I never thought I could have. You gave me hope when I thought it was impossible to hold on. You gave me peace with my darkness."

"Because that darkness is beautiful, too," I whispered.

Dex's eyes glistened, unshed tears gathering. "I love you. I trust you. And I want nothing but you and Owen for the rest of my days."

A sharp bark.

Dex's lips struggled into the barest of smiles, one he fought for amid all the pain circling us. "And Yeti."

My sweet girl. I called Yeti over, but it was quickly followed by a wince.

"What's wrong?" Dex clipped.

"My ribs," I muttered. "I—" A wheeze left my lips.

Dex cursed, glancing at Kol, who was still on his phone. "We need an evac. Now."

"There are two hairline fractures, here and here." The doctor pointed them out on the X-ray.

Dex scowled at him as if he'd personally broken the ribs.

I squeezed his hand, bringing his focus back to me as I lay on the gurney in the ER bay. "I'm okay."

But I wasn't. I was so far from okay. Because all I could hear were Travis's words echoing in my head. *"Want to know where I buried her? Want to know how loud she screamed in the end? Begged for her life? How close you were to finding her? How recently she lost it all?"*

Some part of me still held to the delusional hope that he was lying. That we'd find her somewhere in that cabin or on the property. Some part of me was still waiting.

At least we knew now that Aster was okay. She had a mean bump on her head and a concussion, but she would be all right.

Dr. Gomez turned around, sending me a kind smile that made lines appear in the tanned skin around his eyes. "You are going to be just fine. The MRI we ran shows no injury to any organs. You'll be uncomfortable for a few weeks but should heal nicely."

"Give her the pain meds," Dex growled.

I squeezed his hand again. "We've been over this. Please and thank you and no scowling, glaring, or looking at someone like you're going to remove their limbs from their body."

I wanted to find the humor in Dex's cantankerous attitude returning, but I couldn't. Not today.

Dr. Gomez's lips twitched. "I'm glad you have someone who obviously cares so much about you. I'm going to give you a first dose of pain meds through your IV, along with some anti-nausea medication as a precaution. You really do want to stay on top of the pain because it's important that you continue to breathe deeply, even with it. If you don't, you risk developing pneumonia."

Dex's spine snapped straight. "How do we prevent that? Is there a medication you need to give her? A position she needs to sit or sleep in? What about—?"

When I squeezed his hand a third time, it was hard enough for Dex to say, "Ow."

"I'm going to be okay. Breathing deeply, check. Pain meds, check."

But none of it mattered because the pain in my side was nothing compared to the pain in my heart.

Dr. Gomez administered two injections into my IV line. "I'll prepare all the discharge instructions, but just know that rest is important. No work or strenuous activity for two weeks."

My eyes went wide. "But—"

"No, you don't," Dex said immediately. "You will follow all the doctor's instructions to a T. Wylder will find someone to cover for you. And I will take Owen to and from camp—or Kol will help."

I snapped my mouth closed. Owen, who had no idea what had happened. And I wasn't sure he ever should. Waylon had picked him and Skylar up from camp and had them helping with ranch chores.

A little more reality slipped in. Pain. And not the kind that came from my ribs.

"Okay," I whispered.

Dex was there in an instant. "I'm here. We'll get through it together."

There was still so much we didn't know. But all I could think about were the awful things Travis had said.

I wove my fingers through Dex's, and the steady pressure was there like always. "We get through it together."

His lips brushed my temple, just as someone pulled the curtain back.

My gaze flicked up to find Kol moving into the space. Dr. Gomez took stock of Kol's uniform and quickly excused himself. "I'll just get that discharge paperwork prepared."

"Did you find him?" Dex asked.

Kol shook his head, scrubbing a hand over his face. "Not yet. We've got the county search and rescue team working the river, but the water is high this year. Body could've gotten caught on any number of downed trees or rocks."

A shiver racked me as the image of Travis falling into the river flashed in my mind. The blood spreading out over his chest. The panic in his eyes.

I gripped Dex's fingers harder but didn't take my eyes off Kol. I swallowed hard. "Nova?"

Kol's face hardened, his angular jaw instantly becoming sharper, his cheekbones standing at attention. "We found graves."

The tiny flame of hope flickered as if an invisible wind had picked up.

He stepped closer, pulling an evidence bag from his pocket. "This was with one of the bodies. Do you recognize it?"

I peered through the clear plastic, taking in the dirt-caked item. But I could still make out the purple, pink, and teal strands beneath the soil. The same design as on my wrist. And that bracelet burned now as if made of scalding acid.

"It's Nova's," I croaked. "It's Nova."

The word only lost an *s*, but it changed everything. Nova. My friend. My sister. My other half in so many ways because we'd walked through the hardest parts of life together.

I'd found her. Like I'd always promised I would. But finding her meant losing her forever all the same.

I thought I'd know. Thought I'd *feel* when she was gone. But I hadn't. And maybe that was because she'd never left me. Nova was a part of me. She had been almost from the moment we met. And she would be forever more.

CHAPTER FIFTY-EIGHT
Braedyn

THREE DAYS LATER

"D ELIVERY BRIGADE!" MAV'S VOICE CALLED THROUGH MY CABIN'S screen door. I'd left the front door open. No alarm set. No deadbolt latched. Just a warm afternoon breeze and freedom.

Yeti let out a happy bark as Owen scrambled to his feet from the other side of the coffee table we'd been using to play Monopoly Jr. The interruption was for the best because he was kicking our asses.

Dex's lips twitched as he squeezed my shoulder. "Apologies in advance for what is about to descend on you."

But I knew exactly what he was doing: giving me the family I'd never had, that Nova and I had always wanted. The kind that was there in good times and bad and showed up for you time and again.

Skylar raced inside, Yeti barking and leaping around her. "Let's go play with Yeti!"

Owen glanced at me, looking for permission. "Can we, Mom?"

"Only because you didn't call me *bruh*," I shot back.

He laughed and then raced out the back doors with Yeti and

Skylar. We could see them from where we were, and it was nice that I finally felt safe enough to allow it.

"Little Badass, I come bearing food," Mav called, lifting two massive Tupperware containers.

Waylon ambled in behind him, carrying a large box and wearing his beloved Carhartt overalls. "Don't let him fool you into thinking he made all that. I did."

"Hey, I helped," Wylder called as he moved in behind the group, holding up a bakery box. "And Orion sent chocolate fudge cake."

God, they were all so wonderful. Caring in their own ways. "I think Orion has an obsession with chocolate."

Wylder and Dex shared a look.

"What?" I pressed.

"It's Ever's favorite. Chocolate cake," Dex explained.

That had a different sort of ache settling in my chest. "She's got good taste."

"She does," Wylder said softly as he slid the cake onto the island.

"Where's Kol?" Dex asked, glancing toward the screen door.

"Finishing up some stuff with the, uh, case," Wylder explained. "He said there were still a few loose ends."

Sometimes, it felt like the loose ends would never be tied. The state police had already found six bodies buried on Travis's property, but they weren't done searching. Radar and cadaver dogs were combing the surrounding forest, as well.

Dex's profiler friend, Anson, had driven down to assist on one of the days. He'd been the one to help us make sense of what we could. That Travis had taken people whose cases would be in his direct jurisdiction or close enough that he would have a reason to insert himself into the investigation. He got to see the pain he wrought up close and personal. And he got off on it. That was his high, his release.

But it cost the people around him everything.

So far, three bodies had been positively identified, and two of them were the loved ones of Compass members: Jack's wife, Cynthia, and Alma's daughter, Maya. Their worlds were fracturing, but they would also have closure for the first time since their family members disappeared.

It wasn't just them paying the price. It was those around Travis, too. Roger had gone stonily silent, blaming himself for not seeing it in his best friend and partner. And it hadn't helped that the state police were still uncovering Sheriff Miller's wrongdoings. Every case he'd headed up had to be reexamined, and they were still working on closing down the illegal grow operation.

"Have you talked to Cora?" Wylder asked. His voice had gone quiet, and I knew his mind had gone exactly where mine had.

"Yesterday."

A mixture of pain and worry swept across his face. "How was she?"

She was a wreck. I'd seen it the moment she made her way into my house. Eyes red from crying, dark circles underneath, hollow cheeks. Apologies for wrongs that weren't hers to carry spilling from her lips. And guilt. So much damn guilt.

"I've been to that cabin more times than I can count. How did I not know? How did I not see?" That kind of weight could swallow a person whole, and I was beyond glad that Holly was keeping an eye on her. And I knew Aster would, too, now that she was on the road to a full recovery.

"It's going to take time. For all of us." Because we would all carry brands from this experience and the losses. But I also knew we would make it through—because we had each other.

"I think we need a break from the hard stuff," Waylon muttered, sliding the massive box he carried onto the coffee table. "I made ya something."

My smile came, if not easily, at least authentically, though not because there wasn't still pain living inside me. Because Waylon was quite possibly the best and most adorable caretaker ever. "You've been feeding me for three days. I think that's enough."

"Nope. You needed this, too," Waylon said easily.

I flipped open the lid of the box, and my breath caught. Nestled in paper shreds was the most stunning clock I'd ever seen. About two feet tall and nearly ten inches wide, Waylon had carved an intricate forest scene into the wood. There were tiny animals and birds, trees, and a picturesque creek.

"Waylon," I whispered. "This is beautiful."

"Just you wait." Waylon leaned over and pressed something on the back of the clock. The cave carved into the top of the clock opened, and my very own Bigfoot popped out, a Bigfoot-call sound erupting with it.

A laugh bubbled out of me—the first since I'd been taken. The first since I'd learned Nova was gone.

"Oh, Jesus," Dex muttered. "Is that sound going to go off every hour?"

Waylon huffed out a breath. "You never appreciated the call of the wild."

I pushed to my feet, my ribs twinging, but I ignored the pain and wrapped Waylon in a hug. He returned it, but his grip was feather-light, trying not to hurt me.

"Thank you." Unshed tears stung the backs of my eyes as I pulled back. "All of you." I swallowed down the lump in my throat. "When I had nowhere, you gave me a place to belong."

Maverick pointed a finger at me and waved a hand in front of his face. "Don't you dare."

Wylder slapped him on the back. "This is a good stretch for your emotionally stunted self."

"Hey," Mav shot back, affronted. "I am very in touch with my feelings. I sobbed like a baby when we watched *The Notebook*."

I grinned. "*The Notebook*?"

"Don't even think about it, Little Badass. I am not going through that pain again. That's a one-and-done movie for me."

Dex chuckled and slid an arm around my shoulders before pressing a kiss to my temple. "You've always belonged with us. Just took me a minute to find you."

My eyes filled. "I love you."

"I trust you," Dex whispered back.

"Fuck, now I really am crying," Mav muttered.

Dex's hand lifted to the side of my neck, to that pulse point. "What would you think about hanging that clock elsewhere?"

I frowned up at him. "You can't put my clock in the garage."

"I was actually thinking about hanging it at the house I'm building at the ranch. Talked to the architect about adding on a few rooms. We could even build an agility course for Yeti."

My breath caught. "You want us to move in with you?"

Dex brushed his lips across mine. "Nothing I want more."

"Yes." The word came so easily. No fear, no reticence. Only trust and peace—and hope for our future.

The ringing of a phone cut through my happy haze, and Dex scowled as he pulled his cell from his pocket. A giggle slipped free at the ease with which the cantankerousness returned. The scowl only intensified as he took in Kol's name on the screen.

He hit a button that put the call on speaker. "You know, you're really ruining my moment with Brae, Kol."

"I found her." Kol's breaths were coming in short, staccato pants.

"What? Who?" Dex asked, his brows pulling together.

"I found Nova."

Everything in me stilled.

"Her body?" I barely recognized my voice as I demanded to know, blood roaring in my ears.

"No." Another harsh breath. "*Her*. She's alive. Barely. Medics are on the way. Brae, she's alive."

EPILOGUE
Braedyn

THREE MONTHS LATER

THE FALL SUN BAKED THE GROUND AS IT HUNG HIGH IN THE SKY over Twisted Oak Ranch, as if it knew it needed to shine a little brighter for the occasion. We may have tipped into October, but the sun brought with it enough warmth that we could be outside, scattered on picnic blankets, to celebrate Dex's birthday and the completion of the framing on his new house.

Our house.

Shrieks sounded as Skylar and Owen raced around the yard with Yeti and Lucy, Tink the Highland cow, and Pepper the goat racing after them. Mav gave chase with a massive Nerf gun.

God, they were happy. There was nothing better than happy kids. And honestly, Maverick qualified as one.

Waylon stood behind a grill he'd hauled over here, wearing a Bigfoot apron as Blaze critiqued his grill skills. Wylder chatted with Aster, only pausing when she flipped off Mav after he shouted something at her. I wondered if the two of them would ever make nice. But they hadn't managed to call a truce, even after he rushed to her side in the wake of her attack.

I glanced over my shoulder at the gravel road leading to our property, hoping I'd see a familiar SUV approaching. I didn't. Cora was keeping her distance these days. Aside from work, where we only shared polite chitchat, she avoided me. All of us. It was clear the guilt that wasn't hers to assume had made a home inside her.

But she wasn't the only one I was worried about. My gaze shifted to the fence line, where Nova stood stroking a horse and then scratching behind its ears. She looked better—so much better than when Kol had found her.

The image of her in that hospital bed sent a shudder through me—just like the memory of her screaming when I tried to take her hand did.

But she'd battled her way back to us because our Supernova was pure fighter through and through. Only, I knew she was hiding wounds. And groups like this one today proved challenging for her at times. Then again, she'd lived for an entire year only coming into contact with one person—and a monster at that. She'd had no light, only the exercise of walking back and forth in her prison, little food and water. It made sense that this sort of thing might be too much.

Nova hid it well from most people, though. She smiled and joined in, but I knew there was so much more going on beneath the surface.

Movement caught my eye. Kol shifted ever so slightly, his gaze moving to Nova. I found him doing that often, as if doing a pulse check, making sure she was still there and breathing.

I understood it. He had been the one to find her, after all, nearly starved and dehydrated, more than five miles from Travis's cabin. I had no idea what Travis had planned to do with her out there. But what I *did* know was that her ordeal had changed her forever, as much as she tried to hide it.

Lips brushed across my temple. "Worried?"

I leaned into Dex on the quilt spread out over the ground we were making a home. "I think I'll always worry about her now."

Dex pulled me tighter against him. "She's doing really well, all things considered."

"I know," I whispered. I pressed a kiss to the underside of his jaw. "I'll be right back."

I pushed to my feet, crossing the grass to where Nova stood at the fence. I lifted a hand to stroke the horse's jaw, even though all I wanted to do was pull my best friend into a hug. But that hadn't gone well the first time. "Need anything?"

Nova's gray gaze found mine as the wind lifted her dark, almost-black hair. "All good here."

I knew that wasn't the case. But I also knew she would get there. And I was holding tight to that hope. For both of us.

"Supernova, watch me!" Owen yelled as he executed some sort of flip and roll, shooting foam darts at Maverick.

Nova let loose a laugh, one that felt *real*. Not the kind from our past but one from now—different, huskier. It somehow meant more. "You're a ninja warrior king, Bubs," she called out with a grin.

There was something about the laugh. About her smile. It gave my hope wings.

I had so much to be grateful for. Sometimes, it felt impossible to me that I'd gotten every single thing I'd ever dreamed of. My best friend, my sister, returned to me. My son, thriving and safe. A partner I not only loved but trusted. And the family he'd given me by extension.

My phone dinged, and I pulled it out of my pocket, quickly reading the message from Maren. My jaw went slack. "Give me a second." I crossed to Dex, an incredulous look on my face. "What did you do?"

Dex's brows rose. "What are you talking about?"

"Maren said all of Vincent's accounts were drained." And that was on top of the fact that Vincent was currently in prison, and I'd already received a settlement from the courts, along with sole custody. But I hadn't wanted Vincent's money. So I'd divided it between a college fund for Owen and a trust he'd receive at age thirty. But this was more.

A knowing smile spread across Dex's face. "Hmmm. I wonder what happened."

"Dex," I pressed.

That grin widened. "I felt like some nonprofits needed a little extra funding. One for single parents starting new businesses or going back to school. Another providing educational support and scholarships for kids from single-parent homes. And at least a dozen women's shelters across the country."

"I can't believe you," I whispered. But I could. Because Dex used any darkness he had for good and only that.

Dex's hazel eyes heated. "Justice."

"Vigilante justice," I corrected as I leaned into him.

His lips twitched. "Potato, potahto."

"I love you," I whispered against those lips.

"More than I thought possible." Dex's hand slid into my hair as he kissed me.

I lost all sense of time as his mouth took mine, but I still tried to identify the kiss, classify it. It was still one of my most cherished pastimes. Just like this particular kiss was still a favorite—a blend of heat, comfort, and home.

"Sick," Owen called out, cutting into my blissful haze. "And not the good kind!"

Dex chuckled against my mouth as he pulled back.

"It's romantical," Skylar argued as she wrapped her feather boa around her neck and draped it over the back of her T-shirt that read *If you think I'm scary, you should meet my uncle*.

Owen's face screwed up. "Hard pass."

Mav chuckled. "Trust me when I say, you will be rethinking that in the future, my man."

Aster rolled her eyes as she turned to me. "You might want to watch how much time Maverick spends with Owen. Bad influences and all."

"Ouch, Ice Queen. That hurts," Mav shot back.

"Truth hurts, Satan," she retorted.

Before they could devolve into a bickering fight that could easily get out of hand, I turned to Owen. "Even though we're totally sick in the gross way, do you want to go get Dex's present?"

Dex's hand slid beneath my hair and squeezed the back of my neck. "I said I didn't need any presents."

I shot him a look. "Too bad, so sad, Buttercup."

Owen snickered as he ran to retrieve a wrapped box from Dex's 4Runner. A second later, he was setting it on the quilt. He stepped back, looking suddenly nervous. "I hope you like it."

Dex's expression shifted in that way that said he was paying a little closer attention. "You help pick it out?"

"I helped make it," Owen said softly.

"Then I'm gonna love it."

God, Dex was a good man. The best Owen and I could've ever hoped to find.

Dex deftly unwrapped the robot wrapping paper, revealing a shoe box beneath. He frowned for a moment, then opened the lid. His jaw dropped. "My own custom Converse?"

A grin tugged at Owen's mouth. "I drew a computer and Yeti and your energy drink. And your glasses."

Dex lifted a shoe to hold it up for the group and immediately went about switching his boots to the sneakers. "The best gift ever."

"Really?" Owen asked hopefully.

"Really. Now we all match."

I kicked out my own Converse that Owen had decorated, as Owen put his foot next to mine. "Perfect," I whispered.

"Not quite," Dex said. "We need one more thing."

I frowned as he shifted and pulled something out of his pocket. There was no box or anything for the ring, but the diamond caught the light as he lifted it. It glowed, the large gem in the center surrounded by countless tiny ones, making it seem like it was floating.

Dex's hand slid to the side of my neck. "I want to move into this house as a family in every way. Marry me, Hellion. Plant roots with me. Carve a big, beautiful life with me."

Tears filled my eyes as I took him in, as I felt the family we'd built all around us. "Yes."

It was the only answer.

I locked gazes with those dark-hazel eyes as he slid the ring onto my finger. "I love you. I trust you."

"Love you forever," he whispered. And then Dex's eyes moved to Owen, who looked a mix of excited and unsure.

"Does that mean—will you…will you finally be my dad?" Owen asked.

Dex's throat worked as he swallowed. "That gift…way better than even custom Converse."

Owen grinned huge and leapt on us. We caught him in a pileup that Yeti soon joined with a gleeful bark. And I didn't miss Nova looking on, that new smile stretching across her face.

I knew it then: Nothing was better than this. And it was all the sweeter for everything we'd battled to get here.

ACKNOWLEDGMENTS

THIS BOOK, MAN. IT WAS MY EVEREST. AND AS I'M SITTING HERE, getting ready to send it off for proofreading, I can admit I got a little teary when I tackled the final note. I've never worked harder on a book or bled more for a story. It was a struggle to find myself in a new world, and it took me more than a few tries to get it right. But in the end, it's wonderful to know I gave Dex and Brae my all. Because they deserve it.

This author career is a journey, and I dealt with a lot of self-doubt over the course of writing this book. From the title to the story to the characters, it felt like everything was making me question myself. But I am incredibly lucky to have some amazing women in my life who reminded me to trust myself, trust my gut, trust my path. I'd like to give an extra little shout-out to those who helped me believe in myself when I was doubting: Devyn, Sam, Laura, Elsie, Rebecca, Ana, Lauren, Kandi, Amy, Willow, Jess, and Paige. Thank you for taking me out of spirals and helping me find my path. I love you all.

And an extra special shout-out to Elsie's Baby Silver for helping me get all those slang terms just right! I couldn't have done it without you.

To all my incredible friends who have cheered and supported me through all the ups and downs of the past few months, you know who you are. Romance books have given me many things, but at the top of that list are incredible friends that I am so lucky to have in my life. Thank you for walking this path with me.

To my incredible betas, Glav, Elle, Jess, Jill, Kelly, Kristie, Tina, and Trisha, who read this one at various phases and helped find the characters when I was struggling. And an extra special thanks to Glav, who read this one twice when I begged.

And to the most amazing hype squad ever, my STS soul sisters, Alice, Hollis, Jael, Katrina, Laura, and Paige, thank you for the gift of true friendship and sisterhood. I always feel the most supported and celebrated, thanks to you.

The crew that helps bring my words to life and gets them out into the world is pretty darn epic. Thank you to Devyn, Jess, Tori, Rae, Glav, Margo, Kelli, Paula, Chelle, Jaime, Julie, Hang, Stacey, Katie, Jenna, and my team at Lyric, Kimberly and my team at Park, Fine & Brower Literary Management. Your hard work is so appreciated!

To my team at Sourcebooks: Christa, Gretchen, Katie, and so many others, thank you for helping these words reach a whole new audience and making my bookstore dreams come true. And to my team at Evermore and Century in the UK, especially Claire, Jess, and Rosie, thank you for bringing the stories to stores across the globe.

To all the reviewers and content creators who have taken a chance on my words…THANK YOU! Your championing of my stories means more than I can say. And to my launch and influencer teams, thank you for your kindness, support, and sharing my books with the world.

Ladies of the Catherine Cowles Reader Group, you're my favorite place to hang out on the internet! Thank you for your support, encouragement, and willingness to always dish about your latest book boyfriends. You're the freaking best!

Lastly, thank YOU! Yes, YOU. I'm so grateful you're reading this book and making my author dreams come true. I love you for that. A whole lot!

STAY CONNECTED

You can find Catherine in all the usual bookish places…

Website: catherinecowles.com
Facebook: catherinecowlesauthor
Facebook Reader Group: CatherineCowlesReaderGroup
Instagram: catherinecowlesauthor
Goodreads: catherinecowlesauthor
BookBub: catherine-cowles
Pinterest: catherinecowlesauthor
TikTok: catherinecowlesauthor

evermore

Love, spice and sleepless nights.

The hottest new romance publisher at Penguin Random House UK.

Prepare for excessive swooning, devouring love stories and dangerously high standards for your own happily-ever-afters.

Proceed with caution... and an open heart.

FOLLOW US ON SOCIALS:

  @evermorebooksuk